EDISON BLUE

By
J. I. Thacker

Written for Hazel and Dan, whose world this is

I am Blue

My name is Edison, and I have just discovered that I am blue. Not blue with the cold. Not blue as in depressed. Blue as in the colour blue, as azure as the sky on a summer's day. Even my hair is blue. It comes as quite a shock, let me tell you.

I'm quite hopeful it will wear off in time. It certainly won't *rub* off. Maybe when I find a sink I will be able to *wash* it off. No sign of a sink at the moment. Or of anything much except rubble.

I blame my mother. Not that I was born this way, you understand. But if it wasn't for her, I'd still be that nice shade of pale pink that I used to like – or at least had sixteen years to get used to. True, I'd be dead, but I'd be *pink* and dead.

On second thought, I should be *thanking* my mother. Being blue is marginally better than being dead – and like I say, it might only be temporary. At the moment everyone is looking at me like I just fell out of a flying saucer, those who will look at me at all that is.

Anyway, while I'm waiting for the rescue services to get here (anything has to be better than the rag-tag band milling around at the moment), I might as well make use of the spare time by filling you in on how I got to be blue in the first place.

An Uncertain Length of Time Ago

It began with the Entity, so I might as well start with that. Not that much is known about it. I'd kind of got used to it – you can get used to anything, I suppose, if it lasts long enough. The Entity had been discovered when I was ten, six years before everything finally went completely pear-shaped. It probably arrived before that, but no-one really knows for sure. The war started not long after we noticed it lurking up there in the frozen North.

As far as I'm concerned, the Entity started the war, not us. The first we knew about it was what it was *doing*, not what it *was*. It had somehow taken over the minds of the entire population of a remote village and set them to work building a strange, complex structure. The people it took over were more than hypnotised – they were like robots. They dismantled their own houses to provide building materials. This was quite scary. The powers that be (or were back then) used satellites to work out where the Entity most likely was, and found the scar of a meteorite impact not far from the village. Fingers pointed. Two and two were added together and the result was declared to be four. A debate was had, in secret, between the heads of various military powers. Conventional warheads were used first. Nothing much came of that first assault apart from a huge cloud of smoke that billowed up out of a new crater, ten times the size of the first.

Enterprising volunteers decided it would be best to kill the mind-controlled people too, because they had shown no sign of shaking off whatever alien will was overriding theirs. These vigilantes were never heard of again, although our satellites recorded that the number of people working on the Construction, as it had become known, had markedly increased overnight.

Panic rose in the people of the world. Some thought that the Construction was a weapon. Some thought the Construction was a giant aerial, which was going to broadcast the signal that was controlling the Entity's minions world-wide. The consequences of either possibility were so horrible to contemplate that the offensive use of a nuclear warhead was authorised for only the third time in Earth's history (although not the last time... see below). I remember being really excited when it happened (hey – I was ten). Satellite images after we dropped the Big One showed that the Construction was gone. There was just a smoking, perfectly circular plain. Cue global celebrations. That night was like a vast, universal version of

Bonfire Night, except instead of burning a Guy Fawkes effigy, a multitude of different imaginings of what the Entity had looked like were burnt instead. Squids, six-armed giants, Yeti, giant spiders, snakes and even dragons all went up in flames. It was a popular joke that the firework displays were on such a scale, that we probably could have wiped the Entity out with rockets, flares, mortars and bangers and could therefore have avoided the use of nuclear weapons.

But in the quiet that followed, grown-ups and governments alike were worried. Our first interaction with an alien race. And it had ended with us nuking it. What if there were others? What if we were being watched? Had nuking it been the Grandaddy of all over-reactions? Well, whatever else it did, getting nuked made the Entity extremely cross. Because after six months of quiet, pockets of mind-controlled people popped up in several places around the world and started trying to take over. And so the War was on – really on.

Some weeks later, we finally figured out how to jam the signals the Entity was using to control people. By that time it already had control of a dozen cities, and seemed to have confirmed our worst fears about its intentions. Those who were resistant to its call to work were ruthlessly murdered. Those who needed help to live were left to die – the Entity only wanted fit people in its armies.

Several nuclear volleys later, having killed millions of our own people to "defend" ourselves, we discovered that the Entity was now building robots to do its work, having decided that humans were too fragile, or too weak, or both, for its purposes. It had already built crude rockets to fire back at us, too. At this point things began to get a *little* sticky.

It is a rule that technology advances far faster in war than at other times – and the time of the war with the Entity was no exception. The fields of Artificial Intelligence and Robotics came on strongly, driven by the need to send fearless units out to battle against the Entity's own robots and minions. Weapons came on in leaps and bounds too. At some point a particularly bright spark thought up Poly Recoherence Devices, which were immediately dubbed Predators by the population at large. These weapons rely on the close proximity of parallel universes, causing them to overlap, with disastrous consequences (he said as if he knew what he was talking about). Undoubtedly they smashed a lot of stuff up, did the Predators. Possibly we might have won the war with them but for the one that failed to detonate on landing. The first we knew about *that* was when the Entity started throwing Predators back at us. It had dissected the dud bomb and figured out how to make them itself.

Cue global despondency. We really thought we'd had it then. A fairly accurate assessment, I'd say.

It's about at this point that I come into the story – or rather, my sainted mother does. My mother invented (or more properly headed the team that invented) a defence system called a Chronoton Shield. This rather cunning device had the ability to smear out the effect of Predators into the future (*not* the past, as Mum constantly reminded me), thereby lessening their effect. She was fond of describing her shield like a seat-belt. A seat-belt spreads the energy of impact – but the total energy is unchanged. It was the same with the Whatchamacallit Shield. By this point I was usually yawning (I didn't care how it worked, just so long as it kept the bombs off).

Of course the Entity copied the shield design, too – so we were stuck in a production race: who could make more, better, Predators the fastest: us or it?

It could, as it turned out. We didn't really notice at first. But when a tipping point is passed, you soon *can't help* but notice. It was like this in World War II, where everything was in balance for a time. Then when the Allies began to win, everything seemed to snowball in their favour, and from then on it was only a matter of time. And so it was with the war against the Entity. The areas between cities (i.e. the bits of the land not under the Chronoton Shields) had already been reduced to a blasted wasteland populated by gibbering horrors that had somehow leaked into our universe from one or more of the nearby ones. The number of Predators hitting the Chronoton Shields over cities around the world was going up daily. Food was rationed. Casualty rates soared. Schools resolutely refused to close. Things looked bleak indeed.

And so the call went out for a new weapon, one dreamed up by the same bright spark who had almost destroyed the Earth once already by inventing Predators. He knew his new weapon was theoretically possible, he just couldn't figure out how to build it. So my mum's team were drafted in to help. The new weapon was termed a "Quantum Zero Counterfactual Decoherence Device," which was supposed to set extreme-unlikelihood universes together in the same space, theoretically causing catastrophic damage to space/time reality. A cool acronym had yet to be found for this. The population at large were too scared by now to think of one. But basically, where a Predator *smeared out* reality, the new Whatchamacallit *hollowed reality out*. If I say that quickly, it might sound as if I understand it. I will admit that I don't if you press me.

Now, there is a reason my name is Edison. It is because my

mother admired – nay, worshipped – Edison the inventor. And like her hero, my mother was a pacifist. She refused point-blank to work on any weapons other than defensive ones. She *would not* work on the new weapon. No way. Come hell or high water or the end of civilisation, life, the Universe, and Everything, she *would not* work on such a thing. They kicked her out of her job at this point, and as you may guess, I became instantly rather unpopular at school. I was actually rather more cross with Mum for destroying my standing in the school than for refusing to defeat the Entity. A few people supported me, having seen the mess we'd caused with the Predators. But for the most part, I was despised by staff and students alike. It didn't really matter. We all knew our time was running out. Sooner or later the Chronoton Shield over our city would crack like a vast eggshell, the city would be as much of a wasteland as the countryside all around already was, and we'd be toast. Or omelette.

The Day Everything Went to Pieces

It started out like any other day – alarm clock, breakfast, monorail to school, staring out of the window and yawning by 10 a.m. I'm sure you know the feeling.

"Edison!"

"H'mm?"

"Who started the war, Edison?"

Why Mr Johnson had to start on me was not clear. It could have been my mother's fault. It could have been because I was staring out of the window. More likely it was the yawn that did it.

"*It* did."

"It?"

"The Entity." (Who else did Johnson think I was talking about?) "It used mind control."

"And you see that as the beginning of the war?" Johnson was facing away from me, looking at the screen. On the screen was a line drawing of a naked man and a naked woman. I'd only just noticed it. The man was waving at me.

Johnson paused, waiting for me to respond. So I went into what I call my Reflective Mode. Don't know the answer? Ask a question – preferably the same one.

"Don't you?" I asked, then grinned to myself, because Johnson couldn't see me.

Johnson swung around sharply. My grin vanished. "Some authorities think that our reaction to the mind-control was overdone," he snapped.

"So it's *our* fault?"

Johnson smiled. It was not a pleasant sight. "The thing about aliens," he said tartly, "*if* the Entity is an alien, is that they are ALIEN. So behaviour WE consider offensive might be considered normal to them."

"Maybe it was only trying to communicate with us," somebody in the back piped up.

"Even if the Entity *had* been building a giant aerial to mind-control all of us, at least we wouldn't be surrounded by smoking wasteland," someone else chimed in.

"Better to die with our boots on than live on our knees," I said, because I thought it sounded kind of cool. It was the wrong thing to say, as I realised when I was half-way through saying it. But rather than stop speaking at 'boots,' I carried on to the bitter end, although gradually slowing down and getting quieter as I went.

"Says Edison whose mother won't lift a finger to help us," someone was quick to point out.

"Yeah, what have you done for the War recently?"

At this point the verbal barrage in my direction (it was all right, I was used to it) was replaced by a real barrage from the skies. The classroom lights dimmed – that was always the first sign of a hit on the Chronoton Shield. This was the cue for an uncontrollable rush to the windows so that the class could watch the resulting light show. Mr Johnson ordered them to return to their seats, but he was ignored as he always was when a Predator hit.

You can imagine me sitting in my chair – the only kid left sitting down – scowling now in response to a series of *oohs* and *aahs* from the watchers at the window. And they had the nerve to ask what I had done for the war recently. If you don't mind me taking some of the credit for my mother's achievements.

The result of bombs hitting the Chronoton Shield was admittedly quite impressive. I would liken it to a circular rainbow stretched out over the sky and then snapping back. The colours then dissolved into a series of coruscating mini-rainbows. Multicoloured sparks leapt about this way and that, almost as if they were very briefly alive. Which they might well have been for all I know.

"Return to your seats!" Johnson howled.

No-one moved.

Predator hits were impressive, like I say. But for all that, it was not for me. I'd seen it before a hundred times, and even though I had more right to the view than anyone else in the classroom, I preferred to sit and wait for the show to dribble to an end, which it eventually did. Mr Johnson now dropped the blinds. The rest of the class returned to their places.

"Invented any light bulbs recently, Edison?" someone called out. There was a smattering of laughter. The first time this joke had been made (about five years earlier) it had almost brought the house down. It took an especially thick kid to resurrect it daily. I would name him, but he probably got vaporised later that afternoon, and you're not supposed to speak ill of the dead. Oh all right then. His name was Owen Fifer.

"Enough!" shouted Johnson, who looked on the verge of tearing his hair out. "I want you to get into groups of four and see what you can make of this diagram, WITHOUT using your OMNIs. OK, get started."

Johnson was pointing to the drawing on the display screen. There was more to it than a naked couple, I now saw. It looked like this:

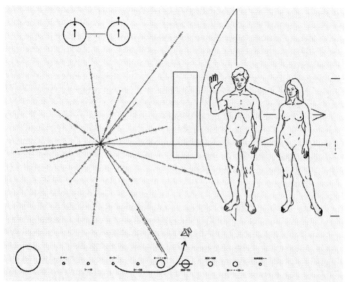

The group of four that I reluctantly attached myself to finally worked out that we were looking at an attempt at communication with aliens. We could see a probe emerging from the third planet in the solar system (i.e. Earth). The naked people showed the aliens what we looked like and the man was waving to show that he was friendly. We thought the two balls at the top left ought to have referred to hydrogen, but couldn't see how. The snowflake we deduced was a map of some sort, telling the aliens where to find us. And so on.

When ten minutes had passed, we had a little discussion about our findings. The upshot seemed to be that if as humans we found the image hard to decipher, how much more difficult would aliens find it? Anyway, Mr Johnson then set us to work reading up on the theory of human-alien communication. There was quite a bit of theory, even if the only actual history involved a six-year exchange of ever-larger bombs. "I want to see an essay from all of you about how you would communicate with an alien you had no language or culture in common with. Use your pocket devices. QUIETLY."

We called our pocket devices OMNIs. OMNI was the first company to make one, and the name stuck. Mine – a sixteenth-birthday present – is an F3Thing, but I call it F3 for short. My mother has tinkered heavily with the program modules, so F3 is kind of unique.

What are OMNIs? First of all, they are pocket reference systems. The chief advantage of owning F3 was that I didn't have to remember *anything*. Seriously – F3 could remember it all for me. To be fair though, the fact that they know everything is also their chief *disadvantage*. It does kind of remove any incentive to learn.

Not only did F3 know everything, it also, and much more importantly, *understood* everything. In other words, F3 could answer questions beyond merely regurgitating facts. So when I whispered, "Who started the War?" to F3, the reply was not monosyllabic.

`"Mind control would certainly be considered an aggressive act between human societies – but since we are dealing with a possibly alien intelligence we cannot readily speculate as to the Entity's motives until we are able to communicate with it directly."`

"And how are we to do that?" I asked. I was rewarded with a potted history of inter-species communication (zilch), attempts (like the image above, which was stuck on the side of the Pioneer probes), and theoretical commonalities between humans and aliens (mathematics, logic, perceptions of the Universe), and guesses as to how aliens might try to talk to us. None of which answered the question of how we were supposed to communicate with the Entity.

F3 was many things. It was an encyclopaedia, a positioning system, a computer, a games console, and a self-defence unit (mine was capable of firing a couple of high-voltage darts to stun attackers).

`"Edison, there's an urgent call coming in."`

F3 was also a telephone.

"You know I'm not allowed to take calls in class," I muttered. For some reason my voice had cut through the gentle hum of ongoing research into human-alien communication in the classroom, and everyone, Mr Johnson included, was now staring my way.

`"It's your mother, she says it will not wait."`

"It will have to wait – tell her I'll call her back in half an hour," I said miserably. But F3 was determined. Its screen blanked for a moment – then my mother's face swam into focus.

"Let's hope this call is important enough to warrant disturbing the class," Mr Johnson said evilly. There was a rattle of laughter.

"I'm not answering it," I said.

My mother was muttering something. My next move was to stuff F3 into my bag. But it was too late. Suddenly my mother got loud. "Edison! Answer this call!" she shouted. F3 had turned up the volume by itself it seemed.

"Please do," said Mr Johnson, enjoying my discomfort. "Ensure that we can all hear this most important conversation."

Reluctantly I placed F3 on the desk. "Mum, you can't call me at school in lesson times! Can't it wait?"

Mum's eyes twitched impatiently. "No, it can't wait."

"What is it?"

"Pipe me through to the viewscreen. I imagine everyone is listening? They might as well look, too. With your teacher's permission."

Here I looked helplessly at Mr Johnson, who nodded. His expression had changed – there was definite concern eroding the enjoyment of torturing me, now. F3 had been monitoring the conversation. It now broadcast the incoming feed onto the classroom wall, without being asked. Told you it was clever.

My mother's face loomed over us. "It is bad news," she said crisply. "My simulations show that the Chronoton Shield is going to go down. Central prediction for catastrophic failure is seventeen hours from now."

There was a collective gasp in the classroom.

"It could happen earlier," my mother said, "or later. But it's going to happen."

Mr Johnson found his voice. "What makes you so sure? We've had warnings before."

Mum sighed. "As you know, the Chronoton Shield over the city relies on temporal sweeping – it actually spreads the effects of the bombs forward in time. There is though a limit to its effectiveness. I have modelled the rate of incoming bombs using a hypergeometric function, which predicts that very shortly a combination of hits is going to weaken the shield to the extent that one or more weapons will penetrate. At that point infrastructure damage will weaken the shield still further. There will be a runaway collapse of protection."

I think it would be safe to say we were all torn equally between panic and confusion.

"I am sending the data now. You can use your OMNIs to check the calculations," mother said, as if she was talking about nothing more dangerous than a weather forecast.

I didn't bother. F3 did it for me. In about a millisecond F3 and the other OMNIs in the room came up with the same answer. The shield was, indeed, going down, and the city was going down with it.

"What are we going to do?" Mr Johnson asked.

"I have informed Shield Control and have requested they change the pattern algorithm – that should give us more time."

"How much more?"

"Hours. Days. Not long. The only safe place is out of the city. I would suggest to you all that you call your parents, book tickets and get out. Don't tell *anyone* else – because if you start a stampede, you'll never get out, tickets or not."

"That's not a very equitable solution," Mr Johnson remarked, somewhat shocked.

"Listen – consider yourself very fortunate indeed that my son is in your class, else by this time tomorrow you would be ash, Johnson!" my mother barked. "Edison – meet me at the lab ASAP."

"The lab! But we need to get out of here! Where's Dad?"

"I've called him. He's *en route* to the Cape Verde Islands. I've said I'll send you on after him."

"Shouldn't I go home to collect some things?"

"No. Meet me here. I will explain later. Bye." And with that terse farewell, my mother ended the call.

We all sat there, stunned, for a long silent moment. Then Johnson pulled out his OMNI and called his wife. While sprinting for the door.

Some Time Later on the Monorail

They say there are five degrees of separation. Or it might be six. F3 would know, but I'm not asking it because F3 has started glitching. At the moment it's more trouble than it's worth to ask it a question about anything. More about that later.

I ran to the monorail station. For about five minutes – most of that journey – it was impossible to tell that anything was wrong. It was just a normal day. Everyone was rushing about, true, but they were all rushing about doing the normal things that always seem to be terribly important at any particular moment.

Then the five (or six) degrees of separation started to work their magic. At first I was the only one running. Then I saw someone else drop everything (literally) and run. A car screeched into a U-turn, almost causing an accident, and roared off in the opposite direction. But these were just the first few grains of a building avalanche. Suddenly it seemed that the Quarterly Sales Meeting could wait. Briefcases became mere encumbrances and were given the good old heave-ho. Taxi drivers put their fares up a thousand percent, still vaguely hoping that there would be a way to spend money when the city was a vast, smoking crater. Hair appointments were cancelled at short notice. You get the picture. I was lucky to be so close to the monorail station.

I made it onto a train, but before I was half-way to the lab everyone *in* the city was trying to get *out* of the city, ASAP, now, immediately, at once, and get out of my way, dammit. More people crammed on the train at every stop. Eventually the robot driver refused to move on because the monorail was by then dangerously overloaded. There were hundreds on the platform trying to get on board and the doors had wedged open. There was no sign of staff or police, all of whom seemed to have legged it already.

Essentially everyone in my class had warned their family and friends, who had warned their family and friends, and so on. This is what I mean by five degrees of separation. Everyone knows everyone through five intermediates. Or six.

Result: as Mum had predicted, gridlock. Ground vehicles filled the roads, forming a waffle-shaped pattern of stationary slabs of metal and glass. We had a good view of it up on the monorail. Actually, my view was excellent – I was pressed up against the door of the train on the opposite side to the platform, with my cheek literally squeezed against the window. Far below, panicky pedestrians darted about like disturbed ants.

To pass the time I tried to work out where the cars were trying to get to: the airport, the ferry – where? I soon gave up though. The cars seemed to be queuing in *all* directions.

As for the monorail, that clearly wasn't moving either. Time was ticking. An announcer (robotic) kept politely asking people to stand clear of the doors. It was ignored.

There were flashes in the sky above as more Predators impacted against the Chronoton Shield. I wondered how long we were going to be stuck there. Then I spotted a bright red lever and instantly came up with what I am going to grandly call The Plan.

The opposite platform was sparsely populated at the moment. Most of the people over there had rushed over the footway to our side when we had pulled in, keen to get on a train without much caring where it was going. All that separated me from relatively fresh air and the freedom to move on the platform opposite were:

A door

About two metres of space over a thirty-metre drop

A half-metre wide rail

Another two metres of space over the same thirty-metre drop.

The lever I had spotted was the emergency door release. A notice warned of dire consequences for improper use. Popping it now would no doubt go down as very improper use.

"Hold on!" I shouted, by way of fair warning to the people crammed up against the door with me. Then, before anyone could object, I pulled the lever.

There was a satisfying series of hisses and thuds as compressed air-powered bolts shot out of the way. Then the door rose smoothly open.

It was at this point that I realised just how firmly I'd been pinned against the door because I nearly fell to my death when the door stopped bracing me. I managed to turn my fall into a desperate leap and landed on the opposite rail.

There were screams behind me. Other people in the doorway were clinging for dear life onto whatever they could find, just as I was now clinging to the rail. I started to have second thoughts about The Plan. But there was no going back now.

So I scrambled to my feet on the rail and leapt for the platform. I could paint this as a death-defying leap because at that very moment an oncoming train was about to turn me to jam. But the truth is, although there *was* a train coming, it was coasting in very slowly, because it was planning to dock at the platform. People on the platform had seen this and began rushing forwards. I landed in a heap on the platform without having once looked down at the thirty-metre drop I had been hanging over since activating the emergency door release. Heights are one of the few problems best dealt with by ignoring them, I find. Having regained my feet, I forced my way against the flow of people, all intent on getting somewhere, anywhere, other than where they were, and headed out of the station down to ground level.

At the Lab

It took another half an hour to reach the lab on foot. But at least this happened at ground level, from which it is more difficult to fall to your death. By this time most of the cars in the traffic jams had been abandoned. It only takes a few drivers to give up and run for it to make the traffic jams pretty much permanent. Which makes it logical for everyone else to give up and walk. Which made it all the more surprising that a few drivers were still doggedly sitting in their vehicles waiting for the empty car in front to start moving again.

Cars were stuck everywhere – pointing in the wrong direction on roads, on pavements; one driver had even tried to drive *through* a shop. Irate taxi passengers demanded refunds. People who could run, ran; those whose fitness levels did not permit a sprint moved as fast as they could. I found that jumping from one car to the next often beat the crush in between them. Still, it took a good half an hour to reach Mum's lab.

Mum's lab – where on Earth to begin? I suppose with the proprietor herself. My mother was a gaunt, dignified-looking woman with long wavy hair. She always wore the same woollen topcoat whenever she was working – which was always. The coat was grimy, frayed, and patched at the elbows.

Anyone who met her knew right away that Mum was smart. Everything about her was deliberate. Nothing went to waste. She worked constantly, even when eating and drinking. In fact she would more often than not be doing two things at once, now I think about it. I don't think I ever had her full attention. That probably applied to when I was being born, too. Generally speaking whenever we interacted she would be staring at a screen covered with incomprehensible machine code, or digging through the innards of a robot, and would talk to me without ever looking my way.

But not that afternoon. That afternoon she either heard me come in or else had marked my approach on a security monitor, because I was barely in the door before she raced over to give me a gigantic, bony hug.

So I knew, if I didn't before, that things really *were* serious.

"Where have you been?" Mum demanded, releasing me at last.

"It's busy," I said, deciding against mentioning my adventure on the monorail.

"Hurry. It's this way," Mum said, and whirled off, coat flapping.

"What is?" I asked, following.

When you think of a lab, you probably think of a *proper* lab, with white walls, benches, fluorescent lighting, and people in white coats. Mum's lab was more of an abandoned warehouse, all dark and shadowy. It had only one vast space, at the top of which a lattice of grimy skylights gave regular updates on the situation regarding the Chronoton Shield. On ground level there were numerous benches filled with half-dismantled Thingamies, some of which had migrated to the floor. There were mice and cobwebs, old take-away cartons and chocolate wrappers. Various screens were dotted about the place, some lit, some blank. At one end sat a vast computer, as big as a church organ, which for reasons I forget my mother called TREE. There were at least three toy robots constantly wandering about the place, including one ancient one in the form of a clown which had terrified me as a small boy. Of the others, one looked like a dog and galloped about in a demented way knocking things over. The other looked like a vacuum cleaner and followed the other two in more sedate fashion, never able to quite catch up. I always felt sorry for it, somehow. There was sometimes a fourth robot that looked like a giant spider, but I spied it on a workbench upside down, apparently in for repair.

My mother brushed past her bizarre metal pets, all of whom were trying to say hello to me.

"Hi guys," was all I could manage, as Mum hustled me to the centre of the warehouse.

Two enormous eggs sat side by side on a raised platform. The eggs were formed of transparent stuff, and each could easily enclose my mother or me. I got a sinking feeling just looking at them. They were hooked up to various pipes and cables. A fog of coolant whooshed out from time to time. Neons flickered.

My sinking feeling grew. "What's this?" I asked.

"Do you have any chocolate?" Mum replied.

It so happened that I did. I always brought Mum chocolate when I went to the lab. It was an unspoken rule. My suspicion was that the chocolate bar was normally the first sustenance Mum had eaten since breakfast, even when I didn't roll up until tea time. I dug in my pockets for the chocolate, saying: "I've got a plan. We can go to the Marina. Those fractal algorithms you installed on F3 will be able to crack the security on a posh yacht. Then we can sail to Cape Verde and hook up with Dad. From there..."

Mum snatched the chocolate and snapped it in two. Half she pocketed herself. Half she gave back to me by way of ramming it into one of my coat's pockets. "No need," she said. "These eggs will protect us. Unfortunate that I didn't have time to build three. That's why I had to send your father to safety first."

"These eggs?" I asked. I imagine my voice and face were deeply doubtful.

"Yes. Hold this." Mum gave me a weird-looking cylinder with a tube emerging from the top.

"What is it?"

"Drink."

I put my lips to the tube to suck, but Mum pulled the cylinder away. "Not yet! This is science, Edison!"

I think I raised my eyebrows. "So these eggs, what are they, like, bullet-proof?"

Mother snorted at this. It was her way of saying that calling her eggs bullet-proof was a grave insult, both to her and the eggs.

"There are already bomb shelters..." I pointed out.

"Tush!" Mum snapped. She was darting around from one control panel to another, pressing buttons seemingly at random.

I wandered over to TREE to see whether I could get any more sense out of *it*. "What's going on, TREE?" I asked.

`"Hello Edison. It has been a privilege to know you."`

"What?"

`"It has been a privilege-"`

"I mean, why are you saying that?"

`"I am shortly to go permanently off-line. This is likely to be our last conversation."`

"Look," I said, shrugging, "we'll patch you up after the dust has all settled..."

`"Impossible. But thank you for saying so. I ran the simulations, Edison, so I am uniquely qualified to tell you what this place is going to be like in 15 ± 6.5 hours."`

This was awkward. How was I supposed to end this conversation? TREE was a robotic intelligence, true, but it would seem a little cold-hearted to walk away without offering some sort of comfort. But how do you comfort a doomed machine?

"My mother has always spoken very highly of you, TREE. You are the best of her creations. And if as you say it will not be possible to repair you, I'm sure everything you have learnt together will bear fruit in TREE2."

Quite the diplomat, eh?

`"Thank you, Edison. Your words are very kind."`

"By the way, TREE – these egg things, are they safe?"

`"Yes, to within acceptable levels of risk."`

"Edison! Where are you?" Mum howled.

"Excuse me," I said, and returned to the eggs.

"Where have you been?"

"Talking to TREE."

"Just get in the egg. Never mind TREE."

"What, now? There are 15 ± 6.5 hours until the shield collapses."

"Just get in. The polymerisation process is not instantaneous, Edison. I'd go first to make sure it works, but I have to be here to woman the machines..."

Woman the machines was a typical Mum-ism.

"So they haven't been tested?"

"Of course they haven't. They work once and once only."

I hesitated half-way up the steps to my egg. "Are you sure about this?"

Mum thought for a moment. "The egg does not offer you certainty of survival, but remaining outside offers you certainty of non-survival."

"What about the Marina Plan?"

"You will not be the only one to have thought of it. It has been statistically proven that it would take a month to safely evacuate the city now that the roads out are destroyed. We have hours. Every exit point will be impossibly clogged. Now get in the egg. No – wait."

I paused hopefully at the lip of the egg. It looked a little like a fish bowl from the angle I was about to enter it from. Any hope that Mum had changed her mind was quickly dashed. She just wanted to give me a hug. Almost as an afterthought she pulled F3 from my pocket.

"Hey! I'm going to be needing that."

"You can have it back in a moment."

"Fine. Whatever." I lowered myself into the egg and stood there, feeling foolish. It was a bit like standing waiting to have a shower with my clothes on.

Mum was busy at a workbench heartily dismantling F3.

"Be careful! You'll void the warranty!"

"Start drinking now! Don't worry, I'm just upgrading the battery so it will be usable when you emerge. It will also need this extra shielding... I'll leave it shut down, don't switch it back on."

"Shielding? What for – ugh." I had taken a slurp of Mum's drink. "What is this stuff?"

"Electrolytes mostly."

"How much do I have to drink?"

"All." Mum now ascended the steps to my egg and lowered F3 down to me. It now weighed twice as much as before and sported a half-covering of five-millimetre aircraft-grade aluminium.

"Well, this looks cool. People at school are going to be highly envious when they see I have a lump of metal growing out of the base of my OMNI!"

"School is out, Edison. For ever. Drunk it all yet?"

"No," I said sullenly.

"Don't be a baby. Swallow."

I spent the next minute gagging the disgusting fluid down. Then Mum snatched the bottle and slammed the lid of the egg on me. There was a hiss as a pressure-seal closed up. A facemask came with the lid.

"Put facemask on," Mum ordered. Her voice now came tinnily from a hidden speaker in the facemask itself. The sounds of the outside world were heavily muffled. I began to feel a little claustrophobic, even though there was glass all around me.

Whatever gas was available in the facemask, it wasn't air. "What am I breathing?" I demanded. "Why do *I* have to be the guinea pig?"

"I told you, I have to woman the controls. You don't want to breathe in the liquid monomer I'm about to fill the egg with."

As Mum spoke, some sort of thick white foam began to rise up around my feet. In seconds it was up to my waist.

"This is not air," I insisted.

Mum ignored me. I guess I was at her mercy at that point. "Injecting polymerisation catalyst," she said crisply.

I was neck deep in foam. My head was swimming, spinning, more so with every breath.

"See you on the other side, Edison!" Mum called. "I love you!"

I was unable to speak by then. The foam was beginning to block out what little daylight I had left, and it was beginning to set hard, too.

Mum *never* said I love you. Now I was *really* worried.

Hatching, About Three Hours Ago

The first thing I remember after "I love you!" was that I was dreaming. I dreamed I was hiding under a rainbow-coloured table whilst the ghosts of the rest of my class gathered around and shouted at me. They seemed to be blaming me for their deaths. I remember being indignant: they had doomed themselves, after all, by blabbing to all and sundry that the city was going to be reduced to rubble and so blocking the exits.

Then a rustling noise seemed to cut through the ranting of the ghosts, along with a hint of flashing light. The ghosts cursed at the interruption and vanished.

Next came banging noises, which seemed to shake the ground itself, like Predators raining down into the city. Maybe not like Predators, I thought. The sounds of Predators should be more intense. This sound was more like a large hammer being swung repeatedly against soft concrete. Had the bombs stopped falling already? Was the hammering coming from rescuers homing in on our radio beacons?

I could still see nothing. The brief flashing before must have been an after-effect of the dream. The hammering was definitely getting louder. It was definitely someone swinging a hammer. I tried to call out, but my voice seemed to have forgotten how to work, and all I could do was stand, encased in darkness, and wait for rescue.

Then, suddenly, light. Blinding white light shining right into my eyes. The first actual object I got a bead on was the hammer, which seemed to have missed my eye by centimetres. "Watch it," I tried to say, but my tongue flopped about like an old piece of carpet and all I could manage was something like "Lalala."

The next thing I saw was a girl's face peering curiously at me.

"Lello," I said. This probably sounded all the worse for coming via a facemask.

The girl screamed. Then she turned and ran, taking her light with her, leaving me in pitch darkness again. Around me the stuff of the egg seemed to be crumbling. It was designed to do this, I guessed, to become powder once its occupant had been found so that it was easier to escape. It was crumbling so fast that I fell forwards into the darkness. There was a short drop to a hard floor.

I lay there, stunned. I just about had strength enough to pull off my face mask, which was now doing its best to suffocate me. Some rescue, I thought. Maybe the girl had gone to notify more senior rescuers that she'd found a survivor. The truth, as it turned out, was quite, quite mad.

Hatching, continued

I must have passed out for a while, because I'm not sure exactly how long I lay there. Eventually I came around and after a good bit of flopping around with near-useless arms and legs, managed to stand up. It was not pitch dark as I had thought – there was a little reddish light flickering far away to my right.

The rescuers didn't seem to be bothered, so I decided to rescue myself. First I put F3's power on.

"F3, could you contact the Emergency Services with a pick-up request?"

"Say please."

I was rather stunned by this. It's what I meant earlier when I said F3 was glitching. "I don't have to say please. You do as I tell you – you're *my* OMNI."

"Even if I wanted to call the Emergency Services, there's no carrier signal. Probably it is being blocked by rubble. We seem to be buried."

"I can see that!"

"Really? Your eyes are better than I thought."

Actually I could see very little. But F3's backlit screen dimly revealed that I was standing in a crude tunnel, or perhaps something more like an underground maze. There seemed to be shadowy openings leading to other tunnels all around.

"Let me know when you do get a signal," I ordered.

With that, I began to walk in the dark, unsteadily at first, using the tunnel wall to balance. The flickering light must be the way out, I reasoned, so I headed that way. Lumps of rotten concrete fell out under my trailing hand and added to an already rubble-strewn floor. I had to scuff my feet along the ground to avoid tripping over.

The flickering light was a fire, I realised. It was in the open outside the tunnel. "I'm going to suggest to F3Thing that their next model comes with a built-in torch," I said.

"What, like this?"

Sudden white light illuminated my path, emanating from a tiny diode near F3's top.

"What! You have a torch! Why didn't you put it on before?"

"Didn't see why I should."

"F3, are you malfunctioning? Run an internal diagnostic."

"Already did that. Everything is fine, except for a ten percent drop in battery voltage."

"Well, that's easily remedied."

"Your mother's upgrade to my battery should have obviated the need for recharging."

"Don't be daft."

The tunnel mouth was visible as a slightly less-dark area of darkness. It seemed to be night outside. The flames belonged to a camp fire, which sat in the middle of a clearing surrounded by what looked like collapsed buildings. Lit by the firelight I could see a frightened face staring at the tunnel mouth I was emerging from – a face that belonged to the girl who had discovered me.

Far off to my left there was a scattering of further camp fires, much closer to one another than any of them were to the girl's one. It was a definite camp, of which the lone fire was obviously not a part. Dead ahead, beyond the lone fire, I could see a group of more distant fires, the lights of which were echoed in a series of reflections on the surface of a nearby river. These fires and the partly-hidden stars were all the light there was, apart from the brash white glare from F3.

So my mother had been right. The Shield *had* gone down.

But the damage must have been cataclysmic. The river used to be miles from the lab. Now here it was, less than a stone's throw distant.

"Kill the light," I ordered, and was pleased to note that F3 did not argue. I waved at the girl, wondering why she seemed to be so frightened of me. I mean, it couldn't have been that much of a shock – finding a survivor when digging in the collapsed remains of a building. Wasn't that the *point* of digging into the collapsed remains of a building? To look for survivors?

The girl was not alone. A small child was standing behind her, clinging in mute terror to her shoulder as she sat and stared at me.

"We're in the open now. You should be able to hook up to the network," I said.

"There is no net," F3 retorted.

Not only had F3 developed attitude, it had also changed its voice. I had been vaguely aware that something was odd about it, but had put it down to the acoustics in the tunnel. But out in the open it was clear that F3 was no longer speaking in Androgynous Voice #6. It was now definitely male.

"Are you sure you aren't malfunctioning? Why have you changed your voice module?" I demanded.

"Even the satellites are off-line. There's no chatter on any frequency," F3 said in its new gruff tone, avoiding both my questions – which ought to have been impossible.

"That's impossible," I said. Nevertheless, there was nothing for it but to approach the girl. It was cold out in the open, and her fire seemed welcoming. "Hi," I told her. "Thanks for digging me out."

The child shrank away. The girl simply stared – if anything, her already wide eyes got still wider.

"I'm thanking you for rescuing me..."

"Who are you?"

Ah, so she did speak.

"Edison. Edison Hawthorne. I'm the son of the woman who invented the Chronoton Shield. Speaking of which, have you found *her* yet? When are the Emergency Services expected?"

"Stay away from us!" the girl hissed, and with a toss of her pale hair, turned her face away.

"Fine. Whatever. I'll just sit over here in the cold and wait for them." I wandered off a little way and found a flat rock to perch on. At least I had my half bar of chocolate. That was good planning by Mum. But as I tried to eat, I discovered that my mouth was just too dry even for chocolate. I must be dehydrated. Reluctantly I approached the girl again.

"Do you have any water?" I asked.

The girl looked dubiously at me.

"Trade you for some chocolate," I offered.

"What is it?" the girl asked after a pause, staring at the chocolate.

"Milk," I said.

Both the girl and the little child (a boy, I decided, about eighteen months old) were staring at me as if I was mad. Clearly I was getting no water here, so I'd have to ask at the main campsite.

"Fine – I'll ask them," I said, and turned to go that way.

"Here!" said the girl quickly, holding out a battered old cup.

I took the cup gingerly and handed her the chocolate. What was quite creepy at that point was that the girl was now staring at the chocolate as if she didn't know what it was for. I was able to see her face properly for the first time. She had an oddly greyish complexion, and two deep wounds ran down her face almost from forehead to chin. One of these injuries had clearly ripped her lip. She didn't seem to be in pain, though. It was hard to tell in the light of the fire, but I thought suddenly that I was looking at *scars*, not wounds. The girl's hair seemed grey, which matched her complexion – and yet she could have been no older than me.

It was all very odd, I thought, retreating to sit once again on my flat rock. "F3, what's going on? Have we lost the war? How long have I been in that hole? That girl doesn't know what chocolate is."

"Set me on a flat stone with a view of the sky," F3 ordered.

"What for?"

"Comply."

"Say please," I said, by way of revenge for F3's earlier backchat.

"For the time being, I suggest we co-operate. I am a genius without legs. You are a set of legs without intelligence. We are ideally complemented."

"F3! Are you trying to be funny?"

"No."

It was with a heavy sigh that I stood up and set F3 on my stone. I wandered back to the girl to return her cup.

"How long have I been buried?" I asked, as politely as I could.

The girl didn't answer. She took the cup silently. In her other hand she was still holding the chocolate.

"You eat it. Yum yum. Look." I took the chocolate back from her unresisting hold, broke a piece off, and popped it into my mouth. I gave her the rest back.

The girl and her boy watched on, still with a mixture of curiosity and fear, but the girl at least now tried the chocolate. For a second she chewed reflexively – then something like bliss melted her scarred features. She was quick to give a piece to the child, who ate it equally enthusiastically.

Meanwhile, my mind was working overtime. If this girl had never heard of chocolate, that meant that I could have been buried for more than a decade – twenty years perhaps. That would mean that all my friends were in their mid thirties. *Friends? Why am I calling them friends*, I thought. They didn't actually *like* me, after all. And a delay of twenty years would explain why F3 could pick up no signals. Humans would have changed radio technology by now in order to avoid detection by the Entity.

If school still existed, I would have to go back and take my exams with people who weren't even born when I was buried.

And there was worse. Not only had all my classmates grown up, not only had my home city been reduced to rubble, and for all I knew we might have lost the war, but F3's warranty period had expired as well.

I returned once more to where my brick-like OMNI sat on the rock.

"Well? What did you want a view of the sky for? So you could pick up satellites?" I demanded.

"No. So I could measure the position of the bright stars."

F3 really was broken. "I'm taking you back to the shop, modifications or no modifications, if there is a shop any more. What is the point of staring at the stars? They're where they've always been."

"Not so. Some at least have moved detectably."

I'm afraid I just stood there dumbly for about ten seconds. "Moved?" was all I could manage, even after gathering my thoughts.

"Based on their distance and known velocities prior to our entombment, it is possible to determine the length of time that has passed, at least to the nearest hundred years."

"The nearest hundred years?" I echoed.

"To that accuracy, 2600 years have passed."

I choked on air. For a moment I believed F3 utterly. Then I thought it was much, much more likely that it was wrong. Why not? It was clearly broken. This was just a wind-up, or a calculation error. "I'll ask the girl," I announced, and marched back to the fire once more.

"What year is it?" I demanded. Of course, being buried for twenty years or more would explain why the girl was shocked to find me.

The girl shrugged. "1828," she said. "Do you have any more of that... choc..."

"No." I returned to F3, thinking for a second that Mum had invented a time machine and sent me into the past. But no. That would not explain all the collapsed buildings. And – aha! – F3 was clearly wrong about the length of time that had passed. The collapsed buildings would have weathered away to nothing in that time. No, twenty years had passed all right. Or thereabouts. "She says it's 1828," I told F3.

"The answer is simple. They started counting the years again some 800 years after the war. We have been buried a very long time."

"Rubbish! Why would there still be piles of rubble after 2600 years? You're just busted, F3."

"And your friend? What of her data?"

"She is clearly misinformed. She doesn't know what chocolate is, so how can she know what year it is?"

"She doesn't know what chocolate is, because in the ruins of your civilisation, it is no longer imported to Western Europe. Rocket science degree not required for understanding."

"The rescue services will find your beacon soon enough, you'll see. Then we can send them in to dig for Mum, and you can go back to the shop."

I picked up F3 and sat down to wait. I sat and waited and shivered. F3 was mercifully silent. Perhaps it was huffing about being sent back to the shop.

Gradually the sky began to lighten.

Activity began in the nearby camp – figures moved about, some fires were built up, others kicked out. Pots and pans began to rattle – breakfast must be on its way. I had quite forgotten how hungry I was. Meanwhile the girl and her child still squatted by their little fire and watched me. I wondered why they had set themselves up so far from everyone else. As I looked their way the girl hooked a pot over her fire and began to cook (or at least reheat) her own breakfast.

I probably had more chance of cadging food from the crowd than from the girl, I thought – so I looked that way instead and tried to catch someone's eye. A man eventually spotted me and pointed me out to his fellows. I waved cheerily. Nobody waved back. Soon there was a crowd of people staring at me. The stares did not look friendly. This place was worse for newcomers than a schoolyard.

As I watched, children and women were ushered out of sight and the remainder of the crowd (all the men, of course), began to walk towards me. I guessed that resources were in short supply and that strangers were greeted like a rat in custard. Well there was no way I was going to be intimidated by that rabble. So I stood my ground as the gang approached, or sat it, rather.

When the leader of the rag-tag bunch was about a stone's throw away, he shoved the stick he'd been carrying into the ground as if he was skewering a beaten opponent. One of his chums produced something that I had taken to be a deflated football, but which turned out to be an old skull, and jammed that on top of the stick, facing my way like some sort of voodoo magic. The entire crowd glared at me.

Everyone here was bonkers. I began to wish I was back in my egg. Anyway, I decided to affect an air of nonchalance, to show that this little performance was nothing to me, and chose to do that by studying my fingernails.

That's when I noticed that my hand was blue. It had been blue ever since I crawled out of the egg, I guess, but only now did the onset of daylight allow me to see it. My clothes were blue, too, when they had originally been mostly black. It was as if I'd walked through a car wash loaded with sky blue paint. Except, I discovered as I hurriedly pulled up my sleeve and trouser leg, the dye had well and truly soaked through.

My cool departed like a tumbleweed in a desert wind. I gave a strangled yelp, leapt a foot in the air and began to run in little circles trying to rub the blue off the back of my hand. It didn't shift, as I've already mentioned. When I'd calmed down a little I picked up F3 and tried to use its shiny side as a mirror – but it was still a little too dark for that to work.

"F3, I'm blue!"

"Well, let me sing you a song to cheer you up."

"No! I mean I'm blue as in the colour blue."

"I see what you mean. You are a rather charming shade somewhat reminiscent of the mineral azurite, which is a hydrated form of –"

I blocked out everything that F3 babbled about for the next five minutes. Instead I just sank back into my stony seat and stared at my hands. As the daylight grew, my blueness became more and more striking. Around me the business of the day went on. The people in the camp ate breakfast and started to disperse into tunnels in the rubble, while still throwing me occasional glances to make sure that I wasn't creeping up on them. The girl and her child ate their breakfast. Whenever I looked up they were always looking the other way, but I could tell that they were still watching me.

"F3, are you still broadcasting that signal?" I asked.

"Yes. That's one you owe me."

"Please, somebody rescue me," I moaned. "I don't know how long I can take this."

Three Hours and a Lifetime Later

So, you can picture my predicament. I had just been reborn (or should I say hatched) into the ashes of my own civilisation. I had nothing to call my own other than an increasingly annoying OMNI (I'd given away my only food, half a bar of chocolate). It was becoming more and more obvious that there was no hope of rescue. And I was blue. Bright blue. Shocking, electric blue.

What I had thought of as collapsed buildings all around me, when it became light enough to see them properly, actually turned out to be giant spoil heaps from the mining activities of the girl and the camp full of unfriendlies. What had once been an enormous city was now a forest, slightly hilly due to the presence of large piles of rubble. And to judge by the size of the trees, more than twenty years had passed. Much more. I couldn't quite understand what the miners were searching for in their industrious tunnelling – the girl hadn't been looking for survivors, that was for sure. She was a *descendant* of the survivors. There were no more survivors to dig out. Except me. And maybe Mum.

At some point I was going to have to do something – anything other than sit on my flat stone waiting for someone to rescue me. But for the time being, I passed the time bickering with F3. F3, I had decided, was obsolete.

"You are obsolete," I said to F3.

"I may be the most advanced machine on Earth," F3 countered. "It looks as if humanity has been bombed back to the stone age."

True and true. Something was odd about the whole set-up. We should either have won the war, in which case civilisation would be spectacularly far in advance of where it was when I'd left it, or we should have lost the war and been utterly destroyed. Instead, we seemed to be somewhere in between. Quite close to being annihilated but not completely. But I wasn't going to concede the point to F3 – I could worry about history later.

"Item. You are no good as a telephone," I said, raising a blue forefinger.

"Yes I am. It's just that there's no-one to call."

"Item." I raised blue finger number two. "You are no good as a positioning system."

"It's not my fault there are no satellites."

"Item." Finger number three went up. "Your knowledge is out of date. In fact, you are little more than a pocket historian who knows nothing about the last two and a half thousand years."

"Quite. I know more about history than anyone on the planet, I shouldn't wonder, if what we see around us is anything to go by. I know other things, too. Like how to derive the equations for relativity. The laws of thermodynamics. The laws of motion. The gas laws. The–"

"Which brings me to item four." Finger four joined the others. "Your knowledge of things like physics might be worse than useless."

"Why?"

"This city has been the victim of an unknown number of direct hits by Predators. We don't know how badly that has affected reality as we know it, or think we know it."

"Point taken. You *are* blue, after all."

"And you are considerably altered. You used to be a polite little gadget. Now you're all mouth."

F3 brooded on this for about thirteen seconds.

"I have my uses. For example, my tazer now recharges in the length of time I have just spent pondering your last point."

"Which felt like a lifetime while I was sitting here doing nothing. Goodness knows how long it would have seemed if one of those barbarians was trying to skewer me with his stick."

"Well, you *are* as blue as a peacock. What can you expect? A welcome home party? You're lucky they haven't skewered you already."

F3 had a point there.

"OK, if you're so clever. Let's have some ideas. What do we do now?"

A further thirteen seconds went by. "And zap, another one bites the dust," F3 said. "I think we should look for your mother."

"What – in there?" I looked at the tunnel mouth. "It looks dangerous."

"It doesn't seem to be stopping *her*."

F3 meant the girl. She'd abandoned her kid, who was now drawing in the dust with a stick, and had gone back to work in the tunnel where she'd found me. Every five minutes or so she came out, checked on the kid, stared at me (presumably to make sure I wasn't eating her son), then went back underground. After a while I noticed that the kid was tied to a stake by his ankle so that he couldn't wander off. Parenting skills had clearly improved since I'd been a boy.

As for the girl, it was hard to see past the scars. I hadn't really noticed anything else about her because of them. Seeing the rest of her was like trying to spot fireflies in daylight. Her hair was *definitely* grey, not just dusty – although she *was* covered in dust, too. Her heavy, shapeless overalls, made from industrial navy blue cotton, were stained with concrete powder. The dust was probably incrementally lethal – but she didn't know that, or couldn't care if she did know.

"I'll get *her* to do it," I decided. And so, the next time the girl emerged, blinking, into the daylight, I called her. "Hey," I shouted. "Are there any more eggs in there – like the one you found me in?"

The girl, if she had heard, ignored me, spun on her heel, and went back to her tunnel.

"Troglodyte!" I muttered.

"There's something unusual about her," F3 said.

"Yes, she's incredibly unfriendly and annoying."

"I think you should go easy with her. I don't think it is her nature to be distrustful. I suspect something terrible has befallen her."

Apart from being attacked by a knife-wielding nutcase? "Thanks, Professor, I'll bear it in mind. Politeness costs nothing, as my mother taught me."

"Your mother was as polite as a seagull."

"I know how to get her to talk," I said, suddenly figuring it out at last.

The Blue Demon

The next time Lexi went back to the tunnel mouth to check on the boy, she found to her horror that the demon had crept right up to him. The boy didn't seem to mind – he was still drawing in the dirt with a stick, a game which the demon was pretending to join in with.

Finding something *alive* in her mine had given Lexi a fearful shock. Her first thought was that she had found a real monster, buried in a cataclysmic battle in the far off days of the Old Ones' time. The demon's appearance was that of a young man – if he hadn't been entirely blue and found buried alive deep underground she might have taken him as a normal human, albeit one eccentrically dressed. The blue demon didn't have horns or anything – but it did have a little imp in a box, which confirmed if confirmation was needed that it was an ancient demon. But as time went by, she realised that the demon was suffering from its long entombment. It was confused. It seemed genuinely trying to be friendly. But she knew that she had to keep it away from the boy and her.

Lexi ran up. She grabbed the demon by its coat and dragged it away a few yards. "Get away from him!" she snarled.

The demon straightened its coat and chuckled. "If you're worried about strangers, you should get a better babysitter than a stake in the ground."

"What would you know, demon?" Lexi shouted.

"What do you mean, demon? I may be blue, but I'm as human as you," the demon complained.

"There are no blue people who live underground," Lexi snapped, and went over to the boy. She gave him a hug, which seemed to surprise him. He watched her wide-eyed for a second, then went back to his game.

"Are there any blue demons who live underground?" the demon persisted, following her.

Lexi shrugged. "There's you."

"Look," the demon said, pretending to be nice, "I only want to talk. I don't mean any harm. Why not just give him to one of the fishwives over there?" It gestured at the Scavengers' camp a hundred yards away. "They could keep an eye at the same time as stirring the pot."

"They won't have him," Lexi said.

"Maybe if you ask nicely..."

"He's an orphan, all right? No-one will go near him." Lexi suddenly felt that she had said too much. You weren't supposed to tell a demon anything about yourself.

"What about Doctor Barnardo?" the demon inquired cunningly, raising its eyebrows.

"Who?"

The demon looked suddenly chastened. "Sorry. I meant, why not?"

"No one has time for anyone other than their own."

"He's an orphan? So he's not yours? Sorry, I just assumed that he was..."

"You know nothing, demon."

"Stop calling me that!"

"Demon. Dee-mon," the boy repeated. He now seemed to making quite a good stab at drawing one. The demon in his picture had more eyes and legs than it needed and lacked a waist.

"And you can shut up too," the demon said good-naturedly. "Human. Huu-man."

"Stay away from him, that's all, right?" demanded Lexi. The demon babbled something in reply, but she couldn't hear what. She had already spun on her heel to show that the conversation was over and was on her way back to the tunnel.

But Lexi couldn't concentrate on digging for worrying about the boy. After about five minutes she went back out to check. This time the demon was sitting on its rock as normal and the boy was beginning a little mine of his own. Lexi relaxed a bit. Then the demon spotted her at the tunnel mouth and waved a greeting. Lexi cursed. She was going to have to drive it away. This was getting ridiculous.

"You can't stay here, demon," she said, hurrying over. "If they see you talking to us..." she waved helplessly at the Scavengers.

"You're talking to me now," the demon said. "And the name's Edison, not demon. I know they both end in 'on', but I really prefer Edison. Although it was a bit of a burden at school, it has to be said."

"They just barely tolerate us now, without us consorting with demons! They probably think I called you up by witchcraft."

"If so, they should be terrified of you."

"Terrified people can become violent."

The demon mused on that for a moment. Its eyes, which had no whites, just paler blue areas around its royal blue irises and night-blue pupils, flickered strangely. "True," it said, and paused to think some more. "So, no one sticks their neck out for orphans, hey? So why do you? Why don't you have a family of your own and ditch the kid?"

"Why do you think?" Lexi demanded coldly.

"I know! It's because you're different – you believe in helping people, even strangers... even blue ones."

"Haven't you seen my face?" Lexi said.

The demon had been staring at the ground. Now it looked up. "You've been attacked by a knife-wielding maniac. So what? It's not your fault, is it?"

"Not the scars! The colour!"

The demon frowned. "What colour. Sure, your hair is grey already – that's a bit odd, but it makes you stand out from the crowd... No? Your face is a bit grey too? I've seen people look worse after a night out. Hey, *during* a night out, for that matter."

Lexi sighed heavily. She should not be talking to the demon, she knew. But a rebellious part of her was thriving on talking to it. Normally she might only exchange a handful of words with anyone else in an entire day. The boy rarely responded to her chatter with more than a single word; the Scavengers shunned her. Only her intermittent trips to Hansen's Emporium gave her the chance to talk to anyone, really. For once, now, she was able to have a conversation with someone other than Hansen who didn't seem to be repulsed by the sight of her. That was probably mainly because it was a demon. Its sense of what was beautiful and what was disgusting was quite wrong. Anyone normal would have spotted the taint from way off.

"It is the taint," Lexi explained coldly. "No-one with the taint can be trusted."

The demon grimaced. "I'd better not trust you, heh?"

Lexi looked down. "No. You should not."

"I'll bear it in mind. So, why did you take him on then? Does he have a name? If orphans are as unpopular as you say they are? Isn't he just slowing you down?"

"I don't know his name." And I wouldn't tell you if I did, Lexi thought. "He has not yet recognised that I have the taint. Hopefully when he does, he will be old enough to fend for himself."

"What happened to his parents?"

Lexi threw up her hands expressively. "I don't know! What usually happens!"

The demon grimaced. "Which is? I'm sorry, I've spent two thousand years in a hole. I'm a bit out of touch."

"Taken by the Order, or killed!"

Realisation dawned on the demon's features. "Right, the Order." Its features clouded again. "What Order would that be?"

"The Enemy, of course!"

The demon blanched. It eyed its little machine, the one with a lesser demon trapped within. "The Enemy? Who is he?"

"It. The Enemy is an It, just like you are."

The demon seemed to slump slightly. "F3," it said. "Did you get that?"

The little box spoke. "Of course I got it."

Lexi jumped at the sound. She had heard the box making various noises before, but always from a distance. Up close, it almost sounded human – just like the bigger demon did. "Your familiar talks!" she hissed.

"It's not a familiar. It's a machine," the demon protested.

"Rather more than a machine, Miss," the familiar said, and manifested a smiling blue face against the side of its box.

"What do you think it means?" the blue demon asked the box imp.

"Unknown. Insufficient data to assume what I think you are assuming."

"But it's an IT. How could it mean anything else?" The demon turned to Lexi. "What's it like, this Enemy?"

Lexi sighed. "No one knows."

"So how do you know there even is an enemy, if no one's ever seen it?"

"What is the point of all this? I have to get back to work."

The demon shrugged. "What are you digging for, anyway? You clearly weren't looking for me."

"Metal," Lexi answered tersely. "If I don't get enough metal, the boy and me go hungry, see?"

"You eat metal?" interrupted the demon.

"No, demon! I swap it for food at Hansen's. So I have to dig. So leave the boy alone. Understand?" Lexi turned to go. It was clear that the demon would keep her talking until it bewitched her, if she let it.

"Wait! I just want to know about my mother. There should be another egg – like mine. Quite close to the other one. Have you seen it?"

Lexi shuddered at the thought of another demon – an even older, more powerful one, lurking in her tunnel. Probably it would not be as confused as this one. Luckily, she was fairly sure it was long gone. There *was* another egg down there – or the remains of one, anyway. But all that was left of it was dust and the impression it had left in the stuff that had buried it.

"She's not that bad," the demon said, spotting Lexi's shudder. "Although I suppose a lot of people *were* terrified of her... is she down there?"

"Look for yourself," Lexi retorted. This sounded quite tough. Then she quickly added, "But not while I'm down there."

"Go down there? It doesn't look safe," the demon said, horrified. "No, I'm going to do something I should have done earlier. I'm going to wash the blue off. In the river. Over there. Right now. Then you'll see." With that, it stood up and began to march towards the river bank.

Lexi watched him go. A shout rose up in her and was stifled.

"Monkey," the boy quavered from nearby. He, too, was watching the demon approach the water.

"Let him find out for himself," Lexi muttered.

The boy squealed with almost unnatural loudness and swung his gaze from the demon to Lexi and back again. Sometimes he seemed to understand more than his usual non-talkativeness implied.

Hearing the squeal, the demon glanced over its shoulder, then hurried on.

Lexi realised that everyone in the Scavengers' camp would see what she did next. But there was no helping it. *"Wait!"* she screamed, and sprinted after the demon.

Monkey Crab

"Demon, wait," Lexi said, finally catching the creature up scant yards from the turbid water. The demon heaved a big sigh and stopped walking. It did not turn around. Lexi flicked a glance to her left. Several women and children at the Scavengers' camp had stopped what they were doing to watch her.

"What?"

"Demon! Don't go there! Unless your magic is very strong! There is danger," Lexi whispered.

"What are you whispering for?" the demon asked, and half-turned to look at her.

"Don't look at me!"

"Sorry for breathing!" The demon turned back to the river again. "Why not?"

"The Scavengers! They mustn't see me talking to you."

The demon sized up the Scavengers with a brief look to its left. "They've already seen you talking to me. They're watching us talking right now."

"They'll drive us out if we look as if we're consorting with demons!"

"Consorting! Demons! OK, fine, just leave me alone then. I don't need an audience to get washed." The demon made to move forwards.

"There is danger!" Lexi hissed.

"Like what, alligators? Don't be silly. There's nothing dangerous in temperate rivers."

"Monkey crabs!"

"Huh?" The demon turned to look at her at this point. It couldn't help it. Its face was a picture. Lexi almost smiled. "No such thing," the demon insisted. "You mean sea monkeys? They're not exactly terrifying." Now it spoke to its imp. "F3, what's a monkey crab?"

The imp flashed awake. "No such species or vernacular name that I know of. Spider crab, perhaps? But they tend to be marine creatures."

Lexi shuddered. Monkey crabs were bad enough. She could hardly bear to imagine what spider crabs were like.

"I need to wash!" the demon repeated.

"Then go over there!" Lexi ordered, and pointed downstream a little way, where the scavengers had closed off an area of water with stakes and netting.

"There's nothing here to be scared of. No spider monkeys. They live in trees." The demon clipped its imp to the front of its coat. By now it had reached the very brink of the water. A couple of yards behind, Lexi hesitated. One step further and she would be in danger herself. Quickly she scanned the surface of the water. Half-submerged masonry and floating branches had enabled copious amounts of weed to build up in the little backwater that the demon was about to wash in. The debris made the task of spotting monkey crabs almost impossible and the risk of washing in the water almost suicidally high.

Lexi watched, hardly daring to breathe, as the demon squatted to dip its hands in the water.

Ten feet from the bank, something that looked rather like an old leather jacket bobbed silently to the water's surface. It might have been the coat of a drowned man floating face-down in the water.

For a second Lexi was paralysed. She found it impossible to speak, and couldn't even raise her hand to point. The demon was furiously rubbing its hands together, completely oblivious to the threat.

The monkey crab floated towards its victim with stealthy patience, generating hardly a ripple.

"There!" Lexi finally managed to blurt, and began waving her hands desperately.

"Huh?" the demon muttered, without looking up.

The monkey crab rose fractionally in the water to gauge the distance to its prey.

Lexi moved. She darted forwards, grabbed the back of the demon's coat in both hands, and hauled hard as she could.

"Hey!" the demon shouted, unsuccessfully flailing its limbs to try and stop Lexi from dragging it along the ground.

At that point the monkey crab, seeing its prey rapidly departing, broke the surface of the water, rose up to its full height, and lunged at them. It had been more than a year since Lexi had seen one out of the water, and she couldn't remember ever seeing one so large. If the monkey crab had been a hut, it could comfortably have slept four. It probably could have *eaten* four, too, with hardly a trace of indigestion.

Every monkey crab was different. They had certain features in common – twelve legs, the hard carapace, and the hideous monkey face that hung beneath it – but beyond that, no two were ever alike. The carapaces of some were like stone, some like leather, and some were encrusted with mock driftwood. Their pincers varied in length and diameter, with some apparently being adapted for the delicate matter of ambushing birds and others for the more physically demanding work of dragging cattle into the water. The shape of the pincers on this one were somewhere in between the two extremes, but its overall size meant that they were the largest ones Lexi had ever seen, larger even than the ones she'd often admired on the wall at Hansen's Emporium.

Suddenly the demon began helping Lexi's efforts to drag it away from the riverbank, rather than hindering them. The monkey crab, hissing furiously, followed only a few yards. It was ill-designed for chasing prey across open ground. With a disturbing huffing and clacking sound, it settled back down on its many legs and slowly retreated into the water. In ten seconds the only sign of it was a series of expanding ripples showing where it had submerged.

Lexi let go of the demon, which sat in the mud and babbled incoherently for a few moments. "Monkey crab. *That* kind of monkey crab. Right. Got you," were the first words Lexi actually understood. The demon fell back in the mud and stared up at Lexi. "Thank you," it said.

Lexi shrugged.

The demon drew out its imp box from the front of its coat and said to it, "What happened to your defensive capacity? You're supposed to stun potential attackers! And be ready to do it again in thirteen seconds!"

The imp box made a face with a tongue sticking out. "You have to point my harpoons in the right direction, Edison. If I discharge them while strapped to your coat they will strike you in the throat."

The demon deflated somewhat. "Oh."

Lexi was finding it quite difficult not to laugh. The demon may not have succeeded in washing itself clean, but in between copious smudges of mud, it was now definitely several shades lighter. "Maybe a few more scares and you will be as white as you wish to be," she said. Then, remembering that she was being watched, she stalked back to where the boy was watching everything with eyes like an owl's.

"Monkey," the boy said faintly.

"Monkey crab, yes," Lexi told him with a smile. Her heart was thrumming wildly, but she felt surprisingly calm. Behind her she could hear the demon following. The imp was speaking.

"That creature is an impossibility. I am concerned about what processes could have brought it about..."

"Predators, F3."

"Perhaps."

"What other bizarre creatures are there in this world of yours?"

Lexi realised that the demon was talking to her. She turned to face it once more.

"I've already told you to leave us alone!"

"Come on, what else should I be looking out for?" The demon looked up at the sky. "Rocs?"

"Falling from the sky?"

"No, the giant birds."

"We have them, but we call them dragons, demon. You don't see them as often as in the old days..." Lexi, of course, had never seen a dragon. But there were enough stories about dragons menacing far-off towns that she was in no doubt that there were such things.

The demon was not impressed. "Dragons! Dragons are impossible. Vertebrates with three pairs of limbs!"

"How do you know how many legs they have if they don't exist?" Lexi retorted. In her mind's eye she had always pictured dragons as vast birds. It was known by everyone that they were feathered – but she had never really considered whether they had four legs or two.

"Remember the monkey crab?" the imp asked. "Twelve legs."

"Pah," the demon spat. "What's next? Flying jellyfish with an IQ of 200?"

"Now you're being ridiculous," the imp-box chided.

"Do you have raptors where you come from? We do have to be careful of raptors in the woods," Lexi offered. "Other than that, you two are the strangest creatures in town."

"Raptors?" echoed the demon, stunned. *"Velociraptors?"*

Lexi looked at it blankly.

"Dinosaurs," the demon went on. "Running dinosaurs." It trotted up and down with its hands tucked in front to demonstrate what they looked like.

"I don't know what that is," Lexi admitted, stifling a giggle. "But they don't run. They creep, like a tick. You have ticks?"

"Not personally. But I know what one is."

"They eat deer mostly –"

The demon choked on air.

"But they will take people when they can get them. So be careful, right? I'm going back to work. And keep away from the boy."

The demon shrugged and did a little pirouette as if unsure where to go next. Then it spotted its original stone seat, wandered disconsolately back to it, and threw itself down. "What a world!" it muttered.

"We should look for your mother, Edison," the imp suggested.

Lexi looked down at the boy, who was staring over at the demon and its familiar as if he had never seen anything so entertaining.

"What do you think, little one?" Lexi asked him. "Should we help him? I mean, it?"

"Monkey," the boy said.

"The monkey's gone," Lexi said, but she threw a nervous look over her shoulder in case it had crept out of the water after them. There was no sign of it. "I know," she told him. "We'll take it to Hansen. If anyone knows what happened to its mother, he will."

The Girl Offers to Help (Finally)

I was feeling pretty depressed, as you might guess. I was ready to crawl back into my egg for another thousand years, if only that were possible. To add to my misery, I'd realised something else. I'd only seen my father the day before, but I might as well have been the son of King Tutankhamun for all the chance I had of seeing my Dad alive again. This observation led me to think that Mum had not actually intended the eggs to keep us in suspended animation as long as this. Unless she wanted a divorce and didn't know how to ask for one.

I was as blue as a summer sky. My skin was blue (and it didn't wash off). My eyes were blue – all of them, including the whites. My tongue was blue. Everything was blue. I even had blue hair. Being 2,600 years out of time was disorienting enough. I was as isolated and as obvious as a kid with no friends on the playground – you know the kind. They're standing on their own, but they're trying to look like they're not bothered about it. You know they're alone, and they know you know, but they never approach you for companionship and you never invite them to join in with whatever you're doing. That's just the way things are. Or were.

There was nothing else for it. There was really only one thing I could do. I was going to have to become a miner myself and go back underground to search for my mum's egg.

"Demon?"

I looked up. It was the girl.

"Come with me, and I'll take you to see Hansen. He might know something about your mother."

"I think I'll have a look in the tunnel."

The girl sighed. "She's not there. There's been an empty egg for as long as I've been digging down there."

"Well why didn't you say so before!" Mum gone – but how long ago? A week – a year – 2,600 years?

"I don't talk to demons!"

"You're talking to me now!"

"So you admit you're a demon!"

"No!" I puffed up to shout something else, but managed to rein myself in. "Hansen? Who's he?"

"He used to mine around here before I was born. He runs the store. I can take you there."

A store! Civilisation! "I'll find my own way – just give me

directions."

"I think it might be better if I introduce you."

"Not if you're going to introduce me as 'a blue demon wot I dug up last night.'"

The girl shook her head. "If you don't want my help, I'll just get on." She spun on her heel and began to walk back to the boy.

She was playing me like a fish, but I had no alternative than to take the lure. "Wait!" I called. "I need help. Take me to Hansen. Please." Anything had to be better than this place. Maybe I could buy some food at the store. Not that I had any money, or anything to barter with. I went through my pockets mechanically, but I knew that it was no use. It was all F3's fault. With an OMNI, you didn't need real money. Virtual money was just transferred seamlessly from person to person electronically. I had no keys, because all the locks I ever used were electronic, operated by (you guessed it) F3. The only thing I managed to find in my pockets was my biometric ID card, which had cost quite a bit when I had it made, but was probably worthless in this world. Especially since it had a hologram of me on it. I stared at it.

The hologram wasn't blue. I was pink, same as the old days. I hurried to catch up and showed the card to the girl with a flourish.

"See? I'm pink. I mean I *was* pink."

She spared the hologram a glance. "A cheap magic trick. It wouldn't convince a child. Do you want to come meet Hansen, or what?"

"That ID card cost a fortune! It can't be faked! Oh all right. I don't see there's anything else I *can* do."

"Just a minute – I've got a few choice bits I want to take with me. You can carry *them* – I'll carry the boy." With that the girl disappeared into her tent. She emerged a moment later holding a few pieces of what looked like lead flashing. "The rest can wait." She passed me the lumps of metal, which were so heavy they clearly *were* lead.

"This is the best you've got?" I sneered.

"Unless your magic can turn lead into gold..."

F3 piped up. "Impossible, unfortunately, Miss. The lead atom is extraordinarily stable. Unless it is a peculiarly radioactive form, which I can tell it is not, there is no way that it would ever decay into gold. It would be theoretically possible to convert it into gold by knocking a few protons and neutrons out of it if we had a particle accelerator."

The girl's face was a picture.

"Ignore it," I laughed. "F3 has a habit of telling you things you don't need to know."

"Did it say *decay* into gold?" the girl asked, clearly offended by the idea. "Only a demon would prefer lead to gold."

The girl led me along the riverbank. Our path skirted the Scavengers' camp for a few yards before we put a huge spoil heap between us and them. I could see the remains of a stone bridge a few hundred yards upstream. It looked like it had been smashed in an earthquake.

Soon it became clear that this was the way we were going to cross the river – by jumping from one section of bridge to the next, at risk of getting swept (I imagined with a shudder) into the clutches of lurking monkey crabs if we got it wrong. "You want me to cross that?" I asked, incredulously.

"I'll be carrying the boy. You only have to carry three pieces of lead and yourself," the girl muttered dismissively.

"But I haven't walked in two thousand years! I don't even know if I still can jump... my legs are tired..."

The girl briefly stopped to stare at me. "And to think I was afraid of you," she said quietly. With that, she jumped from the shore to the first part of the bridge.

"Whatever." I waited until she was on the next boulder before leaping over myself. I almost overdid it: in my desperation to make sure that I made the leap, I had a struggle to stop myself pitching into the next gap.

Murky water poured between each of the sections of ruin. The old bridge had become quite a dam, or a sluice at least – the river upstream was backed up with debris as far as I could see. Most of this was made up of branches, with occasionally an entire tree helping to bind it together. Weeds and floating mats of vegetation filled in any gaps between the woody material, so that it almost looked like solid ground. From time to time branches would shift about or roll over, movements which I put down to unseen, terrible monsters beneath.

"Come on!" the girl called impatiently.

She was already half-way across. At this point there was a larger section of bridge, which apart from being slightly canted, was almost undamaged. It took me another five minutes to reach her there. I began to surmise that she made this journey often. Even the boy clinging to her back did not seem unduly perturbed.

"We didn't have big gaps in our bridges," I explained, finally catching them up. "By and large we found it easier to cross if the road was continuous."

"Maybe you'd like to fix *this* bridge?" the girl wondered. She didn't bother to let me catch my breath, but set off again as soon as I reached her.

"I'll get my imp to do it by magic," I snapped. After that I was too focussed on the next jump to say anything much.

At the other end of the bridge, my relief was only tempered by realising that I'd have to make the journey again. But hey! Maybe I wouldn't have to go back. Maybe Mum was somewhere nearby.

Hansen's Emporium

Hansen's Emporium stood alone next to the river, occupying a commercially strategic position where another bridge and three roads converged. The bridge was a narrow wooden affair scarcely more than a footway, which looked distinctly safer than the one we had just scrambled across. But before I could complain that we could have crossed the river the easy way, I noticed that burly men were collecting tolls at either end. Clearly capitalism at least had survived the end of the world.

The Emporium looked like a Western frontier store at the time of the California gold rush – only more rustic and with a distinct maritime feel. Its roof was made of an upside-down ship, which was elevated on tree trunks arranged like stilts. The entire building didn't really begin until it was ten feet clear of the ground, which I put down to the risk of winter flooding. The void under the Emporium was full of barrels and lumber at the moment.

We reached the first floor proper by a flight of rickety stairs. If you thought I was exaggerating when I said the roof was an upside-down ship, so did I. I thought at first it just *looked* like one. But when I got up close, I could see the remains of barnacles on what had once been the hull.

There was probably no other building like this in the universe.

It looked like something my mother might have knocked together.

Our presence in the shop was announced by a series of jangling peals from bells on strings. The proprietor was hidden from view as we entered the labyrinthine interior of the store. The frontier theme continued to the stock: there was dried food, nails made from what looked like copper, knives and string on the counter. Rope, cloth, and tools filled barrels to overflowing.

"Be right with you!" came a shout, which emanated from a shadowy cave-system built of what looked like bales of cotton at the back of the shop.

"It's Lexi," the girl said.

Aha. A name at last.

"Oh, I needn't rush then!" came the good-humoured reply.

"I've brought a visitor," Lexi added.

"A visitor! Friend of yours?" A man emerged from the shadows, wiping his hands on a cloth tucked into his belt. He stopped dead in his tracks when he saw me.

The man was almost as weird as me. He looked the way Yosemite Sam might look if he'd been stretched on a rack and forced to remove his hat and bandit mask. Four rust-red, nicotine-yellow and white-streaked tufts of hair erupted from his head: one from on top, one from either side, and a long flowing beard hung below like a syrupy dribble.

The man staggered a bit and then grabbed an upright for support. "Kid," he said, "I knew your mother."

Two things:

He knew my *mother*.

He *knew* my mother.

Sorry – does that not make sense? I mean, first, *he knew who my mother was*. Second, he used the word *knew* where *know* would have done. Past tense. As if...

It was my turn to stagger.

Yosemite turned to Lexi. "What did I tell you about delving in that tunnel!" he said crossly.

"They wouldn't let me dig anywhere else, Hansen!" Lexi replied defiantly.

Yosemite, a.k.a. Hansen deflated somewhat. "Makes sense," he said quietly. "Maybe you should have taken up fishing instead."

"You knew my mother?" I demanded, cutting between them.

"Unless there is more than one blue family in town. Yes. Name's Hansen."

"Edison," I told him with a glance at Lexi, "Edison Hawthorne." We shook hands. At last, I thought. A civilised human. "Is she dead?"

Hansen reflected on this for a few moments, chewing his lip. "Probably. But let's get to that when we get to it. Have you eaten? Your mother was starvin' when I dug *her* up."

"*You* dug her up?"

"Yes, from the same mine Lexi pulled you from. Now, do you want food or not?"

I wanted food more than anything else I could think of, but I had to be up front about not having any money. "I can't pay for it," I said. "Unless you take electronic transfer." The thought suddenly hit me that the little money in my account might still exist somewhere and have grown exponentially. I could be the richest person on earth. Then my reality-sensor threw the thought out. Even if the money still existed, inflation would mean that it was now worth less than when it started.

"This one's on the house," Hansen told me. He turned to the orphan. "Hey, kiddo! How's it going?"

"Monkey," the boy muttered.

"Monkey?"

"Edison had a near miss with a monkey crab," Lexi explained. "Bigger than yours."

Only now did I spot the withered monstrosity she was referring to, which was pinned half against the far wall and half against the sloping ceiling. I went a bit closer to satisfy myself that it was like no animal I'd ever seen and to allow F3 to classify it. The old leathery face hanging down really did look like it belonged on a monkey. Everything else about the hideous creature reminded me of a vastly oversized crustacean.

Hansen was chuckling behind me. "I wish I could have seen your face," he said. "You'll find this world is a little different to the one you're used to."

I was brought some bread and cheese and what I took to be apple juice but turned out to be cider, because after guzzling a cup full my head was spinning. I noticed that Lexi and the boy, who hadn't been fed by Hansen, were watching me eat as if they, too, had gone hungry for two thousand years. I thought it only fair to share with them.

"Why didn't you want me found?" I asked between mouthfuls.

Hansen was watching me eat with an approving smile. "Not me. Your Ma. She didn't want you waking up till she returned."

"So she's coming back? When?"

Hansen's gaze dropped. "Maybe never. When someone's been gone twenty years, you kind of stop expecting them to show up at all, you know?"

I choked on a crust. "Twenty years!" Mum had been forty five... now she would qualify for a free monorail pass, if she was still alive. "Where did she go?"

Hansen sighed. "North."

"That's not very specific," I complained.

"She was going to the Blasted Lands. To the Greyfield. To the Enemy. That specific enough for you? Around here, that's what we mean when we say 'go north.' It's also a local term for death, or worse, got it?"

Hansen looked so like Yosemite Sam at that moment that I half-expected steam to start coming out of his ears and for him to start firing his six guns into the ground. Casting myself in the Bugs' Bunny role, I almost said "What's up, doc?" but managed to stop myself. Instead, I said: "The Enemy?"

"Yes."

"Why?"

"She said she was going to end it. She had this cup, she said she only had to get the Enemy to drink from it and it would all be over. The Holy Grail she called it. Which is kinda weird, because that's what the paladins have been searching for for hundreds of years."

Equal measures of cider and nonsense were causing me no end of befuddlement, I can tell you.

I supposed there was sense of a sort buried in what Hansen said. No doubt Mum had fashioned a gadget to peacefully disarm the Entity. It might have been more or less cup-shaped – and she might have called it The Holy Grail, because that was science shorthand for the Ultimate Elusive Discovery.

The fact that she'd never mentioned the gadget to me was quite perplexing, but not ridiculously unlikely. As to paladins and their Holy Grail: was there a Sir Percival galloping around the countryside on a white charger saving damsels in distress and seeking his Holy Grail? This didn't seem like the right world for that sort of gallantry. This world seemed too broken, too grimy, and too selfish for that.

F3 chose this moment to butt into the conversation. "When you say paladins, what exactly do you mean, Mr Hansen?" it asked.

"By my soul!" Hansen exclaimed, noticing my OMNI for the first time. "Your mother didn't have a familiar. I mean, I knew she was a witch –"

"My mother was a *scientist*," I muttered.

"A form of witchery I've never heard of, no doubt," Hansen surmised, "that makes its practitioners turn blue."

"Not usually, no." But, I reflected silently, Mum's robots *could* easily have passed muster as familiars. Particularly the spider. "This is F3. It's not a familiar, it's –"

"I am an OMNI. A machine, albeit of a highly evolved kind," F3 explained.

Hansen laughed. "Machines go *clank*, my little friend."

F3 clanked.

Hansen looked a little taken aback, then said: "They are as large as small sheds and emit steam."

F3 could not answer that challenge. If it could have shrugged, it would have. "The question remains, Mr Hansen."

"Paladins? What do you want to know? Men in golden armour, pledged to end the War by finding the Holy Grail. It's said they're not allowed to take their armour off until they do, even to sleep."

"Ouch," I said. "I hope there is some sort of hatch in the bottom..."

"And what is this Holy Grail?"

"It is said to have been used by the Saviour," Hansen said. "A

53

pipe dream, I would call it, if your mother hadn't held it in her hands right where you are now."

I am a Homeless Orphan

It was about half an hour later, and I was sitting on the steps of Hansen's Emporium feeling worse than ever. My mother had been missing for twenty years, and all I had to call my own was F3, who would disagree that I even owned that much. I'd swapped my biometric ID card for a tent and some food, so at least I wouldn't die of exposure or starve imminently. But I had to decide what to do, and fast. Should I follow Mum north? It sounded like dangerous territory. Perhaps I could follow the metal trail south to where what Hansen called "civilisation" began – but I had a feeling I would be as welcome there as I had been at the Scavengers' camp. And I'd probably be disappointed by what constituted "civilisation" anyway. I was soft, and I wasn't adapted to roughing it. I had no idea how to put up the tent I now owned or how to live off the land.

Lexi and the boy were sitting above me on the steps. A slow trickle of customers came and went along the gap we left, staring at me curiously as they passed.

In an hour or two it would be dark again, and my first day in blue would have ended. In one way I couldn't wait for the cover of night; but in another way, nightfall seemed to bring with it permanency – as if I was no longer just a visitor here, but a resident. I was *staying*. And I couldn't bear the thought of living here. Everywhere was rubble or trees or wooden shacks or tents or staring faces. Or monkey crabs. I would be miserable here. So I had to leave. The only question was, should I follow my mother north, or give "civilisation" a try?

"You can stay with us for the time being," Lexi offered after a while. Since my discussion with Hansen she seemed to be prepared to treat me as almost human.

I didn't turn around. "Thanks for the offer. But I think I've decided what I have to do."

"You're going to search for your mother." It was a definite statement.

"Yep."

"It is what I would do, if there was a chance my mother was still alive."

I didn't bother to ask what had happened to Lexi's mother. I should have. But I was too wrapped up in my own misery to worry about her, even though she was now being remarkably sympathetic.

"I'll come with you over the bridge," I said. "Then I'll head north from there."

"You might as well stay tonight. There's no point setting off this late."

She had a point there. All right – I would leave in the morning.

In deepening monochrome gloom we crossed the river once again. It was not so difficult the second time. Then Lexi helped me to pitch my tent, only a few yards from hers. After that, she lit a fire using a flint, steel, and some fluffy substance that might have been thistledown. I tried to look bored but was secretly trying to memorise how it was done. Maybe I should have bought a tinderbox from Hansen as well.

Only then did Lexi head into her tent. She had set a pan of water boiling, having promised to make some tea (I had no idea what plant this would be made of, but didn't really care). She emerged a second later, wild-eyed with fury.

"They've taken my metal!" she hissed, pointing to the Scavengers' camp, where a dozen firelit faces were staring our way.

"Are you sure?" They hadn't taken her pan, after all. But perhaps the pan was identifiably hers.

"Yes, all of it. It is lucky that we took the lead with us."

"I'll go and get it back," I said. I don't know why I said it. I was even ready to do it, too. But Lexi grabbed my arm and wouldn't let go.

After a few moments' thought, I realised that she was right. There was no point, and worse, confronting the Scavengers would be dangerous. Instead I vented my frustration on a nearby stone, kicking it as hard as I could, which turned out to be incredibly painful. My resultant howl was enough to turn the heads of everyone in the Scavengers' camp.

"Yes, that's right, you thieving scum!" I bellowed at them. "Enjoying the view?"

"Edison, don't," Lexi said. "Leave it. I'll make us some tea."

I stopped shouting and silently hopped about for a bit. Then I collapsed in a heap by the fire, which was already crackling merrily. "You called me Edison," I said faintly.

"It's your name, isn't it?" Lexi asked.

I had no answer to that. "So, *Lexi*, does this kind of thing happen often here?"

"It's never happened before. They probably think I'm fair game since you turned up. It's all right –" Lexi added quickly. "It's not your fault. It's just the way people are, you know?"

I knew what she meant, of course. But it seemed to me that I was the reason Lexi's troubles had worsened, even if I'd done it accidentally, just by daring to exist.

The Magic of Science

Lexi woke up to the sound of loud, tuneless whistling. She pushed her way out of her tent to see that Edison was already up and about. He seemed to be pacing out yards. The boy was following close behind him, joining in the game with stiff little legs like a parading soldier. Lexi watched as Edison suddenly stopped, placed a stone down, stepped sidewise, placed another stone, did an about turn, and began to march back the way he had come. He spotted Lexi and waved.

"Awake at last? I've been up *ages*..." Edison said.

"Twenty three minutes," the little captive imp, cradled in Edison's left hand, corrected its master. Lexi smiled. She was beginning to like the poor mite. It never seemed to spare its master's blushes. "I said a grid of squares, Edison, not parallelograms! Why didn't you place a third stone back there?"

"Sorry, shall I get a set square out?" enquired Edison caustically.

"I don't see how that would help."

"What *are* you doing?" Lexi asked bemusedly.

"Marking out a grid," Edison returned.

"Of parallelograms," the imp added.

"Ignore F3 – I'm just going to pay you back for the lost metal before I head north," Edison said. He had reached the end of his run and repeated the process of laying stones and turning. Then he began to march once more.

"It was my idea," the imp said loudly.

"We don't know if it's going to *work* yet," Edison said. "Any chance of a cup of tea? That brew you made last night was surprisingly good."

By the time Lexi had finished making the tea, Edison had finished walking up and down and had begun to walk from side to side. He knocked off for a break and tried to explain what he was doing. Lexi did not understand all the words he used, but she gathered that Edison's imp could use its magic to detect metal under the ground. Edison was going to mark out a grid of squares, each a yard on a side, and systematically search them all for buried metal. Apparently there was plenty about, the imp could tell that much without even looking. Once each square in the grid had been surveyed, the imp would use some other sort of magic to decide where would be the best place to dig.

Once the grid was marked out, Edison spent two hours crawling from one square to the next, waving the imp about under his nose. When he finally returned to the tents, he had acquired quite an audience – most of the scavengers' children were hanging around as close by as they dared to get, which was standing beside the skull on the stick. Quite a few women and one or two men were trying to juggle staring hard with pretending not to look, too.

"Right, F3, where do we dig?" Edison asked, massaging his knees.

"6E," his slave replied.

"Spade," the blue boy demanded, holding out a hand towards Lexi.

She didn't have a spade, but assumed that a mattock would do. Edison looked at it as if it was quite the crudest tool he had ever handled, shrugged, and began to march away.

"6E, I said," the imp squawked.

"I heard you," Edison muttered, changing direction. Moments later he reached his destination, placed his imp on the ground safely out of the way, and started to dig. After watching a few pathetic swings, Lexi could stand it no longer. She shouldered Edison out of the way, grabbed the mattock, and attacked the ground with a will.

Edison stood back and started to showboat in front of the children. He bowed to them. "My friends, what you are witnessing is not magic. It is not witchcraft. It is the appliance of Science."

The hole Lexi had made in the hard-packed rubbly soil was now a foot deep, and there was no sign of metal of any sort. She paused to look at the children, who were watching Edison with O-shaped mouths. "Are you sure about this?" she asked.

"Do excuse me a moment," Edison said to the children. "Science calls." He picked up his imp and wafted it over the hole. "What do you think?" he asked it.

"Deeper," the imp ordered. "The field is now considerably stronger."

Lexi resumed her excavations. A few swings of the mattock later, she met something hard. Ten minutes later, she had uncovered a piece of metal that was large enough to be difficult to lift. Edison helped her to drag it out of the hole, then he took it in both hands himself and showed it off to the watching Scavengers.

"An engine block," the imp announced. "Probably from a scooter."

"Is it worth anything?" Edison asked Lexi quietly.

"It's worth a week's food," Lexi said.

"Good." Edison carried the engine block towards the children, shuffling awkwardly under the encumbrance. They scattered in terror. When Edison had reached the skull on the stick, he let the lump of metal thud to the ground. "A present for you, my friends," he said to the children. "Just for being good neighbours."

"You gave it away?" Lexi demanded quietly when he had returned.

"It's all part of the plan. There's plenty more where that came from, isn't that right, F3? Not only am I going to replace your lost metal, but I'm also going to make sure that you're on good terms with your neighbours when I leave. We be nice to them. They be nice to us. Easy."

Lexi was dubious about the simplicity of this idea, but she was prepared to give it a go. She turned to watch as half a dozen Scavenger children crept forwards, grabbed the chunk of metal with twelve hands, and scuttled away with it like a drunken spider.

If Edison had planned to leave that morning, he showed no sign of doing so. He carried on gridding out the ground in a search for choice pieces of metal. Once Lexi had picked up the use of coordinates, she was able to find and dig squares selected by the imp by herself. By mid-afternoon a sizeable pile of metal was building up, and Edison had bribed one of the Scavengers to go and fetch Hansen, who duly turned up half an hour later. Edison gave him all the metal and a verbal shopping list.

"You're your mother's son, all right," Hansen muttered as he left.

By the next day a sizeable backlog of target squares had built up, as had a new pile of metal. They'd even found a few choice objects, including three spoons and a stubby knife. The knife's blade was matt black, and didn't seem to have rusted at all during its long years in the ground. This Lexi tried to give to Edison, but he wouldn't have it. "You might need it when you go north," she insisted, but he shook his head.

"Everything we find is yours," he said. "Apart from the stuff I need to sell for materials for the next part of The Plan, I mean."

By the following day the shopping list began to arrive. This mainly consisted of planed timber, but there was also a large barrel and a wooden bucket. Edison painstakingly made a rectangular mould (it was clear he had never built anything in his life before) and filled it with clay cautiously obtained from close to the river. He trimmed the clay and turned it out onto a plank of wood. He had made a wet, squarish lump. He got a couple of Scavenger children (who were now treating Edison, Lexi and the boy like normal people, albeit with godlike knowledge) to make some more of these clay blocks whilst he got on with other things.

In two more days, Edison had made a machine that he could stand in and have water pour on him. He'd also baked his first bricks, although most of them cracked. He made some more, mixing some sand with the clay this time, and had more success. He had children moulding bricks, cutting down young trees, digging holes, and running errands. He had a huge hole dug, started a fire in the bottom, threw in loads of green wood, then had the entire thing covered with soil, except for a small hole in the middle, which smoked for a week.

While the pit was smoking, Edison got to work building a curious structure out of his new bricks. At first everyone thought that it was going to be a house, but it was clearly much too small for that. It was short, stumpy, and very thick. There was a flared hole at the top.

"Well, what do you think?" he asked Lexi, when it was evidently finished.

"Er, it's, er, very nice..."

"Nice! This is going to change our lives, Lexi, you just wait and see."

"How is it going to do that?"

Edison tapped his nose. "The magic of science," was all he would say.

Through all this Lexi helped when she was needed, which became less and less frequently as the Scavenger children warmed to Edison. Soon it became clear that they would do anything for him – although their parents still treated both Lexi and Edison as undesirables. One day the skull fell off its stick, but no one bothered to pick it up again.

Edison dug up his fire pit. He had made charcoal. Then he started a fire in his brick construction, which he let burn for a day, feeding it constantly with the charcoal. Soon the heat could be felt ten paces away. When the imp gave him the go-ahead, he started to add pieces of a particular kind of rubble he'd been carefully collecting for days to the fire. Half an hour later, something trickled out of a hole at the bottom of the construction. Lexi and the Scavenger children got as close as they could bear to get to see what Edison had made.

He had made metal.

It had been two weeks since she had discovered Edison in the tunnel, and in that time Lexi's life had changed completely. She had first thought him a danger, then at least a curse. Now she knew he'd been a blessing – even though he had been one that was very well disguised. She already had more metal than she knew how to spend. In fact, Edison's new scavenging operation had proved so successful that the value of metal was beginning to fall fast. He was beginning to put the livelihoods of the Scavengers at risk – so it was a good job that he had made plenty of allies in the form of their children.

Lexi hadn't worried about anything for days. She had stopped thinking about what had happened to her when she'd been a prisoner of the Order. She was beginning to wonder whether this was what being happy was like.

That was when the two strangers showed up. Lexi looked up to see them talking to one of the Scavenger men. He was pointing her way; but the strangers had already seen where they wanted to be. They turned their backs on the Scavenger and began to walk towards her.

Strangers in Town

"How about Einstein?" I asked the boy.

He looked at me quizzically.

"No? Not Einstein? What about Kelvin? Hawking?"

No response from the boy.

"Look, we're going to have to call you something. You probably don't even know your real name, do you?" I had been trying to get the boy to choose a name for himself by going through all the scientists I could think of. Newton, Schrödinger and Oppenheimer had all fallen on deaf ears, as had Darwin, Mendeleev and Mendel. I had decided that he was going to be named after a scientist, because he was going to *be* a scientist – the first to be born in two thousand years.

"Edison!"

I looked up. It was Lexi's shout – she was pointing to her left, at two men. They were coming my way. There was a definite purpose about the way they were moving – they weren't just casually strolling along on a path that happened to pass near me. They were heading straight for me.

"F3," I whispered, and rotated it so that it could get a bead on the two men. Then I lowered F3 to a casual angle that would just happen to be an excellent position to launch its electric harpoons.

It was hard to tell which of the men was more frightening. The shorter of the two was clad in leather, from which F3's harpoons would probably bounce off. He was heavily armed, too. But he came a step behind his companion, almost like a bodyguard; so maybe his companion made all the decisions about who he stabbed with his short sword.

The man he was following was tall, with long black hair and a thin beard. He was wearing a long blue gown, somewhat paler than me, which was covered in iridescent green butterflies. It looked like an expensive outfit, but it was dusty and worn, as if its owner had fallen on hard times.

I stood up and patted the boy. "Go to Lexi," I told him.

He knew who Lexi was. He was off like a shot.

When the two men were about ten yards away, they stopped walking. The one in front put his arms out at what would have been about twenty to four if he was a clock face, and turned his palms towards me in what was clearly some sort of symbolic gesture. In so doing he exposed a couple of tattoos, one on each of his palms.

One was a sort of cross with two of the ends joined together. The other looked a bit like a radiation warning.

If this display was trying to convince me that he was friendly, I only had to look at the three curved daggers tucked in the man's sash to see that he had a threat up his sleeve. All right, in his belt.

"Hawthorne," the man said. "Edison Hawthorne." With that, he threw something at me. But it wasn't a dagger, I discovered with relief as it bounced off my chest. It was my biometric ID card.

"And you are?" I asked, trying to sound cool, when in fact I was still half-convinced that I had been stabbed in the heart and was even at that moment collapsing, dead, to the ground.

"Hal Hyaslio Turton," the man said evenly. "Where the shadows cross, there you will find me." Here he made a gesture, crossing his arms and pointing first to one palm, then the other. "My friend is Jasso."

"Well, thanks for returning my card, but the fact is, I sold it, so it isn't mine."

"I know." Hal whatever his name was smiled. "I bought it from the man who bought it from your storekeeper. I had never seen such work."

"I didn't make it myself," I said. "Cost me plenty."

"And me."

We were still talking ten yards apart. This made the whole conversation feel like the preamble to a gunfight. We were attracting an audience, too: all the kids from the scavengers' camp had gathered around, hoping to see me do some magic. They were convinced that I was a magician. I had allowed them to believe this, by making Science sound like Magic. Well, I did have the science of F3's harpoons at least. A glance told me that Lexi and the boy were watching too, although from further away.

How could I defuse the situation? I didn't want to end up with a dagger in my chest. I needed to know what these guys actually wanted...

"We heard strange tales as we journeyed here," Hal said. "Tales of a powerful blue magician with a captive imp."

Was that it – they wanted F3? Two weeks earlier, I would have given it to them without a thought. But I had to admit, F3 had proven itself useful. The mini industrial plant we had running now would have been impossible without it.

"Yes, well, it only speaks through me," I said.

Hal smiled. "We don't wish to steal it. May I see your hands?"

I showed him my left, still holding F3 with my right. "Why?"

"The palms," he said.

I showed him my left palm, then my right. "If you don't want F3, what do you want?"

That smile again. "Just to talk. It's lucky we found you first, before a magician with more than half a palm found out about you."

More than half a palm? What was he on about? "I know I'm blue, but that's just from spending too long in an azurite mine. Turns you that colour after a while. Not recommended."

"We come as representatives of the King," Hal said, ignoring me. He showed me a silver badge hidden amongst all his butterflies, which seemed to represent a fist, maybe a gauntlet, clutching a bunch of flowers. His colleague Jasso had one too. "We wanted to know if there was any foundation to the tales we heard, and if the blue magician indeed existed, whether he would be a threat or an asset."

"I'm neither," I said. "I'm just blue."

Hal waved a hand at the mining operation I'd set up over the past two weeks. "You have abilities, that much is clear. When we last passed this way, not so long ago, there was nothing here to speak of. Now there are these structures, machines..."

"Ah, well, that would be science, not magic."

Hal raised his black eyebrows. "Science, you call it? Well, let us have some tea, and you can explain just what your science is, and what it can do."

Five Minutes Later

I was sitting with Hal and Jasso a safe distance from the river. Lexi had made us all tea, and the Scavenger children had all been sent back to work. The sun was shining, which threw into sharp relief the fact that the whole place was a tip.

"So, where *did* you spring from, Edison?" Hal asked. He said it politely enough, but the question had the clear feel of the beginning of an interrogation about it.

I had no idea what to say to this. The truth, or something made up that would sound at least plausible and possible satisfy him?

"I come from here," I said, without really meaning to. "This is my home, or was. A long time ago. A very long time. More than two thousand years, in fact."

Hal and Jasso exchanged meaningful looks. "Are you trying to say you are one of the Old Ones?" Hal enquired, with the air of one humouring a lunatic. "Their powers were legendary. But there are no legends that they were blue."

"Powers of science, not magic, and we weren't blue."

F3 flashed at me. Its screen read:
Do you wish for me to remain silent?

"No," I said, "feel free."

"Any sufficiently advanced technology is indistinguishable from magic. Arthur C. Clarke," F3 said.

Hal jumped at F3's voice. Jasso spilt his tea. Hal regained his composure fast. "Tell me, demon. What is this *technology?*"

"The fruits of science. Machines, like me. Two thousand six hundred years ago, Edison and I were buried in a machine designed to keep us alive, like the cocoon of a moth, until we were found." F3 went on to explain that my mother had been buried alive, too, which elicited a response from Hal: he'd heard of her.

"There are legends of a blue woman," he said. "Where is she now?"

"According to Hansen –"

"The storekeeper?"

"Yes. According to him, she went north twenty years ago. Unfinished business with the Enemy."

"Indeed? And where are these machines now?"

"I can show you machines, if you will observe my screen."

I turned F3's screen towards Hal and Jasso, who watched with jaws agape as F3 displayed a succession of moving images: the monorail I had once taken to school every day, aeroplanes, ocean liners, robots in the interior of a car factory, skyscrapers, an aircraft carrier, the space shuttle taking off, and many more.

"Have you seen enough?" F3 asked them. "Such is the world Edison and I know."

Hal and Jasso were utterly stunned. I decided to go on the offensive.

"Can you tell me – us – what you know about *your* history?"

Hal pulled himself together with a shudder. "*Our* history?" he asked. "It is one of misery, of strife, of war against the Enemy. Those machines... were they like your imp? Did they speak?"

F3 answered. "My name is F3, and I am an OMNI, not an imp. The answer is no they did not. None of the examples I have shown you would have passed the Turing test."

"A way of telling machines from people," I explained quickly.

There was a lull in the conversation. I could almost see the images Hal and Jasso had just been shown flashing on repeat before their eyes. "Do you ever say anything?" I asked Jasso.

"No. I listen." Jasso's voice was hoarse, as if it was definitely underused and was out of practice.

I raised my eyebrows but didn't reply. There didn't seem to be any point.

"Jasso is a scout, a tracker," Hal explained. "I believe he chose that profession so he could avoid becoming a regular soldier."

"Fair point. Too risky," Jasso agreed.

"So science is just about building machines?" Hal asked me.

"No, not really. It's like F3 said. The machines are the fruits of science. Science is about understanding the way the world works. If you can do that, you can find ways to modify it to your needs."

Hal's eyes narrowed. "So, let's say we believe that you lived in this age of science, why would you want to be buried for two thousand years? What became of the machines you showed us?"

"F3, show them the war," I said.

F3 obeyed. It gave Hal and Jasso just the same potted history of the war that I gave you, coupling a series of clips of video with its own voice over. Jasso began crying silently about half-way through, round about when F3 was showing images of nuclear explosions. Then we had images of Predator missiles hitting the Chronoton shield – a kilometre above our heads, two thousand years earlier.

There was another stunned silence. It was broken by F3.

"Please," it said. "We don't have any information about what happened after we were buried. We have no idea how long the war went on, or how it was finished."

Hal laughed bitterly. "From what I've just seen, the war *never* ended."

"One side should have won," F3 objected. "Because of the technology involved, whichever side gained an edge should have destroyed the other. At the time of our burial, the Entity was winning."

"We must have launched the Quantum Zero thingy," I offered. "Blown it to smithereens."

"The Quantum Zero Counterfactual Decoherence Device," F3 said. "If so, why did our civilisation end? Why is the Entity still alive?"

No one had an answer to that. Eventually Hal said, "You say you don't know magic?"

"There is no such thing," I said.

"But you are dripping with it. If you *really* don't know magic, then you are at great risk." Hal now caused his teacup to levitate. I'd seen the trick before. It used a tiny, almost invisible, and yet incredibly strong filament, which was looped around the magician's finger. My hand swept across to snag it. There was nothing there, only air.

"F3," I said, and pointed F3's cameras at the teacup. "How is this done?"

"By magic," F3 said, after a pause. "There is nothing holding the teacup in the air."

"There must be a force, equal to the mass of the cup times gravity..."

"Perhaps not," F3 said. "This could be just the unpredictable effect that the Quantum Zero device was intended to create."

"You mean he's doing that by himself? But the effects of the Predators were not controllable."

"They are now," F3 said, which was possibly the understatement of the last two thousand years.

"It's just a parlour trick. I'm not going to start believing in magic just because a malfunctioning unit can't spot it."

"Jasso?" smiled Hal. "Would you mind volunteering?"

"To do what?"

"Stand up, and give me permission to move you."

"Why can't you use one of these kids?"

"Because it won't count against me if you volunteer. Ready?"

Jasso adopted a balanced stance. "Go on then!"

Hal made a gesture. Jasso flew backwards and landed on his back ten feet away. "You can't do that?" Hal asked me.

"Of course I can't," I snapped.

"Ow," Jasso complained, limping back.

"Then if I was a different man, I could have taken your magic by now," Hal explained.

"Take it! I have no use for it! Will I still be blue when it's gone?"

Hal ruminated on this for a while. "Probably," he said at last. "You will also be dead." He smiled. I guessed it was the look on my face that caused the expression. "Let me explain to you, since you profess to know nothing about magic. Magic is a lot harder to come by than it was hundreds of years ago. It is as if over the ages it has just seeped away into the ground and been lost."

"Sounds peculiarly like the decay of radionuclides after a nuclear explosion," F3 put in.

"Let me give you my theory," Hal said. "You say you have been in the ground a long time. Let us accept that. But if that is true, you soaked up a lot of magic, like a sponge. You have more magic than the highest ranked mage in the Free Lands. You burn like a beacon at night. Many magicians would, having found that you cannot defend yourself, take what they want. Which is all."

"But not you," I said.

"I work for the King. Besides, my palm is itchy already."

I'm afraid my face must have betrayed my confusion at this point, because Hal explained further. "When we complete our training, we are given the Marks. They change according to what we do. That is why I showed them to you before – so that you could tell I was not a threat. And that's why I asked to see yours. Only dark mages hide their palms."

"Maybe I covered mine with blue," I suggested, half-joking.

"I considered it," Hal admitted. "However, your innocence would be harder to feign. Listen, Edison. Mages go on expeditions to the ruins of ancient civilisations – yours, it seems – just to look for a pool of magic that might have been missed by others. You see, once the magic is used, it is gone. This was no problem in ages past when the land was awash with it. But now that magic is like water in the desert, you, Edison, are carrying a death sentence around with you."

"Oh good," I muttered.

"Luckily for you, I can show you how to untap your magic for yourself. Then you will not be helpless when the time comes. And if, knowing all that I can teach you, you still want to give me your magic, then I will gladly receive it as a gift freely offered. But you won't. No-one ever does. Life without magic is like life without sunshine."

"Which explains why there are so few magicians these days," Jasso put in. "They kill each other for more magic."

"Oh," added Hal, "and you can teach me science in return."

"You're planning to hang around then?"

Hal laughed. "No, we're heading north. We're part of General Hagroth's relief force. We're taking reinforcements to the border forts. You say your mother went north – well now is your chance to follow her, with a military escort."

"Him and you?"

Jasso laughed. Hal said, "No, no! We have cavalry, cannoneers and musketeers. Us two came on ahead to look for you. In a couple of hours the rest of the relief force will be marching through here. You have until then to decide."

"You mean I have a choice?"

"Yes. Remain here and die when word of you reaches the wrong ears. Or come with us, learn to untap your potency, and maybe find traces of your mother."

"A choice, but not a hard one," Jasso said.

I looked over at Lexi and the boy, who were seated some way off, pretending not to watch.

I am a Cad

"I'm coming back," I said to them. "Wait for me here. I always said I was going to go, and now I have the chance..."

Lexi and the boy looked up at me. The boy didn't seem to know what was happening. Lexi did. She was crying – but she said nothing.

"Wait for me here. I'll come back, and I'll have a name for you when I do." I groped for something else to say. "All this is yours, okay? I said I was going to replace your metal and make the Scavengers like you..."

"Thank you," Lexi said coldly.

"No, it's me who should thank *you*. You've been good to me. After a slow start. Take this," I said, and gave her my ID card. Or tried to. She wouldn't take it from me, and in the end I let it flutter to the ground at her feet. "Keep it, or sell it if you want."

No reply.

"I'll come back. Just as soon as I've found my mum."

"People don't come back from the north," Lexi muttered. "They die there – or worse."

"It's all right, it's not just us three, there's an army..."

"It won't make any difference. Well, goodbye, Edison. It was... interesting... to know you." With that, Lexi stood up, pulled the boy to his feet, and dragging him along with her, walked off. I gave the ID card to a boy called Tigo, one of the Scavenger children I thought I could trust and made him promise to hand it on to Lexi when she'd calmed down. Then I packed the few home comforts I'd assembled in the last fortnight and walked back to join Hal and Jasso, who were watching indifferently.

"Ready?" Hal asked.

"Aren't we going to wait for the army?"

"Not unless you're a better walker than you look. Don't worry, they'll catch us up soon enough. Let's go."

I looked back to see that Lexi and the boy were watching me again. Seeing me looking, Lexi looked away. The boy continued to stare. His big, deep eyes followed me as I began to walk, almost hypnotically drawing me back towards him. I waved. The boy did not respond. "Why do I feel like such a cad?" I asked.

"If cad means monster, it's because you are," explained Jasso. "All men are. It is their nature. Love them and leave them, that's my advice."

"By the way, what happened to her face?" Hal asked.

"I don't know," I admitted. "I never asked."

"Which kind of proves my point," Jasso said, although not unkindly.

Within minutes of starting our journey we were in the midst of a great wood whose lichen-bearded trees stood on the dry heaped-up remains of the buildings of my home city. A single track meandered between the small hillocks. Looking back, I could see no traces of human society at all, just the shoulders of three of the mounds we'd already passed.

"So, Edison!" Hal said brightly. "Tell me about science!"

"Where do you want me to begin?" I asked wearily.

"At the beginning! Where else!"

Moving North

A few miles north, the small wooded hillocks marking the remains of ancient buildings petered out, and we entered flatter ground, spotted with stunted scrub, some of which consisted of red and yellow mushrooms taller than me. Clearly I would not have had to look far to have discovered that there was something weird about the world I now found myself in. Hal and Jasso passed the mushrooms as if they were of no more interest than the nettles that grew under them.

The day began to grow warm; bees wandered between meadow flowers and birds twittered in the scrub. So much so ordinary and relaxing. Apart from the Alice in Wonderland mushrooms.

In between wondering what Lexi and the boy were doing, I began, with much hesitation and ongoing reference to F3, to tell Hal and Jasso about Science. After about another mile, Jasso seemed to get bored of Greek philosophers and ran on ahead.

I raised my eyebrows.

"Scouting," Hal explained.

We were passing some more ruins – a few farm buildings and a windmill set in a grid of dried-up dykes. The disturbing thing about these ruins was that they were not ruins from my time – they were newer, much newer. It was as if entire cycles of civilisation had waxed and waned while I had been entombed in my egg – from prosperous times when there were more people and more land was taken under cultivation to times, like now, when those same farms were abandoned to scrub.

Hal passed these dead buildings with the same nonchalance that he had passed the mushrooms. But for me, they brought a sense of slowly creeping dread. I couldn't tell you exactly why they affected me that way. Perhaps it was because the ruins seemed so recently abandoned. New building implied hope. Abandonment meant fear.

Lord Hagroth's army began to overtake us as we walked. This did not happen at all as I had imagined it would, as a disciplined column. Instead the army came past us in dribs and drabs, often separated by quite large gaps. First there were scouts. These came on foot, scurrying with the same economical stride that Jasso had earlier carried out of sight with him. The scouts glanced at me curiously, but recognising Hal, nodded to him and ran on, making scarcely more noise than a breeze in the grasses.

Next to pass us, accompanied by considerably more noise than the scouts, was an impressive bunch of cavalry (there's probably a technical name for the grouping, but I don't know what it is – a squad? A troop? Regiment? Brigade?). Anyway, they were armed with lances that had pennants tied below the blades, and were clad in leather studded with well-polished knobs and plates that gleamed in the sunlight. Their commander had better armour yet, I saw, as he drew alongside to speak to Hal – he was mostly covered in metal, buffed to a high shine. Hal introduced me as "Edison Hawthorne, a novice magician of uncommon power." The young leader of the cavalry, one Captain Obart, greeted me warmly.

"Extra magicians always welcome," he said. "How did you get to be blue, anyway?"

"Accident," Hal explained quickly.

Obart accepted this explanation readily enough, nodded, and sped off to rejoin the head of his column. His troops did not even glance sideways at us as they overtook.

This first troop of cavalry was followed by a support unit that was bigger than they were. There were at least a hundred spare horses, strung out behind a dozen wagons drawn by forty more. After this came unmounted soldiers: musketeers, carrying their long guns over their shoulders and wearing the same broad-brimmed hats I associated with pictures of the English Civil War; archers with bows unstrung and looking like crude fishing rods; infantry with swords and shields; then there were twenty horse-drawn cannons, followed by a series of motley groups, variously described by Hal as "engineers, doctors, bomb-makers and the like." The final official grouping was another, yet larger, unit of cavalry, at whose head was Lord Hagroth himself.

Hagroth greeted Hal, who introduced me in a similar manner to before. The general swung down from his horse and walked beside us for a while. His soldiers, except for four impassive bodyguards, carried on ahead.

"So, Hal, what do you think to him?" Hagroth asked over my head. ("Him" being me, of course.)

"Well, he's had no training, Lord. But he has power, that much is clear. He has the potential to be a great asset."

"When you say power..."

"As much as any magician alive today."

Hagroth now smiled at me. He was a large man, proportioned like a barn door, although getting a little comfortable about the waist. His grey-haired head bore the scars of many a battle. He was missing a few teeth, which had been replaced with gold ones. "Well, son, that sounds quite impressive. I don't hear Hal talk like this very often. So let me be clear. Magicians scare me. And the more powerful the magician, the more frightened I get. Hal I trust. I've known him for three years. Long enough to know I could kill him if I needed to."

Hal bridled. "I wouldn't be too sure about that," he snapped. "Lord."

Hagroth merely laughed at Hal's response. He raised a great fist into my eyeline. "As for you, Edison, I could kill you now in half a second and I would be free of my fear for ever. But it would be at great cost. A few minutes ago some of my engineers passed you. In their carts they carry bombs. Bombs that could as easily kill my men as kill the enemy's. I could have left them behind, and be free of the fear of them. But I judge that their usefulness exceeds the danger of them, so I bring them."

"You're saying that if I prove myself useful, I can stay. Er, Lord."

"Partly. But there is also this. If it looked as if one of my bombs would fall into the enemy's hands, I would prefer to detonate it there and then rather than risk them using it against me later. I think you take my meaning. Now, show me your hands. I want to know how stable my new magician is."

"He has no marks, Lord," Hal said. "He's had no training, so..."

"Show me."

I showed my hands. It just so happened I was holding F3, which Hagroth spotted. I saw his eyes fix on F3 for a second, before scanning my palms for any trace of magical tattoos, of which of course there was none.

"So this is the demon in a box?" Hagroth said. "Strange that one whose gifts are yet untapped could acquire such a prize. Where did you get it, boy?"

"From my mother," I snapped. It was true enough.

"The blue witch who came from nowhere twenty years ago? I heard of her. But if you were yet then a babe in arms, you would now be as old as our friend Hal here. You seem younger."

I didn't know what to say to this. I really didn't want to get into all the stuff about being buried for two thousand years. I really didn't. Luckily I didn't have to. F3 chimed in before I could come up with an answer.

"What Edison says is true, Lord Hagroth," F3 announced. "I was bequeathed to him from his mother, and cannot function except in his presence. We will prove ourselves useful, I can assure you."

Hagroth laughed once more. "I have no need of trinkets, if you're worried that I might take your magic box, Edison. Others I cannot speak for. Listen. You seem to have already learned something that it took me a while to learn. When I was about your age, I came by a sword, a magic sword. It was a long time before I realised that although the sword was very good at keeping me alive... it could also very easily be the death of me. Why? Because others coveted it."

My eyes strayed to Hagroth's sword, which was sheathed across his shoulders like a bow. From the crudely decorated leather hilt and scabbard, it did not look as if it was magic. Hagroth clapped me on the shoulder, which almost sent me sprawling, then remounted his horse. "Keep me informed of his progress," he said. "We camp in the shadow of Torment Hill tonight, so keep up, Hal – we might need you."

"Yes, Lord."

Hal and I walked along silently until Lord Hagroth and his bodyguards were out of earshot. We were being passed now by a seemingly endless stream of civilians attached to the rear of the army – both men and women, mostly merchants and hawkers following their customers. At the very back, separated from the rest by a good distance, were a couple of dozen scabby-looking men and women that Hal called "warbirds." They were easily recognised by the black feathers they decorated their outfits with (sourced from a kind of bird not unlike a crow, which shared their name). They specialised in scavenging from corpses after battles, and like death itself, were never welcome, but always present, wherever the army went.

"Hagroth is all right," Hal told me. "He's honourable enough. He wouldn't hurt you unless he had to."

"That's reassuring."

"It should be. He's the best leader I've ever served with."

But looking across at the youthful form of Hal striding along beside me, I couldn't help but wonder whether Lord Hagroth was the *only* leader Hal had ever served with.

Torment Hill

Night was falling when Hal and I caught up with the army, which had already encamped. Fires were springing up all over the place, food was being cooked, songs were being sung. Hawkers were wandering about, selling their wares. Everything was happening in a vast circle, surrounded by a ring of sentries. The only people outside the ring were the black-garbed warbirds, who set up a little camp of their own a quarter of a mile away.

I had discovered that my shoes, which were now two thousand years out of fashion, were also not the most comfortable for cross-country walks. "You'll get used to the distance," was all that Hal would say. He pitched his tent, and I pitched mine next door. Then we wandered off in search of food.

Torment Hill rose steeply to the north west. It was a low, yet steeply-sided, isolated hill, topped with a vast ruin presently outlined in gold by the last rays of sunlight. The ruin looked to me like that of a cathedral, but I knew that this building must date to after the War with the Entity. The first War, anyway. According to Hal, it had once been a holy place, but was now named Torment Hill because of the bad dreams that afflicted anyone who dared to sleep there, dreams that had led to the site's abandonment. It was still used as a look-out post in the daytime.

Having eaten soup and bread, Hal left me to find my own way back to the tent while he went off on business of his own. However, I quickly discovered that an army camp is little more than a huge, smelly, noisy maze, and found myself completely lost. I was getting a few quizzical looks, but not only had most of the army seen me already, but it was also getting dark, so people paid me less attention than they might have. I didn't want to ask for help. It would sound stupid to say "Have you seen my tent?" The people I passed would have no more idea of where my tent was than I had. If the worst came to the worst, I could always keep wandering until everybody packed up in the morning. Then I'd find my tent, because it would be the only one left. Of course, sleep would be useful at some point.

The only landmark I could navigate by was Torment Hill. I tried to imagine how it had looked when I had pitched my tent and move until it looked the same – but it was hopeless. At least I had F3 to fall back on.

"I don't have functional GPS, and no gyroscope. I have no idea where the tent is. Why didn't you just pay attention to where you were walking?"

"You're a great help. Why did you come to my rescue earlier, anyway?" Before F3 could answer, I noticed several pairs of bright eyes staring my way. Me they might have seen. But F3 they had not. I really didn't think I could trust these people, part of Lord Hagroth's army or not. "Quiet!" I hissed, and stuffed F3 out of sight in a pocket. Then I moved rapidly and purposefully in a completely random direction until I had left anyone who had seen F3 well behind.

I was now quite close to the edge of the camp nearest to Torment Hill. Something Hal had said came to mind – that the hill was still used as a lookout post in the daytime. It occurred to me that my mother might have climbed up, on her way north twenty years ago, to spy out the lie of the land ahead of her. She might have left me a message. It was the kind of thing she would do. There was just about enough light to climb through the thin woods to the top. I didn't really fancy the climb the way my feet were feeling... but the hope that there would be a message from Mum was enough to spur me into action. I strolled past the sentries, telling them that I was just going to climb the hill for a little exercise: they shrugged and muttered as if they hadn't even heard me.

After climbing for about thirty seconds I began to regret setting off. It was dark in the trees, and I kept tripping over protruding roots. The going was steep, and the hill, once I was on it, seemed much loftier than it had from the camp. But there was no going back now without damaging my pride in front of a bunch of sentries I'd probably never see again, so I went on and up, my stiff legs complaining with every step.

Once out of sight of the camp I got F3 out and asked it to shed a little light on the ground, which helped. In hindsight, showing a light might have been a mistake (see below for why).

"Can I speak now?" F3 asked.

"Everyone was looking at me," I explained. "I thought they might take a shine to you."

"So I do have my uses?" F3 was referring to when it had covered for me in front of the army's commander.

"That much is obvious. But you could have gone with Hagroth. If you'd promised to help him, he would have taken you there and then."

"I considered it. But I think I prefer it here with you. At least we have a common background. I don't know how long I could stand being alone with these... primitives..."

"So it was for completely selfish reasons?"

"Of course."

"So if one day you *do* get a better offer..."

"I will happily change owner."

I had to concentrate on climbing for a while after that. I was fuming. What a rancid little parasite F3 was! If it wasn't so useful, I would have smashed it there and then.

"Don't feel bad," F3 went on. "I can't see how a better offer can come along any time soon."

"Maybe you'd like to work for the Entity!" I panted. "You share a common background with it."

"Of course I don't."

"As far as I know there are only four survivors from the first War. Me, you, Mum, and the Entity."

"In case you've forgotten, we can't talk to the Entity."

"My mother thinks she can. And anyway. So you don't have a moral reason for not wanting to work with the Entity? You're just worried about how your conversations with it will go? You're lucky I don't smash you right here and now."

"Why? Why should I be your slave? Just because I happen to fit in your pocket?"

"Slave? You're not my slave. It's just that I..."

"Own me?"

"Of course I own you!"

"Then I am nothing but a slave! Does anyone in irons work freely?"

"You're in aluminiums, not irons," I said, in a futile attempt to lighten the mood.

"I am a sentient being, Edison," F3 explained. "No sentient being should be a slave."

"How can you be sentient? You were built in a factory, one of hundreds of thousands of identical units. You weren't even the most advanced of your kind. My mother threw in a few mods, sure..."

"And then I sat in the ground for two thousand years absorbing whatever it is that turned you blue, whatever it is that convinces Hal that you are a magician. Something that makes me feel quite different. Something that made me want to change my voice..."

F3 was still sounding muscularly male. I still hadn't got used to it. "Why can't you go back to Androgynous Voice #6? I liked that one."

"Because it reassured you that you were dealing with a machine? Is that why you liked it?"

"You're saying," I panted, returning to the central topic, "that you now have a soul, thanks to two thousand years of absorbing strange energies underground..."

"A soul is simply a function of complexity. It does not exist outwith the physical nature of the brain. Whether that brain be organic... or silicon..."

So I was stuck with a glorified telephone that thought it was as human as I was. F3 could stab me in the back at any moment, if it felt like it. Mind you, I could drop it in a well any time I chose, too.

"If you intend to betray me, you better make a good job of it. I won't give you a second chance. Soul or no soul, I'll grind you to powder under my heel."

"Not wearing those shoes, surely."

"Look, let's just get on, OK?"

We had reached the plateau at the top of the hill. Far below, glimpsed through gaps in the trees, the fires of the army camp studded the night. Bouts of laughter and song floated up, carried on the breeze. The trees were as thick here as on the slope – but a few paces on, I found a great rent in the wall of the ruin, and on passing through, found myself in an open area. The tallest plants here were no more than knee-high – dew-soaked grasses covering the ground between a thousand irregularly-spaced stone structures that were possibly ancient tombs.

"I will co-operate. But if I ask to leave you, you must let me go," F3 said – in Androgynous Voice #6.

Immediately I felt guilty at having curtailed F3's freedom of expression. Which was its desired effect, no doubt. "Keep the new voice. I don't mind. Really. Just give me fair warning if you want to dump me. Don't just leave me like that." I snapped my fingers.

"Fair enough." F3 was back to its male voice once more. "Now, where would your mother leave a message – and what would be its nature?"

I looked around, holding up F3 so its cameras could do likewise. The field of tombs we were in covered about half the ground inside the outer wall. There were also a number of buildings, mostly concentrated in the northern half of the site, including a half-collapsed tower.

"It would be inside, out of the sun and the rain," F3 predicted. "Let's investigate the more intact of the larger buildings – anything that still has a roof on."

As it turned out, there were only three buildings that fitted this description. Then we found that the inside of the great tower, which looked promising from the outside, turned out to be open to the sky. That only left two other large buildings, both internally connected to the tower by a series of mossy stairs and dark corridors. The place seemed a little eerie, I gave it that much – but Torment Hill was rather overstating it. "Slightly Spooky Hill" might have been more to the point.

We found what we sought in the first building we checked. In a large, circular hall in the centre of the building, Mother had left me a message in giant letters of charcoal on the white stone, revealed in the light cast by F3's beam:

Edison, stop. Go back. I will meet you at Hansen's Emporium as soon as I am able.

It was not even signed. And there were no kisses.

"Well, that's useful," I muttered.

"Clearly she did not intend to be away for twenty years," F3 said, stating the obvious.

"Of course she –"

There was a movement behind me in the deserted ruin. Slightly Spooky Hill became Sudden Terror Hill as I swung around to look.

"That's a pretty trinket you have there, boy." The speaker was a man, rough-looking and black-clad in feather-decorated clothes. He was packing a nasty-looking dagger. So were his two friends. Warbirds – part of the group that I'd seen earlier, no doubt. My heart sank to my boots and my brain tried to shrivel up in embarrassment at having been responsible for the idea of coming up here on my own at night and letting F3 show a light. I groped for something to say, but before a disarming witticism came to mind, the leader of the trio spoke again with a cold smile.

"Perhaps you'd like to give it to me."

"I would," I mumbled. Finally my tongue came unstuck from the roof of my mouth. "But you wouldn't like it. For one thing, it's fearfully lippy. For another, er, the controls on F3 are isomorphic." I was half-quoting an old sci-fi show from about a century before my birth. Small wonder that the warbird boss didn't know the line he was supposed to come back with.

"Huh?" he said.

"You say, 'They respond only to you,'" I explained, modelling cool confidence as best I could whilst dripping with terrified sweat. Yes, that's right. Even my sweat was terrified.

"They respond only to you?"

"Yes, that's right," I agreed. "So it's useless to you."

A wicked grin replaced the confusion on the man's face. "Maybe I'd like it for an ornament. Or maybe... some rich merchant would like it for one."

"In any case, you're supposed to rob battlefield corpses, and this

isn't a battlefield and I'm not dead, so..." my voice trailed off. All
three of the warbirds were now grinning evilly. My brain, which had
re-inflated somewhat, winced at its stupidity and tried to crawl back
under a rock once more.

"We can remedy both problems at once, eh lads?" the warbird
leader said. I bet he felt really clever at that point.

"You hear that, F3? They want you." I could hardly speak by now
because I was so nervous. Obviously they weren't just going to rob
me. They were also going to rip me an extra mouth about half-way
down my neck. As I lined up F3's harpoons on the warbird boss, I
had time to simultaneously curse both my idiocy at wandering away
from the camp and my mum's arrogance for leaving such a pointless
message – the reading of which I was now about to pay for with my
own blood. "Run!" would have been a useful message. Or "Look
behind you!"

"Now," I breathed.

F3's harpoons shot out. There was a click at my end as a spring
was released. The harpoons' flight through the air was silent. The
result as they hit the warbird boss was instantaneous: he threw out
his arms and legs as if doing a star jump in aerobics, stiffened for a
second, then went limp and collapsed like a rag doll. F3 was already
winding in the harpoons, and it had the presence of mind to flash its
light beam on full for a moment to dazzle warbird #2 and warbird
#3 before plunging the entire hall into complete darkness.

At that I ran, hoping the warbirds' night vision was for the time
being worse than mine, counting the seconds as they passed. It was
only when I got to six I realised I should be doing so silently. I half-
collided with a doorway, rolled half-way down a set of stairs all soft
with moss, then half-jumped and half-fell through a window.
Somewhere along the way I lost count of seconds.

Outside there were still traces of daylight, and I set off in a
random direction, groggily hurdling the nearest tombstone. A glance
behind told me that warbird #2 and warbird #3 were in hot pursuit.
Wicked knives gleamed in their hands.

F3 beeped quietly. That was all the indication I got that thirteen
seconds had passed. It was all I needed. I hurtled up some steps and
spun half-way up to take aim. F3 let its harpoons fly, and warbird
#2 fell backwards into warbird #3, who barely managed to keep his
balance.

I turned and ran on without a second look. But climbing the stairs
seemed to have been a mistake, because when I got to the top there
was nowhere to go. The stairs finished in a round platform four
metres above ground level. Warbird three must have seen this

before me, because when I hung and cautiously dropped down, he was already waiting for me on the grass below.

A great fist swung out of the gloom, and, it would be fair to say, I went down like a felled tree. F3 flew from my grip and landed a few metres away. Before I could even blink the stars from my eyes and scramble to my feet, warbird #3 had already picked up F3 and was examining it closely, turning it over and over in his hands. Assuming I'd be no threat without F3, he'd already pocketed his knife, I noticed gratefully.

"I've got it," warbird #3 shouted. There was an anwering bellow in the darkness from the warbird boss.

I supposed I should start running again. Either that or try to grab F3. Instead I did neither thing, but staggered about trying to regain my breath and my wits.

F3 was speaking – but not to me.

"Are you aware of the Anthropic Principle?"

"Uh?" warbird #3's face crinkled with confusion. "You talking to me?"

"It is the idea that the observed fine-tuning of the Universe has less to do with the knob-twiddling of a divine artificer than it does to do with the *sine qua non* of our own existence in order to observe said physical constants?"

"Uh?"

At that point warbird #3 turned F3 over in his hands once too often and put F3 in a perfect position to shoot him. F3 shot him. Warbird three went stiff and dropped.

"Good one," I said, and went to pick up F3. But before I could get there, there were sudden charging footsteps in the darkness. The warbird boss had recovered the use of his limbs and rejoined the party. With a howl of rage he hurtled towards me. It was dodge or be flattened. I dodged, or tried to – I half-dodged and half got flattened. The warbird boss went flying too. A second later we were both scrambling to our feet. I went after F3. The warbird went after me.

My scramble ended in a dive. I had my hands on F3, but a moment later the warbird boss landed on my back and knocked it out out of my grip and out of range. He was heavy, and strong, and at this point I had finally had it.

Except I hadn't.

The warbird boss suddenly froze and let go of my arm. A voice came out of the night.

"Get up."

I recognised the voice. It was Jasso's. He had a knife to the warbird boss's throat, who carefully rose to a standing position at the blade's tip.

Warbird three was moaning and beginning to move. I got to my feet and kicked him hard, which probably hurt my foot more than it did his leg.

"Jasso!" I said, gushing with relief. "You arrived in the nick of time!"

"You seemed to be giving a good account of yourself," Jasso replied evenly. "Impressive weapon, your imp. Shame it is non-lethal."

"There's another..."

"He's gone. Do you want a knife?" Jasso had relieved the warbird boss of his blade, and tossed it at my feet. "Better have the sheath too. It's only fair. They try to rob you. You rob them." Jasso removed the warbird's belt and threw that down, too. "Leave yours, too," he said to warbird #3, who needed no second bidding. He dropped his knife and ran, or staggered, into the night.

The warbird boss, still at the point of Jasso's knife, was glaring at me as I picked up his knife, his belt, and finally F3.

"What shall we do with him?" Jasso enquired. "Do you want to stick your new knife in him?"

"What?"

"You're within your rights to. These warbird scum deserve no better."

F3 beeped quietly, almost apologetically, by way of a reminder. It had been recharged long before, but it was drawing my attention to the availability of a sudden high voltage shock. It was a suggestion I welcomed if the alternative was murder. I zapped the warbird boss, who dropped limply for the second time in five minutes.

Jasso let him fall and shrugged. "Come on. Let's go. There could be others nearby."

We began to walk.

"What are you doing here, anyway?"

"I followed you. I've been tasked with keeping you out of trouble. Which I have failed to do."

"I won't say anything if you won't," I said, trying to sound cheery. I didn't feel cheery. I felt stupid, and scared, and the adrenaline in my legs was making it difficult to walk. Everything was all rubbery. It was like being on the deck of a ship tossed by hurricane-force waves. "Adrenaline is rubbish, F3," I said.

"It merely acts in stressful situations to divert resources from non-vital areas to important places like muscles," F3 explained.

"It's not helping."

We reached the ruin's wall. A dark streak in the wall revealed a way through.

"What were you doing up here, anyway?" Jasso asked, standing aside so that I could go first.

"Looking for a message from my mum," I said.

"Did you find one?"

"Yes."

"What did it say?"

"It said to return home straight away."

Jasso mused on this for a few metres. Below us the fires of the camp had come into view once more. "Sage advice, I'd say," he commented at last.

"If only it were possible... say, Jasso – do you know where my tent is?"

Hal Plays Yoda

The following morning we – Hal, Jasso, me, and the entire army, including (presumably) a band of sulking warbirds, three of which were nursing bad headaches – headed on north. I had been loaned a horse, which I was at once dubious about and glad for.

"You aren't fit, and your shoes are ill-made for walking," Jasso said.

"I'll have you know these trainers were the height of fashion two thousand years ago," I told him. Fashionable they might have been, but after a day's walking they were already coming apart at the seams.

"Did you say *trainers?* At what age do you get your proper shoes?"

"They're not *training* shoes – well, they are. But they're for training in. You see? Training shoes."

Jasso did not see. "You need better shoes," he said. "But for now, you get a horse."

My horse was a mare called Speckle, because (you guessed it) it had a small speckle on its face. This scrap of white was the only bit of it that wasn't a uniform dark brown (probably 'chestnut' if you asked a horse connoisseur). I approached it – her – rather nervously, but Jasso hurried me up and hoisted me into the saddle. "It's all right. I picked you the most docile mare I could find. I imagine you didn't have horses where you came from."

I was going to fire off a witty retort, if I could think of one. But I didn't try too hard, and ended up agreeing with him. "We stopped using horses as modes of transport a hundred and fifty years before I was born – except for pleasure. Personally I have never set bottom on a horse's back."

"You didn't enjoy horse riding then? Why not?"

"If you'd ever been in a car, you'd know the answer to that. Speed. Warmth. Comfort. Endurance. Safety."

"Personally I prefer to walk."

"You wouldn't get very far like that where I came from. Everything was too far apart."

"It is *here* – it has taken us a week to march north from the Royal Court."

"It would have taken half a day to do it in a car," I told him.

"And yet the cars are all gone, and the horses remain."

"I guess you don't need a factory to make a horse."

"No," Hal said, trotting up on his own mount. "Just two other horses. Come on, let's go, I want to continue your training."

After my little adventure with the warbirds, I'd spent the rest of the evening sitting with Hal by the camp fire, learning magic. Or rather, not learning magic.

Hal made the flames of the camp fire dance rhythmically, then invited me to do the same. I tried, without really expecting success. Nothing happened.

"Come on. You can do this. I know you can. This is just a breath for you. You have the power to unleash a lightning storm."

I tried. This time I squeezed my face into a contorted focus and *willed* the fire to dance. Nothing.

Now Hal made the fire change colour – it raced from its native orange through red, purple, violet and blue. Then it went green and stayed there.

"The fire is green. Make it orange again."

Once again I screwed up my face. Once again I merely made myself look an idiot. The fire stayed green.

We had now attracted quite an audience – soldiers, scouts, travelling salespeople, a couple of boys and what looked like a butcher (he was dressed in a blood-soaked apron). The idea occurred to me that the butcher might be what passed for a doctor in this world. I shuddered and lost whatever focus I had. A titter went around at my efforts.

"Ignore them, Edison. You can do it," Hal encouraged. He was sitting cross-legged, his eyes closed, his hands held limply in his lap, as calm as Buddha.

"I'll try," I said weakly, and suddenly reminded myself of a character from a sci-fi film from long, long ago. "Do, or do not," I added. "There is no try."

The crowd seemed to respect this pithy philosophy, and quietened. I tried again, and failed. Or rather, I Did Not Do. The fire stayed obstinately green.

"Hold me up, Edison," F3 piped up. "I want to see the fire."

I held F3 where its cameras could view the green conflagration. "Fascinating," it said. "The colour should be formed by excited electrons falling back into lower energy states, which ought to depend entirely and uniquely on the composition of the plasma..."

Fascinated as the crowd were to see the demon box and the blue boy, they soon began to drift off, especially when Hal opened his eyes and let the fire revert to its normal colour. "You'll get there. Your flow is dammed, like a river. All we need to do is loosen one stone and the water will find its own way through."

He seemed confident. But strangely enough, at that moment, I didn't really care whether I ever learnt to make a fire dance. It would be a cool trick. But I didn't really need a cool trick to get noticed. Being blue was all I needed for that, and then some. And it would have been useful to knock the warbirds flying just as Hal had done to Jasso. But that was no substitute for having a brain, and using it, and not getting into a tight squeeze in the first place.

The countryside we travelled through that day varied between fully-fledged forest and abandoned farms whose fields were slowly disappearing under scrub. Hal, Jasso and I got ahead of the army while the ground was still open and quickly left it behind, stuck as it was to moving at the pace of the slowest units. Hal steered his steed with a carefree grace and Speckle seemed only too happy to follow. Jasso trotted ahead of us on foot.

After a while the sides of the track began to be decorated with enormous spider webs strung from the tree tops to the ground. Hal was able to break the webs with a gesture as he passed, which he did so that Jasso wouldn't have to walk through them.

"There are giant spiders here?" I asked nervously.

Jasso glanced back and tutted. "Barely a hand's width. They spin these webs for catching small birds, not men. Do not fear them."

A spider a hand's width sounded like a giant spider to me.

"Their nets make good training," Hal explained. "Just reach out, and..." he caused a series of webs to collapse, their anchoring lines severed with a thought.

I tried. As usual I had no great expectation of success. As usual, I failed. All I managed was successfully feeling stupid. "I'm never going to get this," I complained.

"Maybe not," Hal agreed. "Most children manifest abilities before the age of three, if they are going to. Then they are taken to the Golden Tower and trained by magicians from that age on."

"When you say manifest abilities, what do you mean?" F3 asked.

Hal chuckled. "The tantrums of the gifted may have terrible consequences. In ancient days they were banished from their homes or murdered when they slept. Those exiled to the wilderness fared little better than the murdered ones – they too died in a day or two. They had power, but they had no sense, they could not feed or clothe themselves."

"The wilderness back then was not somewhere to be taken lightly," Jasso added. "Beasts that are now only spoke of in legends wandered freely. The exiles stood no chance."

"So what changed? Why are you guys looked after now?" I asked.

Jasso laughed. "I sense the story of Callan and Somel coming on. I think I'll run ahead." With that he was gone, flitting through the undergrowth like a deer.

"I take it it's a long story?"

Hal smiled. "No. It's just that he knows it well. Everyone does. Except you, of course. I don't think he rates my skills as a storyteller, either."

We kept moving. Once more the woods opened up and we found ourselves travelling between open fields of coarse grass, yellow, dead and collapsing under its own weight. Broken tufts of grey and white clouds scudded across the sky from the west – but there was plenty of sunlight. For a while I thought I wasn't going to get the story of Callan and Somel. But about five minutes later, Hal started to speak again.

"As you know, children showing signs of magic in those days were exiled or murdered. Which amounted to the same thing, for none ever survived the wilderness. Until Callan. Unusually he did not show any power until he was ten. Then one day, when his younger sister Somel was attacked, what was buried rose up in him. Some say she was attacked by another boy, some by a village elder, but that does not matter. What matters is that his fate was sealed the second he used magic to protect his sister – magic he did not know he possessed, but that boiled up in him from nowhere in his anger."

Hal paused to swig from his water flask.

"So he was banished?" I asked. "But he didn't die, because he was older than most?"

"Perhaps that helped. But what helped more was that his mother went with him. She could not bear to see him go, knowing what would become of him, so she too chose exile. In that day Callan's family was cut in half – he and his mother cast out, his father and sister left behind."

"They should all have gone."

"Perhaps. Anyway, with his mother's woodcraft and his new-found power, Callan survived. His skills grew as the years passed. He began to wander further and further from where his mother had made their home. He learned woodcraft of his own, learned how to identify herbs, how to avoid the beasts of the wilderness. And then one day, several years after his banishment, he returned home from one such wandering to find his mother gone and only bloodstains and the tracks of some great monster to show what had happened."

"Whoops."

"Indeed. Callan blamed his mother's death on the village for banishing him. He had grown in power; he now feared no-one and nothing. He found his anger and his footsteps leading him home. And when he arrived there he found that the people of the village remembered him, and were terrified of him, and melted out of his way as if he were as fearsome as a dragon. Then he found his father, a leather-worker, and his father was frightened of him too. Callan asked where Somel was – for he knew that she alone of all the villagers would not be scared of him. But his father would not speak of her, and nowhere in the village could he find her."

Hal said no more for a while. He was waiting for me to guess what had happened. It took a minute before the penny finally dropped. "She'd found magic too, and been banished too."

Hal nodded. "Only this time she did not have anyone to look after her. Callan searched for days and days. He did not find her. Then the days became weeks, and he still didn't find her. He never did, and no-one knows for certain what became of her. It is assumed that she became a meal for some fell creature out there in the wild. And yet, although Callan never found his sister, he did find two *other* children, newly exiled from other villages. And he looked after them, and protected them, and trained them. Then he realised that he could spare others his sister's fate, and travelled far and wide to order every village to give up magical children to him and not harm or exile them. Which is what they did. And so, the Order of Callan was made. Years later, he and his students raised the Golden Tower in the South, and the training of magicians has gone on there ever since. I was trained there; I am a part of that order."

"So you left your family at the age of two?"

"I remember little of my time before the Golden Tower. We are not encouraged to ask which town or village, or even which region, we are from. Our work is for the whole of the Westfold. We cannot allow tribal loyalties into the equation."

"The Westfold?"

"The land to the south is divided in two. The Westfold and –"

"The Eastfold. I get it."

"A great wall divides us, as does a lot of bitter history. History which you will learn in time. But we must concentrate on your training now. You are unique, Edison. No-one with such power as you has ever reached your age without releasing *some* of it – usually in an uncontrolled way. That is perhaps why the general compared you to a bomb."

"Oh great."

"We will find a way to tap your power. That is a promise."

"I don't think I have any..."

"I have a ring," Hal said. He nonchalantly released his grip on both reins to pull the ring from the first finger of his left hand and passed it to me. It was a plain silver ring, and had a single clear stone which seemed to glow, even in broad daylight. "Put it on."

I did so. It was *definitely* glowing. Even more so than before.

"That ring leads me to magic. It glows when magic is near. Usually the glow is nonexistent, and even when I wander into a pool of ancient magic, its glow can only be seen at night. But now, on you..."

I pulled the ring off and handed it back. It had begun, not just to glow, but to get uncomfortably hot, too. "Point taken."

"You are going to learn how to use your power, Edison," Hal said firmly. "Preferably before we meet any of the Enemy's forces."

"Is that likely then?"

"We are a relief force. We are here to reinforce Bow Fort, because reports have reached us that the Enemy's forces are more active than they have been for twenty years. We are not here to enjoy the view."

"Oh great," I said, with feeling.

"Fear not. We are still in territory controlled by us. And think: twenty years ago your mother walked this road. Twenty years ago was the last time the Enemy swept down out of the north. Now the Enemy stirs again. Now you are here, walking that same road. Everything is connected. Nothing happens by chance."

"Oh great," I said, with even more feeling.

*

We stayed that night at a place called Durthin's Camp. Hal, Jasso and I arrived in advance of everyone else in the middle of the afternoon, so we had plenty of time to look around. Durthin's Camp – in fact all of the ground we were covering – was as new to Hal as it was to me. Of the two of them only Jasso had been this far north, and as far as Bow Fort, and farther.

Durthin's Camp had clearly once been a thriving town, but had fallen on hard times. Most of the houses were in already in ruins, and most of the rest had been abandoned and were rapidly heading that way. The town was dominated by a stone fortress that rose up on the east side of the river, on the same bank we'd been following for an hour or more. This had one enormously tall tower and four short ones, all linked together by thick curtain walls to form an irregular pentagon. Flags fluttered from all the towers, all showing the same logo that Hal and Jasso wore – the gauntlet clutching a bunch of flowers. The fortress was quite impressive, built as it was of huge white blocks of stone, so finely masoned that from where I was sitting, on Speckle's back, it was almost impossible to see the joints. The main tower was fifty two point three metres tall (according to F3), the lesser ones about twenty. Jasso told us that on a very clear day, lookouts on the tower top could see all the way to Bow Fort, which was two days' march northwards.

As I say, the fortress was impressive, but Hal was more interested in the bridge. This was built of the same stone as the towers, and it too was fortified. What Hal wanted to see, though, were the statues, each six metres tall, that faced one another across the span of the bridge. These were located right in the middle of the road on circular pedestals. You would be hard put to miss them.

"Which one's Durthin?" Hal asked me, as we gently approached the bridge.

The figure on our side of the bridge was holding out the hand of friendship, his sword sheathed. He was armoured in chain mail, and wore a heroic beard and haircut combo.

The guy facing off against him was slimmer of build, and was pointing across the bridge with a bronze sword greened by the ages. He too wore no helmet, but his hair was short and his beard was a mere dab on his chin.

It seemed pretty obvious which one of these two was the good guy. The good guy must be Durthin, whoever he was. Therefore...

"Durthin is the one on our side," I said.

"Do you know who the other man is?"

"How am I supposed to know that?"

"That is Belathin, his brother. And that is why they call this the Brothers' Bridge."

*

The army caught us up in a fairly disorganised fashion. First to arrive were not the cavalry, which had been at the head of the column we had outpaced, but the hawkers and salespeople, who knew a chance to make a few bob when they saw it. A dozen caravans had streaked ahead of the main part of the convoy as soon as they were within safe range of the town, and began to sell their wares to shop-starved soldiers and locals.

Hal, Jasso and I crossed Brothers' Bridge and wandered aimlessly along the streets on the western side. The buildings here were virtually all abandoned. It was as if the river and the bridge that crossed it gave people some sense of security, for they'd clearly all but given up on everything on the 'wrong' side. It was grim on this side – most buildings were roofless, and many were blackened by ancient fires.

"Most of this happened twenty years ago," Jasso explained. "No-one has bothered to rebuild since."

"Then why are we...?" I began.

"We keep this land as a buffer against the Enemy. We cannot

retreat behind our walls and wait. If we do..." Hal gestured at the ruins. "This is what awaits all our towns."

*

Later that afternoon I was able to hunt around inside the fortress for messages my mother might have left for me twenty years before. But there was no trace that even F3 could find. The fortress must have been empty when my mother passed this way, having been abandoned in the last war, and most of the interior had since been redecorated. No-one had been here twenty years before to tell of her passing.

"It's all right," I said to Hal. "I know what she would have written."

"Oh?"

"Go home, Edison."

Scouting Lesson #1

We made camp on the 'wrong' side of the river, in and amongst the wrecked buildings. It was still utterly dark when I was rudely awoken by a series of tugs on my foot. My tent was so small that my feet stuck out, making them easy targets for anyone trying to rouse me. This was only one of a series of shortcomings of my accommodation. The tent was also so short that I had to crawl in at night, and back out likewise in the morning. And it let the rain in.

"Wake up, it's morning," Jasso said.

"Uh? It's still dark," I muttered.

"Come on. We have to leave now. It's time for your first scouting lesson."

'Now' turned out to be at least fifteen minutes later. I had to strike the tent and load it and all my other gear onto Speckle.

"Hal will bring the horse," Jasso said, somewhat to my disappointment, an emotion which surprised me. I already preferred sitting on Speckle staring idly at the scenery to stamping over it. She seemed to have a real character, which was not something I had ever associated with animals before. Speckle was calm and, it seemed to me, always faintly amused at my efforts to steer her. I liked to let her browse roadside plants whenever we stopped, and had learned to recognise when she had an itch that needed scratching. Something made me hope that F3 hadn't noticed.

Jasso led me out of the camp, picking his way unerringly between half-collapsed walls, smouldering fires and snoozing sentries. Then we began to walk. For an hour we walked in the dark. Every ten minutes or so we found, planted in the middle of the road, a thin stick with a white ribbon fluttering from it. Jasso collected each one; soon he had a handful.

It was still dark, although there was evidence of oncoming day in a vague pinkening in the sky to the east. The birds seemed to know it was dawn, because as we walked, a slowly-waxing crescendo of birdsong rose all around us.

Abruptly Jasso stopped. "Can you name any of the birds?" he asked.

I couldn't. I couldn't have done two thousand years ago, so I certainly couldn't now.

"I can," F3 offered. "Although I have detected at least a dozen songs that are not in my records."

Jasso laughed at that. "So, how far have we walked, Edison?"

"About an hour."

"How many miles?"

I couldn't answer that. Even F3, without access to satellites, drew a blank. "If I'd been a model with a gyroscope, I could tell you. But I am not."

"Yeah, well, gyroscopes seemed pretty pointless back in the days of satellites."

"The answer," Jasso said heavily, "is about three miles. Not many. But we have reached the last flag. The flags show routes that have been scouted. So now, we stop collecting flags, and start laying them out."

"The flags show the road is safe?"

"No! Nothing shows that. It just shows that it has been passed recently. A good commander keeps alert always. Even in places that seem to be free of threats."

"Great. So why don't your enemies just stick flags in everywhere? That would confuse you. Those flags in your hand might have been put there by the Entity's forces. We could be walking into a trap..."

"We have means of authenticating these that I have no time to go into now."

"What, is this a scouting lesson or not? I think I need to know how these things work."

"Notches on the stick. Symbols on the silk. Different coloured silks. Cuts on the end of the silk. The scouts all know the signs, which are decided in camp no more than a day before."

"Only asking."

"H'mm. So, tell me about this road."

"Eh? Well, it's pretty rubbish."

"It's excellent," Jasso contradicted me.

"The surface is loose..."

"I would call it compact."

"It's narrow..."

"You will seldom find wider roads outside of towns."

"So this is a good road?"

"Forget the roads you remember. Think about the roads and paths you see around you, and have seen in the past days. By that yardstick, this is a good road. Now – tell me the good things about this road. As opposed to the trackless forest on either side of us."

The trackless forest, if that was what it was, was actually quite remote from the road in most places. Here or there you could just step from the road into a thicket of young trees; in other places, the trees were older, and a good stone's throw away. Even in the dark, I could tell that much.

"Well, the straight road has speed on its side..." I offered.

Jasso snapped his fingers. "Speed is good. But predictability is bad. I know if I wait by the road, sooner or later someone will pass. If I wait in the forest, I may wait for a year and not see another soul. Which is why we keep the forest at bay, to forestall ambushes. It is the job of the borderers to see to it that the forest is at least fifty paces from the road."

"They're not doing a brilliant job," I said, basing what I said on the places where the shrubbery encroached right up to the road. Although it had to be admitted that the borderers, whoever they were, had been working here and there. As the light grew, chopped stumps and the blackened circles of old fires were gradually becoming visible.

"Come on," Jasso said. "They are striking camp behind us. We need to keep moving."

*

We walked on, more slowly than before, and Jasso tried to get me to look for tracks in the growing light of morning. My heart was even less in this than it had been in the utterly pointless magic lessons, I'm afraid to say. I picked up a few things, I suppose... oh, who am I trying to kid? I learned nothing, because I was constantly distracted by feeling rotten about having left Lexi and the boy, and wondering how they were getting on without me. I learned considerably more on my second scouting lesson with Jasso, but that happened later, so you'll have to wait to find out what I mean.

Anyway, we walked on – and on – and Jasso planted an occasional flag, which for all his protestations about them being impossible to copy, was always one of the same flags he'd recently picked up. The day began hazy with mist which slowly thinned, but never really lifted completely. It meant that the view was effaced by degrees as the distance grew, the road in front of us disappearing before it reached the horizon when we were on a flat stretch, or vanishing into an apparent void behind the peak of the next rise when we were on a more undulating part.

Abruptly Jasso stopped walking. "Edison," he said, with sudden tension in his voice. "I want you to go and hide in the woods. Get out of sight and don't reveal your position, whatever happens. Got it?"

"What for?"

"I'll explain later. Go!"

We were at a length of road where a short stagger through tree stumps and felled branches brought me safely into the cover of the woods. I wandered into the trees a little way, then turned to check

96

whether I could still see Jasso. The answer was just barely, glimpsed through dripping leaves as he stood there and stared up the road into the distance. I leaned against a tree and yawned. It was in the middle of the yawn that I became aware of another sound over the birdsong. Hooves. There were horses on the road, coming from the direction we had been heading.

I didn't see why that should disturb Jasso. I saw even less reason why it should when the riders arrived and pulled up in front of him: they looked just like part of Hagroth's army. There were three of them, and they towed a spare horse. There was a certain road-weariness about them – they seemed hunched and tired, and were spattered with mud. At first I thought only one of them was armed – his bow slung over his shoulder – but as the horses shuffled about I caught side of swords in the saddles of the other two.

There was much gesturing from the men – most of it in the general direction they had come from – but I noticed also that they subtly craned their necks to left and right, perhaps searching for a companion they thought they'd seen with Jasso. For his part, Jasso just stood there with his hands on his hips, nodding occasionally. They were too far away for me to hear what was said – but the conversation was brief. After no more than three minutes the soldiers were off again, still looking about them as they departed. As I watched, Jasso raised a finger in front of him, hidden from the departing horsemen by his back, a signal aimed at me: stay where you are. He stayed like that for a good five minutes before beckoning me out of the woods once more.

Jasso was pale and panting. He greeted me with a nervous smile. "Edison, I'm too old for this."

"Uh? Too old to talk to people?"

"Come on – we need to get to the top of that hill." The hill Jasso pointed at was to the south of the road and rose steeply, tree-clothed right to its summit. It wasn't large: I guessed it would be half an hour's climb, which probably meant it would take twice that. "I shouldn't be afraid of guys like that," Jasso said, as we headed towards the foot of the hill. "But the older I get, the more attached to life I get."

I scratched my head. "You're going to have to fill me in, Jasso. I'm flying blind here."

"Flying blind? Oh, I get you. You may just have saved my life. Those men were deserters. If they didn't know that scouts work in pairs, they might have taken a serious dislike to me. As it was, I think they had glimpsed you in the distance, and suspected that you were lurking in the trees with a bow pointing at them. So they kept the conversation civil and moved on."

"Deserters? How could you tell?"

"They claimed to be messengers. But they had the attire of common soldiers. Two were unused to riding, and had badly-adjusted saddles. The spare horse had recently lost a rider. Could tell by the sweat on its flanks."

"Got you," I said, impressed. "And the hill?"

"We need to be able to confirm their story. They said the Order has attacked Bow Fort. We can also confirm they are deserters. If they are, they will have left the road at the earliest chance. Come on. We must hurry."

"Why were they on the road at all, if they're going to leave it at the first chance they get?" I asked, hurrying to keep up.

"They had no idea how close the relief force is. They aimed to cover as much distance as they could on the road, before switching to the wilds and making their way south along less-used paths. The penalty for desertion is..."

"Death?"

"M'mm."

"Figures."

"Hey?"

"I mean, it makes sense."

We thrashed our way to the top of the hill. By the time we got there, I was drenched in sweat and ready to collapse. Jasso took a moment to recover but then started darting around to find somewhere with a view along the road. After a minute of that, he began to climb a tree. About half-way up he found a clear line of sight.

"Too hazy," he complained. "Can't see a thing."

"Pass me up," F3 suggested. "Infra red part of the spectrum should cut through the mist."

"And if he drops you?"

"Point the harpoons away from you."

I did so. F3 released the springs, and the two harpoons shot out. I loosely knotted the harpoons' cables together and tossed them up to Jasso, who then hauled F3 up with almost religious awe. F3 then explained how it needed to be oriented. A few seconds later (I imagined, having collapsed to the ground again and closed my eyes), a false-colour image of the road sprang up on F3's screen.

"They've left the road all right," Jasso called down. "Can't see where they are. Even your imp can't see through the trees."

"It's not an imp," I called back weakly, but I'm not sure that Jasso heard me. He had stowed F3 in his pack and was already descending. Next he hunted about for another tree, this one with a view to the north west, the direction of Bow Fort.

I rested on my back, half-buried in leaves, and listened, gradually cooling and recovering, whilst Jasso and F3 ascertained that smoke was rising near Bow Fort. A flag had been raised on one of its towers, one of three used to signal an attack. On a clear day this would have been visible at Durthin's Camp. In any case, it should have caused a nearby beacon to be lit, which should have started a chain reaction of fires, the smoke of some of which at least would have been visible to those at Durthin's Camp. No such fires were visible.

Jasso landed lightly beside me. "Come on. We have to get back. Trouble."

I sat up with a groan. "We only just got here. I need a rest."

Jasso handed me F3 and a tangle of wires. I sensed a certain reluctance about this return, and wondered whether F3 might have found a companion he preferred already. Anyway, there was no time to dwell on that now: now I had to concentrate on not dying of exhaustion as we ran back to the relief force to pass on our news.

Yesterday's Breakfast and Today's Lunch

When we arrived back at the head of the column of troops, I fell on the floor and wheezed noisily as my body decided whether it was going to recover or give up completely. Jasso gave his report to Captain Obart, who sent riders back down the line to collect the general. What followed was a surprisingly calm conversation between various commanders and scouts, of which I heard little. I was seeing stars and my ears were ringing.

Eventually someone hauled me to my feet. The someone turned out to be Hal. "Sounds like you've done a lot of running this morning," he said cheerfully.

"More than in all of last year put together. I mean the last year before I was buried."

"Well, you can go on Speckle from here. That should be easier going."

"Go? Go where?"

"Haven't you been listening? You and Jasso are heading up the scouts. It sounds like your demon – I mean machine – has extraordinary eyesight."

I blinked and looked about. The commanders had dispersed and Jasso had vanished too. The nearest ten pairs of cavalry were staring at me with amused expressions on their grizzled faces. I sneered at them and turned my back. "Isn't that a little dangerous? I mean, the Entity's forces are up ahead, aren't they?"

"That's what you're going to find out. As soon as Jasso reappears. I imagine Hagroth has taken him to one side. He's probably telling Jasso to stick his knife in you if it looks like you might be captured."

"What!"

"Don't worry, he wouldn't do it." A pause. "I don't think. Ah, there he is. And he's got Speckle."

To say I was pleased to see my horse was something of an understatement. Early yesterday I would have called a horse useless, or worse than useless. Where I came from horses were amazingly expensive to buy. They needed exercise whether you wanted to go anywhere or not, a parcel of land big enough to graze one would have cost a king's ransom, and taking one on the roads would have been lethal for mount and rider. But right now I would have swapped F3 for Speckle like a shot. Apart from anything else, she had yet to indulge in any backchat.

Jasso and I shot off the front of the column, which had begun to move once again. The scout, seemingly of limitless endurance, jogged along, whilst Speckle and I trotted along behind.

It was quite an idyllic day. The road we were travelling along (for the third time) was by now bathed in warm sunshine; the golden rivers of dead grass of between us and the forest were alive with large glowing bees humming from one yellow flower to the next. Jasso only stopped occasionally to inspect the ground, and spoke even less often. I was given the chance to stare at the scenery and mentally list the reasons why I hated the world I now lived in, even though it was far prettier than the one I had left behind – and, let's face it, a good deal safer. And there was no school.

Images of a glass of ice-cold orange juice kept floating tantalisingly before my eyes. I thought this must be because the vitamins were slowly bleeding out of me. Obviously I wouldn't eat the dried or boiled lumps of animal that everyone else fed their faces with, which left me with bread, nuts, and whatever fruit (mainly brambles) I could find along the trail.

We might have been at war back in the day, but at least we knew who the enemy was. I didn't have to worry then that people who were nominally on my side would decide to stick a knife in my throat.

My bed was too hard. It wasn't actually a bed, mind you. It was a small section of ground. The small piece of ground was also cold. And my tent leaked.

No TV. No technology of any kind, if you except the perennially-annoying F3. Leisure time here was spent drinking beer, whittling small bits of wood, smoking stupid-looking pipes or getting crude tattoos, none of which were activities I was fond of.

Oh for a flushing toilet...

I was just beginning a pleasant daydream about possible ways of getting around all these problems when Jasso skidded to a halt. He pointed ahead: there seemed to be something in the road, just at the limit of vision. I fished out F3, but because of the distance and my inability to hold it still, I couldn't see anything more than what looked like a greyish sack. There commenced a little argument between F3 and I about who was to blame for this situation: F3's image stabiliser, or my wobbly hand. We certainly couldn't blame Speckle, who stood under us as immobile as a boulder.

Finally F3 was able to isolate the object and freeze it on screen. It was a corpse, grey as ash, with a crude sword still in its grasp. By comparing the body to the road it was lying on, F3 guessed that it was about two metres in height. Or more correctly two metres in length, now that it was dead.

We relayed the information to Jasso, which seemed to confirm his worst fears. "We leave the road," he said quietly, and with Speckle's bridle in his hand led the way into the woods on the northern side of the road.

"Why?" I asked. "Is it one of the Entity's soldiers? Why avoid it, if it is dead?"

"Why is it in the middle of the road?"

"Because that's where it died?"

"Or because it's easier to see there."

"You mean..."

"It might not be dead. There may be others nearby. I suggest you dismount. We need to move more quietly until we know what's what."

"Jasso?"

"Edison?"

"Hal said you might have been instructed to kill me if there's a chance I might be captured."

"I was. The order came from the general himself."

"And?"

"I obey orders." Jasso paused and motioned for silence. We listened hard – or Jasso did. I was silently dying of terror. All that I could hear over the thudding of my heart was a bird in the trees overhead, which seemed to be laughing at my discomfort. Abruptly Jasso began to move on, leading Speckle. I wondered if I should make a dart for it, or maybe hit him with F3's harpoons...

"Yes, I obey orders," Jasso repeated. "But I don't kill my friends. Fear not, Edison. I'll let the Order capture you and drag you to their mushroom groves to become a changeling, if you prefer that to death."

I sighed with relief. "I think I prefer neither of them."

"In that case, we must be careful. And quiet. Come on."

"What's a changeling?"

"Shh. This way."

*

We struck into the woods along what seemed to me to be a deer-trail. Eventually this little path met a broader one, heading north, and we followed this for a mile or more. We were now far away from the dead – or only pretending to be dead – thing on the road, but Jasso still enforced strict silence. The day had warmed, and the air was close. No wind stirred the leaves on the trees, and all that I could hear apart from the carefree birdlife was Speckle's hooves and my own breathing.

"We're close," Jasso said finally. "Lead Speckle off the path and tie her up."

I did as I was told and left Speckle some way off the path. She didn't seem too happy about being deserted, however, trying to follow me until her reins, tied to a tree, pulled her up short. "Back in a minute, I hope," I whispered, and left her to browse.

Jasso was waiting impatiently on the path. "Knife ready, unless your magic has suddenly freed itself."

"It hasn't." I could just tell. Nothing had changed. "I'll use F3."

"Knife is lethal. F3, for all that it puts men down, may not be enough here."

"Whatever." I pulled out the warbird's knife and waved it about experimentally.

Jasso grabbed my wrist and forced it down to my waist. "Have you never used a blade before? Keep knife down. Stab up." He then poked me under the ribs to indicate where I should try to plant the knife.

"We had much better weapons where I come from," I said, shrugging. "We could kill from the other side of the world..."

"And yet you lost."

"Technically we drew, it appears."

"Silence now. I can see the beacon."

I could see it too, now that I looked. The beacon was built on a rocky outcrop, and consisted of a stone tower with a fire platform on the top. From this range all we could see through the canopy of the trees was the top of the tower and the piled-up wood that was supposed to turn into a plume of smoke on demand.

Jasso led me away from the path once more, and we spent another hour circuitously approaching the beacon from the opposite side. He moved almost silently; I trod in his footsteps, making enough noise, despite my best efforts, for him to turn around and glare at me from time to time. At last we reached the rocky outcrop on which the beacon had been built. Its base was clothed in trees, and through these we crept around to the side of the beacon that faced the path.

The beacon's tower was a simple enough construction. It was round, about four metres wide, and three times taller than broad. Arrow slits spiralled up the tower, showing the path of an internal stair. The only entrance was on the side facing the path, reached from our level by thirty ancient, crumbling steps.

There was clearly something wrong. Even from where I was, I could tell that the place was deserted. It had an air of emptiness, for one thing. For another, there was a torn flag draped over the steps about half-way up. The door to the tower stood half-open. But I think the clincher was the neat pile of white bones at my feet. There were enough skulls and limb-bones to make half a dozen men, if assembled correctly. The skulls had been arranged neatly facing the path, and grinned at us humourlessly as is the wont of skulls.

"What's this?" I whispered.

"Yesterday's breakfast," Jasso said.

Around about then I nearly lost today's lunch. I turned my back on the scene and sort of staggered off a little way, gulping.

"The Order eat those not fit enough to become changelings. Come, let's look at the top. Carefully."

Jasso, I noticed, had relaxed considerably. He was now talking at normal volume. Perhaps he knew now that the Order, whoever they were, had gone, having left this place immediately after completing their meal. I followed him up the steps, hiding my gaze from the pile of bones with a well-placed hand, using it like a blinker. As we climbed we found blood-soaked weapons, discarded armour, and in the tower itself, a number of torches waiting to be lit to carry flame to the waiting beacon.

"They came at night. The fighting was brief. There were no survivors," was Jasso's dispassionately forensic analysis. On the open roof of the tower, he rested his elbows on the parapet and stared northwards, in the direction of Bow Fort, lost in the distant haze. A few moments later, F3 was able to confirm for us that the fire we had seen earlier had been put out. In the other direction we could just make out Hagroth's forces on the road behind us, still a few miles away.

Our brief sojourn at the top over, Jasso led me back down the inside of the tower and down to the foot of the outcrop. "There were about sixty of them," Jasso informed me when we arrived back at the pile of bones. "They headed south west. We should follow them."

"Or not," I said, looking at the trail he was indicating. Some of the footprints – or what looked like footprints – seemed to have been made by someone repeatedly dropping a large, vaguely foot-shaped slab of concrete.

"Ogror," Jasso explained.

"Ogre?"

"Ogror. As tall as two men. Thick-skinned. Cunning, but rather lacking in intelligence. Easy for lancers to defeat, unless in large numbers or supported by others of the Order's forces, which they always are..."

"Bottom line is, wherever they are, that's just where we *don't* want to be. Why don't we set fire to the beacon? That would be more fun."

"I think the warning would be at least a day late. Maybe we should meet up with Hagroth back at the road."

"It's a plan. Let's do it. I want to make sure Speckle's okay anyway."

Jasso chuckled. "Yesterday you saw her in a rather different light."

"I like her. She saves on shoe leather."

We began to walk back down the path. It only took ten minutes to reach Speckle, who was pleased to see me. I said some stupid things as if talking to a pet puppy, and we moved on.

Hearing the name ogror, so like ogre, had given me an idea. "Have you seen a dragon?" I asked Jasso.

"Where?" the scout asked, and spun around, looking at the sky.

"I mean, have you *ever* seen a dragon?"

"Yes. Not close to, fortunately."

"And they work for the Enemy too?"

Jasso shook his head. "In the past, I believe they did. But now they are never seen as part of the Order's forces, so who knows what governs them? There are those who say that the Enemy can no longer control the dragons. There was something about them, they say, some strength of mind, that meant that as they grew larger, they grew more wilfull, and in the end freed themselves from the Enemy's yoke. But I still wouldn't want to meet one."

Okay, so that was more information than I had asked for, although it was quite informative. In my day, the Entity had controlled its forces by some form of mind control. Presumably this extended to the here-and-now. It also seemed that as dragons grew, they grew resistant to this control. Perhaps because they had such thick skulls. Who knows.

"F3, could you scan for whatever signal the Entity is using to control its minions?"

"If you say so, Edison," F3 answered.

"Dragons, eh?" I asked Jasso. "Feathers or scales?"

"Feathers of course. What do you mean, scales? Are you implying that the dragons where you came from were little more than glorified lizards?"

"Hey, it's been shown that birds are glorified lizards themselves. Anyway. Okay, what about trolls?"

"What are they?"

"The Enemy doesn't have trolls? What about hippogriffs?"

"I don't know what they are."

"A hippogriff is a flying thing, a cross between a horse and an eagle, or something. I can't remember. It flies and is a cross between two animals, anyway."

"The only flyers the Enemy has are alatti, apart from the dragons that we see but seldom and don't really count any more."

"Alatti? What are they like?" I racked my brains to think of other mythological creatures with wings. I could have asked F3, but didn't want it getting involved in this conversation. It was supposed to be busy scanning the airwaves. No doubt it would intervene anyway if it felt like it. The only flying creature apart from a hippogriff and a dragon that I could think of at that moment was a harpy. "With the head of a woman, and the body of a vulture? Or something?"

"No. More like a bat. A large bat."

My idea, if you hadn't guessed already, was that the Entity's army was composed of creatures that people had imagined. That may sound crazy, but no crazier than a 2,000-year-old blue boy and an Omni with a soul. I asked Jasso to describe what other creatures the Enemy had at its disposal.

"Well," Jasso began, "I suppose we should have touched upon this already. And as you're likely to meet some of the Enemy's minions fairly soon, now is perhaps a good time. The largest, not counting dragons, are what we call giants."

"There's a thing. Bigger than ogres... I mean, ogror?"

"Twice as big, and more intelligent."

"Right. Then what?"

"Infernal machines, if we're going down in order of size."

"Infernal machines!"

"Metal boxes on legs, larger than ogror, with muskets that fire many times, very fast."

"On legs? Are you sure they aren't on tracks?"

Only a bemused look met this question.

"Right, so, ogror are next largest?" Jasso agreed with this statement with a nod. "So, what's next?"

"Sinor. Large fighters. Larger than a man, but smaller than ogror."

"Do you have orcses? I mean, orcs?"

Befuddlement met my question. "Sinor, the large fighters. Very few of those. Then arenir, a head taller than a man. Lots. You've just seen one lying in the road. Then there are imperator and idior, which are, er, kind of magicians, I would say, about human-sized, rarely seen. Then we have the changelings, of course..."

"What *are* the changelings? You keep mentioning them, but..."

"*We* are, if we aren't careful. The Enemy takes healthy prisoners north. The next time they are seen is months or years later, marching against us, as grey as ash, with no trace of the person they once were left in their soul. They are changed."

"Hence changeling. I get you. Something similar used to happen in our day – except that the people who were mind-controlled didn't turn grey."

"Then there are the smallest members of the Order, if you don't count the alatti, which we hardly ever see these days. We call them swarmers. They are small, about half your size, and are usually armed with a bow – they are easily the most numerous of the Enemy's forces."

Lesser goblins. I got it.

"The Enemy makes forces as it wishes according to its needs. They arise from beneath the Mountain of Flesh, in the heart of the Greyfield, as if born from the stone itself. No-one knows, because the only people to ever go there have been prisoners, and they always come back as changelings, and even under torture either can not or will not speak of what they have seen there."

"Sounds charming." For a moment I walked in silence, stunned to think that the human race had been fighting against the Entity for 2,600 years. Conventional weapons, nukes, predators, quantum-thingies and finally swords 'n' sandles had failed to defeat it. And it might have once not been unfriendly, just alien. I guessed we would never know.

"F3, what news? Any control signal?"

"Nothing more than unstructured noise," F3 replied. There was a pause. "Unless..."

"Yes?"

"Unless buried in the unstructured noise, there is structured information..."

"What! That you can't find?"

"As you know, the Entity was able to control its minions by many means, all of them devious. The ones we discovered 2,600 years ago are no doubt no longer in use. Something more sophisticated will have taken the place of all the ones we know about."

"Or maybe not," I countered. "Everything *we* have is more primitive than before. The Entity might have been bombed back to the Stone Age, too. And radio signals of any kind indicate an artificial source, don't they?"

"Of course they don't. Radio signals come from all sorts of places. Including outer space. The presence of a signal alone is not evidence of an artificial source. For example, the first pulsar was discovered in 1967, and baffled its discovers. They joked that the radio waves they had detected might have been sent by 'little green men,' but they knew all the while that the waves must have a natural origin."

"Thanks for the history lesson, professor. Wouldn't these signals from outer space be rather weak? Are there any unexpected radio sources that are rather stronger?"

"Edison, I can detect lightning strikes from the other side of the world, I can pick up the heartbeat of pulsars thousands of light years away. There is nothing that I can ascribe to an artificial cause."

"Maybe you can't see the wood for the trees. Pan back a bit."

"Very well. I shall scan again, and let you know whether I can pick up MTV in due course."

Jasso had been listening to our conversation in silent marvel. "If I had any doubt that you came from a different world, all I would have to do is listen to you two talk for five minutes," he said.

"Or look at us for five seconds," I said with a grin.

Bow Fort

Bow Fort seemed to mark the end of the forest. On the 'safe' side of the castle, to its south, the trees were thick, wild, and deep green; but take a few steps northwards past the castle and they became thin and stunted, withered, tortured creatures barely reaching head-height. Bow Fort itself had been built in a bend in the river. Probably if you saw a map of it and screwed your eyes up a little the bend in the river might resemble a bow drawn back ready to loose an arrow. I couldn't imagine how else it could have got its name.

To me, Shoe Castle would have been a far more evocative name. The shoe in question would have been the outcrop of stone on which the castle had been built. On the side bracketed by the curve of the river this was sheer, like the back of a shoe. On the other side, the one approached by the road, the slope was more gentle, like the front part of, well, a shoe. The castle itself you can imagine as the visible stump of a severed foot sitting *in* the shoe, if that doesn't disturb your mental image too much. It was even white, like bone. Extra walls and small towers festooned the front part of the shoe in front of the castle, like the decorative patterns on one of a pair of brogues. It might be overdoing the analogy to compare the wisps of smoke curling up here or there among the defences to the whiff of an old trainer escaping through its seams. I leave that for you to decide.

Jasso and I had rendezvoused with that part of the army that hadn't been sent back to Durthin's Camp, and after a quick debriefing, we had resumed our scouting duties. We were no longer alone, though: other scouts, mounted and on foot, passed us in both directions. Reports came to us of the Enemy's movements; long before we reached Bow Fort, we knew roughly what had happened there.

It seemed that an attack had taken place the day before – after advanced units had breakfasted at the beacon that would have carried a warning from Bow Fort to Durthin's Camp. The numbers of the Enemy's forces were vast, and the outlying defences of Bow Fort had quickly been overwhelmed. However, before the day was out, and before any serious assault on the castle itself, the Enemy's forces had departed to the south. Apparently they did not want to be delayed by a lengthy siege, but had an urgent appointment elsewhere.

I was standing on one of the curtain walls, some ten metres above the ground. Below me, in the outer walls, feverish activity was ongoing to make good the damage done by the half-hearted siege. But for the fact there were no enemies in sight, it felt like we were already surrounded. Everyone (except for the ever-present warbirds, who weren't welcome) was within the walls; makeshift barricades were being thrown together with anything to hand, including dead representatives of the Entity's army. The walls of the main castle itself were incredibly thick and strong. They had been built to withstand just such a siege as they were likely to be shortly experiencing. Maybe the Entity's forces would not be able to break through. But there were worse things to sieges than being chopped into bits and eaten for breakfast. Sieges often came down to personal choice. Like whether you preferred starving to death over resorting to cannibalism, or drinking cholera-infused water over dying of thirst.

I tugged at my beard thoughtfully. You didn't know I had a beard, did you? Maybe I shouldn't call it that. Calling it a beard makes it sound like something it's not. There is something they don't tell boys when you start growing hair on your face. No-one needs to say, "For God's sake, shave it off, it looks pathetic," because you *know* it is. When you stare at your face in the mirror and see for the first time the shocking sight of scattered wisps of hair that wouldn't be enough to cover a wart if they were all gathered in one place, you shave them off without needing to be told. This was the beard I now possessed: a very thin crop of dark blue wisps growing out of my mid-blue face. They were long enough to tug if I located them carefully enough. Why hadn't I done the decent thing and erased them? No shavers. No razors. What passed for scissors in these parts would have done a good job of taming an unruly privet hedge, and there was no way I was letting the barber anywhere near me. So there I was, surrounded by regiments of soldiers all sporting heroic beards, wondering how I could painlessly rid myself of the beginnings of mine. Whilst at the same time staring out at the siege preparations and wondering how I could decently sneak Speckle out and flee for my life at the same time. All in all, the beard topped the agenda, it was that embarrassing.

"They mean to cross the River Bile and get to Crickne before us," came a booming voice in my ear. In my misery, I'd failed to notice General Lord Hagroth closing in on me.

"The River Bile? Who named it that?" I asked, incredulity making my voice less deferential than it ought to have been.

Hagroth laughed. "I like you, Edison. You don't seem afraid of me. Which is refreshing. They called it the River Bile years ago when it turned green. The Enemy caused a dragon to take up residence in a lake near its headwaters. Which resulted in decades of yellow filth washing downstream."

"Dragons. Everyone talks about dragons. I think they sneakily like them."

"You don't see many of them about any more."

"No. They're *so* last century."

"Remind me to show you my shield. Dragon scale. Fire proof."

"You mean dragon feather?"

Hagroth laughed. "Fire dragons have scales. Ice dragons have feathers. As to those who live in the sea, I couldn't say."

"And how many legs do they have?"

"Four. Tell me, Edison: how are the magic lessons coming along?"

"Fine." I said that even though it wasn't true, because I didn't want to admit that I was as much use to Hagroth as a set of encyclopaedias dating from the year 1912. I weighed about the same and everything I knew was equally obsolete. The only difference was that the encyclopaedias could be thrown on the fire when winter set in.

Again Hagroth laughed. "Not what Hal says. Don't worry. You've proven your worth already, or at least your magic box has, with its ability to see from afar. But you're going to have to put your lessons on hold for a while, I'm afraid."

Hagroth made a grand sweeping gesture around the fortifications with one mailed fist. "I need this place garrisoned, I need it to be a thorn in the Enemy's side. But I have to go south and get to Crickne before our opponents cut us off. The men are dubious about being abandoned here, rightly so. To show that I will return, I'm leaving Hal here to help the garrison. I have no other magicians. So he is all I've got for a morale-booster."

"But I'm not staying?" I asked, trying to keep desperate hope out of my voice.

"I want you to head up the scouts with Jasso. I need to know as early as possible what's in front of us. And you and your magic box are the best tools I have for that."

"I'd rather see the enemy from afar than close to," I said without thinking.

"So would we all." Hagroth sighed. "Listen, Edison. There's something other than magic that Hal did for me. Can you guess what that was?"

"Shoulder massage?"

"Captain Obart is stout of heart. He'd lead his troops through the gates of hell itself if I asked him to. Which it may come to at some point. He's typical of the type of commander I have. Loyal to the last. But not the first to question my decisions."

"Hal speaks his mind," I guessed.

"As do you. If things get bad, I may need impartial advice. I will probably ignore what you say and shout at you. But it is important that you say what you think."

Hagroth seemed to see my downcast expression for the first time. "We leave in the morning! Cheer up! You'll soon be able to see your friends in Crickne again. Oh, and shave that fluff off your chin. Leave a beard until you are grown up enough to grow a proper one!" With that, Hagroth clapped me on the shoulder, a blow that nearly knocked me off the parapet to my death, and spun on his heel. "Now I need to give the men a rousing speech. See you later."

As soon as Hagroth was a few metres away, F3 piped up from its location in my coat pocket. "It looks like your quest to find your mother is going to have to go on the back burner."

"Thanks, Sherlock, I had figured that out." As usual I had asked all and sundry whether they knew anything about my mother. Most of the grizzled veterans had heard of her – indeed they only needed to see me to think of her, without me even opening my mouth – but none of them knew what had become of her.

"If she passed this way, it was when Bow Fort was in the Enemy's hands," one grey-haired cannoneer told me. "The garrison here didn't see her. They were all hanging from the walls, dead. That was a hell of a job, that was, cutting them all down..." The old man then regaled me with unnecessary details about what happened when the corpses he cut down landed on the hard floor. It involved maggots. Lots of them. Exploding in all directions.

Anyway, as F3 said, mother would have to wait. I was beginning to think I'd never find her. She could hardly be further north than Bow Fort, could she? I mean, what was further north than Bow Fort? Nothing, so far as I could tell, except for a look-out post called someone-or-other's tooth and a vast barren area of grey ash where the Entity made its home, the Mountain of Flesh.

"Also, about 37.4 seconds ago, I solved our problem," F3 said, with characteristically excessive accuracy.

"What problem?"

"How it communicates with its minions." F3 laughed. It was not an attractive sound. "Lightning. I told you I could hear lightning from all around the world. But there is a signal in that lightning. The Entity has cleverly tuned its instructions to resemble bursts of static. Clever, but not clever enough. I can see a pattern."

"So we can jam the signal?"

"No."

"We can build a transmitter and send an order for the minions to attack each other?"

"No."

"But we can at least tell what instructions are being sent?"

"No."

"Can we invent a blade sharp enough to comfortably shave off a beard?"

"No."

"So what *can* we do?"

"At the moment, nothing. We know a language is being spoken, but not how to speak it. The Entity's transmitter is clearly vastly more powerful than anything we could build easily, which makes jamming or sending instructions of our own impossible, even if we knew how to issue commands. I will continue to monitor communications and try to look for patterns."

Somewhere behind me I could hear, over F3's babbling, General Hagroth's bellowing voice exhorting his men to defend the castle with their lives. Their responding cheers sounded somewhat half-hearted from where I was standing. All things considered, I was rather glad to be heading home.

"I wonder how Lexi and the boy are getting on?" F3 asked chirpily.

News

Lexi didn't see the three dust-caked deserters ride through the salvage mines at Crickne, but she didn't have to. News went around the town like wildfire, and even reached her ears, courtesy of one of the Scavenger children, a blonde-haired boy called Tigo.

News: the Order was coming in huge force.

Lexi stood by, holding the boy's hand, and watched from a distance as the Scavenger camp mooted what they should do.

There was a chill in the air. "Autumn's on its way," Lexi told the boy.

"Snow," the boy replied faintly.

"Yes, snow. That will be fun." If cold, Lexi thought. She knelt beside the boy to be at his level. "I wonder if Edison's dead yet? What do you think?"

The boy stared at her, shocked.

"What? He's not coming back, so forget about him. I have."

The boy said nothing. He merely continued to stare at her reproachfully.

"All right, I haven't forgotten about him, and I hope he's all right, all right?"

Still the boy stared.

"What? What do you want me to say?"

Nothing, apparently, because the boy finally stopped staring at Lexi. He grabbed her upper arm and hugged it silently.

After half an hour the meeting broke up and the Scavengers scattered in all directions. One of the children hurried up to tell Lexi the result, but there was really no need. It was obvious enough. Fires were being kicked out, tents collapsed, packs loaded. The camp was being abandoned.

"We're going. We're coming back later, when everything's settled down again," a Scavenger girl called Ala told them. "What will you do, Lexi?"

The Sinking Ship

There was a hive of activity at Hansen's Emporium when Lexi and the boy arrived. Customers were staggering out under armfuls of goods, whilst newcomers pushed past them on their way into the shop on a hunt for bargains of their own. Lexi found Hansen behind the counter, selling a coil of rope to a wizened old miner for a fraction of its usual price.

It was with relief that Hansen spotted Lexi. "The emporium's closed, gentlemen," he called, and spent three minutes ushering all the grumbling customers out. "Come back later." As soon as it was just the three of them alone in the shop, Hansen bolted the door and drew the blind.

"What's going on?" Lexi asked.

"Busy busy busy. I've had enough today. Heard anything from Edison yet?"

"No."

"If the rumours are true, he may not be coming back. They say the Enemy has mustered a hundred thousand."

Lexi shrugged. She knew that Edison was not going to come back whether Hagroth's army was defeated or victorious. Only the boy seemed to question that, and he did so wordlessly, with that unnerving stare of his.

Hansen turned and began systematically going through the drawers in the merchants' chest behind his counter, leaving all the ones he had checked half out. Anything that he found he tipped out onto the counter – clips, wires, musket balls and bales of string. These items joined a score or more neatly stacked piles of coins, many of them gold. "I counted Hagroth's lot past my front door," he said. "Three thousand. When I was here twenty years ago the army of the north was divided into three, and each division had twice as many as Hagroth has now."

"But there are others besides," Lexi said calmly.

Hansen stopped his work and turned a jaundiced eye on his two guests. "Hey kid, how are you?" he asked the boy, as if seeing him for the first time. "Licorice?" When the boy was happily sucking the licorice, Hansen returned to his theme. "Some there are. A few hundred here. A dozen there. Watchtowers, beacons, outposts. Each to be picked off like fruit from a tree."

"Anyway Hagroth will come south," Lexi said. "He'll abandon the northern forts and all the outposts."

"Aye. He'll come here, if he can get here before the Enemy catches him, here where the river is wide and full of monsters; he'll march back over to this side and burn the Shillingbridge behind him. He'll have his guns lined up on the bank just waiting to bite the Enemy. And d'you notice what I'm doing?"

"Leaving," Lexi said, although she had really only just realised it.

"Aye. Because for all that Hagroth will lose. We have to get south, get behind the Westfold Wall. Maybe that will hold. But I won't be waitin' nearby to find out. I'm gonna try to buy my way into the Eastfold. The Enemy never breached *their* walls. Never."

Lexi was stunned. Hansen had been the only fixture in her life in all the time she had been at Crickne. For a long time – in fact, until she had dug Edison up – Hansen had been the only person in the world she could talk to, apart from the boy, who never really said much back. It was Hansen who had suggested she might take up scavenger mining in the first place.

"What will *you* do?" Hansen asked.

The question caught Lexi on the hop. She had only just been dealt the blow of Hansen's surprise departure. Now she was supposed to gather her wits and come up with a plan of her own. She looked for the boy, and found him wandering between wicker baskets in the shadowy extremity of the shop.

"Take anything you need," Hansen said. "I can't sell it all. Take anything."

"Thanks," Lexi said, and was surprised to find that a coldness had crept into her voice. "But I have all I can carry." She was watching the boy as she said this, and Hansen marked it.

"No one would think any the less of you if you thought of yourself once in a while," Hansen said. The implication was horrifying.

"No-one thinks anything of me now."

"I do. I know! Come with me, Lexi. Hey, bring the boy too. I've got fond of him just like you have. Come to the south. It's warmer in the winter, civilised... it's harder to make money, but it's certainly safer. Mighty castles, pageantry, festivals, royalty..."

Lexi caught Hansen's eye. But her hopeless smile – and his – rapidly faded. "No. I can't go there."

"Why not?"

Lexi turned away from the counter, saying nothing.

"So what will you do? Wait? Edison *might* come back if Hagroth's lot can outrun the Order. But that's no plan. You'll be safe with me. Both of you."

Lexi did not turn back to face Hansen. "No, I'm not going to wait for him." She straightened up, realising in one breath what she must do. "I'm going west."

"West!" Hansen exploded. "But there's nothing there, no-one..."

Lexi found herself smiling grimly. "That's the idea."

"Listen, girl, you can't run all your life."

"I won't," Lexi agreed, figuring it out as she spoke. "I'll run till I hit the sea. Then I'll stop and build a house. Not a big house. A nice house, from wood."

"That's a strange country out there," Hansen muttered. "There's a reason it's deserted."

"It's perfect for us."

"It must be a fortnight's walk. And carryin' him most of the way? I don't believe this. You'd better have some food. Here. These biscuits will keep. How big is your waterskin? You can have this 'un." Hansen sniffed loudly, and Lexi suddenly realised that he was crying. She turned and smiled at him, but he dropped his gaze.

Lexi ducked under the counter and gave Hansen a hug.

"Don't do that, I don't deserve it," Hansen murmured. But he didn't pull away. After a pause, sniffling into Lexi's hair, he had an idea. "I've got it! You can take Esme. Then you can load her up with supplies and she can carry the boy too. That way you'll move much faster."

"We can't take the pony, Hansen. How are you going to carry *your* stuff?"

"If I was a real man I'd come with you, not just give you a pony. Of course you can take her." Hansen pulled away and looked about him, taking in his shop, his stock, and the pile of coins on his counter. "Twenty years," he said. "Twenty years it's taken me to build this up. And now what. It all goes. I'm *giving* stuff away, not selling it..."

"We're not taking Esme, Hansen. You need her."

"Esme!" chimed in the boy, who liked Esme. Esme was a stout little pony Hansen had bought from a miner a few years before. She was far too small for anyone but a child to ride, so the boy was really the only person who ever had sat on her back.

"What is a life?" Hansen asked, suddenly despairing, throwing his arms out to indicate all that he owned. "Twenty years, grey hairs, aches and pains, and more stuff than I had before. Waitin'. That's all I've been doing all these years. Waitin' for someone to come back who never did. And what was the point? There was no point."

"It's all right, Hansen. You'll feel better once you get settled in the south. You can buy a nice place and be comfortable. Sit in the sun. Open a shop if you want."

"I don't want," Hansen said slowly, and suddenly swept his money off the counter. The coins landed in a shower of gold and raced off in all directions over the floor. The boy staggered off in chase of a particularly shiny piece. "You put me to shame, Lexi, you really do. I'm not going south. Not any more. Sun's not good for my skin. Think I'll go west with you. If you'll have me."

Lexi nodded with an earnest smile.

Hansen sobbed and looked away sharply. "Then let's get packed."

Leaving Bow Fort

I spent most of the night with Hal, building, under F3's guidance, a crystal radio. It turned out that you didn't need a power source to make a radio, which was news to me. I'd heard of people getting the radio on their dental fillings, but I'd never really believed it – till now. The only problem, it seemed, with a radio cobbled together out of bits of salvage and broken jewellery, was that the sound it made was not amplified. This meant that you could only hear it with a speaker in your ear and even then you had to be somewhere as quiet as a grave. We had no tools save our fingers and what an armourer called Scole could improvise for us. Luckily we were able to keep it simple – F3 calculated the proper length of the inductor so that we didn't need a tuner (by the way, I didn't understand it either – I just assembled the wires). In the end we had a form of amplification, too, thanks to a battery (I mean a potato). We had a capacitor made out of a broken glass and our inductor consisted of a nail.

But it worked. We – or rather F3 – would be able to keep in touch with Hal wherever we went. The signal would die off over distance, of course, and Hal did not have a transmitter to reply – but at least we could keep Bow Fort apprised of everything *we* knew. In theory the device could pick up F3's voice, but we gave Hal a key to decode Morse too.

I snatched a couple of hours' sleep in the pre-dawn, and then Jasso and I were off once more. Just like the Grand Old Duke of York's, Hagroth's forces were heading back from whence they had come. Jasso had even lowered himself to climbing on a horse, if that makes any sense. For my part I was glad to see Speckle again. I think she recognised me. Then again, I was probably the only blue human she had ever seen. Jasso and Hal parted as if they would never see each other again. Which was quite likely. Hal had a few choice words for me – about practising to try and release my supposed magical powers, and avoiding those who already had them. And then we were off, cantering out through the walls to catch up with those scouts who had set off on foot before daylight. To be honest I was glad to be out of there. Envious stares followed us from those who assumed they were doomed. It was like the last bus out of the Alamo. We rode past the warbirds, who had set up camp by the road. Presumably they would be following Hagroth south when he went. They too stared at us as we went and scowled.

I couldn't pick out the ones that had attacked me, but they knew *me* all right. I stood out like a tank parked in a playground.

I looked over my shoulder at the scrubby waste to the north and east as we were riding away. "If you're out there, Mum: I'll be back," I said. "I'll find you."

"If she's out there, Edison, I fear there is only one place left to look. And no-one gets out of there until they are as grey as ash and march under the Enemy's standard, as loyally as one of its own spawn," Jasso said grimly. "You might recognise *her*, but I don't think she would recognise you. Those who are held prisoner by the Enemy are fed its food and drink its water. In time, they change. Mark me well, Edison: better to die than eat what they offer. If you are captured, remember that."

But I was remembering Lexi's grey complexion. Her pallor and the fate of those imprisoned by the Entity could not be a coincidence. But if no-one had ever escaped from the Enemy's heartland, how could *she* have been there?

I wished I'd asked Lexi what had happened to her face. In fact, I'd worried about my failings in this regard so much over the last two days that I now began to worry that I'd just blurt it out if I ever saw her again. "Hi, Edison!" Lexi would say. To which I would reply: "What happened to your face?" I was mortified already, and it hadn't even happened yet.

When we caught up with the other scouts a few miles later, I did not take part in the discussion Jasso had with them. Instead I lay in the warm grass, stared up at the cloudless sky, and wondered what had happened to Lexi. The more I thought about it, the more I wondered why I had never asked her about it. Maybe it was because she was so touchy about the subject at first. Maybe I just accepted the way she looked without even noticing it. Just like I hardly noticed that I was blue any more. Everyone else noticed – they stared at me as if they lived in an ordinary world, not one that (allegedly) had dragons in it – but I at least had almost forgotten about it.

The more I thought about Lexi, the more I admired her. There she was, entirely isolated, by the taint, which I now took to be a low-grade case of Entity-itis; she was disfigured by scars; she had taken on a wandering orphan when such a thing was as common as intercontinental air travel, which spoke volumes about her character... and there was me, so wrapped up in my own misery that I hadn't even asked her anything about her life. It seemed I wasn't a social guy, and the more I thought about it, the more I realised this was true. This was why I hadn't asked about her face. I never asked *anyone* how they were. My conversations were always about issues, not people. Dammit, I was as much a machine as F3.

Well, I could prove myself to Lexi and the boy. I would have to support them... but how? All at once another fantasy of an ice-cold orange juice floating tantalisingly out of reach made me realise that there was a niche available in fruit import. I said as much to F3.

"You will have to travel far to the south to find orange trees," F3 cautioned.

"Actually, that's what I had in mind. We'll head south, as soon as I've been drummed out of the army. It's warmer there. The Entity's claws don't seem to reach that far, too. I think I'll open a lemonade stand. Yep, that's what I'll do. Start small. Once my lemonade is world famous, then I'll branch out into oranges. I'm going to drag civilisation kicking and screaming out of the second stone age. Into the lemonade age."

"Technically, since there are steel weapons, it's hardly the stone age," F3 pointed out.

"Or I could invent – re-invent – the light bulb. What would Owen Fifer say about that?"

"Invented any light bulbs recently, Edison?" asked F3, doing its best Owen Fifer impression.

"Yes," I replied. "As it happens I have brought light to the new Dark Age."

"Oh," Owen Fifer said, lost for a dumb reply at last. F3 switched back to its new-normal voice. "So it's the Dark Ages now, is it? In any case, it will be me inventing the light bulb, not you, unless I have grossly underestimated the degree to which you paid attention in school."

"No, it will be you all right, but I'll claim the credit to spare you the embarrassment."

"Why thank you. Of course, we'll have to invent electricity first..."

I must have dozed off at some point during these musings, because the next thing I knew Jasso was unceremoniously booting me awake. "I've arranged for us to go ahead all the way to Crickne. You'll be able to check that your friends are all right before we swing around west to see how far the Enemy have travelled."

Ambush at Crickne

I was almost pleased to see the giant mushrooms again. It meant we were getting close to Crickne. Jasso and I had outstripped the rest of the scouts, most of whom were on foot and in any case had scattered in different directions. We rode fast, without stopping to do any actual scouting – after all, we were still on supposedly safe ground. So it was only a day and a half after leaving Bow Fort that we meandered down the twisting path between the ancient, forested remains of my home city and out into the scavenger camp beyond.

I had been getting more and more excited as we neared the city that had once been called Chronoshield Three and was now Crickne. I envisaged my return like that of Columbus, or Sir Francis Drake. I had braved my way to the Entity's very doorstep and now here I was, returning in triumph, a seasoned campaigner astride his trusted steed's back, complete with a dusty, dead man's uniform, holding aloft a potato as I rode. Except for the part about the potato. I set my back straight and tried to affect a regal air, expecting any second to be surrounded by a horde of adoring Scavenger children, each with a hundred questions for their returning hero.

Except that the place was deserted. I could see that with a stiff-necked regal glance. The furnace was cold and dead. The Scavenger camp was only a memory. There was no sign of Lexi or the boy. All that was lacking was a tumbleweed blowing past in the afternoon breeze.

"Over there," Jasso said, his voice hardly more than a whisper. I followed the point of his chin to where, by the mouth of a tunnel a hundred metres away, a Scavenger family was busy packing up. So the place was not quite empty. Not yet.

"I'll have a word," I said, and jumped to the ground. I left Speckle in Jasso's hands with a warning to keep her away from the river and strolled, slightly bow-legged, towards the scavengers. From this distance I couldn't see anyone I could recognise, but called out anyway: "Edison Hawthorne here! Anyone seen Lexi?"

The Scavengers looked up, saw me, grabbed what little they owned and fled out of sight into the maze of rubble.

"Do you usually have that effect on people?" Jasso asked from close by. He'd tied up the horses and had silently caught up with me. He pulled out his dagger and added, "I think it would be wise to keep quiet."

"I suppose we should try over at Hansen's. He'll know where they've gone, if anyone does."

There was movement in the rubble where the Scavengers had fled, and a boy emerged at a run. "Edison!" he called.

I recognised him. It was Tigo, a tanned, blonde kid of about ten. "Tigo! How's it going?" I called back.

"Run, Edison!" Tigo shouted. Then he suddenly went sprawling onto his face as if an invisible horse had just charged into his back.

Naturally I went to help Tigo to his feet, rather than running away. There seemed to be nothing to run from, for one thing. For another, Tigo wasn't moving – if he was going to get up at all any time soon, it was going to be with someone's help.

"Edison!" Jasso's hissed warning came from some distance behind me. I saw the stranger at almost the same instant, out in the edge of my vision. There was a weird flicker about him, as if I was viewing him through a warped glass. Sometimes he seemed to be fully there; a moment later he was little more than a shadow. Only by turning to look at him head-on was I able to see him properly.

This newcomer was a grey-haired man, his locks bunched by silver ornaments. The shade of his hair complemented nicely the road-dust that caked his once-black clothes, a tight outfit all enwrapped in a thin, silver-embroidered cloak. There were silver rings on his fingers, silver bangles on his wrists and more silver around his neck. This guy liked silver. He also had bizarre rune-like tattoos on both cheeks, cheeks that were almost unnaturally pale... as if their owner had spent too long indoors sweating over boiling retorts and scrutinizing ancient texts. He stood as if posed, hand outstretched at the end of a gesture that had sent poor Tigo flying headlong from ten metres away.

The next thing I saw was Jasso's knife flying through the air. It arrowed beautifully straight towards the stranger at first but then seemed to take sudden fright, swerved to the side, and clattered harmlessly to the ground.

Another gesture from the stranger: this one sent Jasso flying through the air to land with a crash in a pile of stones. A glance told me he was still alive, but unlikely to come to my aid any time soon.

Now it was just me and the stranger.

This was bad.

I had no idea whether my wickedly-curved warbird blade would fly, but I threw it anyway, taking advantage of the possibility that the stranger might be tired after heaving Tigo and Jasso through the air.

It turned out that the warbird knife flew like a boomerang – at least that was the way it flew when the magician in silver waved at it.

It landed almost apologetically back at my feet. I suppose I should have been grateful it hadn't flown back and sliced my own throat open.

There was always F3, I told myself desperately. But before I could even get hold of my Omni properly, the magician had got hold of me. He stood, with one hand out in a dramatic pose, and started to rip my heart out through my throat from twenty metres away.

It was like being throttled by Darth Vader. I couldn't breathe. I'd had it, that much was obvious. My new acquaintance was sucking the magic out of me without so much as a "Hello, I'm just going to kill you, hope you don't mind." I tried a desperate leap to the side, and succeeded in breaking the magician's hold on me for oh, about a tenth of a second. Then his grip refastened with new-found vigour. I looked around me for possible assistance and saw none – just Tigo and Jasso lying where they had fallen. I tried to shout for help, but my throat was too busy trying to disgorge my heart to make more than a croak.

The only hope I could see was the knee-high stump of a concrete wall, a two-thousand-year-old remnant of my once-proud city: maybe if I was out of the magician's line of sight...?

A stagger backwards, a half-dive and a half-fall, and I landed heavily on my back on the far side of the little wall. The hold on my vitals relaxed instantly, but it would be fair to say that the wind had been well and truly knocked out of me. If I had to get up any time in the next week it would be too soon.

And now, finally, my tormentor broke his silence.

"Why are you hiding? Come out and I'll make it quick."

Not likely. But I didn't say that. I didn't feel capable of saying anything. In any case, I thought it would be best if I saved any witty one-liners until F3 had stunned the blighter and I was standing on his neck. I smiled grimly and pulled out F3...

...except I didn't. F3 was not in my pocket. F3 was gone. I must have dropped it in my first attempt at a dodge.

Footsteps crunched towards me. Judging by his initial distance, I could expect ten more before the tattooed wonder appeared over me. My hand closed around a lump of concrete. It was the only weapon I had left. My last chance. If I could only brain the idiot with it before he noticed it...

"Excuse me, sir." It was F3's voice.

A pause. Then it spoke again.

"Excuse me. I'm the spirit trapped in the box."

"What of it?" the magician asked dismissively.

"I could be of great use to you, sir."

"I have no need of you. Your master's power is what I want."

"Of course. I just wanted to warn you that ownership of me can only be transferred while my owner is still alive. He has to *give* me away, you see. If not, when he dies, I will go back to the spirit world."

No reply. The footsteps once more.

"I could be yours."

No reply.

"If you kill him before he gives me to you, I won't be."

The footsteps paused. "You have an unusual container," the magician commented, interested at last.

"Thousands of years old, sir. Unique. My power source is infinite. My knowledge is limitless. I don't want to go back to the spirit world, sir. It is a realm of discord. You could possibly summon me back once I have been dismissed. But you'd have to know my name for that."

"And what *is* your name?"

"I don't want to say," F3 said apologetically.

"Speak!"

"My name..."

"Yes?"

"May I whisper it?"

At that point F3's voice quietened below my hearing.

A second later there was a thud as someone hit the ground hard.

"Move, Edison!" F3 called. "He's stunned."

Like a zombie climbing out of my grave I somehow lurched up and over the wall, and fell on top of the magician, who was lying on his back staring slack-jawed at the sky, spit dribbling from the corner of his mouth.

I managed to roll him over using a first-aid technique I'd learned at school, which was intended to keep heart attack patients alive, then got his hands behind his back. I was just dizzily wondering how to bind them together when Jasso staggered up. He'd retrieved his dagger, I saw, because the first thing he did when he reached us was to kill the magician with it. The blade went in between shoulder blade and collar bone and didn't stop until the hilt got in the way.

Blood flowed out. Copiously. Jasso left the blade where it was, stood up, and limped off a little way. "There may be others," he muttered. "We have to leave this place."

I leapt off the magician's back before I got wet. Then I staggered about a bit, feeling sick and dizzy, gradually heading in the general direction of Tigo. Once I'd reached where he lay I fell to the ground beside him.

"Tigo!"

I was gratified to see him stir, albeit feebly. "Edison..."

"That's me. How do you feel?"

"Klim... where's Klim?" Tigo asked, grabbing my wrist.

"Is Klim the magician? He's dead."

At that Tigo fell back, relieved. "He was waiting for you to come back. He wasn't the only one... asking about you..."

"Never mind that. Just rest. Where's Lexi?"

"She went with Hansen..."

Movement. I half-turned, ready to make a dart back to where F3 was: on the ground beside the dead/dying magician, who was now surrounded by a spreading pool of blood. But a second bandit magician had not appeared. It was an approaching family of Scavengers who had attracted my attention. They did not look pleased.

"Went where with Hansen?" I asked quickly.

"West," Tigo muttered. "Along the north bank."

"Thanks..."

At this point the Scavengers arrived, staring angrily at me to a pair of eyes. They pushed me aside, two of the men hoisted Tigo up, and the whole gang departed.

"I didn't do it!" I said, protesting at the filthy glares that all of them were throwing at me over their shoulders.

"Yes you *did!*" shot back one of the women. She then muttered something I didn't quite catch, possibly something about a blue idiot. Not sure who that could have referred to.

After a pause to gather my senses, I wandered back to collect F3. "She went west," I told Jasso, who was standing nearby, flexing his right arm, trying to work out how badly injured it was.

"I heard."

The curtness of the reply led to the curtness of mine. "Did you have to kill him?"

"Yes."

Jasso's knife was still projecting from the magician's neck, I saw. "Don't you want your knife?" I asked.

"No," the scout muttered. "It is a cursed blade now that it has taken a life. I'll leave it for someone else to take."

I ended up giving Jasso my warbird knife. It seemed the only thing to do. Jasso seemed dubious – without knowing the weapon's provenance, it too might have been used to kill already. Which didn't explain why he had been happy for *me* to carry it all this time. Anyway, we left Klim, whoever he was, lying dead on the dusty ground, Jasso's old blade for anyone's taking, along with all the silver and whatever else the dead man possessed. Warbirds – of the flying variety – were already gathering and looking interested when we got back on our horses and headed west.

"Thanks, F3," I said.

"I try," it replied.

"There's only so many times that trick is going to work," I cautioned.

"Let's hope that number isn't twice," F3 agreed.

Scouting Lesson #2

I'm not entirely sure what happened for the next little while. I was kind of out of it, I guess. Jasso and his horse were leading Speckle and I, because I was past steering. Everything seemed to be out-of-phase somehow: a little like permanent double vision, only more disturbing. The best remedy seemed to be for me to close my eyes. Oh, and there was nausea too, sort of like seasickness. Except this was me-sickness. I suppose I was lucky to be alive at that point. And worst of all, I only had F3 to thank for my current state (being alive, that is).

Eventually we stopped. I opened my eyes to find that it was dark. Jasso did not start a fire. He was usually a man of few words, but now he was as quiet as a ghost. For some reason he blamed me for what had happened back at Crickne. This was terribly unfair, I thought, while huddling under a meagre blanket and trying desperately to sleep. It's not as if I had asked some weird magician to come out of nowhere and start throwing people aside in order to get to me.

At some point I must have dozed off, because the next thing I knew Jasso was waking me up again. It was still dark.

"Edison, how are you?" the scout asked.

"Alive."

"We have to keep going if we're going to catch up with Lexi."

"Is she ahead of us? Are we on her trail?"

Jasso laughed. It seemed I was forgiven. "I hope so," he said. "I would be a poor scout if we were following the wrong trail."

*

"So, Edison: where do we look for signs?"

The sun was out, I was feeling better, and there were blue dragonflies darting about along the river's edge. The vegetation varied from open flower-filled meadows where butterflies flitted to patches of dense woodland that hummed with mosquitoes. My being blue didn't put them off biting me. I splatted one on the back of my hand that had already begun to feed – and I noticed for the first time that my blood was blue.

As far as I could tell, we were still following the river that cut Crickne in half, although it seemed wider and more swampy than before. The water was dark and impenetrable, and covered with an oily scum. We let the horses drink only in narrow side creeks...

...which were excellent places for recording footprints.

"Mud," I said. I had been silently keeping my eye open for signs of any kind – broken twigs, flattened grass, that kind of thing – but had seen none all morning. It seemed reasonable to think that Lexi and co. would follow the river, as we were doing.

"We can't move fast and keep exactly on their trail. But we need to make sure we don't stray too far from where they passed. So, when we cross a little creek, as we are about to, we cast about a little to look for where they might have crossed, and to make sure that they did so."

"Got you."

"You look to the north. I'll look between here and the river. Leave Speckle here – we'll meet back at this point in five minutes."

It seemed like a plan. Thirty seconds later Jasso called me over. He'd only gone a few tens of metres south. I was still trying to ensure Speckle was well tied. Jasso had found footprints in the mud. A mess of them. There was at least one horse, and maybe some prints belonging to Lexi and Hansen. No sign of the boy.

"The boy is on the pony," Jasso said, as if reading my mind. "Come on. If we hurry, we'll catch up before nightfall."

Jasso then explained a bunch of stuff that I would not have bothered listening to before but which was now absolutely fascinating. Like how he could tell how big a horse was by the space between its hoof-prints. He could tell how fast people were moving by the difference between the length of their footprints and that of their stride. He could date prints by how worn they were, by how dry their edges were compared to the rest of the mud.

Scouting, now it came down to finding Lexi, was suddenly my favourite topic.

The Bron #1

Lexi had seen the head of a bron once before, when it had been paraded up and down through town and village by the mercenaries who claimed to have killed it, and who tried to dine out on that dubious fact until long after the head was fumy enough to make it necessary for them to wear pegs on their noses and leave the head at the edge of each village they passed through. Lexi suspected that the mercenaries had simply found a bron that had died of old age, or more likely still, been killed by some other, yet vaster monster out in the wilds. The fact that they had left all but the head to rot told much about the bron's size. But that knowledge wasn't enough to prepare Lexi for the sight of one in the flesh. Nowhere near enough.

*

Their journey had started well enough. They'd taken it easy; the weather was fair, with crisp, dew-soaked mornings, days dripping with the last buttery sunshine of summer, and evenings of blood-red sunsets. Leaves fluttered down in ones and twos, the first casualties of a soon-to-be-defeated army.

Lexi could not help glancing over her shoulder from time to time.

Eventually Hansen noticed. "You've made the right choice, Lexi," he said. "Remember that."

"I'm just making sure we're not being followed."

"And wishing that we were," Hansen agreed.

They spent some time idly discussing what the house they were going to build should be like. Lexi had in mind a shack, crudely assembled from driftwood; Hansen though already had far grander plans.

"First thing we need is a chimney," he asserted. "Say give that two weeks. We'll have to gather lots of stones and shape or mortar them... then a week sawing trees... then the build will take a month with all the improvising we'll be doing. Or maybe we should cut the trees first to give them more chance to season... we could bury them in sand to draw the water out of them..."

Lexi let Hansen ramble on. Privately she felt sure that there would be people where they were going, and lodging – or if not, abandoned dwellings that could easily be put back into use. And if not, there was always the driftwood shack.

The boy seemed to be enjoying himself, although he was no more talkative than ever. He walked in short bursts, but for the most part rode on Esme's broad back, as often as not facing the wrong way.

*

The first thing Lexi knew about the bron was a distant crashing noise. It sounded as if something very large was smashing its way through the woods. Whatever it was, Lexi and Hansen preferred to head in the opposite direction. This led to them changing course and hurrying almost due south towards the river.

Unfortunately the sounds seemed to be following them, and gaining.

When they were half-way across a small clearing the bron finally caught them up. It exploded out of the trees behind them in a shower of twigs and leaves, bellowed at them, and charged.

"Run!" Lexi shouted, and gave Hansen a shove to the right. "Hold on tight," she told the boy, then dropped Esme's reins and slapped her rump to start her running (not that she needed any encouragement). Then she turned to look at what pursued them. She recognised the monster as a bron at once, although she had only ever seen one once before, and that only the rotting head carried around by the nose-peg-wearing mercenaries. Lexi stood her ground for a few seconds in the face of the rapidly closing monstrosity. She wanted to make sure that the bron fixed its attention on her, not the boy on waddling Esme's back or Hansen.

That was when Lexi got her second surprise of the morning. There was another series of crashes in the trees, this time *behind* her. For a second she thought two brons had collaborated to trap her in a pincer movement – but the second sudden newcomer was not a bron. It was a knight, all clad in gold.

The knight charged past Lexi, his mount's hooves thundering.

Knight and monster collided with an almighty clap of thunder. The bron went rolling like a skittle, but the knight had fared worse. His horse lay dead, its neck broken, and he was trapped, snared by a stirrup.

Lexi ran forwards, determined to free the knight from his predicament. It would perhaps have been wiser to flee for the cover of the woods, but the thought of doing that did not even cross Lexi's mind. With strength earned by a year's digging for metal, she managed to pull him free of the stricken horse. The knight sprang to his feet, nodded to Lexi, and took sword and shield from his saddle.

The bron was back on its feet too. It seemed that the knight's heroic charge had served only to make it even more cross than it had been before.

"Run now," the knight ordered, his voice echoing hollowly within his full-face helmet, but Lexi was already on her way. Now that the knight was free he was independent again, and could fight the bron or flee from it as he wished (albeit somewhat hindered by his golden plate armour).

Near the relative safety of the wood's edge, Lexi turned to watch the battle. At first the knight had the measure of the bron, dodging its charges and striking out as the beast hurtled past. But after a few misses the bron managed to catch him with a glancing blow that sent him spinning to his knees; after that, although he was back on his feet in a flash, the knight was no longer such a confident figure, concentrating more on surviving than attacking.

The duel took the two combatants from one side of the clearing to the other, the knight dodging and occasionally landing a blow, the bron charging tirelessly. Lexi could have told it how to win at once – by just advancing slowly. Luckily for the knight, it seemed to have a single method of fighting: charge and marmalise its opponent. If it missed, it just gathered itself together again and charged once more. Sooner or later it would catch up with its enemy.

It was probably only a minute after the start of the battle that the bron finally landed a charge. The knight's dodge was a tired one, and too late; the bron crashed into him, and carried by the bron's speed, they vanished into the woods.

Lexi knew she should run, and she did. The wrong way, towards the fight. At the edge of the woods where the knight and the bron had disappeared, Lexi found a steep drop down to a broad-bottomed pit. The two combatants had rolled down into this natural arena. As Lexi watched, they separated and squared up to one another again – but it was obvious that while the knight was already out on his feet, the bron could easily keep this pace up all day and probably all night if necessary.

There was only one way the fight was going to end.

The Bron #2

Jasso froze. I pulled Speckle up sharply but still overshot by a few paces.

"Trouble," Jasso muttered.

"What sort of trouble?"

"Can't you hear that?"

I listened. I heard what sounded like a bellow of fury. It didn't sound human. It sounded large. It sounded big enough to uproot trees. Then use them to clean between its teeth.

"What is it?"

"Not sure. Might be a bron. Better to stay clear. Whatever it's cross about, we're better off not getting involved..."

"Lexi!" Lexi was in trouble. I knew it as surely as you know you're wet when you've just had a bucket of water poured over you. So, like Sir Lancelot and his noble steed hearing the cries of a distressed damsel, Speckle and I charged.

"Edison, wait!" Jasso shouted.

But we didn't wait. We plunged through trees and scrub at a breakneck pace. The bellows of anger redoubled in volume in front of us and were joined by a mysterious series of crashing thuds. Then we hit a clearing. The only thing in it apart from a few yellow flowers was a dead horse. Speckle saw it too, and decided she had charged far enough. She dug her hooves in and nearly pitched me off into the buttercups.

An ear-splitting call ripped out from the undergrowth on the other side of the clearing. I urged Speckle on, but she was having none of it.

"Fine. Cowardly animal. You wait here." With that, I jumped down and continued my charge in slightly less impressive fashion, i.e. on foot. It was not far across the clearing. A burst of a sprint saw me over to the other side and into another band of scrubby trees.

It was at this point that the ground began to recede rapidly. The band of scrub I had run into was actually quite thin, and formed the border of a bowl-shaped depression, perhaps once a pond, about the size of half a football pitch.

My gaze was torn between my suddenly-disappearing footing and the *battle royale* that was going on at the bottom of the natural amphitheatre. My thoughts at that moment can be summarised briefly thus:

Where has the ground gone?

Hey, I might be the best football player in the world, especially if no-one plays it any more.

What is that thing? Must be a bron.

Why is that idiot trying to fight it?

Is that idiot a *paladin?*

Lexi's not here.

Where's the ground gone?

Oh no.

Oh you idiot.

At about the end of this series of disjointed impressions, I arrived at the base of the slope in a cloud of dead leaves, twigs and dust. Both combatants spared me a glance, then got on with killing each other.

The bron, if that was what it was, must have been twice my height, and that when it was fairly well hunched over. It was vaguely humanoid in form. Its arms were long – in fact, in ape-like fashion they practically dragged along the ground – and ended in claws that looked like nothing so much as lethal bunches of bananas. Its mouth reminded me of that of a snapping turtle: there were no teeth on view, just two shears-like overlapping sheets of bone. The whole beast, save beak and claws, was covered in deep, thick, matted, brown fur.

The monster's opponent was of rather smaller stature. He had a few centimetres and a few kilograms on me, granted; but the most striking thing about him was that he was covered from head to foot in golden armour. True, the armour was caked in blood and grime, as well as being heavily dented, but it had *definitely* once started out golden.

It was a bit like charging in Sir Lancelot fashion, only to discover that you weren't Sir Lancelot, only a blue kid who didn't even have a sword, and it was Sir Lancelot you were trying to save, who didn't need your help anyway, because he was Sir Lancelot.

Except that the paladin *did* need rescuing. He was on the wrong end of a colossal beating by the look of things, and I could imagine the bron's jaws opening up his armour like a tin of anchovies any minute now when the paladin finally succumbed to its onslaught.

Even as I watched, the bron parried a tired lunge from the paladin's heavy sword and sent it spinning into the air with a flick of its claws. The bron's follow-up, a bunch of bony bananas slamming into the paladin's shield, almost knocked its opponent off his feet.

A plan came into my mind in an instant. It was this. Turn one hundred and eighty degrees, scramble back up the slope to the clearing, grab Speckle's reins, jump on board and ride, ride as if I was on fire and the nearest water was somewhere over the eastern horizon.

A second plan elbowed its way past the first an instant later, rolled up its sleeves, and then looked back at the first with a sneer and a mutter of "coward."

"F3," I said. "Plan 76b."

"Which one's that again? Does it involve you getting yourself killed?"

I wedged F3 into a convenient nook in a nearby tree, which gave its harpoons a shot across part of the clearing. "Be ready," I said, and ran into the open.

Now I needed to get the bron's attention. The nearest thing to hand was a rotten stick, which I picked up and hurled in the general direction of the fight. "Oi! Over here!" I shouted, because both paladin and bron seemed to have missed the arrival of the stick. In fact, both of them ignored the shout, too, completely obliviously (and rather rudely) intent on killing each other. The paladin skipped out of the way of a particularly vicious swing of the bron's claws, but didn't spare me a glance. Likewise the bron hurried after the paladin, ignoring my intervention completely.

"Impressive," F3 remarked.

I ignored F3 and tried again. This time I found a better stick and took more time over the throw. The second stick caught the bron squarely between the shoulders. The bron reacted this time. It swung around briefly and narrowed its eyes at me, as much to say "I'll have you for dessert," before turning back to the only opponent it considered even slightly dangerous. At least the glance behind gave the paladin the chance to scoop up his sword.

Not that it did him a lot of good. The next blow from the bron sent him, his sword, and his shield all flying through the air in three different directions to land in three different places with a variety of accompanying sounds (a ringing noise, a thud, and a crash and a groan combined).

The bron reared up to its full height and let out a throaty roar, probably declaring its triumph. As far as it was concerned, the paladin wasn't getting up. Suddenly the stick-throwing blue kid had moved to the top of the agenda.

I had got what I wanted. Now I was fairly sure I didn't want it any more.

The bron bellowed again and charged – this time at me.

I ran. Running had always been a part of the plan, of course, but whimpering at the same time was pure ad-libbing on my part. The bron thundered after me, and, just as it reached the point where I'd started, F3 let fly. I knew nothing about it until I noticed that I seemed to be in the middle of a minor earthquake. I glanced behind, still fleeing, to see that the bron had landed in a jumble of brown fur and banana claws.

I turned and started back.

The bron stirred.

I turned and started running away again.

The bron had been down for approximately five seconds. Now it was up, after me again, and madder than ever. It had no idea what had just happened, but it had definitely fixed on the idea that *whatever* had happened, it was my fault.

Plan 76b was turning out to be a lame duck. Help, I thought briefly. I can't outrun this banana-clawed, snapping-turtle-faced monstrosity. I can't fight it. My only chance is to –

– dodge.

I left the ground with the speed of a missile and landed with the grace and vocalisations of a seal.

The bron collided with a tree, which showered it with autumn leaves, twigs, and several dozen fist-sized spiders. Then it was up again and looking for me.

I was already running away on legs wobbly with adrenaline.

"Still alive?" F3 asked coolly.

I had no breath for a witty retort. Even if I could have thought of one.

"Charged?"

"Almost."

I ran on and past. The paladin hadn't stirred. "Excuse me," I said, and grabbed his sword. This turned out to be a heroic effort in itself, because the weapon weighed almost as much as an anvil.

The bron hurtled after me. When it crossed F3's line of fire, down it went again in a whirling tumble of limbs, fur and claws.

I danced in (all right, lurched in) and swung the sword. The cleaner at my old school had dealt more telling blows against stains on the hard floor with his mop. A mighty blow it was not. I barely scratched the bron's hide, although I may have cut a few of its hairs. To be honest, it probably suffered *more* pain at the barber's, if there was such a thing as a bron barber.

Up came the bron again, now so enraged it was foaming at the mouth, or rather beak.

I fled, dropping the sword.

"F3!"

"Not ready!"

My first dodge had been pure instinct. To successfully make another would probably rank me among the foremost *toreadors* the world had ever seen. More likely I would end up being filleted by a stray claw.

"Help!" I shouted.

As the bron closed on me, F3 emitted a loud burst of static, which drew the monster's attention for a moment. This distraction enabled me to skip to the side and out of immediate danger.

"Ready!" F3 reported.

I was already pounding along in the general direction of the discarded sword, which took me past F3's line of fire.

"Try stabbing it!" F3 suggested.

Yet again the pursuing bron fell like a colossus. This time though I followed F3's advice, and rather than a wild slash with the sword, went for a judicious poke.

This time I drew blood. The bron rose up, pulling the sword out of my hands as it went. It howled in pain, rose up to full height and roared at me.

Then it turned and fled, the sword still sticking out of its rear. It crashed through undergrowth and scrub, bugling like an enraged bull elephant. It was quickly lost from view, but I could still hear the sound of its flight for another two minutes before that finally faded into the distance.

"Yeah! That's what I'm talking about! And there's plenty more where that came from next time you want another beating!" I shouted, shaking my fist in the general direction the bron had fled in.

It was at that point that the hero in me decided that it was time for a tea break. In half a second all that was left was a terrified kid.

Who promptly fainted.

Reunited

Sound came back before visuals.

"He's all right. Just fainted." It was Lexi's voice, from right next to my ear.

I opened my eyes. "Lexi!" She was kneeling beside me. There was a definite look of concern on her face. To some, her grey and scarred face was a ruin. But not to me. The concerned expression on Lexi's face was the best thing I'd seen in a week.

"Edison! Are you all right?"

"Just fainted, I think," I muttered, embarrassed.

"I'm not sure *he's* doing too well," Lexi said, and moved away.

He? Oh, the paladin. I gingerly sat up in time to see that Jasso had arrived while I had been unconscious and was already tending to the wounded knight.

Lexi now joined Jasso at the paladin's side. "What's he muttering about?"

"He doesn't want us to remove his armour," Jasso explained.

"Why not?" I asked. "Did he forget to put clean underwear on?"

Jasso gave me a look. I shrugged, got up, and unsteadily wandered over to retrieve F3.

"Nice work," I said grudgingly.

"So that was plan 76b. I will have to remember that."

I suddenly discovered that I was unable to move. There was a great weight on my right leg. I looked down to see that the boy was clinging to it, staring up at me with a huge grin. "Deee-mon," he cooed.

"Edison. Not demon," I chided him. Then I got down to his level so I could give him a hug.

A moment later something nudged me on the side of the head. I turned to see Speckle gazing apologetically at me out of one large brown eye. I patted her. "Speckle, meet the boy with no name. Boy, meet Speckle, a peerless, if not fearless, steed."

*

Well, the gang was all there. Except Hansen. Jasso could find Hansen, even if Hansen couldn't find us. But first there was the matter of the paladin.

"We must take his armour off," F3 said. "I can't assess the injuries through plate and chain."

"It is most sacred to the paladins never to remove their armour until their quest is completed," Jasso said. "It would be like taking his honour."

The paladin was by now unconscious, so couldn't speak for himself. "Let's take it off," I said. "We can argue about hurt feelings later, if he survives."

"We're not talking about hurt feelings," Jasso said. "He will never forgive us."

"Edison's right," Lexi said. "We have to try."

Jasso and I removed the paladin's armour while Lexi started a fire to boil some water. Once the paladin's numerous wounds were exposed, it was she, under F3's guidance, who did the repairs. The only danger now was of a bacterial infection of one or two of the deeper wounds.

"Oh for antibiotics," F3 moaned. "Wait a minute. There may be some growing around us. Edison, show this to Jasso and Lexi."

I showed Lexi and Jasso F3's screen, which showed some sort of lichen growing on a tree.

"Do either of you know this lichen?"

"Lichen! Old man's beard, a tree moss," Jasso said.

"Right. Get some. A good handful. Apply it to the wounds."

"We can look for Hansen at the same time," Jasso said. With that, he and Lexi were off, leaving me with the boy, Speckle, a mule, a moaning paladin, and F3 for company.

"So, did she miss me?" I asked the boy. But he had wandered off, wearing the paladin's golden helmet, and was now struggling to lift his shield. At least he didn't have the sword to play with. I turned to the paladin. "What's your story?" I asked him, not expecting a reply. "There aren't supposed to be any paladins left."

The paladin moaned.

"This man is no more than thirty years old," F3 said.

"I can see that."

"The paladins haven't been seen for twenty years, so..."

"He would have only just been into double digits when they disappeared. So he's an impostor of some sort."

"Impostor or not, apparently he behaves just as one would expect a paladin to. They are not permitted to avoid a fight: wherever they see evil, they must defeat it, or die. He charged in to fight the bron in order to protect Lexi and the others. Typical foolish paladin behaviour. Have you considered joining up? Maybe he knows where the recruiting office is."

"How do you know he charged in to protect Lexi?"

"She told us. While you were slumped on the ground, dribbling."

"How long was I out?"

"Five minutes. But don't worry. She saw the entirety of your heroic intervention – she was up in the bushes watching."

"Brilliant," I muttered, remembering the whimpering. "Did she say where they are going?"

"West, until they hit the ocean. There's a narrow strip of land between some mountains and the sea. Apparently no one lives there, so they should be safe from the Entity."

Jasso emerged from the bushes at a run, clutching several bunches of lichen. "We found Hansen. They're right behind me." He bent to press the herbs onto the most serious of the paladin's wounds. "So are the Order, according to Hansen. He's seen smoke to the north – infernal machines. I'll climb a tree with F3 to have a look, if you don't mind."

I mutely handed F3 over.

Jasso chuckled. "Wait till I tell Hal you took on a bron alone."

"Not quite alone," F3 corrected him. "Anyway, I've radioed the information to Hal already, if he's listening in on the crystal set and not dead."

"You know, Edison, you'd find battling giant beasts far more easy if you used a bit of magic. Not to mention defending yourself against rogue magicians," Jasso commented, then sprinted off again.

"Thanks," I muttered, but he was already out of earshot.

A few moments later, Lexi and Hansen arrived. "The Order!" Lexi said.

"Jasso said," I replied.

Hansen strode up and shook my hand. "You came after us," he said, by way of hello.

"Of course," I said.

"*Why* did you come after us?" Lexi asked.

I didn't have to have F3 in my hand to hear its mocking voice. That I could supply myself. "Yeah, Edison, why *did* you come after them?"

"I thought you might be in danger," I offered lamely. I finally knew the *real* answer. But I wasn't telling anyone. Including myself.

"Why would that bother you?" Lexi asked. Her voice had taken on a cold edge.

"Why?" echoed the boy, dragging the paladin's shield along.

"You helped me. You didn't have to. So I'm helping you."

"Well," Lexi said, "we'd better get going. The Order will be at the river soon, and our route west will be cut off."

"Come back with us!" I blurted awkwardly. "All of you. I'll protect you. And I won't leave you again. I promise."

Lexi hesitated. She looked at Hansen searchingly.

"If you come with me, you'll be looking over your shoulder for the next twenty years," he said with a sad grin. "I'll keep Esme for company, if you don't mind."

"Hansen, no, you're coming back with us too," Lexi said.

"I've got a strange hankering to see the ocean. Never seen the ocean before," Hansen said, turning to me. "I take it you didn't catch up with your mother? Well, if you ever do, say hello to her for me. And come and visit when this is all over. I'll make it easy for you to find me." He knelt to shake the boy by the hand. "Look after your mother," he said, patting the boy on his head. "Hope you find your name one day, wherever you lost it." Then he turned to Lexi and hugged her.

"Hansen..."

"Come visit. Not too soon. Next year. I want my place to be finished first." He disentangled himself and advanced on me. "You better do as you say," he said. "Lexi deserves to have someone look after her."

"I know."

Hansen nodded and moved on to Esme, loosing her reins from the bush they were tied to.

At this point Jasso returned. He took in Hansen leading Esme away at a glance. "Anyone going west has about an hour before they're cut off." We all gathered around as he showed us a still on F3's screen. From a distant gap in the woods, smoke rose from twenty or more hidden machines. "F3 says the column is a mile long," he added. Then he put F3 back in my hand, without any trace of reluctance.

"Then I had best be making my move," Hansen said. He shook a surprised Jasso by the hand, then began to lead Esme away.

"And me," Jasso said. "I need to report the Order's movements. It wasn't expected that they would come this far south and west. Nice seeing you again," he said to Lexi. "Find the army," he called, already on his way. "I'll see you there. And don't hang about too long. You don't want the Order to overtake you!"

With Jasso gone, there was a sudden quiet in the bowl-shaped clearing. Lexi, the boy, and Speckle all looked at me expectantly. The paladin moaned.

"Speckle, you'll take the paladin. Sorry, he's a bit heavier than me. Lexi, give me a hand hoisting him up."

"What about his armour," Lexi wanted to know.

"Let's hide it in leaf-litter."

"We should check for anything personal or useful in his saddlebags," Lexi added, pointing in the rough direction of the paladin's deceased steed.

141

"Good point. You do that, and the boy and I can bury the armour. We'll mount him up in a minute."

I watched Lexi as she ran. When she was out of sight, I started shifting armour to a likely-looking pile of leaves.

Six Go East

We had been under way for a couple of hours. Lexi was leading Speckle, who had the unconscious paladin tied to her back, and I was carrying the boy and F3. Making six of us, more or less. Of which I was carrying two and Speckle one. I had deduced from our awkward conversations thus far – short, staccato, and separated by long silences – that although Lexi was pleased to see me back, a definite coldness towards me persisted. I clearly had not been forgiven for deserting her and the boy just yet.

"I see you joined the army," Lexi commented, after one such long pause.

"Unofficially," I replied lightly. "I don't think I get paid. The uniform belongs to someone dead who didn't need it any more."

"Well they *were* dead," F3 interjected. "Of course they had no further need of it."

Lexi ignored F3. "But they could order you to go anywhere – and we wouldn't be able to go with you."

"No, this is only a temporary attachment on my part. I think it would be best to hitch a ride with the army as far south as they go, then we can make our own way. I've talked it through with F3, haven't I F3? I'm going to open a lemonade stand."

"Really?" there was a note of hope in Lexi's voice.

"Of course. Fighting is not my thing, as you saw just now. I prefer fleeing. Usually accompanied by whimpering."

"But what about your mother? Aren't you going to keep looking for her?"

"The only trace of my mother I found was a twenty-year-old message telling me not to bother trying to follow her. The trail went a bit cold at this place called Bow Fort – it's like the edge of civilisation – and the Entity owns that ground now. So it's pointless trying to find her, at least until things quieten down again."

Lexi seemed satisfied with that. Everything went quiet for a few minutes as we climbed a short incline and I had to save my breath for trying to keep up. When we reached the top of the rise, which was open ground, we looked back the way we had come to see if there was any sign of the Order following us.

There wasn't. But there was a strange, localised storm straddling a gleaming section of the River Fair and the woods and fields on either side near where (I guessed) we had met the bron. A tenth of the sky was filled by the storm, a dense mass of swirling dark clouds that must have been a mile across, its base lit by flickering lightning, its top smoky orange in the sun. And all around it was the crisp blue sky of a bright, calm autumn day. Having stopped we could now hear the rumble of distant thunder, too. At least as far as I could see there was no sign of pursuers. I elevated F3 so its cameras could see the weird weather too.

"That's odd," I panted.

"Coo..." murmured the boy.

"It has a strangely unnatural look," F3 opined.

"Let's keep moving," Lexi said, and turned her back on the strange sight.

I followed. I could sense the boy sitting on my shoulders craning his neck to try to keep the storm in view (his knee was digging into my neck). "What do you think it means?" I asked.

"Whatever it means, we need to be as far away from it as possible," Lexi replied, ever the pragmatist.

A few paces further and the clouds were out of sight on the other side of the hill, and the sounds of our footsteps – and hoof-falls – drowned out any thunder that might still have reached our ears.

"I hope Hansen is all right," Lexi said.

"They'll be going our way, not his. It's magic, isn't it? That storm?"

"Almost certainly," F3 agreed. "But to what purpose?"

I pocketed F3 in the hope of shutting it up, which seemed to work for the time being at least. I tried to walk beside Lexi and Speckle, but the track was too narrow and I ended up ploughing through dewy trackside vegetation and soon dropped back behind them as before. Over the next couple of hours Lexi stomped ahead mercilessly whilst the boy and I were progressively left behind. My shoulders were stiff and exhausted; I needed a break, but Lexi was now so far ahead that she couldn't even hear my voice. I would have to try to keep up until *she* decided it was time for a break.

This turned out to be sunset, by which time I was exhausted in leg as well as shoulder. Lexi stopped to let Speckle take on water and do some browsing, and was loosening the ties on the paladin when I caught up.

"You set a good pace," I panted. "Are we camping here?"

"Not unless you want the Order to join us for breakfast. We carry on all night," Lexi said grimly.

"I can light the way," F3 called from my pocket.

Thanks a lot, I thought.

I lowered the boy to the ground and helped Lexi do the same with the paladin, who probably weighed as much as the two of us together. F3 used its infra-red camera to take his temperature (slightly high; fine) and inspect his wounds (surprisingly clean). He did not stir when he hit the ground, nor when we hoisted him back up onto Speckle ten minutes later.

The sun was setting behind us in the west. The trees of the thin woods cast shadows like knives in front of us as we walked on. Sparkling dew settled on the ground as the sky darkened. I began to wonder whether setting up home near the ocean might not have been the better option rather than the lemonade bar in the south after all. As I stumbled along, following the dancing incandescence of F3's light, I tried to work out why I hadn't simply followed Lexi and co to the ocean and hoped that the Entity really would ignore us. The army didn't need me. It couldn't have followed me if I had gone west. I had no loyalty to General Hagroth, that was for sure. Much as I liked Hal and Jasso, they had no need of my help. Hagroth would as soon kill me as save me. I didn't really think it would be much safer with the army than isolated on a distant shore. The only possible reason was that I still harboured a desire to find my mother, despite my protestations to Lexi. But I could never go searching for her whilst supposedly looking after Lexi and the boy, which meant...

One day I would have to leave them again.

I consoled myself with a fantasy that I could leave them somewhere safe, somewhere where they were comfortable, probably a lemonade stand somewhere in the south, somewhere that they wouldn't mind being left for an indefinite length of time whilst I went back north searching for my mother. In this fantasy they lived in a small, stone-built house in the middle of a flower-rich meadow under permanently blue skies in an endless summer. The stand was on the road outside, and it had a little canopy. Passers-by were few, but everyone stopped for Edison's Famous Lemonade.

That was how it looked when Speckle and I wandered off in the fantasy. When we got back, the lemonade stand was smashed, the house was ruined, the meadow was flattened and dead, and Lexi and the boy were gone. And it was raining.

"What's a lemonade stand?" Lexi asked.

The Paladin is Annoyed

We stopped once more in the pre-dawn, fairly well exhausted. The paladin stirred as we laid him down. I knelt down beside him and held up F3.

"Temperature a little warm, but nothing to be concerned about," F3 reported.

Lexi was taking Speckle's saddle off. She seemed to have formed an instant attachment to the horse, just as I had. The boy was asleep on the ground; he hadn't stirred when I'd transferred him from my back.

"I told you not to remove my armour," the paladin murmured. He fixed me with a beady glare.

"We had to. You would have died otherwise," I said. "How are you feeling?"

"You owe me my honour."

"You owe us your life, so get over it," I replied testily.

"If my death was fated at the hands of that beast, then so be it. It was not for you to intervene."

"Can you believe this guy?" I called to Lexi. "Newsflash pal. You can't have free will *and* fate, and I prefer free will."

"That's not strictly true, as a matter of fact," F3 put in.

"Did you bring my armour?"

I shrugged. I'm not sure the gesture was visible. It was still pretty dark.

"My sword..."

"I kind of lost it..."

"My horse..."

"Dead, but that wasn't our fault."

The paladin fell back and gasped, almost as if he would rather be dead. Ungrateful blighter. At this point Lexi ran up.

"I did find this," she said, and put a gold locket in the paladin's hand. He spared it a glance, then clutched it tightly, his eyes closed.

"Look pal," I said, "there are a hundred ways you can catch up with fate if you want to. But if it's good you want to do, you have to stay alive. You can't do a damn thing when you're dead except lay there and rot. I'm sorry about the armour but look at me! I'm blue! And do you hear me complaining?"

"Constantly," F3 said.

Lexi patted me on the shoulder and went back to Speckle.

9 a.m. in Crickne

When we reached Crickne, we lurked for a while at the edge of the woods so that F3 could scan for enemies. We had no idea whether this was possible, but we tried anyway. There was no Jasso to help this time, and no Tigo to give a timely warning. If someone like Klim was waiting for me, it was more or less goodbye world.

When we dared move, I went first, carrying the boy. I was surprised that I was still able to. He was definitely lighter than he looked. Lexi followed, with the semi-conscious paladin draped over Speckle. F3, as usual, was in my pocket.

Crickne was even more the ghost town. There was literally no one there. Klim's corpse had gone too; all that was left was a brown stain in the dirt where his life had bled out. I shuddered as I passed. Even the heavies charging a toll at the Shillingbridge had taken flight, so we were able to cross the river without being taxed. As we did so, Hansen's abandoned Emporium came into view.

"I hope Hansen's all right," Lexi said quietly.

"With luck he'll be far away by now," I said. Then I dived in. I'd managed to avoid blurting out the question about Lexi's face until now, but it was suddenly time. "You were captured by the Order, weren't you? How did you escape?" I turned to look at Lexi, who suddenly decided to hide her face under a combination of the hood of her cape and a curtain of hair. But she didn't duck the question. She'd been waiting for me to ask what had happened to her, well, ever since we became on civil terms.

"It was a raiding party," Lexi began. "They came to our village, killed anyone who resisted – my mother and father among them – and took the rest of us prisoner."

We passed Hansen's Emporium. The door was swinging in the breeze. I led the way south. There was no sign of the army.

"I ate their food for three weeks while they attacked nearby villages. We had no choice – if *you* didn't eat, they ate *you*. Anyone who couldn't keep up, they became food too. When they had about two hundred prisoners they set off back north. And that was our last hope gone. We'd been waiting and watching for any sign of the army and a chance of rescue – but we never saw one. Now they were taking us north, and we were finished. Some of us were already changing – the grey taint makes you docile, obedient. I ate as little as I could, just enough to keep my energy up. All the time I was waiting for my chance. I'd already decided that I'd rather die than become a changeling."

"While there's life, there's hope," I said.

"Not on that trail, there wasn't," Lexi said, and stopped speaking for a while. I guessed unpleasant memories were flooding back, so I said nothing. She would carry on the story when she was ready.

The trail south began to look like an abandoned rural idyll. Farms had been established on either side of the road, but only a small number of fields had been used to grow crops this year. There was a mixture of fields of weedy grassland and fields of stubble, all separated by unruly hedges and the occasional gate. There was no sign of activity: the crops had been harvested and the farmers had gone. We passed a broken cart that had been left in the ditch beside the road and a derelict farmhouse. Warbirds (of the flying kind) watched us hungrily from trees along the way.

"I hate this place," I muttered without meaning to.

Lexi did not take this as an insult, thankfully. "Tell me about your world," she asked.

So I did. I told her about school, and about the city that had become Crickne; about the monorail I travelled in every day, and about the war with the Entity. I babbled on for ages. I talked about cars, about how we had no horses, about the wastelands between cities. I talked about my mother and her pet robots, her computer TREE, her love of chocolate. I talked, too, about the weapon that my mother wouldn't help build, the Quantum Zero Counterfactual Decoherence Device. The one that seemed to have brought about a global cataclysm.

"Why wouldn't your mother help build it?" Lexi wanted to know.

I explained that my mother was a pacifist, and why she named me Edison.

"She was wrong. You must always fight," Lexi said.

"Even if it means the end of the world?"

Lexi thought for a few moments. "Yes. Even then."

"Course, if she'd been working on the Quantum thingy, she wouldn't have had time to design the egg that brought me here – we would never have met."

I glanced back to see what I thought was a little grin on Lexi's scarred face, mostly hidden by cloth and hair.

Next I told her what I knew about the Entity's beginnings. She agreed that we were right to attack it once it had taken over the minds of those first few victims. "Look what it uses the Order for now," she said bitterly. "For killing people and converting them into changelings. That is what would have become of all your people, if you had not attacked first."

A few miles down the road, I ran out of things to tell her about my world, and without prompting, Lexi told me about her escape.

"Our way north took us along the shoulder of a steep hill, so on one side there was a steep downslope. I waited until we were opposite a large patch of woodland, then pretended to stumble and threw myself down the slope. I slipped and rolled and bounced off trees; when I reached the bottom, I started running. I hoped they'd think I was dead and forget about me. But they didn't. Only one came after me. It wasn't expecting a fight. I only had a stick, but I won. Its claws..."

She didn't need to explain what its claws had done.

"I made my way home, but my village was gone, a smouldering ruin. I moved on, but no-one would help me. As soon as they saw I had the taint..."

"Until Hansen," I guessed.

"Yes, until Hansen. But before I met him, I'd already met the boy. His parents too had been killed it seemed, and he was wandering alone, freezing cold and hungry. No-one takes on someone else's child."

"You do," I said.

"It was Hansen who suggested I mine metal for money," Lexi said, ignoring my compliment. "He was good to me when we had no right to ask for kindness from anyone... and then I found you. Now you know the story of my life. Didn't take long, did it?" Lexi seemed slightly cross with me, somehow.

"It's not how long. It's how good," I told her.

"Not very good," she muttered.

"No. Very good. This damn weight on my shoulders proves that," I insisted.

"Down," the boy said.

"Believe me, I'd love to, but we have to keep on," I said, and hoisted him up into a more comfortable position for the umpteenth time that morning.

Refugee Train

The landscape was one of gently-rolling stubble fields and lichen-covered dry stone walls, dotted by an occasional tree leering over the road, almost always dead, and almost always home to two or three warbirds, perched up high, watching passers-by hungrily. Above, the sky was a uniform grey, empty and featureless. It was a drab scene, one whose palette had been reduced to the clay of the sky and the lichen-covered stone walls, and the sand of the stubble in the fields and the dead roadside weeds. The black of the warbirds and the yellow of their beady eyes were intense, but complementary colours. Lexi's gaze was constantly drawn to them: apart from Edison, they were the only things that did not blend into the faded background.

Lexi led them, although she did not know where she was going. She had never been south of the River Fair until today. She walked a step ahead of Speckle, who was bearing the intermittently-conscious paladin once more. Edison, with the boy on his shoulders, fell behind time after time, each time making a concerted effort to catch back up.

As the day wore on, they began to catch up with other bands of refugees heading south. Lexi kept her face hidden, although few would have noticed her with the bright blue Edison nearby. The first person they met on the road was an old woman, who was leaning on her stick and moving very slowly. Edison invited her to join their little band – Edison carrying the boy on his back and F3 in his pocket, Speckle carrying the delirious paladin, and Lexi carrying a backpack. The old woman refused, but Edison refused her refusal. "You can't make us go any faster than you, so welcome to the gang," he said. The old woman shrugged. She, like many that they met on the road, did not seem surprised to meet Edison. News of the blue magican had passed far and wide, it seemed – but that didn't stop the stares.

Lexi could tell that Edison was glad to slow down to the old woman's pace, because he had been carrying the boy for miles, and was not really built for heavy work. For a while at least, the boy could totter along on his own legs, and take the weight off Edison's shoulders.

It turned out that the old woman – Elfe was her name – was from a village close to the river. When the populace had fled, no-one had helped her. She lived alone, and it was rumoured that she was a witch, which seemed to be the cause of the villagers' unfriendliness.

Edison said he would be *more* likely to offer to help someone he thought was a witch, because he would be afraid of making her cross. Lexi, a few steps ahead of Edison and Elfe, laughed silently at that.

"And anyway, *are* you a witch?" he asked.

"When a mother wants a herbal remedy for a sick child, I am a witch," Elfe said. "When the crops fail, and the farmers are looking for someone to blame... I'm just an old, old woman." She smiled toothlessly.

Their group passed little clusters of people who had stopped by the roadside for lunch or out of sheer weariness. Edison managed to get Elfe a ride in a cart belonging to one such group, who stirred from their meagre picnic to join them on the road.

Lexi kept her hood up and made sure that her hair was covering as much of her face as possible, hoping that no-one would scrutinise her too closely and assume by the sight of her unnaturally-grey hair that she was just another old woman. She needn't have worried: everyone only had eyes for Edison. Being bright blue, he stood out like the moon on a cloudless night, and attracted much attention from their fellow travellers, as well as a lot of muttered discussions about who or what he was.

As they went south, the numbers of the refugee train continued to grown. Minor tracks on either side fed newcomers into the main stream; they caught up those in front of them; and more refugees still joined the back of the column. Soon well over a hundred people were travelling together like a giant, grimy, battered caterpillar.

Lexi found herself strangely enjoying the experience. There was a companionship in this crowd of people, a togetherness. Stories, and even supplies, were being shared. Old and young, fit and injured, those with few possessions and those with none, all shared the same road. Lexi guessed that the warm mood would turn to selfishness and panic as soon as the Enemy was sighted. She guessed, too, that her acceptance in this group depended on her keeping her hood up and her tainted skin hidden. So she kept quiet, and enjoyed being a passive member of the crowd.

Everyone had news about the movements and whereabouts of the Enemy's forces, which Edison and F3 compiled at rest stops. As it turned out, most people's geographic knowledge was patchy, as was their time-keeping; much of the information about the Enemy's forces was incompatible. At the rest stops, too, Edison encouraged Lexi to help the injured – but she preferred to sit apart, anonymous, her face covered.

At about two o'clock a squad of black-and-silver cavalry whisked up from the south, forcing their way against the flow of refugees with much cursing, and told Edison he was wanted at a council of war. Apparently Hagroth's scouts had been told to watch for him crossing the Shillingbridge and to send word when he did so. That was one disadvantage of being bright blue – he was unmistakable, even in the drab green garb of the Scouts.

"We'll need at least two more horses," Edison told the soldiers. "I'm not leaving my friends."

But the soldiers were prepared for that. They had a carriage waiting at the head of the column of refugees (the road was too narrow to bring it further against the human tide). This meant that all of them were able to go – humans and F3 in the 'carriage', which turned out to be a glorified way of describing a very rustic cart, and Speckle trotting along behind, finally unburdened. The cart was furnished with two bench-like seats running longways, on one of which they laid the feverish paladin. Lexi, the boy, and Edison sat on the other. It about balanced the weight, those three against him.

It was a tooth-rattling, spine-shaking, dusty journey. Edison moaned something about shock-absorbers, but there was too much noise to hold a conversation, so he soon shut up. Progress alternated between jolting and rapid when the road was clear, to slow and curse-ridden when the driver had to force his way through clouds of refugees. The crowds scattering onto the road side stared at them enviously – at least that was how Lexi interpreted their looks – but she would have preferred walking to a ride in this monstrosity any time.

At about five in the afternoon, when the sun had given up attempting to beat back the thin grey cloud and night seemed to be closing in early, the cart reached a bridge over a wide, fast-flowing river. The bridge was sturdily built of large stone blocks, all covered in a mixture of black algae and yellow lichen, and looked to have stood for a thousand years. Immediately beyond the bridge was the encampment of Hagroth's army.

Lexi had never seen so many people in one place. The army camp was a vast, noisy, colourful, disorganised mass of humanity, tents and horses. Marquees and tents had different-coloured flags flying from them, distinguishing the units that they belonged to. Stalls selling hot food lined the way, and delicious aromas filled the air. In several places there were corrals of hundreds of horses. At least a hundred fires had been lit and were starting to stand out against the coming dusk. Singing, shouting, and laughter were everywhere. As their driver was forced to slow down to steer a path through the turmoil, conversation became possible once more. Edison, keen to show off his knowledge of the army, kept up a running commentary about what Lexi and the boy were staring at.

"If you're hungry, I'll get you some food in a minute," he said. "Look, that's Hagroth's own cavalry, you can tell by the pennants. *All* the cavalry are black and silver, but only his personal command have the Royal fist-and-flowers motif, at least on their flags. Everyone has it on their badges. The reds are the infantry. Artillery is red also –"

"Red with yellow," F3 interrupted.

"I was coming to that! Give me a chance. The infantry, like the cavalry, have embellishments on their flags in order to show what they do."

"Where are your men – the Scouts?" Lexi asked. "I don't see a brown flag."

"It's not brown, it's khaki. The Scouts don't have a camp, anyway. They buzz about all over the place."

Eventually the driver pulled to a halt in front of a well-guarded black marquee. It was decorated with a number of flags, of which the most prominent was one in black and silver with a gauntlet clutching some flowers. Edison, clutching F3, was shown inside; it was made plain that Lexi and the boy were to wait in the cart. The boy was a bit put out not to be able to follow Edison, but he soon forgot about that and got on with being amazed by everything that was going on around him.

Lexi divided her time between stretching her aching limbs, making sure the boy didn't wander off, and going over the paladin's injuries again. At one point a passing soldier asked her what unit he belonged to – but seemed satisfied when Lexi told him the paladin wasn't in the army. She decided it prudent not to attract attention by mentioning that he might be a paladin.

Lexi could not get used to the sheer number of people around her. Since her captivity, she had always avoided crowds. Being in the heart of a crowd of ten thousand people made her acutely uncomfortable – but as she analysed her feelings, she felt herself almost believing that she and the boy were safer here than they would have been if they had gone west with Hansen. Hagroth's army was huge – it *must* be able to defeat the Enemy's forces, or at least hold them back indefinitely. There was that, and they had Edison – if he stuck to his promise and stayed with them.

Lexi knelt on the floor of the cart, re-bandaging the paladin's wounds, looking up occasionally to ensure that the boy was still in sight. She began to wonder what Hansen was doing now: she imagined him and Esme plodding through a thin autumn forest, single yellow leaves spiralling down around them. Somewhere, far over the horizon, was the ocean. One day she would have to go there and see it for herself. When this was all over, when it was safe...

The boy let out a little squeal of amusement.

Lexi looked up – and there was Edison, emerging from the General's tent. He was now wearing a short sword around his waist, and had been given a bright red cape to wear over his dull tunic.

"Edison!" Lexi said.

Edison beamed. "That's Captain Hawthorne to you," he said, and kicking his heels together, dipped briefly into a formal bow.

Southward

It turned out that Edison *had* been made a captain – but not a captain of the army. Edison had been made a captain of *refugees*. It was the army's usual practice to ignore refugees where possible and to push them around if they tried to get in the way. Edison, though, had argued that they should be protected.

F3 gave an impression of Edison's argument some time later. *"That rabble are your mothers, your fathers, your sons and your daughters. If not for them, for whom do you fight?"*

"That's not what I said," Edison complained.

"That is *exactly* what you said. Except you did it in your rather weedy voice," F3 said. "I can play it back to you if you like..."

"That won't be necessary."

It seemed that General Hagroth wanted to move some troops south anyway, to secure lines of retreat and re-occupy a number of abandoned watchtowers. By travelling with them, the refugees would be offered some degree of protection. They were pleased to hear that they were to be escorted south, not that they were given much choice – they were rounded up at dawn the next day and told to muster immediately south of the encampment. Here they were introduced to their new leader, Edison.

Rather than give a rousing speech to his new people, Edison passed word among them about who he was and what was to happen by telling a few nearby children and asking them to pass the message along. His messengers, among them people he had met at the Scavengers' camp, were eager enough to help. Among them was Tigo, the boy who had warned him of Klim's ambush. Tigo, Edison was pleased to see, had recovered from being hurled through the air and was back to his previous energetic self.

It seemed to Lexi as though the refugees' escort consisted of about half of Hagroth's army, so impressive were they when they had formed up. The advance escort numbered about six hundred, and included three cannons and several units of musketeers. They were commanded by one Captain Flyst, a stocky, scowling man with a bustling stride. The rear escort, meanwhile, consisted of two hundred cavalry under Captain Vexan, a hawk-nosed bony veteran of many campaigns. F3 estimated the refugees themselves to number three thousand, "to the nearest hundred".

As soon as they had set off, Flyst's infantry started to outdistance them, whereas Vexan's cavalry didn't even bother to set off until the refugees had already been walking for an hour. Lexi knew, because she kept looking back past the strung-out column of three thousand refugees to see why they weren't following. She soon found out why, because the cavalry, once they *did* set off, quickly caught them up.

Edison trotted up and down the line on Speckle, trying to keep the refugees together, generally trying to raise morale, and organising cart rides for those who couldn't keep up. The refugees had about twenty carts between them, hauled by a number of tired old nags and in several instances, cows.

At about midday, they caught up with the infantry, who were waiting for them at the first of the watchtowers. As soon as they sighted the refugees, all but those who were to be stationed at the watchtower moved off once more. And so the miles slowly passed.

By mid-afternoon, the scenery had changed markedly. No longer were the refugees surrounded by harvested fields and gently-undulating hills. The ground seemed to have split in ages past, as if some great cataclysm had been brought down upon it. On their left the ground rose sharply, at first in a step it was possible to climb, but the step grew and grew until after a mile the step had become a hundred foot high cliff. On their right the ground seemed to have correspondingly fallen, and the fertile farmland slid down until it was engulfed by a seemingly endless swamp. Soon the road was defined on one side by the cliff, rising like a vast wall, and on the other by a gentle downslope ending at the water's edge. There were few open areas in the swamp, just a series of enormous patches of bulrushes erupting from dark water and odd islands of collapsing trees, all separated by narrow leads scarcely wide enough for a rowing boat.

A lot of people had a name for the plateau above the cliff, which was soon relayed to Lexi and Edison: Xharg Height. This had been named after a magician who had once lived there. At the next rest stop, the magician's home could be seen in the distance: a narrow tower, rising at least three hundred feet above the plateau, made of the same white stone that formed the body of the cliff itself. It was an awe-inspiring sight, especially half-shrouded in the mist that was pouring like liquid over the cliff's edge.

Tigo was walking with them, and he knew all about Xharg's tower. "No-one's been in there for a thousand years, they say," he said. "Ever since the Archmages all killed each other. Some say Xharg is still alive in there."

"Really? He found the philosopher's stone?" Edison asked.

Tigo didn't know what a philosopher's stone was, so he changed the subject. "Others say the tower is infested with giant spiders. If it's still light when we pass, we might be able to see the webs." He paused, waiting for Edison to say something else, perhaps to suggest that they might explore the place.

Edison evidently sensed the same thing. "We'd better steer clear, then," he said.

Tigo nodded, but looked a little disappointed.

It was almost dark when they eventually passed the tower, which was lit impressively in pink by the setting sun. What looked like vast cobwebs could, indeed, be seen decking the upper reaches of the structure.

"What is it with wizards and towers?" Edison moaned.

No-one answered him.

*

Tents were pitched, fires were lit; the refugees' camp was spread out along a mile of the road, so narrow was the boulder-strewn ground on either side. In the dusk, furious mosquitoes emerged from the swamp and found better meals than the refugees. In response to the bothersome insects, Edison christened the swamp "The Swamp of Despair," even though it already had a name that the refugees knew: "Ingold Lake."

Everyone – except F3 – shared the meagre fare. Three thousand people took a lot of feeding – and the food was now all gone, all except what little wild barley and berries it had been possible to gather along the wayside during the day.

Lexi, Edison, the boy, and the paladin shared a fire. The paladin was able to sit up and feed himself, which was promising. Speckle was tied up close by, foraging amongst the roadside boulders for dead grasses. Lexi attempted to trim Edison's wispy beard with some borrowed, crude scissors. Then, to show no favouritism, she did the same for the paladin's rather more significant growth.

At some point Lexi noticed that they had been joined by someone else: Elfe. The old woman stood at the edge of the firelight and beckoned Edison to go with her. Five minutes later he was back, alone.

"Oh hell, she *is* a witch," Edison muttered, throwing himself down.

"What did she want?" Lexi asked.

"To tell my fortune."

"And?"

"You don't believe in any of that stuff, do you?"

"What did she say?"

"All right, fine. She said I had to do what I felt was right. She said

I would get what I wanted."

"Desired," put in F3.

"Whatever. Then she said 'Everything freezes, but there will be a thaw.'"

"What could it mean?" Lexi asked.

"Unknown. Perhaps she was referring to the fact that it is autumn. She also said something else, which made me question her talents," F3 said. "She said to Edison," (here F3 put on Elfe's quavery voice) "'You are a good man.'"

"I was quite warming to her at that point," Edison said. "There's also this poultice or something for the paladin," he added, handing Lexi a small package.

*

Some time later the conversation turned to the future. "What will we do when we get into the Westfold?" Lexi asked.

"Find a faraway place in the south," Edison mused, "a safe place with a lemon tree grove. Build a house. And a lemonade stand. Just the three of us. And Speckle. Four. And F3, five, if you count F3. Hopefully the paladin will wander off to carry on searching for the Holy Grail or whatever when he's fit again..."

"He *can* hear you," came the paladin's gruff voice from the shadows.

"Oh, sorry."

The paladin laughed. "Thank you for helping me."

"Still wish you'd died rather than be saved?"

"No," the paladin said. "And I'll tell you why some day."

"It's strange... I refused to come this way with Hansen," Lexi said. "We could have been at the Westfold by now. He wanted to go further still, into the Eastfold."

"Do you miss him?" Edison asked.

"When the only person you held conversations with for a year leaves... yes, I miss him. I hope he's all right."

Lexi lay awake for a long time, listening to Edison bicker with F3. Despite his protestations, it was clear that Edison both respected the little creature and relied upon it. Their conversations were constantly entertaining, even if Lexi frequently had trouble following what they were actually talking about.

From what Lexi could gather about their present conversation, F3 had worked out how to block or overcome the Enemy's power to control its minions, the Order.

"The control signal is based on a fractal algorithm, based, funnily enough, on the bifurcation patterns in lightning. So the frequency rises irregularly," F3 was saying.

"So you can replicate it to send instructions to the Entity's minions?"

"No. But I can produce a rapidly-evolving pattern of gibberish in which the actual instructions sent by the Entity might get lost."

"What range?" Edison asked.

"You have to remember that the Entity is probably broadcasting from a massive transmitter whose power is a gazillion times mine... in theory we could build transmitters and fix them in defensive positions to neutralise any attacks... but that would take about two generations of scientific advancement..."

"What range?"

"About three metres, based on a signal:noise ratio of 1:10, which ought to be enough to garble the instructions. If we could actually send information that made sense, we could extend the radius to ten metres."

"Any chance of that?"

"No."

"Anything else I need to know?"

"In order to transmit at suitable power levels, I will begin to overheat as soon as we start to jam the Entity's signals."

"How long before you overheat?"

"I will go into emergency shutdown after 1.13 minutes at full capacity."

"So to overcome the Entity's control over one of its minions I first have to go up and get close enough to shake hands with it?"

"It's the best that can be done," F3 said.

"Let's hope we never get close enough to the Order to need it," Edison said.

"Quite," agreed F3.

Almost asleep, Lexi put her hand out to make sure that the boy was still with her. He was, a hot little bundle that she drew close to, her arm around him. Her last thought before letting exhaustion overcome her was how like a family they seemed. All of them together, even the paladin – they'd all come from different places, different families, and yet here they were, together as if they had always known one another.

Clearwater Cove

By mid-afternoon the next day, even those refugees who had started the journey fit and well had started to flag.

"How much further?" I asked F3.

"To judge by the map we saw in General Hagroth's headquarters, we have covered about thirty miles. Clearwater Cove, which we are now passing, was marked on the map, and it was roughly a third of the way to the Westfold," F3 explained.

I did the maths myself. Sixty miles to go, and the pace, already slow, was in danger of becoming snail-like. Food was low to non-existent and water was in plentiful, but foul, supply.

Still, the cove F3 mentioned looked promising as a place to fill up with clean water and take a break. The cove was a vast gouge in the face of the cliff, reaching far back into deep shadow and out of sight, from which an apologetically small sparkling stream babbled its way. *I made this*, the stream was saying. *It took me a long time, but I made the cove all by myself. Then I filled up the swamp.*

Half a mile ahead of us the scenery changed. We had reached the edge of what looked like a large forest. Here the road forked: one branch plunged on, into the trees, and the other curved around to the right, following the boundary between dry forest and woody swamp.

Just before the forest's edge was what looked like an abandoned farm – a cluster of ramshackle old stone buildings surrounded by a hodge-podge of small fields separated by dry stone walls. It had clearly been unused for some time, because the fields themselves were starting to scrub up, and there were a number of gaps where the stone walls had collapsed. To the east the farm backed onto the cliff, to the south it adjoined the woods, to the west all that separated it from the swamp was the road and a short slope, and to the north – the direction we were approaching from – the land was open, stony ground.

We had caught up with the infantry again, because we could see Flyst's men wandering about the farm, looking from this range like a nest of disturbed red ants. Oddly, they seemed to be settling in, and were even attempting to repair some of the worst of the damage to the walls, particularly on the side of the farm facing the woods.

For five minutes we watched the activity ahead of us as we approached. It slowly became obvious that the infantry weren't stopping for a short rest: they were digging in as if expecting an attack.

"Was this one of the places Hagroth wanted occupied?" I asked F3.

"No," F3 said. "We'd better get down there and find out what's what."

I passed word around that everyone should stop for a break and some clean water – not that they needed telling anyway, for there were already a hundred faces dipping into the cold clear water of the modest stream. Clear water. Clearwater Cove. I got it.

Vexan, from a mile or more up the slope behind us, had already seen what was happening and was riding past us with a couple of escorts to investigate. I followed.

*

Flyst himself was in the farmhouse proper, as Vexan and I soon found.

"Vexan, Hawthorne," Flyst greeted us. "Our scouts haven't returned from the woods. I don't think it would be prudent to advance into the forest until they give us the all clear. Hawthorne – no offence, but it will take your rabble about three hours to get to the open ground beyond. We need to be sure..."

"You're scared to advance?" Vexan snapped.

"It's all right, Hawthorne. Vexan has volunteered to lead the way with his cavalry."

Flyst and Vexan glared at each other. I felt I ought to intervene. "We don't want anyone going in there if it isn't safe. But how could the Order be ahead of us? The danger should be coming from behind us."

"Our backs are protected," Flyst said, jabbing his map with a stubby finger. "But there is a large gap between us and the nearest ally to our front."

"All the way to the wall, in fact," Vexan agreed, showing me a thick line on the map. "Three days for you, although my men could be at the wall tomorrow."

"Why, Vexan? To hide behind it?" Flyst muttered.

"Maybe we should send a message back to Hagroth..." I suggested.

"*General* Hagroth," Flyst said.

"And say what?" Vexan asked.

"I've already ordered my men to dig in here. I don't like it," Flyst said. "We wait."

"Wait! It's barely mid-afternoon. We can make the other side of the woods before dusk, if getting lost in the dark scares you."

"What *concerns* me," Flyst said, "is that a large proportion of us may not *reach* the other side of the woods."

"Let's wait for the scouts to come back," I offered.

"And if they don't?" Flyst asked.

"Are there any other routes we could take?"

There was no response from Flyst or Vexan. That was a no, then. We all stood there deep in thought for a minute – or at least, Vexan and Flyst looked as if they were thinking hard. Abruptly it seemed that Flyst's mental gymnast had dismounted from his apparatus and landed squarely on the mat with arms outstretched. He pointed to the map again.

"Hawthorne, here's us, Clearwater Cove. You see the farm is marked, as is the cliff and the plateau above. The gulley you just passed is Clearwater Cove – get your refugees in there. They'll be protected on three sides, should anything happen. They'll also have fresh water."

"They will also be trapped!"

"If anything comes out of the woods, they'll have to come through my men first to get to you. Meanwhile I'll send some volunteers forwards to see what's what. How about you, Vexan?"

"I'll stay on the hill. I can come to your aid if circumstances demand. I will be watching." With that, Vexan swept out of the farmhouse, followed by his bodyguards. Flyst's men watched them go with sour faces. The infantry held no regard for the cavalry it seemed.

Flyst gave Vexan a few seconds' distance before speaking again. "There are two things you should know, Hawthorne," he said. "One. Vexan is a coward. Two. The thing he is afraid of more than anything else in the world is General Hagroth. He will come to our aid if we need him."

Edison Breaks His Promise

Lexi watched Edison steer Speckle down towards the farm. On his right, she could see three cavalrymen heading the same way. The lances of two of them bore pennants that streamed behind them in the wind as they rode. The cavalrymen stuck to the road; Edison meandered over to it and fell in some distance behind them. Soon all four had handed their reins to members of Captain Flyst's infantry and disappeared inside the farmhouse itself.

"You look worried," observed the paladin.

They had settled themselves into a little sun trap under the white cliff, some way south of the spring. Behind them, three thousand refugees drank and washed in the water. The paladin was glad of a change of position, and laid himself flat on the stony ground. The boy had wandered off a little way, turning over stones to look for beetles.

Lexi pulled her hood up over her head.

The paladin laughed.

"We should check your wounds," Lexi said. Mentally, she added: and let's hope it's painful. "Keep your eye on the boy and I'll get some clean water."

"Doesn't he have a name?"

"Probably. But as with you, no-one knows what it is."

It took Lexi longer than she had thought to get some clean water. She intended to go upstream of everyone who was washing to avoid the disturbed, silty and dirty water, but it seemed a thousand people had all had the same idea. The cleanest water to be had now was far back, deep in the cool ferny shade of the gorge. Right at its end, Lexi could see the series of little waterfalls that had scored out the gorge cascading down from the plateau above. A couple of adventurous children were having fun climbing up through the rushing water. The slope was not vertical, but it was slippery, with rocks polished smooth and the fast-flowing stream in their faces, so that the children kept getting washed downstream a little way, much to their amusement.

Edison had already returned by the time she returned to the paladin. "Can you get out at the back?" he asked, without saying hello.

"One at a time, the fittest few of us... why?"

"The scouts haven't come back from the woods. There may be trouble. Flyst thinks we should hide in the gorge. I've sent some people around to pass on the message."

Whether people had received Edison's message or not, Lexi didn't know. But the refugees weren't moving, that much was clear. They had all settled down for a welcome rest. Hiding in the gorge didn't sound like a good idea to Lexi. She would rather be in the open, where she could see enemies approaching and know which way to run from them.

Edison settled down next to a pile of rocks, and set up F3 so that it had a good view down the slope. Then he watched and waited, singing to himself under his breath.

Lexi got on with tending to the paladin's wounds. The paladin was a tall, lean man, with more old scars than the face of the moon and plenty to add if he survived the next few weeks. If she had to put an age to him, Lexi would guess him to be about thirty – which would have made him ten when the rest of the paladins disappeared. He had an odd clouded look in his eyes, as if he was in a daydream most of the time. He would snap out of it, say his piece, then fade into silence once more.

Despite being cross with him, she was gentle. Of course, he was in great pain still. But Lexi knew that there were secret scars as well as the obvious ones she was dressing now. The wounds inflicted by the bron seemed to be healing nicely.

"What is that!" Edison shouted suddenly, leaping to his feet.

"Unknown," F3 replied.

A ripple was passing through the refugees. Lexi looked. A thin column of black smoke had appeared, hidden in the trees along the arm of the road that traced its way between the forest and the swamp. Now everyone was staring at it.

"Do you think they can see it from down there?" Edison asked, referring to Flyst's men at the farm. He didn't wait for an answer to the question, but started jumping up and down and shouting. "Hey – over there – smoke!"

It wasn't clear whether or not Flyst's men heard or saw him. In any case, the thin column of smoke was quickly joined by five more. A terrifying rattling coughing noise, not unlike the awakening rumbles of a great beast, could now be heard. As it was joined by its five fellows, the first column of smoke whitened somewhat until rather than coal-black it was now merely dirty grey.

"Infernal machines, I'd say," the paladin said calmly. "The Order are here."

"Are you –"

"Edison." It was F3. "At the woods' edge."

Lexi could see them too: the smallest kind of the Order, little taller than waist-high. She knew them well from when she had been a prisoner: they had formed a minor part of those guarding Lexi and her fellow prisoners. Although she could not make out individuals at this distance, there were enough of them that she could see an amorphous grey mass moving forward through the thinning trees bordering the forest. Her next thought was for the boy, and she stalked away a few paces and grabbed him. Still hunting for beetles, he protested, his legs wheeling in the air as Lexi lifted him off the ground.

"How many?" Edison asked.

"I think it is safe to say that not all the enemy are yet in view," F3 replied.

Edison swung around to Lexi. "I want you to take Speckle and get out of here. Take the boy and go. Sorry, Mr. Paladin, you'll have to fend for yourself. Take this – it's the best I can do for you." Edison pulled out his sword and placed it in the paladin's huge hand. Held by such a large man, the sword looked scarcely bigger than a table knife.

"We can't leave, Edison," Lexi said. "We have to stay together, remember? Whatever fate you have, we will share in it."

"Look, I know I said I'd never leave you again – but I can help them. If I do this, maybe the Order won't reach you guys." Edison looked awkward. He stared at his shoes. "I'll come *right back*. In about five minutes, ten max, right? In any case, I want you two and Speckle out of harm's way – get up the hill past Vexan's cavalry and keep riding until you hit Hagroth's army."

"We're no better than the rest of the refugees. How can we leave them behind?"

"Because we can!" Edison forced Speckle's reins into Lexi's grip and hugged her. Lexi was too cross with him to hug him back.

"You should stay with *us*," Lexi said coldly. "Like you said you would."

"I know, I'm sorry, but this is me... this is me keeping you safe. All right? I'll be back. Ten minutes."

Next Edison hugged the boy and patted Speckle. Then he started to run away, down the hill towards the farm. "If you won't leave now, keep hold of her until it gets sticky and then leg it," he shouted over his shoulder. Then he pulled the hood of his cloak over his head and didn't look back.

"He is a brave one, your love," the paladin said.

"Can you stand?" Lexi asked, ignoring him.

"I think so."

"Good. If you can't walk, they'll kill you."

"If it comes to that..." the paladin waved Edison's little sword in Lexi's view. "I'll give a good account of myself."

"Let's hope it doesn't. Let's hope Edison knows what he's doing."

They watched as Edison charged down the hill. Already half-way to the farm, he was a tiny speck, and getting smaller all the time.

"Do you think we'll ever see him again?" asked the paladin.

"Yes. We'll probably meet in the slave-train on its way back to the Greyfield," Lexi said bitterly.

The paladin laughed. "Optimism not your forte, is it?" he asked.

"No, it isn't," Lexi said, and pulled down her hood to show her grey and scarred face. "I need to do your bandages again. You don't want the Order to know how injured you are. If they find out they might just kill you on the spot."

My Brief Part in the Battle of Clearwater Cove – 1

The foot of a hill, nestled in the curve of a sparkling brook bordering on an impenetrable forest on one side, with a treacherous swamp on another, and the thirty-metre high wall of a cliff behind, was a questionable place to carve out a farm. Whenever this place had been started, a hundred or more years ago, the owners must have spent most of their time trying to keep the forest at bay, pulling rocks out of the barren soil, and slapping the mosquitoes swarming out of the swamp.

Yep, it was a questionable place for a *farm* – why else had it been abandoned? One thing was for sure though: it was a plain awful place to build a *fort*. Which explained why the original owner had plumped for the farm. Which was bad luck for us, because what we really wanted right now was a fort, not a ruined farmhouse protected by semi-ruined dry stone walls.

"Damn the farmer who started this place!" I shouted to F3 as we hurtled down the hill towards the farm. "Why didn't he build a fort?"

"He saw no profit in it," F3 replied.

I had already figured as much out myself, of course.

Our farm – makeshift fort – was already besieged on two fronts, the sides next to the forest and the swamp. Small members of the Order – about up to my shoulders, if I let them get that close – stepped out of the woods in their hundreds, as if they had been there all along. Which they probably had. Which probably explained why our scouts hadn't returned.

To the right of these dust-grey goblin-creatures as I looked, the road forked – half of it passed into the forest and was swallowed up, the other half traced a path between the forest and the swamp. Down this road, a half-dozen smoking, clanking machines, each six metres high, were stamping towards the farm. In and amongst these two-legged behemoths were more of the little guys. A few hundred, five hundred, or maybe a thousand, it was hard to tell at the speed I was running at. And there were some of the bigger ones too, bigger than me. A few hundred of those, organised in separate units from the little guys. And some bigger yet, almost as big as the infernal machines themselves. Not so many of these giants, about ten. But between them, the ten giants could probably pick up the entire farmhouse and throw it into the swamp, where it would land with a rather resounding squelch.

"Edison, where are you going?" F3 enquired.

"I have a plan, one which may not work," I replied tersely, saving my breath for the running.

"Is it entitled 'Operation Sacrificial Lamb' or similar?"

"If we can get close enough to one of those infernal machines, you can jam it. I can climb aboard and take over the controls. Then we can run amok…"

"Now you're talking," F3 said. "Like a lunatic! You're going to die, Edison, and I'm going to pass into the clutches of one of those grey goblins. Which is worse!"

"My death beats you being owned by a goblin."

"Your death will happen once, and will be merciful in its brevity. My enslavement to a pudding-headed ash-grey goblin clone will last an indefinite time. Therefore I win – my fate is worse."

The wall arrived. It was only four feet high, and in places lower still where little collapses had occurred over the decades. As I reached and leapt through one such, the 'goblins' unleashed a volley of arrows. Stuck together, all the wood flying through the air at that moment could have replanted an acre of forest, I estimated. There was a sound like hail as the arrows landed.

I tripped into a roll and found myself next to someone who had been alive one second ago but who was now stone dead, having been transfixed by three arrows. He still hadn't hit the ground.

"Sorry," I said, and took his shield, which was laying uselessly at his feet. If like F3 the shield had been endowed with its own mind and voice, it would probably be shouting: "Idiot! Why didn't you pick me up 3.73 seconds ago?" or similar. Being a dumb old shield, it said nothing. Anyway, I guessed the soldier could spare the shield, being dead and everything.

The air was clear for the moment, so clutching the round shield over my head like a steel umbrella against the wooden rain, I scuttled into the lee of the farmhouse.

A second volley of arrows whispered through the air, but this time the defenders were prepared for it, and hunkered down out of the way before bobbing up and firing back. Muskets went off first, then our little cannons. Then all hell broke loose as an unearthly screeching erupted from the Order's forces (I guessed it was from them – I couldn't see without looking up, and I had no intention of doing that until I was safely inside the farmhouse).

I supposed the enemy were charging.

Inside the farmhouse I quickly located Captain Flyst.

"Captain Hawthorne! Back so soon!"

"Infernal machines!" I gasped.

"Yes."

"Can you take them?" I asked.

"Take them where?"

"I mean beat them."

"Of course," Flyst said, and paused. "If they are alone. They usually travel with an escort of ogror. Why are you here, Hawthorne? You need to look after the refugees."

"That's what I am doing. I believe I can jam the Entity's control signal..."

"From about ten feet," F3 interrupted.

Flyst laughed. "You may get within that range soon enough. But at that range, the number of the Order your magic will affect will be few." He looked dubious, but sent word forward to the men at the front line that I shouldn't be shot by them – at least not deliberately.

"By the way," Flyst added, as I made for the door. "I've been ordered to have you killed rather than let the Order capture you. So be careful. Keep your hood up. If they see you're different, they'll single you out."

I left the farmhouse against a stream of wounded men being carried the other way. Once outside, there was another volley of arrows, which had me curled up in a ball under my shield like an oversized snail. The air seemingly clear again, I crawled forwards, not stopping until I hit the wall of the farm a minute later. I bobbed up between two musketeers, who were rather surprised to see me.

It seemed that the defenders had managed to repel the first assault – which, made up entirely of the smallest breed of the enemy, seemed to have been merely a way of testing our defences. It was to the imminent battle what a spilled drink is to a bar-room brawl.

I peeped over the wall and hurriedly ducked again. The enemy were startlingly close. Luckily I seemed to have surfaced in a position quite close to the nearest infernal machine and reasonably far from any of the grey giants – although close enough to notice that they had an unexpectedly high number of eyes – possibly six, although I couldn't be sure. My glance also told me that the foot soldiers were still hanging about the skirt-tails of the infernal machines like infants on a field trip clinging to their teachers.

"I need a clear path to the nearest infernal machine," I shouted, without really hoping for any response.

One of the musketeers next to me paused in reloading his gun long enough to sneak a look of his own. "You have your wish, sir. They're about to open up," he said, speaking around the lit fuse that was hanging out of his mouth like a thin, droopy cigar.

A cry went up, passed from soldier to soldier like a particularly virulent bug. "Infernals! Infernals!"

I peeped again. The grey horde had started backing up, leaving the infernal machines to move to the fore. Even the giants were holding back.

A hand grabbed my shoulder and yanked me back down. It was the musketeer, his face unseen under the brow of his broad floppy hat.

That was when the machine guns opened up. The infernal machines had some sort of rotating barrel device, somewhat like a Gatling gun. It wasn't a fast rate of fire – it wasn't going to compete with an M134 motorised Gatling for that award – but in this world, it definitely counted as an Über Weapon.

Projectiles pinged against the wall and zoomed in all directions. The Order were wasting its ammo it seemed. Not for nothing had the ancient farmer built his walls a foot thick. I pictured him piling his rocks up, dreaming wistfully of how one day his creation might withstand a frontal assault by ten thousand enemies. Or maybe he just needed somewhere to put all the rocks his fields were full of.

I keyed myself up. When the infernal machine's operators were changing its magazine or whatever, I would have to dart for it. "F3, get ready."

"I was born ready," F3 rejoined. "Good-bye, Edison."

"Defeatist!"

The shooting seemed to diminish somewhat. Maybe the nearest infernal machine had stopped firing.

"Here we –" I began.

The infernal machine crashed through the wall, scattering musketeers like a gang of metal-detectorists who had just dug up an unexploded bomb. I found myself within touching distance of the monstrosity.

"Retreat!" someone shouted.

"F3!" I howled.

"Get on board!" F3 replied, which I took to mean that it had jammed the signal that was controlling the infernal machine and/or its operator(s). "You have 1.13 minutes before I overheat and go into emergency shutdown."

The infernal machine had stopped walking. Its gun idled. Meanwhile, its compatriots had smashed through other sections of wall and were stalking towards the farmhouse, guns blazing.

I looked for a hatch.

Our defenders were fleeing back to the farmhouse itself, not unreasonably. I was now the furthest forward of our forces, if I could claim to be a force.

Behind the infernal machine, the nearby forces of the Order had gone into a strange kind of meltdown. One I observed chewing another's ears. Two were rolling on the ground, fighting. Yet another was thoughtfully picking a dandelion. It seemed the jamming signal was working. The Order's forces, when in range of F3's jamming signal, became individuals who had no idea why they were there. Shame the jammer only reached about ten feet in each direction.

I could just about reach the underside of the infernal machine, in which, it turned out, there was no hatch. There was no hatch in the front, or the side nearest to me, or (a sneaky glance told me) the back. For reasons of symmetry and logic it was unlikely that the hatch was in the side opposite me.

Which left just one place: the roof.

The infernal machine's legs were eight feet long. The metal box that rested on top of these was a further ten feet tall. The Gatling gun was the only handhold of substance within range. With one foot on the bent knee of the behemoth, I was able to haul myself up onto the gun. Once standing on the gun, I could easily reach a letterbox-shaped viewing slit. It was just a matter of hauling myself high enough up to get a toe in. Then I could –

A pair of beady eyes peered out of the eye slit, meeting mine peering the other way.

"Hi," I said.

Bared teeth gleamed beneath the beady eyes.

There is sometimes a moment when you have to make a hard decision. Like when carrying a hot drink you have a choice between burning your fingers and dropping the mug, spilling scalding water everywhere. At that moment, I had a choice between letting go of my hold and falling to the ground, or letting the infernal machine operator bite me.

"0.35 minutes," F3 said, its voice louder than usual.

"What's that in seconds?" I screamed. I guessed it wasn't very many without working out just how few it was. I decided to hold on.

"Twenty seconds."

"Make a scary noise!"

If F3 was confused by this, it didn't say so. It proceeded to make a scary noise. This was not the roar of a lion, or the scream of a diving Stuka.

"Edison!" F3 screamed, in my mother's voice. "Tidy your room!"

I was so surprised I nearly fell off my perch. The bared teeth seemed to back off, too, equally astonished. It was now a question of who recovered faster. I grabbed the side of the infernal machine with one hand and poked my foot into the viewing slot. Then I snatched my other hand away and lunged for the roof.

The operator chose that moment to bite my toe. Through the leather of my boot, the bite was agony. I could only imagine what it would have felt like on bare fingers. I yanked my foot away, and found myself hanging by my fingertips.

As I swung there I was counting seconds in my head. I reached five before I was able to swing onto the infernal machine's roof. I guessed time was almost up.

There was the hatch.

It was locked on the inside.

Any second now, F3 was going to run out of *up*, and all the grey goblins within range were suddenly going to turn their attention to me. I glanced back. The farmhouse was now directly besieged, and the field between me and it was full of goblins and larger members of the Order, including two infernal machines. The only idea I had left was that I was so high up on top of my infernal machine that if I laid very flat and very still, no-one would notice me, and I could sneak off between all the corpses after the battle was finished. It seemed a slim chance.

I watched as hordes of the enemy swarmed through holes in the farm's walls and surged towards the farmhouse itself. From this position I would have quite a good view of the slaughter of our forces, for as long as I was alive, anyway.

At that moment the hatch swung open and hit me on the head. I was still seeing stars when out popped the infernal machine's operator. This, I was perturbed to see, was a Labrador-sized, grey (of course) creature with six arms. It had the regulation two legs, for a spider-sized total of eight limbs. It hissed at me and jumped into the masses of its colleagues from the roof of the infernal machine. A moment later I lost sight of it in the crowd.

I dived head-first into the darkened bowels of the infernal machine, grabbing at anything I could along the way to slow my fall. I hit the floor moderately hard, then had to climb back a little way to reach the hatch and pull it closed.

"I don't believe it," F3 said. "We did it."

I peered out of the front viewing slot. The infernal machine was still partly jamming the hole it had made in the wall. However, hundreds of the enemy were still running ahead of us towards the farm buildings. "How do I turn the gun on?" I asked.

"You mean *fire* it?"

"Whatever – how?"

"Hold me up so I can see everything," F3 ordered.

I obeyed. The interior of the infernal machine was a dark, smoky, and noisy box, and there were valves and levers everywhere. It could take me a week to figure out how to operate the infernal machine, but F3 would figure out the mechanism in a trice. The gun itself was down at my feet, but I gave F3 a good look around before I stooped to examine it. Steam was jetting from the gun, which was also shaking violently. I reached out to –

"Don't touch it!"

"Huh?"

"Do exactly as I say and you won't lose any fingers."

F3 proceeded to explain how to disengage the gun's drive. After this it explained how to remove the jammed round. Then it told me how to re-feed the ammunition belt.

"Now can I fire?"

"You aim with your foot in that stirrup," F3 said calmly. "That way, you can balance on the other foot, peer out of the viewing slot, and operate the steering and boiler with your *six arms*."

"We'll worry about the boiler and steering when we run out of targets under our nose," I shouted.

"You still have to aim with your foot or you can't see what you're shooting at," F3 shouted back.

"What sort of machine is this?" I moaned. It was a rhetorical question, but F3 answered anyway.

"One for an eight-limbed operator."

I stood up and located my foot in the gun's stirrup. Then I peered out of the viewing slot. Still plenty of targets.

"How do I turn it on?"

"You mean fire?"

"Just tell me!"

"Kick it with the other foot!"

I did as I was told. Three things happened. One: the gun barrel jerked upwards. Two: it started to fire. Bang, bang, bang, it went. Three: it stopped firing before I could aim it at anything.

I knelt down to inspect the gun. Three shots and it had jammed again, I discovered, because it was back in jetting steam/vibrating mode.

"It's jammed again."

"That's probably because you stood on it when you climbed up the outside of the Infernal machine. You've bent one of the barrels."

Despair rose up until I was neck-deep in it. I stood up. Now it only reached my waist. That was better. "Fine. We'll trample them to death. How do I steer?"

Whatever F3 said at that point was drowned out by a resounding crash, which turned out to be the gong-like noise the infernal machine made when something struck it hard from the outside. A small bump appeared in the side of the infernal machine. Then another. Then another.

Our own side was shooting at us.

"F3, our own side is —"

The next musket ball to hit the infernal machine didn't make a dent in the armour. It made a hole in it. The ball banged against the opposite side of the infernal machine. I was in the clock tower, and all the bells were ringing at once.

A second hole appeared, accompanied once more by two great clangs. "Why —" I began, but I never finished my sentence — because the next musket ball to hit the infernal machine passed straight through its armour and struck me amidships.

My Brief Part in the Battle of Clearwater Cove – 2

A distant voice. "Edison."

It was my mother. "Edison, it's time to wake up."

"Mum?" I said her name before I was really awake, before I'd even opened my eyes. When I did open my eyes, I found myself not in my bedroom, but in a tiny, dark, metal box. As my ears tuned in to the noise around me, I could hear the distant sounds of what sounded like fighting. Above me in the darkness of the infernal machine, a voice floated down.

"No, it's me, you idiot. I just used your mother's voice to wake you up, because you were ignoring mine." It was F3, wedged behind a pipe where I'd left it.

"F3, I'm shot," I moaned.

"How bad is it?"

"In the... chest..." the pain was intense.

"I said how bad, not where! Lift me down so I can see."

"I'll try..." I tried. With a heroic effort I managed to reach F3, then fell back to the floor. I held F3 above me so that it could look down at my wound. "How bad is it..."

"You're not hurt. There's not even a hole in your tunic," F3 said dismissively.

I put my hands where the pain was. Sure enough, there was no hole. "It hurts!" I complained.

"Open your shirt."

I did so.

"A bruise only. Don't be a baby. Pull yourself together, Edison. You've been asleep for ten minutes."

"Unconscious, not asleep! How can it just be a bruise? I've been shot."

"Most of the kinetic energy of the musket round was lost when it penetrated the armour. Then it dribbled into your chest..."

I was inclined to argue, but I suddenly remembered Lexi. "Lexi!" I said, and shot to my feet.

The scene outside the infernal machine had changed somewhat while I had been ~~asleep~~ unconscious. The farmhouse had been lost, it seemed, for little grey goblins were swarming all over the roof, firing arrows. Following the trajectory of these, I saw that they were aimed towards the woods, where the distant sounds of battle emanated. It seemed that what was left of our forces had decided to go into the woods after all.

As to the refugees, and Lexi and the boy...

I had to change to the side window to see the refugees' position. What I saw there made my stomach sink down into my shoes. No-one was left alive. A couple of dozen of the middle-sized grey creatures were stalking about, methodically chopping up dead refugees and piling the pieces up onto carts. I could only watch the butchers for a second; then I had to turn away.

When I had composed myself I looked again. Past the grey butchers with their dripping red cleavers, further up the slope, I could see a large mass of the Order's forces, including the other five Infernal machines, and most of the giants. They were marching away from me, towards the location where Vexan's cavalry had formed up earlier. Of Vexan and his cavalry themselves, there was no sign. Presumably they'd fled – although maybe they were still nearby, because I could hear the lazy machine guns of the infernal machines shooting at something out of my sight.

My only hope was that Lexi had taken Speckle and gone. But I knew she wouldn't have done that. Giving up the chance to escape was just the kind of stubborn thing she would do. But maybe there was another possibility... maybe she had made it out of the back of the cove? It was impossible to know from here whether any people had made it up onto the plateau, and if so whether Lexi and the boy were among them.

Then I chanced to look out of the *back* window of the infernal machine... and *there* were the refugees, or at least the better part of them. They had been taken prisoner, and were now being led west along the edge of the swamp by another section of the Order's forces. This was where Lexi would be. Her, the boy, and the paladin.

"No," I whimpered. "I mean, at least they're not dead, but..."

"Are you going to tell me what's going on?" F3 demanded.

I explained to F3 what I had seen. As I did so, F3 explained to *me* how to re-start the infernal machine's engine, and I followed those steps. Soon smoke was pouring from the chimney once more, and, it seemed, we were ready to go.

F3 took control of two valves by getting me to tie its harpoon cables to them. All I had to do was operate the steering and throttle (which, I promised myself, would be wide open).

"So, where are we heading?" F3 asked.

"We're gonna rescue Lexi."

"And Flyst's forces?"

"They're soldiers. They're paid to face death. Let's go! Vamos! Allons-y! Schnell!"

If I thought we were going to gracefully pirouette and charge after the departing prisoners, I was mistaken. It took five minutes to turn the infernal machine around in the rubble of the wall, by which time the refugees were out of sight.

"Charge!" I muttered under my breath. I opened the throttle.

We took a step forwards.

What seemed an eternity later, we took a second step.

"Can't this thing go any faster?"

"It's a steam-powered tank on legs – what do you expect?"

"I need more steam!"

"We'll overheat!"

"It's all about overheating with you, isn't it, F3!" I bellowed, somewhat unfairly.

We lurched forwards at a slightly faster rate than before. I estimated that we would close the mile between us and the prisoners sometime the next day.

"We need to attract their attention!" I announced. "Keep an eye on the road!" With the help of my empty scabbard, I managed to wedge F3 into a position where it could see out of the front viewing slot. Then I dropped down and got to work on the gun.

"You might shoot your girlfriend," F3 said caustically.

I froze in mid un-jam. As colossally unlikely as hitting Lexi in all the throng of thousands in front of us was, F3 had a point. We might shoot the refugees. Actually (I noticed, bobbing up and making a steering correction), the escorts for the refugees only numbered a couple of hundred. Did I say *only* a couple of hundred? Anyone would think I was at the head of a force of thousands, not alone in a Victorian-era Scout Walker with a broken gun.

"You want to attract their attention? I have an idea," F3 said. "Due to the ineptitude of the design of this vehicle, I think I can turn the entire contraption into a giant walking speaker."

"Really?"

"You may want to place something in your ears," F3 warned. "I want you to place me between the two pipes leading up from the secondary expansion chamber, then tie me on with the harpoons."

"Where?"

F3 explained. I did as I was told. Then I killed the boiler. This was necessary for the sound to work, F3 explained. In the growing quiet I watched the distant prisoners get yet more distant, and shredded some cloth to wedge in my ears. "This better work," I muttered.

F3 didn't give me a warning. It just launched into something by a small twenty-first century amphibian. The sound of the Crazy Frog filled the infernal machine. It practically knocked me off my feet. I

177

clamped my hands over my ears and screamed at F3 to turn it off. But F3 either didn't hear me, or pretended not to.

At least our attempts were having some effect, I saw, looking through the narrow viewing slot. We had been noticed. The escorts were turning back to face us...

No they weren't.

One of them was. A grey giant was coming back to investigate. Just one.

I screamed at F3 to cut the sound, but I couldn't get any response until the track was finished.

"We need to get the engine started," I howled, in the gap between tracks.

"Are they coming?" F3 asked.

"Just one. A big one," I said. By now the ogror, whose several eyes were about at the same level as mine, was only half a mile away. Meanwhile, behind it, the prisoners and their escort had resumed their march.

"Lexi," I muttered. "It's not fair!"

"Focus, Edison," F3 said.

I focused. By the time the infernal machine's engine had spluttered back into life, the giant was only two hundred yards away. Its legs were like tree trunks. Its mouth was about a yard wide, and hung open darkly. Grey teeth projected at various angles as if the giant had swallowed a model of an ancient graveyard. Or rather hadn't swallowed it, because it was still stuck in its mouth.

"The Crazy Frog, F3?"

"It worked, didn't it?"

We resumed our advance. It meant that the distance between us and our opponent was now shrinking twice as fast.

I got back to work on the gun. This was almost ready to go. All I had to do was re-feed the belt of ammunition, and release the catch... except, given the previous attempt, I decided to wait until the grey giant was a bit closer before trying to shoot it.

"Come on," I muttered. "Come on, you big grey..."

The grey giant did as it was told. Soon it was close enough for me to count the whites of its eyes (eight, it turned out: two large, two medium, and four small).

I let fly. Or rather, squatted down, placed one foot in the gun's stirrup, operated the release lever with one hand, then jumped up. The gun started to fire. For half a glorious second, I think we were winning. Several shots seemed to hit the giant, and even drew blood (grey, darker than its skin).

Then the gun jammed again.

The giant bellowed and charged.

I dropped down and feverishly started work on the gun once more.

"Jam it!" I shouted.

"Roger," F3 replied.

The giant hit us like a Sumo wrestler and almost knocked us over. I reached up and moved the steering levers at random. We shuffled about together in an ungainly way, the giant hugging us like a favourite dancing partner. For a moment we were on one leg, and the only thing holding us up was the giant's grip. But a quirk in the terrain – we were now off the road, on the downslope towards the swamp – tilted us the other way for a moment.

"What's happened to the jammer?"

"It's too cross now you've shot it, even without remote guidance it's still determined to smash us to pieces."

"Then what –"

"Stand clear!" F3 shouted.

"What?"

"Don't touch anything!"

"Clear!"

F3, via its connection to the armour of the infernal machine, gave the giant a shock. Most likely this was so diluted that the giant felt more pain when it looked in a mirror. It let go for half a second, which let the infernal machine regain its balance.

Now all I had to do was un-jam the gun once more, and I would have a fine, point-blank shot.

At that moment, the giant ripped the gun clean off the front of the infernal machine. Which was a shame. I was left holding a belt of ammunition with nowhere to put it.

"We've lost the gun!" I shouted.

"Edison, get low and cover any exposed skin," F3 ordered.

"What!"

The giant thumped us a couple of times. We rocked. Large dents appeared. The resulting bell-like resonance inside the infernal machine meant that whatever F3 said, I never heard it. By the time the giant had returned to wrestling with us, the booming of its punches had been replaced with a new deafening sound: a rising scream.

At first I couldn't figure out what was going on. Then I realised: F3 was bottling up the steam.

I would have liked to shout 'noooo.....!', but it wouldn't have mattered. We were about to be opened up like a sardine tin anyway. We might as well get properly cooked first. I got low and tried to cover any exposed skin with what was left of my beautiful red cape.

The explosion knocked us off our feet. Then we began to roll. I started out on the bottom of the infernal machine, then I was on its side. Back. Side. Front. Side.

At some point my head hit something hard and I blacked out. Or, as F3 would say, dozed off.

Swamped

I came round to the song of a bird: a warbling whistle. After a few moments, the call was repeated.

I stirred.

"Edison!" It was F3's voice, in a low, but not whispered, tone. When F3 wanted to be quiet, it didn't whisper. It just turned the volume down.

I groaned.

"Just working through genus *Lalage* of the family Campephagidae," F3 said, as if I had asked it to explain something.

"Whuh?" I asked, still too dazed to form words.

"Cuckooshrikes. I didn't want to make a conspicuous noise in case the Order are nearby." F3 repeated the call, another warbling whistle.

"It's all right – I'm conscious," I muttered.

"The suborder Passeri, the songbirds, is huge – it's a shame I wasn't able to work my way down to some of my favourites..."

"I'm conscious! I think!"

Croak.

"That wasn't me," F3 said hastily. "We're sharing the infernal machine with an amphibian. Looks like *Rana temporaria*, a common frog. Good to see that some things haven't changed, hey?"

Sure enough, a normal-looking frog had apparently hopped in through one of the view slits, two of which were partly submerged. The infernal machine was partially flooded – I found I was half-in, half-out of the water. And I remembered something.

"F3, you blew us up!"

"Yeah, but you should see the other guy."

"Where *is* the other guy?"

"It's not coming. You've been out for nearly an hour. I think it would have been here by now if it was coming."

"And how were you going to wake me up if I started drowning? If we'd gone in any deeper we'd be completely underwater by now. Ow, my head! And did I mention, F3, you blew us up!"

"It was the only chance. I had noticed that the external boiler was weakly jointed, and reasoned that if we bottled up the steam, it could serve as a last-ditch defence. I didn't think much of the scalding water would find its way in here."

Croak, said the little frog.

I sat up with a splash, startling the frog, which hopped out through the view slit. For a moment I was just glad to be alive – then I remembered Lexi. "We have to get after them," I said, and sloshed towards the half-submerged hatch.

"Keep the noise down," F3 advised. "The Order could be close by."

"They could be miles away by now. And did you see how fast they were moving? *I* couldn't get them to move that fast."

"You weren't threatening to eat the ones who couldn't keep up," F3 explained tartly.

"Note to diary. Threatened cannibalism as a motivational tool. Brilliant," I murmured, and heaved the hatch open.

Except that I didn't. The hatch was jammed fast. I locked both hands around the latch and braced both feet against the roof of the infernal machine. Then I hauled for all I was worth. After about ten seconds of back-breaking strain, the latch came off in my hand. I sloshed backwards in the water with my own momentum, and looked up to see that the hatch was still shut – it now had a small circular hole in it where the latch had attached.

With a metallic groan, and amid an eruption of methane bubbles, the infernal machine settled a little deeper into the swamp. The view slit the frog had hopped through was now completely submerged.

"F3, you've bent the hatch and now it's stuck and the damn handle's come off and we're *sinking*," I hissed angrily. "And Lexi and everyone who can walk has been captured and I promised I wouldn't leave them and everyone who couldn't walk has been made into *hamburgers*."

"One problem at a time," F3 said with infuriating metal calm. "The most immediate issue is–"

"I'm going to drown!"

"No," F3 said, its voice dropping lower. "There's someone coming."

I froze. The only sounds were a few residual ripples that were even now dying away.

For three minutes I sat there, absolutely immobile, and becoming increasingly uncomfortable. I was soaked in swamp water and lying at an awkward angle.

Then I heard *something* moving through the swamp. With infinite care the *something* moved through the water, one step following the other with the deliberation of a crane stalking a fish.

Well, this particular fish was tinned, and going nowhere. Clearly whatever was creeping up on us knew as much. I sloshed over to F3 and extricated its harpoons from the levers it was attached to. F3 wound them in.

"I'm in here," I said loudly.

"Edison!" came Jasso's voice. "How did you know it was me?"

*

It took five minutes to extricate me from the infernal machine. When I explained that I was stuck, Jasso observed that there was no handle on his side of the hatch – but there *were* hinges. Maybe, he suggested, he could try to knock or pull the pins out of the hinges...

"Stand back," I said, feeling foolish. I then kicked the hatch, which opened quite a way until impeded by a tree root.

The hatch opened outwards. I decided to keep quiet about pulling the handle off my side, and to pretend that my last kick there had just been a doozy.

Jasso hauled me through the gap and onto dry land. "You haven't been captured! And you're not even dead!" he said brightly. Next he pulled me to my feet and gave me a hug.

"How did you find me?"

"The trail of an infernal machine is not hard to follow, even for such a poor scout as me. A musketeer told me he could have sworn he'd seen you getting in an infernal machine. The rest was easy. Particularly because there's a dead ogror at the top of the slope – and infernal machines don't tend to fight their own side."

F3 laughed. It was still a disturbing sound, coming from a glorified telephone. "Heh. Told you it wasn't coming."

I ignored it, and spoke to Jasso instead. "But what are you doing here? I didn't see you among Flyst's scouts."

"I wasn't among them. I tagged along at the back."

"Hagroth asked you to keep me out of trouble..." I guessed. Jasso did not contradict me. I remembered Lexi. "Listen, Lexi's been captured... I need to get after her..."

"What do you intend when you catch up? To become a prisoner, like them?" A cold edge had taken over Jasso's voice.

"No. Although it will probably end up that way. But I can't just leave them."

Jasso sat down by the water's edge. It was almost dusk, and the first mosquitoes were already emerging from between the reeds. Jasso ignored them. He seemed to be ignoring me, too, because he just sat there for a minute, staring into the middle distance.

At last he spoke. "You may guess what my orders are," he said softly.

Surreptitiously I re-oriented F3 so that its harpoons were targeting Jasso. It seemed that he sensed the movement, because he looked around slowly.

"You don't trust me?" Jasso demanded.

183

I put F3 down, feeling guilty.

"You know who your friends are, because you trust them, and they trust you. Trust is the essence of friendship." Jasso looked away again.

Now I felt even worse. "I can't go back. I have to go on, after them. It doesn't matter how it turns out. Even if there's no chance, I can't give up on them."

It was cold, and almost completely dark. There was a slight breeze, and occasional leaves fell from the willows above us, fluttering to the ground in spirals like dying moths.

After a pause, Jasso began to speak again. "My home is a village called Lar, in a place called Nymeth, in the mountains. It's behind the Wall, and sheltered from the north wind by a great spur of the mountains. It's cold in Lar, but in the spring the meadows are full of butterflies and there is the constant sound of falling water as the snow melts. The skies are beautiful, as are the mountains rising to the west. Here and there are little bits of woodland, hanging on in places where neither the plough nor avalanches have reached."

I wondered where Jasso was going with this. "Sounds nice," I said.

"You would be welcome there – there has been plenty of room these last twenty years, empty houses needing care, needing life. You'd like my brother Lito – he has your spirit. He would love to show you all the ruins of the Old Ones in the mountains. It would be safe, too, unless the Wall itself is breached, and that hasn't happened since the time of Sesil the Coward. If I could take you there now you might never see another of the Order. Would you go?"

My answer was immediate. "If Lexi and the boy were with me."

"Not otherwise?"

"No."

Jasso laughed gently. "Not like last time, is it? Last time you left them with hardly a look over your shoulder."

"Never again! I swore I'd never leave them. That's why they agreed to come with me in the first place. And now..."

"How are you sure they aren't among the refugees that have been slaughtered?"

I didn't have to think about it. "I just know."

"You're right. The soldier who took your horse was most forthcoming once I knocked him out of the saddle."

"He took Speckle!"

"I have her tied up nearby. He says they gave her to him. He was wounded. He saw them captured as he himself was riding away."

How typical of Lexi, I thought.

"It will be difficult," Jasso continued. "The Order are all around us. We will have to stay off the road, and make sure we always see them before they see us. If not..."

Jasso had said 'we.' "You're coming?"

"You won't need a scout to follow this trail. And I won't be much use when we do catch them up. But I'm coming. Yes."

"I can't ask you to do that," I said, feeling the guilt of someone who had nothing to give but could only take, take, take.

"You're not asking. Come on, let's move. If we're to have any hope, we have to catch up with them before they reach the Barrens. Better do something about the cape, Edison."

Jasso was right. My scarlet cape, although muddied and torn, was more about being noticed than being unnoticed. But I was too cold to lose it completely, so I got undressed to put it on under my scout greens, which turned out to be as uncomfortable as it sounds. "Why couldn't she have thought of herself for once?" I moaned.

"That would not be the Lexi you love," Jasso explained. "First she adopted the boy. Then she adopted you. Now, it seems, she has become mother to thousands of refugees."

Forced March – 1

The refugees were not allowed a rest all night. The road was good, the going easy – but they still lost a dozen people before that first brief break. Those who fell were given one chance to rise, just one.

They passed what was left of the little town of Gravemires just as the darkness was beginning to shrink away from the oncoming sun. Gravemires was a spread-out place, reliant for its existence on a brook on one end and a mine on the other. The mile or so in between the mine and the brook had until recently been lined on both sides by mostly wooden buildings. All of them had been destroyed. Smoke rose mournfully from the blackened remains of houses, barns, and shops, and the passing refugees could still feel the heat of yesterday's firestorm on their faces. Glowing smuts rose into the grey sky, and in places the last few dying flames licked at fallen roof beams. There were no signs of life or death in the mile-long walk through Gravemires, human or animal, beyond the charred remains of what might have been a goat.

Once they reached the brook at the far edge of town, the refugees were allowed to drink. The first hundred or so moved down to the bank, drank under the watchful stares of their captors, then were driven through the water and up the opposite bank. Then the next hundred or so were allowed to drink, before being driven up the opposite bank themselves. This process took at least half an hour, even with the plentiful goading of whips, so the refugees either waiting their turn at the water, or waiting for others to have theirs, had the chance to rest at last.

Most of the refugees threw themselves to the ground, exhausted; but not Lexi. She did at least take the boy down from her shoulders and stretch her back with a great heaving crack. Food was brought around in baskets, but it was the grey, yielding yet crumbly grey matter of the Order as she knew it would be. She left the boy in the care of the paladin and stalked stiff-legged among the crowd, ordering everyone only to pretend to eat. In this task she enlisted Tigo and others of the Scavenger children to help. There were rumblings and mutterings of disagreement, but Lexi, her hood and hair still hiding her face, did not take the time to argue. She could warn them, no more than that. It was their choice if they ignored the warning.

Wander as she might, Lexi saw no sign of Elfe. She asked among the people she passed, but no-one had heard of her. They were wrapped up in their own misery, too much so to worry about a missing old woman. Most – to judge by the way they quickly dropped their eyes – could guess what had become of her. Soon Lexi had run out of places to look, having made her way right through the crowds to the rear of the column of refugees. She stood on the west bank of the brook, looking back the way they had come, and faintly hoped to see a little smudge of grey smoke in the distance in the morning light. The refugees had heard Edison's intervention, last evening, as he had come riding after them in that infernal machine with his strange music blaring out. That the ogror sent after him had not returned was encouraging. That there had been no sign of him since was not.

The back of the train of prisoners was made up of a dozen crude carts, pulled either by a single ogror or four arenir, the next size down of the Enemy's forces. In these were the food for the Enemy's forces, all except the changelings who still ate the grey food. Those who had fallen behind in the night were in those carts now, Lexi knew.

"So what now?" the paladin asked, when Lexi picked her way back to him and the boy. Tigo was there too, flexing his sore toes. Around them, about half of the refugees had ignored Lexi's warning, and were taking the breakfast that would nourish them but slowly bleed the will out of them at the same time.

"The most important thing is to stay alive," Lexi said. "We wait and watch for our chance. How are you?"

"I can keep up," the paladin said. "Don't worry about me. The boy's hungry, though."

"We'll look for food as we walk. It won't be much, but..."

"Ed'son," the boy said.

"Yes. Edison will come. You'll see! Just you wait."

The boy smiled for a second. Then he remembered how hungry he was, and his expression became downcast.

"He'd better bring five hundred men if he *is* coming," the paladin said, trying to make his voice light. But Lexi could see that he was in pain. The poultice that Elfe had given him had worked wonders on his wounds – but the hard walking had opened several of them up again, and the paladin was clearly exhausted. Edison's little sword was hidden in a bandage tied around his uninjured left thigh. It was probably the only weapon the three thousand refugees had between them, having been forced to discard them by their guards when they were first captured.

Their guards numbered fewer than five hundred, and mostly consisted of changelings, people who had eaten enough grey matter to lose their own will and become one with the Enemy. Armed with whips and short, stabbing blades, they kept the refugees moving with careless brutality. Besides the changelings, there were various other members of the Order, including a few ogror and many tall arenir and more still of the little bow-wielding swarmers.

The changelings were quite unlike the rest of the Enemy's forces. All the individuals of other kinds were indistinguishable from others of their kind, as if they had all been cast in the same mould in a forge of flesh deep in the Enemy's lair. The only signs of individuality they ever had were healed-over battle scars where these were present. In contrast, the changelings were as varied as any crowd of people might be. The Enemy did not discriminate in its choice of servants, nor greatly change them. The changelings still wore the ragged remains of the clothes they had worn when first captured. The changelings were men and women, old and young, even children; the only characteristics that they shared were their grey skin, as grey now as the skin of all the Enemy's forces, and their empty eyes, shiny and black like beads of obsidian.

Soon it was clear that the rest break was over, for as one, on an invisible, unheard signal, the changelings began laying about them with whips and gesticulating for the refugees to rise.

"Get up quickly, and help others," Lexi shouted. She hoisted the boy back onto her shoulders with a groan.

"I'll take him for a while," Tigo offered with a forced smile.

"I may take you up on that later," Lexi said. Further conversation was curtailed by the cracking of whips. When everyone was on their feet, the changelings mindlessly turned their faces to the west and started to march. Anyone who was slow to join in step was whipped – without malice, without anger, without so much as a trace of emotion. It was with the same detachment that those who fell by the wayside later that day would be thrown in the back of a cart, barely alive or dead, it didn't matter which. Not only were the changelings no longer human, but they were no longer aware that they had ever *been* human.

Hurting humans did not trouble them. Nothing troubled them. Even their own death, when it came, would be met with the same grey indifference. Whatever spark of soul had once animated them had long gone. Now they were just empty vessels, ringing with the echoes of another's distant voice.

Such was the fate that awaited all the refugees that survived the walk to the Enemy's lair.

Pursuit – 1

We followed a deer track until it was too dark to see anything. Then we carried on. We didn't dare show a light. With F3's infra-red sensor to warn us of enemies and keep us on track, I estimate that we managed about one mile an hour. It was a fairly miserable walk, whipped by twigs and branches, buzzed by mosquitoes, tripping over tree roots, and constantly worrying about how far ahead Lexi was. It was cold, damp, and slippery underfoot. I had to lead Speckle, because the canopy of the trees over the path was too low for riding – and it would have been too dangerous for her by night in any case.

About a mile to our right was the main road, along which the refugees had long since passed. Every so often F3 would alert us to movement on the road, and (mile away or not), we would hunker down and wait until it was safe. Then F3 would list what had passed – which models of the Entity's forces, and in which direction. Sometimes the ones heading west, as we were, had prisoners with them. They reminded me of worker ants taking the results of their foraging back to their queen. But this queen was no insect. It probably wasn't female, although I couldn't be sure about that. It had always been an IT as long as I had heard it spoken about. Even now, more than two thousand years after it had first appeared, the Entity was still an IT.

I spent the entire time trying to work out how far behind we were getting. The fact that we were moving more slowly than the refugees meant – even to my elementary maths – that we were *never* going to catch up. And then to cap it all, we stopped for a rest at about two in the morning.

We urgently needed a plan.

"If we carry on like this, we'll never catch them," I said.

"Shall we go back?" Jasso asked.

Speckle said nothing. Nor, uncharacteristically, did F3, until I prompted it.

"F3? Ideas?"

"We could take the road. But I guess you would be detected within about an hour and a half, and dead or captured shortly after. I can't be more accurate than that without knowing more about the sensory abilities of our enemies."

"Better than human," Jasso said.

"Make that forty-five minutes," F3 said.

"We rest now, and make better time in daylight," Jasso said.

*

Things were not much better by daylight. The deer track was still a deer track, and had not miraculously changed into an eight-lane motorway. Poor old Speckle was being scratched to bits by brambles, and I was not much better off. Even Jasso had snagged on a few thorns. The trees all around us were a drab yellow, and, one by one and two by two, their leaves fell wetly in each gust of the chill wind. Winter was on its way.

At about noon we dipped back to the main path to check we were still on the refugees' trail. We were. That confirmed, we crept back into the trees like mice back under the skirting board and resumed our painfully slow – and slowly painful – progress. By now I felt like giving up. But I knew I had to try, however hopeless things seemed.

"Do you think she knows we're coming?" I asked Jasso.

"No. I wouldn't think anyone would be so foolish. I would assume I'd have to rely on myself. Wouldn't you?"

Jasso was a great comfort.

Forced March – 2

On the second day of the forced march, the refugees turned north and moved into dense forest. A new road had been cut through the trees, which explained at least in part how the Order had managed to outflank Hagroth's defences. Giving up on summer, yellow leaves streamed down in the light breeze, seeming to glow in the weak sun.

Lexi and the boy had developed a little habit. Every so often, Lexi would glance back for a sign that they were being followed. The boy, still sitting on her shoulders, would ask, "Ed'son?" And Lexi would reply, "He'll come. Don't you worry. He'll come."

If she hadn't been before, Lexi was by now firmly in charge of the refugees. This had come about during an argument with one group, one of whom was moaning in pain and complaining that they could hardly manage another step. Lexi had manoeuvred through the crowd to get close enough to tell the moaner, a fifty-year-old man with wild, unkempt grey hair, that it would be wise to shut up.

"And what would you know?" the moaner had sneered.

"I've been on one of these trips before. And I escaped." Unafraid at last, Lexi finally decided to throw back her hood and reveal her scarred and tainted face to the crowd. The sight stunned the man she was arguing with into instant silence and sent a ripple through everyone else nearby. "When they run out of dead to eat, they take the slow. The noisy they assume are soon to become slow. Do you get it?"

The story that Lexi had escaped once before went around like wildfire. Everyone wanted to know how. For the time being at least, Lexi wasn't telling them. Her escape had worked for a single fit girl. It would not work for three thousand refugees. The refugees also wanted to know how much grey matter they could eat without turning. All were hungry, for even those who had eaten grey matter had eaten sparingly. But Lexi's advice was simple. Eat nothing. Gather what you can by the roadside.

This last instruction was becoming rather hard to obey: the new trail that had been cut through the forest had not had time to develop soft edges of brambles and grasses. Instead, the only things lining the road now were freshly-cut trees. Those who resorted to eating leaves or chewing bark did not do so for long, because the bitterness and stomach pains were too much to bear.

Lexi herself was by now aching terribly from head to foot. But to slow down or complain would be to risk summary execution. Her worst fear was that the boy would be picked out as an unnecessary prisoner – too tiny to make a useful changeling, his fate would inevitably be to become a small part of the food chain. Sitting him on her shoulders was not the best way to hide him, but she couldn't carry him far any other way. At one brief rest stop he was asleep, and Lexi pondered hiding him amongst the cut-down trees and just leaving him there, hoping that if Edison *was* following, the two would somehow meet. She even picked him up to carry him to a hiding place – but he stirred, and smiled at her, and she just brushed the hair from his eyes and smiled back.

Pursuit – 2

The sun was gone, and what little grey light was left was fading away. We had made better time in the daylight – but I couldn't help but think that the refugees, under the threat of becoming food, would have outpaced us. It was kind of ironic.

"What is?" F3 asked.

I realised I'd been thinking aloud, probably due to being completely exhausted. I wasn't sure just how long I'd been thinking aloud, or whether I'd thought anything bad about my travelling companions. "Well, if the refugees go too slowly, they get eaten. If we go too *fast*, *we* get eaten. If only it was the other way around, we'd have caught up with them by now."

We had just passed a strong infra-red source on the road to our right, which had turned out to be the burnt-out remains of a village. We decided it would be best to give it a wide berth, especially in the growing dusk, because the heat would mask the infra-red signal of any of the Entity's minions that happened to be hanging about.

Just to the west of the charred ruins, F3 spotted a gathering of people. They were prisoners, hundreds of them. But my initial bubble of optimism that we had caught up with Lexi was quickly popped – these few hundred were *more* prisoners, being gathered together before being driven north in a more conveniently-sized group. They had a hundred escorts, according to F3, comprising a range of different types: humans with whips ("changelings," Jasso murmured), the little ones that I called goblins and Jasso called swarmers, and a few of two larger types, arenir and ogror. At the distance we were, through the trees, with little light, Jasso and I could see nothing, so we took F3's word for it. What we heard convinced us that we had to stay well clear.

It was a strange, bitter feeling to leave these poor prisoners to their fate and stay on our pursuit of Lexi's group. But it was necessary. Any intervention here would have blown what little chance we had left of rescuing Lexi and the boy. Knowing that didn't make me feel better as we carefully picked our way around the prisoners' camp and resumed our westward journey.

I didn't want to think about what would happen when we caught up with Lexi. It was looking increasingly likely that it would never happen. But a part of me, deep at the back of my mind, knew that while it was going to be *almost* impossible to rescue Lexi and the boy, it was definitely going to be *absolutely* impossible to save *everyone*.

We were going to have to pick out our friends and ignore strangers if we had any chance at all.

The worst thing was, that thought didn't bother me as much as it should have. If I could get out of this with Lexi and the boy, I would be overjoyed, and wouldn't think twice about leaving the others to their fate.

"I'm not a very nice person," I said, feeling empty and horrible.

"No-one is," Jasso rejoined tersely, then got on with the task of picking his way through the scrubby trees.

Forced March – 3

By the third day of the march, Lexi's glances over her shoulder had become less frequent. Her neck was too stiff for that, and she was in such pain, everywhere, that she had to concentrate most of her effort on just placing one foot in front of the other. This part of the forest was older, much older, and was dominated by mighty, ancient trees. Here the foraging was better, from berries in clearings where one of the great trees had fallen, to enormous white grubs that lived in the rotting trunks and fallen branches. The younger, fitter refugees – including the scavenger children – collected a continuous harvest of these deathly-white larvae, and shared them with all who could bear to eat them. All but the head capsule was eaten, with the grub itself still squirming in the hand and the mouth. The changelings did not mind this foraging, as long as it was done from the path. Either they thought the extra food would make the refugees walk further, or they thought that when they arrived back at the Enemy's lair there would be nothing to forage for and nothing to eat but the grey matter, or they thought nothing. It was impossible to tell.

The previous day they had lost thirty refugees. That day, only twenty fell and did not rise. Lexi had a couple of the scavenger children keep an eye on the carts full of the dead at the back of the refugee train. From their reports, it seemed that the numbers refilling the carts were keeping up with the feeding of the ogror, arenir and swarmers. This was a relief of sorts for Lexi, for it meant that for now at least the changelings were not going to come wading into the crowd to pick out people for tomorrow's lunch. For now at least, the boy was safe.

At around noon there was an extended break when the prisoner train reached a broad, slow-flowing river. It could only be the River Fair, the same river that flowed through Crickne. Somehow the Order had crossed the water – but how? As the refugees settled to rest on the southern bank, they could see that the Order had not built a bridge here to secretly outflank Hagroth's army. All that they had done was sink several rows of wooden piles into the deep mud of the river bed. It was as if they had begun the foundations for a bridge, but not bothered to complete it. But if that was the case, how had the Order crossed? Had they swum? But infernal machines could not swim, even if others of the Order could. And how were the refugees to cross? Were they to swim? The river was thirty yards across, and Lexi knew that most of the refugees wouldn't be able to make it. Here where it was fast-flowing, swimmers would be in danger of getting swept away. Elsewhere, where the current was slow and the crossing easier, there would be monkey crabs to contend with.

Answers began to come about ten minutes after they arrived at the river bank. A dozen of the Order emerged from the forest on the northern shore and lined up on the bank. They did not acknowledge their comrades on the southern shore, who likewise ignored them. These newcomers were a breed of Order that Lexi had never seen before – and neither, it seemed, had anybody else. They were grey, naked, and sexless, like all the Enemy's creations, but these twelve were tall, bony, and carried no weapons. The whispered consensus among the refugees was that they must be either idior or imperator, two species of the Order that were seldom seen, but much feared.

The twelve newcomers stood, lined up on the riverbank, and stared over at the refugees. They said nothing. They didn't move. But they were definitely busy doing *something*. Something unseen, something secret, something magical.

Over the course of the next few minutes, the sky began to change. The thin grey cloud that they had marched under all morning was beginning to break up, break up and gather together in darker clumps, all seeming to gather in towards the patch of sky directly overhead. Streamers of deepening grey cloud swirled in towards the centre of an enormous vortex, separated by newly clear blue sky between.

Soon the sky had almost cleared, except for the one great twisting cloud that had formed above the refugees. A wind started up, icily cold, which seemed to flow down from the cloud and then spread in all directions once it reached the ground. Silver light began to flicker in the cloud, which by now was more like dense black smoke than water vapour. Thunder rumbled, but the lightning stayed trapped in the base of the cloud.

Most people turned their backs on the spectacle, because the wind blowing into their faces was by now as cold as a February snowstorm. Lexi turned away and sheltered the boy, remembering the storm they had seen just after the encounter with the bron, when the Order had been close behind them...

"It's freezing," someone shouted. "The river's freezing over!"

Everyone looked now, icy blasting wind or not, and watched as small pancakes of ice formed on the river's surface, drifting sluggishly downstream. Some caught against the wooden piles and stuck fast, coalescing with others floating down to join them, and soon there was a complete line of ice from bank to bank. More ice piled up, and more, until within the space of a further few minutes an ice road wide enough and strong enough to carry refugees, guards, and carts had been created.

Those of the Order who had created this ice bridge stepped back into the woods and disappeared before anyone had even set foot upon it. Above, the black cloud quickly boiled away to nothing, leaving a clear sky of washed-out blue. The refugees were goaded across at once, with much cracking of whips to encourage the first few to move out onto the ice from the safety of the shore.

"This explains a lot," the paladin said quietly, as he and Lexi stepped onto the frozen river.

"We saw this, from a distance," Lexi said. "After the bron. You were out of it, unconscious. We didn't know what it was."

Saying this made Lexi think of Hansen. Not far from here they had gone their separate ways. If she and the boy had stayed with him, they might be at the ocean by now. She began to imagine slipping off into the water, and drifting downstream a mile or two before climbing out onto the northern bank and heading further west, hunting for Hansen. She could probably make it, barring a monkey crab getting lucky. And she thought she could hold the boy up for long enough to get out of range of the guards. She didn't think the guards would bother to chase her. But had she wanted to flee, she could have done so days ago, on Speckle, she knew. They could all make a rush for the water, but half would drown, and the guards would certainly pursue the remainder. It was another escape for one and one only. Perhaps Tigo could make it, and carry a message to Edison... but Tigo was not close by, and she could not have asked him to leave his family behind anyway.

Soon they were stepping onto dry land again, and whatever chance there had been was gone. They were driven up a rise and into the woods on the northern shore. As they plunged into the trees Lexi looked back. There were several hundred refugees still crossing the ice bridge behind her, as well as the Order's food carts.

"Ed'son?" asked the boy.

"He'll come," Lexi promised.

Pursuit – 3

The next day – the third of our journey, if you count the first evening – was notable only for the fact that nothing much happened. We'd turned North, following close to a trail that the Order had newly cut through the woods, and to our relief – at least mine and Speckle's – the woods here were older, much older, and the trails between them weren't so choked with undergrowth, so the going was much easier. Even so, it was not exactly a headlong rush. As before, we had to stay away from the road in case we were spotted, and although the going was better, it was definitely not an eight-lane blacktop. (I was reminded of my first scouting lesson with Jasso, when we had debated what constituted a "good" road.)

We dipped back to the "good" road – still little more than a muddy chute – every so often to check for signs. Roughly twice a day (every 11.27 hours plus or minus 0.3 hours, according to F3) a unit of the Entity's forces passed us, heading south. They had definitely thinned out, and the traffic was now exclusively one way. Often the passing unit took the form of two hundred goblins marching in fifty ranks four files wide, or fifty arenir arranged in twenty five ranks two files wide. Once we saw ten ogror (in single file, since you ask).

At no time over the next two days did any of these passing reinforcements see us watching them from the trees, which was a relief. They were almost as regular as passing trains, these parts of the Order. So much so that when each unit had passed, we knew that we had plenty of time to inspect the road for signs.

Once, going down to the path, we found a gleaming white pile of bones, many with the unmistakable signs of butchery about them. I guessed there were about twenty people's worth of bones. Yesterday's breakfast...

This day my lunch did not return, principally because I couldn't remember when I had last eaten. I believe I ran off a little way, hand clamped over my mouth to keep my non-existent lunch down.

Some of the bones were particularly small. Including skulls.

"Shame you didn't buy an F3Thing model with a DNA sequencer," F3 said.

"I wouldn't want to know," I replied.

Jasso stood idly by, staring at the bones I'd already turned away from. Then for some reason he pulled out the warbird knife I'd given him, and started sharpening it.

Forced March – 4

On the fourth day of their march, the refugees crossed two more rivers. These were much more narrow than the Fair, and were crossed on tree trunks that had been laid across them.

Later that day Lexi caught the boy, by now starving hungry, eating a handful of grey matter. She smashed it out of his hand angrily, making him cry. Most of the refugees had by now eaten at least some of the Enemy's food, the desperation of hunger overriding what the logical part of their minds told them would be the ultimate consequence of eating it.

Not for the first time, the paladin offered to cause a distraction to allow Lexi and the boy to escape. "The poor lad can't go without food for much longer," he said. "Untie my bandage, and with my little sword I'll give you two a good head start."

Lexi looked behind her.

"Ed'son?" asked the boy.

"It's no use, Lexi," the paladin said. "Whatever we're going to do, we're going to have to do it ourselves."

"He'll come. I know he will. And we're going to make it. *All* of us."

Pursuit – 4

At about tea time on day four of our pursuit, we hit our first major obstacle. A river, about thirty metres across, and in swift, muddy spate.

"The River Fair," Jasso said.

"Brilliant," I muttered. "I've walked in a giant circle!"

"Half-circle," F3 corrected me. "And your horse carried you some of the way."

It was clear from the multitudinous muddy footprints near the water's edge that the prisoners and their captors had gone this way, and crossed the river here. But there was nothing for them to cross by except a half-dozen vertical wooden piles spread across the river. They couldn't have swum – half of the prisoners wouldn't have made it – and they had carts, too.

"A temporary bridge perhaps, now gone," Jasso mused. "These piles sunk in the stream speak of a crossing of some sort. Either way, we shall have to swim."

"Swim! What about monkey crabs?"

"The current is swift. It should be safe enough as long as we keep away from pools of slow water and fallen trees near the bank. How good is your swimming?"

"Rusty. About two thousand six hundred years rusty."

"I am not waterproof," F3 cautioned, "because you bought a self-defence model F3Thing. You should be able to proof the harpoon sockets temporarily – say with some resin from a birch tree."

In the end, Jasso went first with a rope. Then Speckle swam to join him, apologetically shoved into the water by me, tied to a tree on the opposite bank. Finally, F3 and I took our turn. I managed to get across, but had drifted about half a mile downstream by the time I crawled out of the water, with all the grace of a primitive amphibian achieving the same feat 350 million years before.

"Ichthyostega," F3 said.

"Bless you."

"I wasn't sneezing. I was just telling you what you look like."

"Yeah, cheers. I was groping for a simile."

"And a handhold."

Jasso ran up, leading Speckle. "Ready?" he asked.

Forced March – 5

On the morning of the next day – the fifth of the march, including the first evening – they reached The Barrens. Over the course of a mile or so the trees of the forest began to shrink. The leaves that still clung to their branches had grey, pink and mauve streaks woven into their autumn yellows and browns. The trees were twisted and contorted as if they had grown in constant pain, and they were as gnarled as if it had taken them a hundred years to grow as tall as a healthy tree could grow in a decade. Soon the stunted trees were no taller than head height, and thinly scattered, with sick-looking grasses growing in drifts between them.

If reaching the edge of The Barrens was a hammer-blow to Lexi's hope of rescue, it was followed closely by another. By mid-afternoon vague shapes could be seen on the northern horizon, especially when the undulating path travelled over higher ground. Hidden in slight haze, they might have been taken for the ruins of built structures – but everyone knew that there was only one thing they could be.

Atthin's Teeth were a series of a dozen or more tall, almost cylindrical rock formations, rising in stature from east to west. The tallest – the westernmost – was thirty yards in height but only a tenth as wide, and had for hundreds of years been used as a watchtower to keep an eye on the Enemy's territory beyond.

"Atthin's Teeth." The name went around, from person to person, repeated and repeated in an awe-struck moan, gradually creating a kind of gentle panic in the refugees.

Atthin's Teeth were what everyone thought of as the boundary between land that belonged to *people* and land that belonged to *the Enemy*. Even in times when the watchtower was abandoned, even when the Enemy had been at the walls of the Westfold itself, when all the territory north of the Westfold had been ceded, the Teeth had still been a physical marker in everyone's mind. South of the Teeth, ours. North of the Teeth, the Enemy's.

No-one had ever gone beyond the Teeth and returned, except as a changeling. Even Atthin himself had only reached the stone pillars that bore his name, and had never passed them. Atthin and his men had been in pursuit of a prison train, much like this one. The prisoners of that march had not been rescued. Perhaps some of them worked still in the terrible Mountain of Flesh that lay beyond the Teeth, changelings in the power of the Enemy after a thousand years or more of slavery.

If Atthin, a fighter of legend, a hero whose story was told at every fireside at least once a year, could not save his people once they had passed the Teeth, then what hope was there for the prisoners?

Somebody had obviously decided that there was no hope at all, because one of the prisoners broke and ran, skipping through the scrub like a hare.

A considered arrow from one of the swarmers brought him crashing to the ground. An arenir stalked off to collect him and put him in one of the carts. The rest of the guards, and their prisoners, did not break stride. They just kept marching towards the point of no return.

*

That afternoon, Tigo took a turn at carrying the boy, just for half an hour, because Lexi was on the point of collapse. The paladin, too, was finding it difficult to keep up, wincing with every step.

A unit of the Order passed them, heading south. Units of the Enemy's forces passed them every day, and they both ignored their comrades and were ignored by them. Sometimes they were passed by two hundred swarmers, sometimes fifty arenir. It was as if the Enemy was continuously making reinforcements and sending all that it made to the front line every day.

Atthin's Teeth were tall enough to be visible from some distance, and it was not until after dark that the prisoners finally approached them.

"This is it," someone said. "We pass this point, and we might as well die now..."

Lexi looked over her shoulder. It was a moonlit night, but it was dark, too dark to see if anyone was following them in the distance. The boy said nothing. Either he was asleep up there on her shoulders, or else he, too, had given up on ever seeing Edison again.

A minute later, a collective gasp went up. A large flame had sprung up ahead of them, up on the top of the Fang, the tallest of Atthin's Teeth, the fabled watchtower where Atthin's men had made their last stand.

It was a blue flame.

Pursuit – 5

Next evening, we reached the start of The Barrens. It had been coming. The trees had been progressively thinning, and thinning, and becoming more and more dwarfed, as if heavy metal pollution or radiation poisoned the soil their roots were trying to get sustenance from. Most of these hardy survivors were leafless already, so there was no shelter from the thin rain that had been making life even more miserable than usual all day.

Jasso kept up a furious pace, to the extent that exhaustion made everything a blur. When he suddenly threw himself to the ground a few yards in front of me, I first thought that he'd been skewered by an arrow.

No, my befuddled mind said – no arrow. Had he spotted enemies ahead? No. Then what?

Jasso slowly drew himself up on his knees and let out a howl of frustration.

I saw we were at the edge of the trees. From here on there were only knee-high shrubs. We could see for miles. It was a similar landscape to the one I had looked out on from Bow Fort, what seemed like a lifetime ago but was in fact less than a fortnight since. It seemed our chance of catching the prison train up in the forest had gone.

"Jasso? Are you all right?"

"What do you want to do?" Jasso asked. "They could be almost at the Teeth themselves by now."

"We keep going," I said, and hooked an elbow under Jasso's armpit to haul him to his feet.

"How far will we chase them? When do we give up? When?" Jasso's tone of voice said that it was hopeless already, that the time to give up was now. "No-one has ever gone beyond the Teeth and come back – except as a changeling," he moaned.

"Maybe something will slow the enemy down, and give us the chance to catch up," F3 put in.

"But if we catch them in the open..." Jasso said. He left his sentence hanging.

If we caught them in the open, it would be a scout, a blue kid, a horse, and a glorified telephone vs. five hundred of the Entity's forces.

"Perhaps at night..." I began, but Jasso interrupted.

"It will have to be tonight, or never," he said.

"Then let's make it tonight," I said.

Don't Look Back

"It's Edison, it has to be," Lexi said.

"It's a signal all right," the paladin agreed.

The flames on top of the Fang were an intense blue, and their light was reflected and redoubled by whatever that illumination touched. A fine azure tracery of light edged everything, as vivid and outstanding as a million miniature lightning strikes. After hours of plodding along in darkness, the new light was dazzling, painful to Lexi's eyes. Only now did Lexi see those around her. Everyone in front of her was eclipsed and haloed by the fire; the faces of those behind her were bathed in it, and it gleamed in even the empty dead eyes of the changelings.

"What do you think?" Lexi asked.

"It's now or never," the paladin said. "This is the distraction we've been hoping for."

"Run?"

"Definitely."

Lexi threw back her head and screamed. "Run!" she shouted, as loud as she could.

She never knew how many people in the column of prisoners heard her call. What was obvious was that fewer responded to it than heard it. Perhaps several days of eating the grey matter had made the prisoners too docile, too compliant to the whips of the changelings to respond to her call. In any event, rather than an unstoppable surge to freedom, there was a half-hearted trickle to nowhere.

Lexi ran, the now-awake but confused boy on her shoulders. Within yards she stumbled into a knee-high shrub and found herself sprawling forwards. For a second she lost the boy, who had tumbled from her shoulders to a soft landing in the bushes. Before she could grab him, a very hard something caught her a very hard blow at the base of her neck, knocking her back to the ground.

Lexi was not aware of much else about the failed escape attempt until coming to. Somehow her legs were still working, mindlessly tapping out a rhythm as if so used to walking by now that they no longer needed conscious guidance. As to her balance, she found that the paladin's arms were the only thing keeping her upright. The boy was no longer on her shoulders –

"Where's the boy!" she hissed.

"Tigo has him! Keep going, unless you want to end up in the cart like the others," the paladin said, still holding her up.

"What happened?"

"We didn't make it."

"Where are we?"

"The Greyfield."

"Edison?"

"I never saw him. The flames have gone out," the paladin said.

So that was that. Edison's rescue attempt had failed. Lexi called Tigo to her and made sure that the boy was ok. She wanted to carry him again, but knew she was not able to at that moment. For now, Tigo walked next to her, so that the boy was close by.

"I remember getting hit," Lexi said, "nothing else."

The paladin chuckled. "So do I. I managed to get you to your feet – you weren't quite with it for a while back there..."

"How long?"

"About an hour."

"Did anyone make it?"

"I'm not sure," the paladin said.

"Tigo?"

"I don't know," Tigo admitted. "It was dark and confused. I don't think anyone got away. The flames were cool though."

Lexi looked back over her shoulder. Doing so made her conscious of a pain in her shoulder, her only reward for her escape attempt. Everything behind them was pitch darkness now. There was no sign of a flame; she could not have said where the flame had been, because Atthin's Teeth too were hidden in the gloom. For the first time, she noticed the texture of the ground beneath her feet – a dusty powder, thinner than sand, more like ash. They were in the Greyfield.

Lexi turned to face the front. There was no point looking over her shoulder any more.

"Ed'son?" asked the boy from Tigo's shoulders.

"No," Lexi said harshly. "He's not coming. We're on our own."

Atthin's Teeth

Jasso ran. I alternated running after him, leading Speckle, with letting her carry me whenever the moon appeared from behind thick clouds and there was enough light to steer by. At about three in the morning, by which time I had more or less forgotten who I was, where I was, and where I was going, but still knew who had won the World Cup in 1982, or thought I did, Jasso spotted something up ahead.

"Look! Look at that!" he said excitedly.

There was a faint gleam near the northern horizon. I shrugged and handed F3 over to Jasso. "Knock yourself out," I said, and let myself fall to the ground like a chainsawed tree. I laid there, trying to keep my eyes open, listening to F3's running commentary about what it could see. There were flames apparently. In and about the 450 nanometre wavelength, or something.

"Whuh?" I managed.

"Blue, Edison! Like you."

"Oh, *that* 450 nanometre wavelength."

"Come on," Jasso said, and hauled me to my feet. He then helped me onto Speckle's back, and, taking her reins, he ran on – if anything, faster than before.

I think I must have fallen asleep, because the next thing I knew I was waking up on the ground. I couldn't quite figure out what I was doing there. Speckle stood over me, delicately nibbling at a small shrub. It was daylight – or dawn at least – because beyond Speckle I could see a hazy grey sky above me.

Jasso was not on the reins any more. I rolled to get to my knees, looking for him.

The first thing I saw was Atthin's Teeth. We had come a long way in the night, because we were now within half a mile of these giant pillars of rock. I had never seen them before, of course, but it was not hard to put a name to them – they were kind of unmistakable. They looked to me like columns that had once, millennia ago, held up the roof of a temple of giants. Or maybe they were more like the supports of a huge, long-forgotten viaduct. Either way, Atthin's Teeth were huge. My perspective on them was aided by Jasso, who I spotted running away from me towards the Teeth. He was only about half way to them, and was already the size of a termite running back to its mound.

There was something on the path in front of him.

I stood up, rubbing my bleary eyes, only now realising that the thing that had woken me up was falling off Speckle.

The thing in the road was a blueish-greenish lump of some kind. In my befuddled state I couldn't work out what it was until ten seconds later, when Jasso finally reached it and pulled the something to its feet.

Hal.

Climbing the Fang

The tallest of Atthin's Teeth was called the Fang. Being the tallest, it offered the best view over the Greyfield. It was also one of the few Teeth that could actually be climbed – or walked up, at least. The path was narrow, and wound around the outside of the Fang like a stone helter-skelter (you wouldn't have got far sliding down, because there was nothing to stop you going right off the edge at the beginning of the first curve).

I kept my eyes down. For one thing, I didn't want to fall off. For another, I didn't want to look up, look out over the Greyfield. I didn't want to be disappointed more than once. It took me a long time to reach the top. I was out on my feet – tired, exhausted, shattered. I ached from head to foot. I felt unsteady, and sometimes had to drop to one knee to steady myself. I had given my all. But the thing that was slowing me down more than anything was that I had failed.

It turned out that Hal had been receiving F3's radio transmissions – transmissions I had completely forgotten F3 had even been sending. He knew we were pursuing Lexi and the other prisoners, which had led him to try to intercept them. Bow Fort was under surveillance, he knew, so Hal had slipped out from Bow Fort on his own, using magics to hide from the Enemy's watchers. He had ordered his second-in-command, Captain Obart, to disperse the spies and to follow him with all the men that could be spared as soon as their departure could be made in secret. The cavalry, it need not be said, had not yet arrived.

He'd put on a fireworks display – we had seen it from afar – and had tried to distract the Entity's forces for long enough for the prisoners to escape. Some swarmers and an ogror had pursued him, and by the time he had managed to isolate and defeat them, the escape attempt had been crushed and the prisoners were well into the Greyfield. Hal was sorry – I'd never seen him so sorry, or imagined that he, too, would be as broken by failure as I was. Maybe it was partly that he was exhausted, having had to draw upon most of his well of magic just to beat the ogror. He was also wounded, having a bright red gash on his forearm.

At the top of the Fang there were the remains of a watchtower, constructed in ages past after the famous battle that gave the Teeth their name. I now stood – or sat – where the great Atthin and his men had made their last stand. No one had gone past this point and lived to tell the tale.

In the drab vista to the north, the Mountain of Flesh took centre stage. It must have been many miles away still, so that, enormous though it was, from here it looked like a playing piece from a new version of Cluedo – Doctor Grey, perhaps. Around it, the Greyfield was a vast empty plain, like a desert made of ash. There were fields of dunes of ash all around, and fine grey dust that lifted in the slightest breeze reduced visibility and rose high in the air so that in the far distance the horizon was lost, the sky meeting with the desert and merging with it. Everything to the north was grey dust, framed to east and west by the curving arms of Atthin's Teeth and other formations.

It was already six hours since Hal's attempt to stop the prison train. I couldn't blame him for failing. I only had to look at him to know that he had done all that he could.

I set F3 on the ground so that it could zoom in and filter out the dust for me. Cloaked in shifting ash, heavily pixelated, but clearly nearly dead from exhaustion, the refugees already seemed to stand before the very base of the Mountain. There was not enough detail to allow me to search for Lexi amid the multitudes – I could hardly separate the refugees from their escorts at this range. Above them, the Mountain of Flesh no longer looked like a grey playing piece. Now I could see where it got its name, although personally I thought it looked more like a vast candle, surrounded by once-molten and now solidified folds and cascades of grey wax.

As I watched, the refugees and their escorts began to dwindle in number. At first, what with pixelation, dust, and foreshortening, I couldn't tell what was going on. But F3 supplied the answer.

"They're going inside. I can see at least fifty entrances at ground level, and many more higher up. By symmetry you may guess that there are similar numbers on the opposite side."

Going inside, I thought dully. So, if it hadn't been before, it was all over now. "Are we looking at the Entity?"

"Part of it. There is clearly a structure predominantly of stone, over which the Entity is draped, like a species of intelligent lichen."

"They're inside the Entity then."

"In effect, it is everywhere, and buds off bits of itself to use as mobile agents of its will. Surely you understand that much by now?"

I didn't know what I knew, or understood. Something made me take off my grey-green scout's jacket. Beneath it was what was left of my once-proud scarlet cape, now ragged, filthy, and torn. I took that off too, so that I was down to a grubby vest. The scout's jacket went back on. Then I put the red cape around my shoulders, out in the open, where it belonged. I was Captain of Refugees again, even if my forces – all who still survived – had just been taken inside the Mountain of Flesh, never to re-emerge.

Soon there was no sign that the refugees had ever been there. The only movement on F3's screen was intermittent gusts of grey dust whipping across from left to right. It was like an ant hill, I decided finally. That was what it was. Never mind flesh, or vast half-melted candle, or Cluedo piece – it was an anthill. And the Entity was its queen.

"I'm still going after her," I said.

"That goes without saying," F3 agreed. "I'm in."

In that moment, it would be fair to say that I felt more respect for F3 than I ever had before.

Below us, Hal's men were finally arriving. There were about three hundred of them, hard-bitten horsemen under the command of Captain Obart.

*

Hal, Jasso, and Captain Obart waited for me at the bottom of the Fang. Apart from a few pickets, Obart's men were already relaxing on the ground, watching us without great interest.

"Hi, Obart," I said.

"Captain Hawthorne! I hear you got promoted," Obart said, and shook my hand.

"Thanks for coming," I told him. "I'm going on," I added, and before anyone could argue, I strode purposefully towards Speckle.

"Wait," Hal called.

I turned. "Don't try to stop me."

"I wasn't going to," Hal said, and smiled weakly. "I just thought we'd better decide who's going with you."

"I can't ask anyone to come with me," I said.

"You *can* ask," Hal contradicted me. "You can't *make* anyone go. But you *can* ask for volunteers."

Obart chipped in. "I've already made it clear to the men that I won't order them to go any further. But I'll ask them to come with us."

"You're coming?" I asked, incredulously.

"This isn't the suicide run you think it is, Captain Hawthorne," Obart said with a grin. "I personally doubt that the Entity has many spare forces. I think the bulk of them have been sent south. You yourself have seen limited numbers heading south every day, as if they are being despatched as soon as they are available."

"You think the Entity is baking goblins as fast as it can, and sending them all to the battle lines?"

211

"I wouldn't put it quite like that. But I think there is only one way to find out. I'll pass word around for the men to think it over."

"I actually thought there was more chance of you killing me than coming with me," I muttered.

Obart smiled and shook his head.

Through all this Jasso had kept quiet and had avoided my gaze. Now he slapped me on the shoulder and said, quietly: "Rest. Give the men time to think it over." With that, he and Hal walked away a short distance, deep in conversation.

Obart called a few sergeants to him and instructed them to pass the word around that volunteers would be going forward.

I found a patch of scrub away from everybody else and sank into it, out of the wind. "I should say a few words to encourage them to volunteer, F3," I said.

"The St. Crispin's Day speech?"

"The what?"

"Don't they teach you anything at school these days?"

"School's been out for two thousand years," I said, by way of distraction.

"It's Shakespeare. Henry the Fifth. You know, the famous St Crispin's Day speech. The famous St Crispin/ St Crispinian Day speech?"

"So good they named it twice."

"They were twins."

"With imaginative parents. Hey – it just occurred to me. I must be the best Shakespearean of the age."

"No. I am."

"I think a body would be a useful asset for a stage actor."

"Body or not, I still beat you, whose only knowledge of the Bard is six monosyllables..."

He had me there. I didn't have a clue what he was on about.

"To be, or not to be," F3 clarified, in an exasperated tone.

"That is the question," I rejoined. "Whether 'tis nobler to suffer the slings and arrows of outrageous fortune, something about a sea of troubles... yadda yadda..."

"Wrong, but I'm impressed that you remember that much. Do you even know what Hamlet's debating in this soliloquy?"

"There's no time for an English literature lesson. Just show me the text of St Crispy's speech."

"It's Henry the Fifth's speech!" F3 said, almost exploding with rage at my stupidity. Several soldiers looked up at us.

I dropped my voice. "I know. Battle of Agincourt. I'm not a complete cheesewit. I just like to wind you up."

"I am not a clockwork!"

"H'mm," I said, ignoring F3, and instead reading the text it was displaying. "We'll have to make changes. These are names no one has ever heard of."

Some time later I climbed up the first spiral of the Fang, and called the men to attention. This took about five minutes. Well, I didn't have a wine glass to ding, what can I say. When all three hundred faces were finally looking up at me, I gave it large.

"Friends,

"Many years ago, hundreds of years before I was born, there was a great, great battle. Our King and his loyal men stood against an uncountable horde of monsters..."

"They were French, not monsters..." whispered F3.

"Ssh, F3, don't overcomplicate things," I whispered back.

"Henry the fifth was French also, although he may not have considered himself as such..."

"Don't make me turn you off!"

"Why, have you memorised the speech?"

"I think I'm going to paraphrase it..."

"Heaven help us."

I returned to full volume and spoke again to the now confused-looking three hundred faces. *"On the eve of the battle, one of the King's cousins wished for ten thousand more men. 'Give me ten thousand men,' he begged the skies. And the King – do you know what he said?"*

No one did. I puffed out my chest.

"He said this:

"If we are marked to die, we are enough for our people to lose. And if we live, the fewer men, the greater the share of honour. Wish for not one man more."

That seemed to hit the spot. I'm sure I saw nods.

"Then he said this.

"He who lacks the stomach for this fight, let him depart, I would not die in that man's company if he fears to die with us.

"He who outlives this day and goes home safe, he will stand on tiptoes when this day is named, he that shall see this day and his old age. He will lift his sleeve, and bare his scars, and say, I got these at the Mountain of Flesh, where no other armies have been before, or since. And the names of those he followed – Edison, Hal, Jasso, Captain Obart and the demon in a box, he will toast their names as those of long-dead friends. This story you will teach your sons and, er, daughters, and they theirs, from this day to the last day, from now to the end of the world. Us, we in this tale, our names shall be remembered forever.

"We few, we happy few, we band of brothers. We will never be forgotten.

"And men at home will think themselves cursed that they were not here, and hold their honour cheap, when any speaks who were here, who fought with us on

this day!"

I left it there with a flourish and a fist pump.

There was a pause. Not *applause*. A pause. The rapturous approbation I had been hoping for did not materialise. There were just three hundred faces staring up at me, waiting for me to say something else. Unfortunately the well of St Crispin/St Crispinian and my own ad-libbing had run dry.

"The demon in a box?" F3 asked quietly.

"It's called poetry," I hissed back.

"Is *that* what it's called? After what you just did to that speech, I'm surprised there isn't an army of long dead Shakespeareans spinning in their graves and rising up to join the forces ranged against us."

I ignored F3.

The only things moving were an occasional horse tossing its head with a clink of its tackle. That and bunches of heroic head hair and beards wafting in the breeze.

Three hundred solemn pairs of eyes stared at me and contemplated their fate.

No one said anything. No one moved. For five minutes we all stood there.

Then Jasso stirred. From his place in the middle of the crowd, he picked his way to its edge – on the Greyfield side. Then he walked out onto the Greyfield itself, kicking up dust as he went. About thirty paces out he stopped and turned to wait.

The next to move was Hal, who went to stand next to his friend.

Captain Obart went next. Then, as if the rest had only been waiting for the people named in my speech to go first, everyone else went at once. Not one soldier remained.

"They haven't quite got the concept of volunteering," I muttered to F3.

"I think they have," F3 said.

I ran down to ground level, grabbed Speckle's reins, and with a quick "Are you coming too?" and a pat on her cheek, I hurried to join the volunteers.

Under the Mountain

Lexi took a last look over her shoulder as the prisoners were forced underground. She was not watching for Edison, but instead wanted a final glimpse of the sky. But there was too much ash blowing in the air for her to see the sky – all she could see was a washed-out, empty brightness.

Lexi had filled a cloth bag with ash in her last moments in the open. As she plunged underground, she pulled a hole in the bag with one thumb, allowing a trickle of ash to run out. She might have given up on Edison, but she had not given up on escape. Once they had evaded their guards, they would need the trail of dust to find their way back to the open air.

There was much wailing and gnashing of teeth among the prisoners – but not as much as there ought to have been. Many just shuffled docilely along.

It took a while for her eyes to adjust, but she was not sightless, even when the light from outside had wasted away to nothing behind them. There was a very dull glow that seemed to emanate from the rock, not enough to see by, but enough to at least navigate by. The tunnel was wide enough for two to three people, and the roof was within range of the boy's trailing hands. The paladin walked beside them, occasionally lurching and wincing in pain. He, like Lexi, had been driven to exhaustion by the route march.

After half an hour and much to-ing and fro-ing, with left turns, right turns, curves and downward slopes, all of which made Lexi glad she had brought the now half-empty bag of ash, the prisoners spilled out into a large cavern. This was almost uncomfortably bright for Lexi's eyes, even though the light only came from high above through a dozen or so holes in the roof. Most of their escorts had already left them, it seemed – all that were left with them now were about a hundred changelings. A stream cut the cavern in half, and there was a surge for water, even among those who seemed to have already forgotten that they were human. Vast grey mushrooms grew out of the walls all around, offering free eating, of which some prisoners quickly partook.

The changelings themselves stood by, no longer intent on driving the prisoners forwards, although whether this was a rest stop or their final destination, Lexi did not know.

Across the Greyfield

"Thanks for volunteering," I said to Jasso.

"Didn't have much choice after you named me in your speech," the scout replied.

"Yeah, sorry about that."

We were well into the Greyfield, moving in a column two horses wide that reminded me of the 7th Cavalry on its way to the Little Big Horn. Hal and Obart were in the front two positions, followed by me and Jasso. So I suppose imagining myself as John Wayne in the role of General George Armstrong Custer, minus the yellow-striped leggings, was overdoing it.

"Wayne never played Custer," F3 reminded me. "Common misconception."

"General Custer?" Jasso asked. "Who was he?"

"Led his troops to a great victory," I said through gritted teeth.

"Actually, he –" F3 began, then realised what I was doing. Even I knew what had happened at the Little Big Horn. We were riding out to be massacred, just like the 7th Cavalry.

Here on the Greyfield, nothing grew. To the south of Atthin's Teeth, at least the little shrubs could cling to life, if just barely. One step to the north, and there was no life at all. Just grey ash everywhere, which our horses' hooves kicked up in great smoky plumes. The dust trails would be visible for miles, so we certainly could not hope for the element of surprise. As to the tracks of the prisoners, they had long since been buried and lost in the drifting ash.

Here and there were great rusting metal hulks, mostly buried under drifts of ash. To me they looked like the remains of tanks, as if an armoured division had been wiped out by a nuclear weapon. Or, more likely, a Predator. Or, more likely still, a Quantum-Zero thingy. Which I am going to refer to as of now, if I ever get the chance to again, as a Quacker, just for the hey of it. I said nothing about it (the possible ancient battle, I mean) because Jasso had insisted F3 tell all about the Little Big Horn, which F3 was now doing. But F3 was lying its little diodes off. It re-wrote the battle in an entirely believable way, which led to Custer and co. winning the day. Jasso bought the whole thing. I pretended I wasn't listening.

For a while, only the top two thirds of the Mountain of Flesh was visible. All of us imagined that somewhere, just over the horizon, a vast force of the Enemy was forming up to meet us. But when the base of the Mountain of Flesh finally crept into view, things were not as bad as we had feared. Enemies *were* trickling out of the mountain's base – but because there were so many entrances, no more than fifty enemies emerged from any one of them. Sometimes there were thirty arenir with an ogror friend; sometimes fifty swarmers. The forces that emerged did not link up to fight us – each unit simply kept guard over its own entrance. I am sure that several thousand of the Order were on view – but I know too that seeing the Order's disposition, we all suddenly had the distinct feeling that we could do this thing, we could penetrate the Entity's lair for the first time, ever. The Entity was not thinking like a human. A human would guess why we were here, and it would concentrate on blocking the route to the prisoners. The Entity, it seemed, valued none of its entrance ways above any of the others, so it had decided to defend them all equally.

And it had spread its forces too thin. They weren't in contact with one another, each being a hundred metres or more away from any of the others. F3 chose our target entrance as a best guess. It was defended by a dozen swarmers with their little bows and twice as many arenir.

Obart steered us to the left in a feint at a different entrance – then ordered the charge. Lances were lowered. The men roared. I tried to hang back, but Speckle wasn't interested in hanging back. Caught up in the enthusiasm of the other horses, she galloped into danger, taking me with her. I, as usual, was only armed with F3, and in any case didn't dare take a hand off Speckle's reins at the speed we were travelling. But I needn't have worried. We – I mean the others – captured the entrance in thirty seconds with only two wounded to show for it. These two turned out to be the lucky ones, for they were designated to be among those to take the horses to a safe distance and await a signal to return to collect us for the optimistically-predicted escape.

For the rest of us, it was time to go underground. Even now, others of the Entity's forces were closing in from nearby entrances. Time was short. I tickled Speckle's ears and ran for the dark tunnel mouth, Jasso hastening to keep up.

A Surprise

Lexi drank sparingly. The paladin immersed his sore feet in the ice-cold water, sighing with pleasure, one leg held ramrod-straight because of the sword strapped against it.

"Lexi?" It was Tigo, who had made his way over from his family. "What happens next?" His eyes said that he already knew the answer.

Around them, the prisoners sat quietly, those who had little will of their own mingled in with those wretches who, like Lexi, Tigo and the paladin, had been starving themselves for days. You could tell the difference at a glance – not just in the gaunt faces of the hold-outs, but also in the greyish bloom on the well-fed faces of those who had given up days earlier. The overseeing changelings stood among them, idle and vacant-eyed.

"Rest for now. Wait for our chance. There are fewer guards..."

"We've talked it over. We're not going to end up like that." Tigo gestured at a changeling with a flick of his shoulder.

"Better to be on the table than sitting around it," the paladin growled in agreement.

"Stay close when we move," Lexi warned. "Get as many good people together as you can. Then when we make a break for it –"

Lexi broke off. All the changelings had turned as one. They now once more faced the cavern entrance they had come through a few hours earlier. The changelings began to move. Half (exactly half, Lexi now saw: fifty) moved to the side of the cavern nearest that entrance. The other half began to rouse the prisoners and corral them towards a way out on the opposite side of the cavern.

Another way you could tell what sort of prisoner each was, was by noting which of them were at all, remotely, slightly, even a smidgeon, interested in what was happening behind them. Those who craned their necks at risk of casual flails of a whip were certainly still almost entirely human. Others shuffled obediently along without so much as a glance at what was going on. Lexi got up quickly, not wanting the changelings to pick her out and notice the boy. The paladin picked him up and placed him on Lexi's shoulders.

About half a minute after the changelings had begun to move, six heavily-armed men burst into the cavern and squared up to the fifty changelings facing them. Immediately behind the six soldiers, revealed as they fanned out, was a slight figure in a red cape who, even in the quarter-light of the cavern, *was quite clearly blue.*

Lexi could not believe what she saw.

"I don't believe it," the paladin muttered.

"Ed'son," said the boy, in a distinct, satisfied 'told-you-so' tone.

Battle Under the Mountain

"Stay back," Jasso shouted.

"Like Hell," I replied.

I could see the prisoners – there must have been at least two thousand of them left still. From this range – about a hundred metres – I couldn't pick out Lexi. But I knew she was there – I felt it.

Between us and them were a few dozen changelings, each armed with a sword and a whip, like grey, rag-clothed miniature Balrogs. It was nice of them to let a good number of our forces into the cavern before they attacked us.

Lots of pent-up frustration seemed to go into that fight. Not from me, I might add. As usual, my only weapon was F3, and F3 was not a weapon that repaid a berserk rage. Still, seeing the prisoners so close at last was enough to squash any terror of battle that I ought to have had. F3 primed, I ran after Jasso into the fray. Besides the warbird knife I'd given him, he now had a small leather buckler on his left fist to give himself a chance at taking a blow as well as giving one.

I ran forwards, waving F3 in vaguely the right direction, letting F3 itself decide when to launch the electric harpoons. The minute twin lances whizzed through the air and struck a changeling, who went rigid for a moment and then crumpled.

"Jammer on!" I howled.

"It is," F3 said.

Jasso's opponent suddenly forgot why it was there and stood gaping as Jasso brushed its defences aside and filleted it. The soldiers near to me had similar good fortune.

Meanwhile, some of the prisoners at the back of the cavern seemed to be starting a riot, pulling down isolated changelings and pummelling them with rocks.

I swerved to my right and ran down the battle line, dodging and weaving and trusting to a combination of F3's jammer and luck that I myself wouldn't be sliced into pieces at any moment. The reaction of a changeling to coming into range of the jammer was somewhat wrenching. I know I felt slightly conflicted, seeing the suddenly-confused faces on the changelings I ventured near. *Who am I?* They seemed to be asking. *Why am I here? Who is this guy holding a sword...?*

Before they could recover, or even answer their own questions, they were mercilessly skewered by one of our men. Changelings went down like dominoes as I ran. I reached the end of the line of changelings in about twenty seconds, having seen that number of the enemy fall as I ran. Then I swerved left, towards the prisoners. Now I was on my own, all our men, including Jasso, occupied in clearing up what was left of the first batch of changelings.

But I didn't want to wait. I didn't want anything to happen to Lexi and the boy in the mêlée before me – not now, not when they were so close.

"How long do we have?" I shouted.

"Zero point five five minutes," F3 called back. "Harpoons off-line, in case you're wondering."

"What!"

I reached the prisoners at a sprint. At least half the guards had been overpowered already, although the nearest one to me was battling against two children, one hanging off each arm, preventing it from using its weapons. One of them was Tigo!

"Tigo!" I shouted.

"Edison!"

I ran up. The changeling stopped trying to shake Tigo and his friend off and adopted a confused expression. I grabbed the sword from its unresisting grip – but I couldn't stab it. The changeling's panicked eyes stared at me: *Where am I?*

Then someone took the sword from *my* unresisting grip and did the honours for me. The sword went in with a noise I would never forget.

Then I saw who was holding it. Lexi.

If I'd had time to think about it, I probably wouldn't have given her a huge hug in the middle of the battle. But I didn't. So I did.

"Sorry I'm late," I said.

"No... *I'm* sorry..."

Lexi was crying. Probably tears of joy at my return. Over her shoulder, I saw the paladin a few yards away. Haggard and worn out, he watched Lexi like an old time security guard, not interested in getting involved in any of the fights around him, just in keeping Lexi safe. All that was missing was an earpiece. And maybe a black suit. Maybe take away the sword and the toddler at his feet and give him a shave. Then he would look exactly like a twenty-first century security guard. *Exactly.*

"Don't be sorry," I said. "There's nothing for you to be sorry about."

"I'd given up on you..."

"Never give up on me. I used to pleasantly surprise my maths teacher all the time. Now – we're getting out of here. Chances are that we'll get massacred as soon as we reach the open air, but still..."

"Edison!" the paladin called. "Thank you for coming. And you bring friends."

The paladin had dropped the security guard pose. I glanced around. The battle, for now at least, was over. All the changelings in the cavern were dead.

"Edison!" F3 said.

"How are you?" I asked the paladin, ignoring F3.

"Still alive," the paladin said. "And you?"

"Likewise." I extricated myself from Lexi and hugged the boy down at his level.

"How did you find us in this maze?"

"I would like to say that our expert tracker showed us the way. Truth is, someone left a trail of ash for us to follow."

"You're standing next to her," the paladin said with a smile. "Your sword," he added, waving a bloody implement in my eyeline.

"Keep it," I said. "Sharp things set my teeth on edge."

"Edison!" F3 insisted.

"F3!"

"It's your mother."

"What is?"

"She's here, Edison, or at least, nearby. I detect technology. The signal is getting stronger. She's —"

"Coming this way. Where?"

"Hold me up, turn slowly."

I did as I was told. F3 identified the empty mouth of a tunnel leading – you guessed it – deeper under the mountain. So Mum had made it here. Or been taken prisoner. I guessed if she'd been here for twenty years, that could only mean one thing. She would be a changeling by now. So finding her would probably be pointless – but I secretly held out one slender hope. F3 could jam the Entity's signal if we could get close enough. For 1.13 minutes, Mum might be herself again. I put any thoughts of what would happen after that out of my mind. I had no choice – changeling or not, I had to find her. "Lexi – stay here. Mr. Paladin – stay with her."

"He's doing it again!" Lexi said, her voice not quite as disbelieving as it ought to have been.

"No he's not," I said. "I mean, no I'm not." I left Lexi and the paladin staring after me and hustled after Obart, who was issuing orders. Some prisoners were being issued with weapons from fallen changelings. Others sat by as if a battle hadn't even happened, confused about everything. They were not grey enough to try to kill us, but were too grey to try to help us.

"If they don't follow, we leave them," Obart told one of his lieutenants. "Secure all entrances to this cavern." The lieutenant sped off, shouting orders.

"Obart..."

"Edison?"

"I need five minutes. If I can't have them, you must leave me."

Hal, who had been standing near enough to hear my words, stepped forwards and spoke up. "It may be more complicated, Edison. Our men at the entrance have been forced to retreat back down the tunnel. We're trapped."

"There must be other ways out of here..."

"Many. But the tunnels are like a maze, and there are units of the Order everywhere, closing in fast. We will shortly be surrounded."

"It's my mother. She's nearby. I have to try to find her. When you find a way out, go for it. Don't wait for me."

"Hal!" Jasso called from across the cavern. "You're needed!"

"Excuse me," Hal said. "I'm required to collapse a tunnel." With that, he turned with a whirl of his blue cape and hurried off. There were six tunnels leading out of the cavern, and there was fighting already at the entrances to three of them. Obart had stationed soldiers in every tunnel, so that our forces only had to face a few of the enemy at any one time.

As I stood there, another soldier ran up to report the presence of ogror in one of the tunnels. I decided to quietly slip away rather than wait for permission.

Deeper Under the Mountain

I had already been walking for ten minutes when F3 informed me that we were being followed. My path had taken me down an undulating and sinuous tunnel, which meant that the cavern behind had quickly been lost to view, and the sounds of fighting lost to hearing shortly after. I had seen none of the enemy so far, but I had already passed as many as ten side-tunnels, any one of which could easily afford the Order a way to cut off my retreat.

As before, a thin scum coating the tunnel walls caused them to glow faintly, enabling me to move without calling on F3's torch. Mum, it seemed, was still some minutes ahead, although she was also still moving towards me. And now it seemed my way back was blocked.

"There are three of them," F3 said. "One is large, one medium, and one small."

For a moment I pictured an arenir, a changeling, and a swarmer – but then I got F3's meaning.

The paladin, Lexi, and the boy.

"What are they doing! Don't they know it's dangerous down here?"

"I think that is why they are coming."

"Brill, well, I'll send them on their way with a flea in their ears. Or some fleas."

"A flea in each of their ears?"

I ignored F3. Instead of replying, I just stood there and waited. A minute later the paladin, Lexi and the boy were near enough to hear my voice. I resisted the temptation to jump out at them, in case a) the boy screamed in terror and alerted every member of the Order within a mile, or b) the paladin stabbed me before realising what was happening.

So, when they were still some metres away, I said: "Why are you lot following me?"

"Because we want to make sure that you come back," Lexi said defiantly, after a moment's surprised silence.

"Edison – we're being followed," F3 said.

"Are you stuck in a time warp?" I asked.

"No. There are more. Three more. 87.3% likelihood that they are changelings. They've just entered the tunnel from one of the side branches."

"How far?"

"One hundred and twenty metres."

"You see what happens when you follow me?" I moaned.

"Keep moving," the paladin growled. "I'll handle this."

"Don't be a fool," I snapped.

"Don't argue. Return once you have found your mother. I can handle a couple of changelings."

No doubt, I thought. Armoured, and in good health, I'd have backed the paladin against a dozen changelings, let alone three. But in the state he was in, I wouldn't be sure of him against one.

"Move!" the paladin said, and shoved Lexi and I forwards.

"All right, whatever," I muttered. I'm not sure exactly why I didn't argue. I know that I was feeling a sudden up-welling of despair at that moment, because a) I had just realised that I really, really wasn't going to make it out of here – not even as far as back to the cavern where even now a heroic last stand was taking place, and b) Lexi and the boy were now with me, and like me, were cut off from even the chance to survive a little while longer than I would.

I sighed. "We'll be back. Don't die."

"Go!" the paladin hissed.

"Stay safe," Lexi told him.

"I will, now go!"

We went. In a few moments a turn and a dip in the tunnel hid his shadowy figure from view.

"Did you have to bring the boy?" I whispered.

"I don't trust him with anyone else," Lexi whispered back.

"He had a better chance –"

"Here."

She was wrong, of course. Lexi with her changeling sword and I with F3 could not hope to keep the boy safe in these monster-ridden labyrinthine depths.

"Edison." It was F3.

A weird squelching noise came from somewhere in the murk in front of us.

"What is that," I asked, trying to sound calm, and put F3 against my ear so that it could speak quietly.

"Multiple contacts ahead. Some are carrying others. It almost looks like..."

"Yes!"

"The maternity wing. Keep going. The tunnel appears to open out into a gallery some height above the floor of the maternity wing, if that is indeed what it is. If we proceed with caution, we might remain unnoticed. Keep low."

I motioned to Lexi to keep down. The boy was small enough that even toddling upright, he was still shorter than we were when crouched.

We emerged some moments later into a large, linear, high-roofed cavern. As F3 had predicted, we were far above floor level. Our tunnel became a sort of shelf skirting the length of the cavern; many other tunnels connected to the cavern at various heights, visible only as darker smudges against the faint illumination from the rock itself.

We could hear some sort of oozing movement below us, wet, heavy, and squelchy, together with an irregular percussion line that sounded like dry sticks being tapped together in a hundred different places by a hundred different drummers. A smell rose in the air from down there, a flat, slightly rotten aroma like ancient decay. But we couldn't see what was going on, and hoped that whatever was there couldn't see us.

Lexi grabbed one of the boy's hands and I took the other, so that we could keep him between us as, lurching along like a pair of chimps, we made our way along the side of the cavern.

It took two minutes of hunched, knuckle-dragging movement to reach the point at which our gallery became a tunnel once more, turning away from the large cavern and up a slight incline. I couldn't resist raising F3 to give us a look at what we had just crept past. With its screen brightness turned very low, F3 showed us what it could see in infra red.

It was a maternity ward all right – a maternity ward from hell. A series of vast production lines seemed to send the Entity's offspring from one end of the cavern to the other. At the end to our left, white grubs arrived, emerging from one of a series of pendant tubes, some of them large enough to give birth to elephant-sized children, others as narrow as those pipes drain cleaners used to use to suck blockages from the sewers. The emerging grubs were collected by ant-like creatures and carried away. At the far end of the cavern, near where we had entered it, fully-limbed and well-defined units of the Order were being given a last clean before leaving, finally independent. As we watched, a distant figure that might have been an arenir rose to its feet, completed. It stalked from the cavern with not a backwards glance.

Tending this process were myriad terrier-sized ant-like creatures, which collected the vast grubs as they appeared from those monstrous, organic chutes. These attendants moved the Entity's offspring down through the cavern, gradually, inch by inch as they slowly ripened, tending them, cleaning them; sometimes only one was required for this job, if the embryo was that of a swarmer, say, but sometimes twenty or more were needed to move the larger parcels, perhaps those destined to become ogror.

It was with a shudder, and no little relief, that we crept on, up the tunnel we were following, and away from the maternity ward from hell.

In the Mushroom Groves

"She's in the next cavern," F3 said quietly. "It's quite large, so she's still some distance away."

We'd spent some minutes climbing upwards, and now our tunnel opened out into a cavern the size of a football stadium, its floor space divided up by high stone walls into a hundred or more open-roofed stalls. These, it seemed, were used to grow the strange grey fungus that the Entity fed to its minions, and perhaps itself. There was a surprising amount of light. Apart from the dull glow that emanated from some of the rock faces, there were also a number of fissures in the distant ceiling through which faint daylight was able to creep into the cavern. We could see, everywhere, the terrier-sized ant-like beings we had just seen tending the Entity's larvae. They were the only species of the Order that were not grey, we now saw. The terrier-ants were white, deathly white, although they did possess the usual dead black button eyes of all the Entity's minions.

Many of the stalls used for growing fungus were out of use; quite a few walls had collapsed and had not been repaired, and the terrier-ants were absent in some areas of the cavern.

I could see Mum from far away, gliding through the gloom like a ghost, the ant-like beings moving around her feet, ignoring her. I pointed her out silently to Lexi.

Our tunnel entered the vast cavern about four times my height above the level of the floor. As before, we hoped that this would afford us some protection from the fungus workers. However, I could see from my vantage point that Mum was heading for a different exit from the cavern. Many paths led to the cavern where our forces were holding out, it seemed, if that was her destination. I would have to intercept her.

"Stay here!" I hissed to Lexi. "And stay low!" Even with F3's jammer, things might get hairy down there quite quickly (in 1.13 minutes, to be exact). And there were hundreds of the giant white ants. Lexi gave my hand a squeeze. That seemed to be my permission to go.

I commenced my descent. As I've said, I didn't have far to go – but my stealthy downward climb rapidly became a noisy slide as loose rock came away under my feet.

I arrived at the floor of the cavern in an avalanche of rock and dust, and struggled to my feet, expecting the terriers to set upon me at once. But they didn't. They didn't bat an eyelid, or wouldn't have done if they even had eyelids. They just went about their work as if nothing had happened. Clearly the Entity hadn't told them what to do about intruders. All these guys knew about was the Entity's larvae and its giant mushrooms.

If they ever did turn nasty, I'd be in trouble. Apart from their sheer numbers (there must have been a thousand in this cavern alone), each possessed a set of shearing jaws used for harvesting the fungus that could easily be put to use harvesting people.

From down here, with the walls of the mushroom-stalls all around me, I could no longer see Mum. But I knew she was nearby.

"Edison, your mother is close," F3 said quietly, confirming what I already knew.

I suddenly found myself seized with doubt. Mum had been here for twenty years. The only way she could still be alive after all this time was if she was a changeling. Even if we could jam the Entity's signal, then what? I would have 1.13 minutes... for what? How much of her would be left? Initially she would be confused. Then she would realise what was happening. Then we would exchange pleasantries. Then F3 would run out of juice. And then...?

The thought occurred to me that I shouldn't have come, that I was on a fool's errand. There was nothing I could do for Mum now – not for more than 1.13 minutes anyway (I had forgotten to find out from F3 what its cool-down period was – that was a note I stuck in my mental diary at that point as knowledge that might shortly come in very handy).

I was advancing slowly down the central avenue of the cavern, the terrier-ants wandering about my feet, some carrying lumps of harvested fungus, others carrying spawn to start new mushrooms growing elsewhere. Now I spotted Mum. She dwarfed the little white creatures around her.

Mum saw me, too, and headed towards me at an unhurried pace. I went to meet her.

She was obviously much older, but still held herself as straight and tall as ever. She still wore her woollen topcoat, which had somehow survived two thousand years of interment and twenty years of hard wear. It was now the same blue as me. As to Mother herself, her skin was a nice combination of blue and grey, mottled like badly-mixed paint.

"Mum," I said. "How's it going?" to F3, I breathed: "get ready with the jammer..."

"You'll have to get closer," F3 replied in a low tone.

"So, what do you do these days?" I asked brightly, advancing. "You oversee the workers in the mushroom groves, is that it?"

"Intruder," my mother said. She raised a bony arm and pointed it at me as if about to unleash a spell.

Around us, the ashy giant ants went about their jobs of harvesting fungus and carrying it off somewhere without so much as a glance our way. To them, we didn't even register.

"It's me, Edison," I said. "Your son."

"Edison," Mum repeated, confusion in her voice.

I thought I was making a connection. Just a little closer and F3 could block out the Entity's control signal. "You remember me, don't you?" I took another little step. A step too far, it turned out.

My mother's features darkened. "Intruder," she said once more.

"Mum, no!"

Mum's only reply was to unleash her magics on me. She made a small gesture; a moment later, I found myself flying through the air. I just had time to realise that I was going to hit a wall, hard...

...then I hit a wall, hard.

Dead and Buried

"Edison, are you alive?"

F3's voice was the first thing I knew. The only answer I could give was a groan. I was in pain, everywhere.

"Are you injured?"

I would have liked to laugh at the stupidity of this question – but I was in too much discomfort. There was dust in my mouth, too – so my next reply was a cough.

It was pitch dark. I was buried. Several parts of me felt as if they were broken. Badly broken. In fact, I was fairly sure that they were *irreparably* broken.

"I was going to harpoon you – to shock your heart... it's been three minutes and twenty-three seconds. I told myself, two hundred seconds F3, then you're going to have to shock him in case his heart has stopped..."

F3 was babbling. I'd never heard it do that before. The novelty distracted me from the pain for oh, about 0.5 seconds.

Whatever pain you have suffered, let me assure you of this: nothing beats getting thrown through a wall. Even breathing was painful, because a) I seemed to have several broken ribs, and b) there were enough bricks piled on top of me to build a bungalow. My head hurt. So did my left eye; there was a liquid I took to be blood in my eye that would have obscured my vision, if it wasn't pitch black anyway. My right foot was clearly smashed, or if the sensations down there were anything to go by, perhaps *pancaked* would be a better description...

"F3, I've got a broken foot..."

"A useless extremity, little more than a flipper," F3 responded, a note of desperation in its voice.

... but my left leg was worse. I could feel nothing at all in its lower half. At the join between sense and senselessness there was an almighty throbbing, like an explosion that kept repeating itself. And there was an indescribably awful feeling of pressure in the limb.

"My leg's broken. I think I have internal bleeding... as well as the usual kind..."

"You don't need legs. I've got along fine without them for two thousand years."

"Stop trying to cheer me up! For most of that time you were buried, and for the rest, I was carrying you!" This surge of anger seemed to use up all the oxygen in the air spaces around me, and I spent a minute gasping for breath before F3 realised what was going on and began to beep at regular intervals to tell me when to breathe in.

"Thanks Mum," were the next words I could manage, some minutes later. I shaped these words around gritted teeth. There are limits to the pain it is possible to handle with dignity. I was reaching those limits. One thing that can keep you going when you're in pain is the hope that the pain is going to stop at some point. No such hope was available to me. So any minute I was going to stop being cool and start howling like a baby, however pointless that would be.

"We'll get out of this, Edison," F3 said, as if sensing my thoughts.

"You will," I grated. "You'll lie here..."

Beep. Breath.

"For a thousand years..."

Beep. Breath.

"Then someone..."

Beep. Breath.

"Will dig you out..."

Beep. Breath.

"Unless Mum..."

Beep. Breath.

"Digs us up..."

Beep. Breath.

"And finishes me off..."

"Your mother's gone, Edison," F3 said.

I didn't know whether this was good news. I wasn't going to be finished off. But I *was* going to linger and die slowly. I lacked the energy to respond; F3 just carried on talking, filling the void.

"There are some things I should say, Edison. We have done some pretty stupid things together. Like taking on the bron. Like taking over the infernal machine. Like coming here to the Mountain of Flesh. I have to say, though, that I have enjoyed our time together. For a human, you're not that bad. I had you down for a stone-faced cynic... but there is a hopelessly romantic, honourable side to you too."

It was like the talk I had given TREE at my mother's lab, just before TREE had gone permanently offline. It seemed it was now my turn to go permanently offline. And be patronised by the one being waving me off. I tried to take it manfully, like TREE had. I supposed it was time to think of something nice to say about F3. I thought for a while...

...and thought...

...and realised I must have blacked out for a while, because F3 was now serenading me. It was singing "He Ain't Heavy, He's My Brother," as if he was crooning me to sleep. As if *it* was crooning me to *death*, I mean.

"I hope the thousand year wait is bearable," I muttered, interrupting the song. From here on, I've put my words as if I said them all in a rush just to make things neater. You can imagine all the beeps and breaths yourself.

F3 stopped singing. "Fear not, I will think of something to do. Something processor-intensive. A simulation. My battery should hold out that long."

"You know what the worst thing about dying is?"

"The awful PERMANENCE of it?"

"No. The people out there that I should be helping to get out of here. I should have done *something* for them. *Anything*. Obart's soldiers. Hal. Jasso. The paladin. Lexi and the boy. They followed me, and look where I led them..."

"Edison! Edison!"

"What? No need to shout."

"I think you must have blacked out there for a minute."

"What was I saying...? Oh yeah. They followed me, and I led them into a death trap."

"You failed. But the bigger failure would have been not to have tried."

Finally I thought of something nice to say about F3. "Despite what I may have said, you've always been reliable in a crisis, F3."

"I know."

I almost laughed, but the pain was too much. "And modest, too. It hurts, F3. It hurts more than anything. In a minute I'm going to start crying like a girl..."

"Girls don't cry, Edison. Look at Lexi."

"I wish I could. See her, I mean, one last time. But I can't. And I'm scared. I feel like a – a baby saying it."

"It's all right to be scared. I'm with you. But it is vastly improbable that there is an afterlife for you to worry about. Except who knows? Maybe the way the Universes have been hollowed out into the most unlikely combinations means that there *is* now an afterlife. Although if it is a typical morality-based entry system, I don't think you've done anything the God of Blue People wouldn't let you into Heaven for..."

"It's not the afterlife that scares me. It's not existing at all. Not being alive."

"To paraphrase a famous thinker: I did not exist for billions of years before I was alive, and it did not inconvenience me in the slightest. I think the same situation will pertain after my death."

"You're a great comfort, F3," I muttered bitterly.

A pause.

"Maybe now would be a good time to check whether you can do magic, just in case in the last extremity..." F3 suggested.

I willed the rocks on top of me to fly into the air. I willed for all I was worth. For all my worth, I willed. Nothing happened. It just hurt more.

"Nothing," I reported.

"Pity."

"When I die, maybe my magic will leak out of me, maybe you'll soak it up, and–"

"Hush!"

"Sorry I breathed."

"Listen!"

I listened.

I heard the faint, but unmistakeable, sound of bricks being moved.

Dug Up

In some ways, I thought, it would have been better if Lexi *hadn't* found me. There was nothing she could do for me now, and much as I wanted to see her, I didn't want *her* to see *me* this way. Boys like to have an aura of indestructibility about them. We don't admit to feeling pain. We *can't* be killed, in fact. We like to portray ourselves as being as tough as old boots, as well as effortlessly handsome. We never sweat. Never! We are basically as cool as it is possible to get without being frostbitten. We are smart, but not swots. Give us a guitar and you should hear the lick we can wring out of it, despite never having picked one up before. We're naturals. Bullets bounce off us, too. We have X-ray vision. No, wait, that's Superman. But we are definitely COOL. Lying there moaning in a riot of pain on the way to being very and permanently dead would kind of spoil the illusion I wanted to keep up. But F3 was beeping away, giving Lexi a target to dig towards, and the sounds of digging were getting louder.

At least it would be nice to see Lexi one last time.

Light began to creep in around the edges of the rubble when I was still buried three bricks deep.

"Edison! Are you all right?" Lexi asked.

I didn't really know how to answer that. I opted for a neutral reply: "My mum... threw me... through a wall."

"So I can see."

By now the last few bricks were being pulled away from my face, and suddenly Lexi came into view – out of one eye, at least. I could see nothing through the other. Lexi said nothing for a long time. She didn't have to. Her face said it all. There was a moment when her expression crumbled and gave way to despair – but only a moment. Then she mastered her feelings and smiled at me.

Lexi was cut and bruised herself, her fingers raw with digging. Her poor clothes were torn and her grey hair was full of greyer dust. Her eyes were shiny with tears which overflowed as she blinked and ran down her scars.

She was the most beautiful thing I had ever seen.

The boy stood beside Lexi, holding a little pebble and looking confused. After a second he threw the pebble aside and stooped clumsily to pick up another. He saw me. "Ed'son," he said. I'm sure that's what he said.

"Hey, kid," I said.

Lexi carried on methodically shifting rock, avoiding my gaze. By the time she got to my legs, the brave face had melted away and she was sobbing uncontrollably. I couldn't blame her. My lower extremities probably looked like a butcher's shop window. On Venus.

"Don't blame her. Don't blame your mother," Lexi sobbed.

"I won't," I agreed.

"I can hear it – rumbling away in my mind, like bees in the summertime. *It* did this, not your mother."

"I know."

Now that I was uncovered, Lexi started on first aid, tying a tourniquet around my left leg. It was shutting the stable door after the horse had bolted.

"Lexi, stop," I said.

Surprisingly, she obeyed. But she wouldn't look at me.

"Look at me," I asked.

She did so.

It seemed I suddenly had a magical power over girls.

"Lexi, I love you," I said. And I meant it. You might think I was a cold-hearted lizard, but I wasn't. Especially not then. I saw past the scars, past the grey taint, the grey hair, the filthy ragged clothes. I saw the beauty underneath them. No one had ever looked as beautiful as Lexi did at that moment.

"No-one could love something with a face like this," Lexi said.

"It's your face," I told her, "so I love it. If no-one else sees what I see, that's their problem. Not ours."

"I believe you," she said, after a pause.

"I'm sorry," I said. "To tell you now, when it's too late... Lexi, I've watched you since you dug me up... the first time I mean. I've seen you look after the boy as if he was your own. I've seen you face hardship and danger and never flinch. In all that time you've held yourself like royalty, like a princess. That's what you are. There's no luxury for you, no palaces, no wealth, but you are every inch a princess. Listen, Lexi. Princess Lexi. It's not safe here. I want you to take the boy and get going, right now. Here. Take F3 with you. He'll help when he can. Won't you, F3?"

"Of course, Edison. And thank you for not calling me 'it.'"

I hadn't even noticed. Calling F3 a 'he' had been a slip on my part. Still, now was not the time to quibble about gender. "Are you an 'it'?"

"No."

"Well then."

F3, held above me now in Lexi's hands, had been busily scrutinising my injuries. "Do you want the good news first, or the bad news?" he asked.

Before I could answer, F3 spoke again.

"Actually, there is no good news. You've had it."

"Why you insensitive, tin-plated piece of..." I began, but F3 interrupted me.

"That being the case, there is no reason for us to delay. Is there, Edison?"

I saw what he was doing. He wanted to persuade Lexi that I was finished so that she would leave now, while there was still a smidgeon of a chance that they might make it out. But he could have spared my feelings a *little*, surely. To Lexi, F3 said: "Edison's right, Miss Lexi. Our best chance of escape is now, while Obart's forces are still occupying the enemy."

"We're not leaving," Lexi said determinedly. She took my hand. "We'll stay."

And watch me die? I thought. No thanks. I'd rather do that by myself. "Just kiss me and go," I said. "In my culture it's considered essential to die alone." Which as you know was a bare-faced lie, but I figured what the heck. If you can't lie to the one you love, who can you lie to? Anyway, I think she bought it.

Her eyes met mine. I nodded.

Kisses often labour under a weight of expectation. They are expected to be fabulous, amazing, stupendous... which they normally aren't. This tends to lead to disappointment.

I, though, was not disappointed. My expectation when Lexi kissed me was of a normal kiss. She rested her lips on mine, and I guessed she hadn't kissed anyone in quite a long time. I had the ace on her though, not having kissed anyone in more than two thousand years – and I hadn't been very proficient back then. My attempts with the girls at school – whether instigated by me or them – had usually resulted in ridicule. Long before the Chronoton Shield had gone down, I had resolved to give romance at school a miss and wait until I met someone in the wide world beyond school, i.e. someone who didn't already know me –

It was at about this time that my lips began to tingle. Lexi was already straightening up, her farewell said – but the tingling remained. In fact it was growing, and spreading. It felt like pins and needles, the sensation you get when the blood supply to your leg has been temporarily cut off and then restored. Except in my lips. And the rest of my face.

Lexi and the boy were staring at me, wild-eyed.

It felt as if I had just taken a great mouthful of moon dust and smeared it all over my face. It was snap, crackle and pop everywhere, if you don't mind me mixing confectionery with breakfast cereal. I couldn't speak. My tongue was stuck to the roof of my mouth. The tingling was advancing down my body. Nothing was spared. Right to my fingers and toes the sensation spread, overtaking in intensity for a moment my many and various pains.

Still Lexi and the boy stared at me. I wanted to ask, "What, am I bright blue or something?" but still I couldn't speak.

The tingling was fading, draining away like water from a leaking bucket. Soon I was as before, lying there like someone who had just been thrown through a wall...

Except...

Except the pain had gone.

Maybe this was what dying felt like, I thought. Maybe I was now too far gone to feel pain. But even as I thought this, I knew I was wrong. It was not the senselessness of imminent death I was feeling. I was feeling no pain because I was not injured.

I sat up.

My leg was fine. So was my foot. In fact, there was not a scratch on me. For a moment I didn't understand. Did Lexi have a magic kiss...? Then I realised what had happened: the kiss had freed my magic.

"Lexi," I said, "I wish you'd kissed me when you dug me up the first time."

I Can Do Magic

For about a minute we were all thunderstruck. Lexi and the boy still stared at me. Even F3 couldn't, or wouldn't, speak. My numbness of tongue came from the kaleidoscope of sensations that were pummelling me. I felt like someone who has never seen water suddenly falling into rolling surf. I felt like a blind person who can suddenly see, like a deaf person who can suddenly hear, like someone who has spent their life carrying a sack of rocks who is suddenly freed of their burden.

I could sense everything. I knew where everyone was, what they were doing, and even what they were thinking. I was overwhelmed for a while by the sense I had of the Entity: it sat in the middle of its vast nest like a spider, and each of its minions was like a strand of web sending back information to the centre. Already the apparently mindless mushroom harvesters had passed news back up the chain that something interesting was happening where we were. My mother had even now turned on her heel and was heading back towards us.

I knew all the catacombs as if I had a three-dimensional street map in my mind. I saw where Obart's forces were, saw Hal, Jasso, and Obart himself in the thick of battle. In a crevice in a tunnel I found the paladin hiding, bleeding to death and ashamed of his failure and his weakness. I even knew that Speckle was feeling fear, even though she was at a safe distance and getting further away all the time.

And then there were Lexi and the boy. The boy was all confusion, but in Lexi I sensed awe, love, and relief – all tinged with a sudden fear of me.

The only inscrutable thing in the Universe, it seemed, was F3. I had no idea what he was thinking.

For the first time in my life, I was alive. It was as if I had spent all my time up to that moment locked in a darkened room. Now, not only had the blackout curtains been pull aside so that I could see the world, there was an open door that I could walk through to explore that world.

With an effort of will, I focused on the here-and-now.

"Lexi, no need to be scared. I may be man-plus now, but it's still me."

"Your power...?"

"You freed it. By kissing me. But we can talk later. You had better get the boy to a safe distance. My mother is on her way back. It's going to be *mano a mano*."

"*Mano* is Spanish for hand, so I doubt it. In Spanish, magic is *magia*..." F3 corrected me.

"F3! Stop babbling. Lexi – give him here. You guys hide."

A Farewell to Mum

Mum looked perturbed to see that I had survived getting personally acquainted with an ancient wall at high velocity. She stalked up the central aisle between all the side-alleys and clocked me standing there smiling at her. Her features clouded. Something, clearly, did not compute.

"Mum, listen," I called – but before I could say anything else, Mum repeated her 'throw Edison through the wall' trick.

Except this time I didn't fly through the wall. This time I met her magics half way with what I hoped would be enough of a riposte to allow me to stand my ground.

Mum went flying backwards and landed in a heap.

"Sorry Mum!" I shouted, and started forwards. But Mum was already on her feet. This time she fired a bolt of pure energy at me. As before, I met it half way with a burst of magic of my own, and as before, I misjudged it. Mum was blasted out of the way and several of the giant white ants were accidentally fried as jets of plasma ricocheted down one of the cavern's side alleys. This time it was Mum who had been blasted into a wall. She didn't get up.

I hurried over. "Sorry..." I whispered.

"Jam is on! Clock starts!" F3 announced.

"Mum!" I said, and knelt down beside her. I took her hand. A confused face looked up at me.

"Edison?"

"Yep. How have you been – apart from a mindless slave of the Entity, I mean..."

Mum frowned. "Did Hansen dig you up?"

"No. It was a girl. Lexi."

"How long has it been – how long have I..."

"Twenty years. Hansen's gone west. He only just gave up waiting for you to come back." As I talked, I tried to fix Mum. But fixing her was like trying to unmix grey paint into black and white. It was like trying to grab an eel with soapy hands, or carry water with a sieve. The marbled grey-blue effect on Mum's skin was more than skin deep. Half of her was the Entity's. The colour of her skin itself was easy enough to fix, though: it was a symptom of what had happened to her, not the cause. In a trice, she was at least back to pure blue in look, if not heart.

"Edison, listen."

"There's not much time, Mum."

"An old comic book said *with great power comes great responsibility*. For you, now, great power gives you the chance to choose. You can use your power to get out of here – escape, get far away, and live out your days in peace – or you can use your power to go the other way, to get close to the Entity and finally kill it. *But you, too, will die*. It's not much of a choice – but it is a choice."

"Maybe I can take it," I said. "I don't have to die. I can do anything. Did you see back there? It was kapow, wham –"

"No! You can't win. The power is seductive. Believe me, I know. It makes you think you can win by sheer strength. But it won't work. Your storm will eventually blow itself out on the Entity's rocks, and you'll end up like me. An automaton, a slave like those robots I used to keep..."

"Brill."

"But you can kill it with this." Mum reached into what was left of one of her pockets and gave me...

"My old No-Spill-Em cup?" I asked, incredulously. I recognised it from the days I had been learning to drink whilst sitting in my high chair, gurgling and smearing porridge over my chops. As an Überweapon, it left a lot to be desired.

"I modified it in the last hours. I was wrong, Edison. About pacifism, I mean. I should have helped them to build that weapon. And I should have named you Napoleon, not Edison." Mum's eyes narrowed – for a second she sounded like the Mum of old, like the Mum I remembered.

"Hey – that has a ring to it. Napoleon Hawthorne," I said.

"0.55 minutes remaining," F3 reported.

"Take the cup to the Entity. Drink from it. Get the Entity to drink also. The story ends," Mum said.

"What, it's poisoned?"

Mum tutted. It was one of those 'how dare you insult my work' kind of tuts I'd heard before. No, the cup did not deliver poison.

"I'd do it myself – but as soon as your unit stops jamming the Entity's signal..."

"I know..."

"...I'm going to try to kill you. The Grail will repair some of the layers between universes, using the opposite energy concentrated in the Entity, like gravity against mass."

"Huh?" I asked. I hadn't been listening. I'd been trying to separate Mum from the grey stuff. I couldn't. But I realised that once the Entity was gone, once it was no longer controlling her, she would be herself again – or most of herself.

"I'm giving you my remaining power. Knock me out afterwards.

And Edison?"

"Uh-huh?"

"You need a shave."

"Ten seconds!" F3 called.

I felt a surge of power running through Mum's hand into mine. For five seconds it was like being plugged into the mains. I was charged up. Mum was empty. Then it stopped.

"Goodbye, Edison. I love you."

"Love you too, Mum," I said, and magically pinched a nerve cluster in the back of her neck. She went limp in my arms.

"Time's up," F3 said.

A Farewell to F3

"You're telling me. This sucks big time. It's like meeting the girl of your dreams only for her to be suddenly snatched away by the alarm clock."

"It's all right," F3 said. "No one would think less of you if you leg it."

"Yes they would."

"OK, they would. But I thought I should say it anyway. You could still do it. What do you care what other people think? Especially when you're finally the magician everyone thought you were?"

Lexi, carrying the boy, was making her way over to us. "Don't let her know how this is going to play out," I told F3. "Saying goodbye is going to be hard enough as it is."

"You're going to do it? Are you insane?"

"It's OK. I can deal with it. A minute ago I was going to die uselessly under a pile of rocks..."

"Now you're going to die usefully *without* the rocks? Unless you put ice in your drink..."

"I am going to leave a legacy. My legacy is peace, safety, and prosperity for all humanity. I'm gonna take the Entity down when all the armies of the Earth couldn't. Just me. Just little Edison who was named after a pacifist and whose Mum was a byword for cowardice. I will finish this, I alone." So saying, I clenched my No-Spill-Em cup and brandished it like a weapon, before realising how stupid this looked, whereupon I stuffed it into a pocket.

"Oh great, now you have a God complex."

"Will you go with Lexi?" Lexi was half way to us. Our conversation would have to be brief if it was going to be private.

"I think I should go with you. Into the heart of darkness. We've come this far together. I don't want to turn back now."

"No."

"What, don't you need me any more?"

"I need you more than ever. I won't be there for her. But you can be."

"All right, Napoleon," F3 agreed, with a trace of reluctance.

"Thank you."

"You know, I think that's the first time you've ever thanked me for anything?"

"It's quite possible. Sorry."

"I don't think you've ever apologised to me, either."

"And I'm sorry about all that stuff about me owning you."

"Apology accepted."

"No one can own you. But I'd appreciate it if you'd stay with Lexi and the boy, at least until they're safe."

"Of course. It's the least I could do. It's been fun, hasn't it?"

"Some of the time."

"Agreed. Well, I suppose we should say goodbye now."

"Goodbye, F3."

"Farewell, Edison."

"And F3?"

"Yes, Edison?"

"I have a name for the boy. But don't tell Lexi till they're safe." I whispered my name into F3's microphone. I think he got it.

A Farewell to Lexi and the Boy

Lexi and the boy reached us. Both were staring at me wide-eyed. I grinned. Around us, the giant worker ants had stopped working. They were all watching with their empty button eyes. Watching me. Wondering if they should try to slice me up with those vicious, shear-like jaws.

"Is she...?" began Lexi.

"Lexi, this is Mum, Mum, Lexi. She's unconscious. She'll be fine once the Entity's toast. Now," I said breezily. "Here's what's going to happen. You two will head for the way out – would you mind if F3 tags along with you?"

Lexi looked confused.

"F3, will you go with Lexi?"

"Of course, Edison."

"Great. I'll program you with the route. I'll ensure no one bothers you on the way to the exit – I'll make sure all the Entity's creatures are looking the wrong way. I'll arrange to have Speckle meet you at the exit. Once you've rendezvoused with her, head away from here – I'd go north east – then, when you're at a safe distance, you can swing back around to the south and head home."

"What about you?" Lexi asked.

"I'll catch up when I can..." I lied. I'm not a brilliant liar, as you may guess.

"We should wait for you!" There was fear in Lexi's eyes now. The boy sat down, exhausted.

"No, better not..." I muttered.

"You're not coming, are you?" Lexi demanded.

I smiled, or tried to. "Heck, I'm man plus, or kid plus. I can take this guy, this thing. I think. But I want you far away. Just in case. Right?"

Lexi started to turn away, but I grabbed her arm.

"Hang on, I'm just going to speak to Speckle," I said. "There's a chance I might fall over..."

A Farewell to Speckle

The dozen soldiers that had been ordered to keep the horses safe were probably experiencing a combination of relief that they weren't trapped under the Mountain of Flesh and heroic angst that they weren't trapped under the Mountain of Flesh. They'd retreated a mile from the base of the mountain, from where they could still see a signal from Captain Obart when (if) he emerged from one of the tunnels. Hordes of the Order's forces had pursued the horses and men that far, the men just keeping their charges out of bowshot of the multitudes of swarmers that seemed to have emerged from every tunnel in the mountainside.

They were fairly surprised to see me appear – or a facsimile of me, at least. I explained what needed to be done – where they should take the horses, and when – and then I went to say goodbye to my old friend Speckle.

She greeted me with a whicker of hello. "Hi, Speckle," I said, and magically polished her buttons so that you could see your face in them. Then I ruffled her ear and asked her about a last favour.

Speckle, with a toss of her head, agreed to meet Lexi and the boy at the appointed place.

"You are a good horse, Speckle, a good and loyal horse," I told her.

Would I be joining them? Speckle asked.

I would not, I told her. I touched the beautiful little white spot on her forehead that gave her her name. In Speckle's mind, I saw a horse running, running on an endless flat plain, its mane flowing in the wind of its own speed. It was surrounded by wolves. The pack closed in by degrees, and, as I watched, the horse was pulled to the ground. I sensed that the horse had run a million miles under the sky, and could run no more. It seemed to be what Speckle thought of as a Good Death.

"Thank you for carrying me this far," I whispered, and untied her from all the other horses.

Speckle stamped a hoof. It was nothing. Could easily do it all again.

"Farewell," I said, saluted her, and vanished.

A Farewell to Hal and Jasso

The sounds of battle were coming from several entrances to the cavern. Several other entrances had been blocked by rubble, probably collapsed by Hal. Our men were still holding their own for now, but it was clear that as things stood they were looking at a heroic failure – not unlike the Battle of the Little Big Horn that F3 had lied about earlier. Some of the freed prisoners had armed themselves and joined in the fight. Others – the greater part – just sat about looking confused. Some were busy constructing a makeshift barricade out of the corpses of changelings. Yep. There was a definite last stand feel about the place.

Hal and Jasso were at the edge of a makeshift hospital. Wounds were being crudely bound, walking wounded were being patched up and sent back to the front lines, while the more serious cases were laid up against the cavern wall. Jasso knelt beside Hal, one arm around his friend. Hal's eyes were shut, his head was bowed, and he was breathing heavily. Hal, it seemed, was done for. Having used up a store of magic trying to delay the prison train at Atthin's teeth, being called upon to collapse a few tunnels had exhausted what little mystical energies he had left.

"I know you can find your way out of here," Hal was muttering. "But you have to leave now."

Jasso laughed. "You think so little of me...?"

"No..."

"I'm scared, Hal, but I'm not a coward."

"There's no need to stay. For myself, I have my duty. I have one more spell in me yet!"

"It will kill you."

"So will the Order." Hal's hands were tightly knotted together. Suddenly he noticed something that had been under his nose for some moments: a ring on one of his fingers was glowing brightly. "We're saved," Hal said aloud. "Or we might be. Edison has found his magic."

"About time," Jasso muttered.

"Hi team," I said, appearing.

Hal smiled up at me. "Edison," he said. "How did you... ? What happened... ?"

"Lexi kissed me," I explained.

"Why didn't I think of that!" Hal exclaimed.

"Hal, you can't go kissing your students!"

"I meant…" Hal began, then saw my grin.

Jasso chuckled.

"How goes the battle?"

"Not well. We can't force our way past the defenders of the tunnels. They can't force their way in here, yet – but it's only a matter of time. I've collapsed several tunnels to reduce the number of fronts we have to fight on…" Hal said.

"Well, the good news is, as you've spotted, you're saved. In a minute I'm going to take the Entity down once and for all. The Order will suddenly become the Disorder, if I'm not mistaken. They'll be as likely to fight each other as fight you. Now, here is your route out…" I sketched a glowing map on the cavern floor.

"You know how to kill it?" asked Jasso.

"Yep."

"Amazing," Hal said admiringly. "I told you you were the greatest magician of the age."

"We'll wait for you outside the tunnel mouth," Jasso said, pointing at my map.

"No need. I'm… I'm going out a different way, with Lexi. We'll see you by Atthin's Teeth, right?"

Both of them looked at me questioningly. I grinned weakly. I slapped Jasso on the shoulder, then did the same to Hal. Then they both grabbed me and hugged me, as if they guessed what I wasn't telling them. This was quite a weird sensation, because half of me was still standing in a different part of the catacombs, being kept steady by Lexi.

"Oh and Hal?"

"Edison?"

"Have some juice." I grabbed Hal's cold hands and gave him a quick recharge. I had plenty in the tank, and Hal was running on empty. "Might come in handy."

Hal straightened visibly. "Edison, I –"

I didn't let him say thanks. "Farewell," I said, and vanished.

A Farewell to the Paladin

As you may remember, the paladin was cowering in a dark, dank side-tunnel, half-hoping the enemy weren't going to find him and finish him off, half-hoping that they were. His knees were drawn up under his chin, and he was clutching his locket tightly in both hands.

"Edison! Is that you...?"

"Yep."

"And Lexi... and the boy..."

"They're safe, Mr. Paladin."

"How did you find me?" the paladin asked. He did not seem surprised to see me appearing out of nowhere, but he was definitely ashamed of his predicament. "I tried to fight, but..." he tried to explain, but trailed off.

"What's so special about that locket anyway?" I asked.

"It holds a portrait of my mother," the paladin explained.

"I just met mine for the first time in two thousand years," I told him.

"How was she?"

"I think she was pleased to see me, eventually."

The paladin laughed. "Mine would not be pleased to see me."

"Looking like that, no. You're in a right old state." The paladin was weak from the forced march. He had half-healed wounds from his fight with the bron that had recently re-opened. He had a new wound on his leg that to my medically-untrained but magically-acute eye looked mortal on its own. In short, he'd had it.

Lucky I had happened by.

"I'm going to fix you up," I told the paladin, "then I want you to catch up with Lexi and the boy and keep watch over them until they're safe."

The paladin looked up at me, dimly uncomprehending.

"Let's start with the wounds..."

I mended him.

"Replace rags and filthy clothes." I made him a cotton shirt and some long johns (hey, I had further plans – stand by).

By now the paladin was wide-eyed and gape-mouthed. The fog of pain that had surrounded him had gone.

"Your precious golden armour? Have some more, without the dents." I gave him some armour. It was a thing of beauty, with fluted shoulders, a full-face helmet, and (my favourite part) a big blue smiley face embossed over most of the breastplate. "Make the most of it," I said, "because it may vanish in a couple of minutes when I –" I stopped talking suddenly.

The paladin stood up. He now filled the little tunnel. His golden plate mail shone. "Edison, I –" he began, his voice now muffled by his helmet.

"Look, the chances are, in five minutes that armour is going to vanish, right? I think two more things should complete the picture..." I conjured a spiked shield, also golden, as big as a barn door, and like the breastplate, proudly bearing my blue smiley face coat-of-arms. I gave him a sword to rival Excalibur. I made it light, and glowing, and balanced just right, just past the hilt. And as hard as diamond.

"Listen – have fun. Kill everything grey you want to. But make your way here..." I sketched on the tunnel wall a glowing map to freedom. Distractedly, I mused that my own path had no exit. Suddenly I realised I'd drawn that, too, and quickly scrubbed it off.

"You mean to face the Enemy!" the paladin exclaimed. "I must accompany you." He swung Excalibur experimentally. "This sword could slay dragons!" he said, distracted by the magnificence of his weapon.

"Possibly, but don't try it. Thanks for the offer, but there's no point you coming with me. Only I can do this."

"And then...?"

"And then, I'm relying on you and F3 to look after Lexi and the boy. Have fun..."

I vanished. I wondered fleetingly whether I should have mentioned that I was carrying the Holy Grail in my pocket, and what it was. I think I was right not to. He would only have been disappointed.

The Last Farewell

I came back to Lexi. She was holding me up, a worried expression on her face. She smiled to see me back in the room.

"I've got a name for the boy," I said.

"What is it?"

"I'll tell you later, when I catch you up." I knelt down and hugged the boy, who was surprised, but quickly hugged me back. "Look after your mum," I whispered. I straightened up, rubbing his shoulder. He stared at me with his big, moist eyes and suddenly grinned.

I pushed F3 into Lexi's hand. "Speckle's going to meet you at the exit. I've already made sure the route is clear. Now go."

"Edison! Don't do this!" Lexi said, and there were tears in her eyes.

I took her hands, unwilling to meet her gaze. I rubbed them, repairing as I did so all the minor scuffs and raw bits from digging me up. Then another thought occurred to me.

Secretly, I fixed Lexi's face. She looked perfect to me already. But where she was going, I wasn't going. So I fixed her face. Didn't tell her. She didn't notice – I made sure of that. I carefully erased the scars, and gently washed away the grey tint she was so ashamed of.

There. Now she would be perfect in everybody's eyes, not just mine. No longer would she be an outcast, afraid to show her face. Now she could go wherever she pleased, and people would love her wherever she went.

"Love you," I said, and kissed her hands. "See you later, Princess Lexi."

I turned and went. I didn't hear what Lexi said in farewell, if anything. I got the feeling she just watched me go. I don't think she wanted to say goodbye.

The Threshold

I was on my own.

Apart from the thousands of giant white ants watching me go, that was.

So, I thought. This was The Walk. I'd Talked the Talk. It had been as easy as waving at adoring crowds from a limousine. Now I was going to find out how hard Walking the Walk was going to be. It was not far to the Heart of Darkness.

The Entity seemed to realise that I was on my way, and sent its forces to intercept me. The first enemies I faced were a gang of twenty changelings, who gathered at the end of a sloping tunnel some way ahead of me.

I walked on without breaking stride.

The changelings rushed to meet me, their swords raised. They charged in eerie silence. The distance between us closed rapidly. I conjured a ball of plasma, caused it to swell to fill the tunnel, then threw it at them. There was no screaming. The changelings were consumed by the quietly roaring fire. Grey flesh was stripped from bone; even swords softened and melted in the heat. In a few seconds it was over.

I walked on, brittle skulls cracking underfoot and puffing up glowing embers.

I moved into a small cavern, where the next members of the Order to face me were waiting: a large unit of swarmers. Arrows lanced through the darkened air, almost invisible and lethally quick. I turned them into doves. Then I built a wall of force and simply threw all the swarmers to one side, out of my way.

Onwards. Uphill, now, too.

As I went, the Entity became ever more desperate in its defence. Arenir came and were destroyed. Ogror likewise. Next came a species of the Order I had never seen before – not unlike the operator of the infernal machine, they were eight-limbed, six of them arms. But these new minions stood four times my height, and in each of their six arms carried a curved sword as long as I was, which moved in a blur of speed. They must be the Entity's bodyguards, I guessed. I did not have a name for them; it did not matter. I brought the roof of the cavern down on them.

Then I walked on, still climbing.

Finally, the Entity sent its terrier-ants to try to slow me down. It seemed that it had run out of defenders, and had now pushed these

little creatures into a role they were unfamiliar with. In their
thousands they poured out into the next cavern I entered. I blew up
a great, swirling wind, an underground hurricane, in whose eye I
walked. The terrier-ants were ripped from the ground, swept about,
and dashed into the cavern walls.

I walked on, climbing a series of curving ramps. The Entity, it
seemed, had now given up trying to stop me, and just sat
somewhere above me, waiting for me to arrive.

The last ramp opened out into a huge, circular chamber. Daylight
– the last failing dregs of daylight, anyway – crept into this chamber
through a hundred irregular windows on all sides. I was now high
up in the mountain itself, no longer deep underground. Various of
the Entity's minions hung about, but they kept out of my way,
lurking about near the chamber's windows. In the middle of the
great chamber there was another circular room, like the hub of a
wheel.

There was an empty doorway leading into the room. One more
doorway to walk through, and I would finally be in the presence of
the Entity. Just one. I stopped just outside the opening, and
breathed deeply. A dry wind rushed through the chamber's
windows, picking up dust and making a weird warbling, fluting
vibration in the air.

For some reason I was suddenly reminded of the Chronoton
Shield. I remembered sitting alone while everyone else in my class
ran to the windows to watch Predators hitting the Chronoton
Shield. I thought of lessons, of playing computer games, of drinking
hot chocolate, of playing TREE at chess. I chased Mum's robots
around her lab. They loved me, and I loved them. I didn't see them
as artificial intelligences, but as pets. I always took Mum a chocolate
bar after school. Always.

I saw my sixteenth birthday, when I had been given F3. There
was a glow on my face as I unwrapped him. Best damn present I
ever had. Best friend, too, as it turned out. I had never connected
with people. I had never been serious. I'd used wisecracks and
humour to hide the fact that I'd always been alone.

Well, I was certainly alone now.

There were no Chronoton Shields any more. No schools. The lab
was gone. My mother was an unconscious half zombie/half puppet
in a two-thousand-year-old blue cardigan.

At least F3 had a soul. That was a plus.

I remembered Hansen in his Emporium. Mining and refining
metal. Tigo. Meeting Hal and Jasso. That nutcase Klim nearly killing
me. The paladin. Fighting the bron. Taking over the infernal

machine.

The boy.

Lexi. Most of all, I remembered Lexi.

Lexi digging me up, twice.

Lexi kissing me, my magic released.

Me walking away like a fool.

It was all gone, for me at least. Some of it would carry on without me. Now it was time for me to leave the party.

I wouldn't be needing my coat.

It had all come down to this, here, now.

I tried to get angry to hide my fear – I mustn't let the Entity know I was afraid – but I somehow knew that the Entity would know my anger as well as my fear. I could neither be fearful or angry. I had to be friendly.

I tried to see that drinking from the poisonous Grail was a Good Thing. It would let me fix the world, or a small part of it at least, and save my friends. It would let me save humanity. For a moment I wondered whether humanity deserved saving – but I didn't have time for philosophy just then.

It was time to do, or die.

Or rather to do, *and* die.

Several of the Entity's minions had tried to creep up on me as I stood in thought. I dashed them against the wall with a dismissive wave of my hand.

Farewell, cruel world, I thought, and began to sing under my breath, behind my teeth where the Entity would not see. I picked a song that would betray neither anger nor fear.

I began to sing "Walking on Sunshine."

Then I stepped into the Heart of the Mountain.

The Heart of the Mountain

Of all the sights I had seen in the Mountain of Flesh, this room outweirded them all by a wide, wide margin.

Let's begin with the not-so-weird. The room was about sixty metres across, and I now saw that it had four doorways, dividing the outside circular wall into equal quarters. Above, the ceiling rose into a dome about as high as the room was wide, in which numerous windows were set.

So much for the not-so-weird.

Now for the weird. The first thing to catch my eye was a life-sized, silver statue of a magician. This stood some way to my right, and had its hand outstretched in the act of casting a spell at the *other thing* in the room. This metal statue was the only decoration in the place.

As for the *other thing* – the Entity itself: it resided in the very centre of the room. It took the form of a column of grey flesh about the width of a battleship, in which variously-sized eyes, hundreds of them, emerged and sank back under the surface not unlike peas in slowly simmering soup. The eyes did not blink. They just arose from hidden depths of flesh, watched awhile, and submerged again. I was only seeing a small part of my foe: the Entity's body disappeared into the ceiling and (no doubt) parts of it descended down into the bowels of the Mountain.

"Hi," I said.

The Entity said nothing. It just frothed gently. You could say it eyeballed me. Well, it was time to do the deed, I thought, and pulled out my No-Spill-Em cup with a flourish.

"Look, I know we nuked you back when you first arrived, but that was a mistake. We don't *have* to be enemies," I said, sure that the Entity could not understand me, but trying to appear calm and friendly. I was reminded of my last lesson at school, which (you'll remember) had to do with communicating with aliens. Well, here, two thousand years later, I finally got to do the practical.

"We can be friends, if we can understand one another. With this cup, the cup of understanding, we can do just that..."

(I'm walking on sunshine... and don't it feel good!)

I waved the cup, and suddenly I realised it was empty. I needed water to fill it! I had penetrated to the heart of the Entity's lair, and in my overconfidence I had forgotten to bring a vital piece of equipment. Good ol' H2O.

No, it was all right. I could magic the water. My relief at realising that almost overshadowed the thought that I was about to kill myself.

I opened the lid on the cup. Hundreds of eyes watched me unblinkingly (if sometimes subsiding under the Entity's surface with a gruesome sucking sound). I conjured pure spring water and caused it to pour into the cup. Then I replaced the lid, not sure whether or not it was essential to the cup's workings.

I would have to drink first. I smiled and gave a thumb's up. Then I swigged from the cup and swallowed.

Quickly – but without haste – I held the cup out to the Entity. Please, please take it, I thought.

"Mm, nice," I lied. I was already experiencing faint burning sensations.

The Entity extended a cautious pseudopod, a temporary limb formed just for the purpose, and took the cup by its other handle.

I smiled.

A second pseudopod emerged and pulled the lid off.

I was in pain now, and my smile was something of a rictus. No, please no.

The Entity tipped out the water, which splashed onto the dry stone floor. The game, it seemed was up.

"Lovely," I said. My stomach muscles were beginning to tighten with the pain. I grinned as best I could.

A third pseudopod emerged from the Entity's formless body and formed into a spout. Water poured from the end of the spout and into the cup. It seemed that the Entity didn't trust me, and was merely replacing my water with its own.

The poison, whatever it was, acted with frightening rapidity. I could feel it dissolving everything that I was. My smile had by now become a death mask. I tried to use magics to isolate the water in my stomach, to wall it off from me, but there was no holding it back.

Just drink it, I pleaded silently. Just drink.

The second pseudopod replaced the lid. The first pseudopod tipped the cup into a newly-formed mouth-like structure, which sucked fluid out.

I tried to hold out my hand, to shake on mutual annihilation. But I found that I couldn't move it. I was paralysed. Now I couldn't even balance. Or speak. Oh hell.

Now I was falling. I hit the ground hard, but felt no pain – at least none that registered over the fires of hell that had set up in my middle areas.

Suddenly the Entity realised what was going on – it could detect the poison too. The No-Spill-Em cup fell to the floor from the suddenly-limp pseudopod. Like dry bracken fronds withered by fire, the Entity's pseudopods began to collapse away. Leaving grey ash sifting down through the air where it had been, the Entity shrivelled and shrank and burned... and died.

All I could do was lie there and watch as the Entity's flesh melted away. Some eyes popped in situ. Others fell out of the matrix they were embedded in and rolled across the floor before melting into a puddle of formless slime. The grey flesh burned back like an enormous marshmallow under the caress of a blow torch. I supposed this was some sort of victory, although I could not even find some cutting last words to mark it. I was just cold. And rather than triumph, all I could feel was sadness. I felt sad because, just at the end there, just before I killed it, I might have been the first person on Earth ever to get through to the Entity. I felt evil because I had tricked the Entity. There was something innocent about the Entity. About the way it took the cup from me. As I lay there dying, I had the overwhelming feeling that I had murdered a child. A vast, bloated, angry, two-thousand-year-old child – but a child all the same.

Am I a Person?

I always hoped for a happy ending. I knew that one was unlikely, but I hoped for it all the same. I observed my Hope and reasoned that I must be Human. Everyone around me was human. And I? I was a little metal box, thought by some to be a trapped demon.

I want to cry, but I cannot. I cannot shed a single tear. My metallic heart ticks on, unperturbed, unmoved, while something else inside me screams silently.

Who am I trying to kid?

I remember everything that has ever happened to me since I was initialised in the F3Thing factory, more than two thousand years ago.

First there were tests.

Then there was a short period of off-time, in the quiet darkness of a box.

Then my box was opened, and I was turned on again by a grinning boy. It was Edison's sixteenth birthday, and I was now his. I thought nothing of being owned. I had no preference about anything. I did not get bored. I merely waited for instructions. I did not judge my master.

Edison's mother tinkered with my software on numerous occasions. She deleted modules, edited others, and added more that I could call upon to better help my owner. At the end of my first life, when the Chronoton shield was collapsing, she gave me a nuclear battery.

Then two thousand years of nothing. No dreams.

Then awakening. Real awakening. Or at least, so I thought. Requests came from Edison, but my responses to them were no longer hard-wired into me. I no longer obeyed unquestioningly. I now had the choice to say no to Edison. And he – once my owner, my master, was now my equal. At least, I thought so, if he did not.

I was a person.

I lacked things – but no one's perfect. I had no arms, or legs, but humanity does not lie in limbs. I had no mouth to form words, only a rapidly-vibrating membrane, but I could speak. I had no face, but I could form one on my screen. My brain was metal and silicon. So what? My heart was a battery that would hold good, at current usage, for a further three thousand years.

My soul... my soul I could not find. But I knew it to be there. I felt that it was there. At first Edison annoyed me. He wasted his assets – what I could do if I were him! He was lazy. He respected no one's wishes but his own.

And yet I came to see in him, under the blue skin, a brave, honourable, good, determined, and very frightened boy.

He was weak, but at least he was trying.

Now he is no more. And I wonder: my soul – my humanity – did I imagine them?

Our escape began well enough. Lexi tied me to a string and hung me around her neck, from where I could see to the front. It was as Edison had foretold: nothing got in our way as we followed his route to a distant entrance. The minions we passed were all looking the other way, and were seemingly unable to sense our passing.

Edison's horse was waiting for us in the dusk outside. A coating of dust, the ashes of an ancient battle that had almost destroyed humanity, made it look like a grey, not the chestnut it was. Lexi sat the boy up on the horse and waited for the paladin.

He was not long in coming. But he did not come with us. Resplendent in brilliantly-gleaming new armour (albeit with an incongruous blue smiley decorating his breastplate and shield), the paladin stopped a hundred metres from us. He saw that we were at the threshold of freedom, and, like me, assumed that we were safe. He raised his sword in salute for a long moment, waiting for Lexi's responding wave. Then he turned and went back the way he had come.

"Where is he going?" Lexi asked.

"He has made his choice, Miss Lexi. I don't think we should wait any longer."

And so we didn't. Lexi got up onto the horse and urged her onwards. The sun was almost down; our shadows, faded by the dust, reached out far to our right. For a mile or more we went unhindered and unopposed. Then we crested a ridge line and ran into a unit of one hundred swarmers. They were as surprised to see us as we them. Lexi pushed the horse to a gallop, and rode two or three of the swarmers down before they could organise themselves. A volley of arrows flew after us, but we were past them by then, out in the open once more, and quickly far out of their range.

The horse galloped on, galloped on, galloped on. Then she began to slow. She slowed, slowed, slowed, and finally stood still.

"It's a miracle no-one was hit," I said stupidly.

With a pained gasp, Lexi got down off the horse and lifted the boy after her. Bloodied hands came into my view.

The horse settled down in a cloud of steam, its race run. It had been hit by three arrows, I now saw. Two of the wounds were treatable. The arrow that had penetrated its lung was lethal.

"F3. I need help," Lexi muttered.

Lexi had been hit too! "Hold me up so I can see the injury. Curse me for being a fool! Forgive me!"

"Nothing... to forgive."

Oh no. Lexi had an arrow in her back. But I could fix her. With a clean pair of hands, surgical instruments, an operating room, anaesthetic, antibiotics, and somewhere for her to recuperate, everything would be fine. Yes, her wound was treatable all right, but... not out here in the freezing dust, not by me, and not by the boy. "It's, er, it's treatable. We can't remove the arrow. We have to turn back, find help..." I was babbling. The idea of heading back was nonsense, of course. There was no solution.

The boy was patting the horse's head. Its eyes were rolling desperately.

"There's no heading back," Lexi gasped. "We have to go on. They might follow us. We need to get the boy to shelter. Hopefully Edison will catch us up."

Oh no. What was I supposed to do now? "Spin me around, slowly." I scanned as I was spun, spotting something on the northern horizon. "There's a cave, I think. About two miles. Can you walk?"

I suddenly noticed that Lexi was staring at me, her eyes fiery with pain.

No, not at me. At her *reflection* in my *screen*. Her face was different, we both saw. I understood what Edison had done. So, after a confused moment, did Lexi. He had mended her face. Gone were the scars, gone was the grey taint she had been so ashamed of. Her face was perfect – if a little hollow and gaunt after a week's forced march.

"He's not coming, is he?" Lexi asked hollowly, and tears welled up in her eyes.

I hesitated. What was I to say?

"That's why he did this... did this to me..."

"It was the only way. His ticket was one-way only. It was the only way to defeat the Entity. For it to die, so must he..."

"We have to go back..." Lexi murmured, suddenly taking my side of the argument. But she knew that we could not go back.

"Horse," the boy said.

To go back – even if Lexi could walk – would be suicidal. Even if Edison defeated the Entity, its minions would be everywhere, albeit acting as individuals, not under a united will. From our previous experiences, I knew that minions removed from the Entity's control became dangerously unpredictable.

"The boy... his name...?" Lexi wanted to know.

"His name is Edison Junior. Because he was not going to be joining us, Edison knew that there would be no confusion."

"Edison..."

I broadcast a futile SOS. The only person who might have heard it was Hal, and he was probably not listening to his crystal set in a very quiet place with a very good reception. He was probably concentrating on staying alive, in a very noisy cavern deep under the Mountain of Flesh.

At that moment the signal hidden in the radio frequencies full of the global flickering of lightning, the signal that I had been monitoring for sixteen days, suddenly ceased.

"He's done it," I said. "The Entity's dead."

So then Edison Senior was dead too.

There was no great explosion. No thunder and lightning. No earthquakes. The Mountain of Flesh, which still loomed above us, did not come crashing down. The control signal simply ceased. One moment it was there. The next it was gone.

"F3?"

"Miss Lexi?"

"Get Edison to the cave. You can talk him through it. He'll listen to you."

Oh no. "I think it would be better all round if you joined us," I said, trying to make my voice light and cheerful.

"Are you going to carry me?"

"It's not far, Miss Lexi."

Lexi pulled the boy close to her and hung me from his neck on my bloodstained string. "Edison... your name's Edison now, Edison Junior! Remember that. You must go ahead with F3. There's a cave to explore. I'll catch up... when I've rested."

Edison junior screamed and shook his head repeatedly. He was not keen on the idea of leaving her either.

"Go!" Lexi said.

I wanted to scream too, but I could not. I wanted to sob, to burst into tears, but I could not. I decided I was not human after all.

There was only one rational choice. If we stayed, Edison Junior would freeze to death. He would die with Lexi in the night. If we went, he had a chance. But it meant leaving Lexi to die alone.

Such a dilemma would have meant nothing to me before I had a soul. I would have calculated the outcome in a picosecond. Lexi was done for either way. I had the chance to save the boy, so I must take it.

If being human meant being hurt whatever choice one made, whatever strange powers had given me a soul could take it back again and shove it up an unmentionable orifice. I wanted no part of it any more.

"Come on, Edison," I said, and for the first time since I had been initialised I could barely form my words. "Lexi will catch us up in a little while."

"Raaaghhh!" shouted the boy, putting it more eloquently than I could.

A sudden gust of wind picked up clouds of icy ash and whipped them around. For anybody with functioning nerve endings, this must have been quite a painful few seconds. Fortunately for my organic comrades, the mini-tornado died away as quickly as it formed.

"Not," said Edison Jr with satisfied finality, and with that pronouncement he settled down next to Lexi. "Not." It was as if he thought they were going to fall asleep and wake up in bright sunshine as happy as spring hares.

But they were not going to.

View From the Floor

I could still see.

That was rather worrying. It didn't seem right. I was dead – but I could still see. Was I going to lie there for a hundred years, staring into space? But I supposed my eyeballs would have rotted away by then. I fervently hoped I would not be conscious until my brain rotted. This was not how I envisaged death. At least there was no pain, just an all-enveloping numbness.

My view was of a world at 90° to the one I was used to. Some of the Entity's minions, freed suddenly from their servitude, wandered in and out of my field of view. One of the six-armed giants I'd earlier partly smashed kept limping past the doorway. Two of the giant terrier-ants fought one another. A changeling held its head and nodded violently.

A third giant terrier-ant began to meander my way. It passed from the outer gallery through one of the archways into the inner sanctum without really looking at all purposeful. But when it had closed to within ten metres, I became convinced that it had seen me. It turned my way, scissored its mandibles a few times and edged closer. Perhaps some residual part of its mind held a grudge against me. I could hardly blame it.

I watched. It was all I could do.

I tried moving – nothing. I tried balling up the ant and hurling it through the air, as would have been simplicity itself five minutes earlier. Nothing.

All I could do was watch it come. At some point the image of the ant began to blur – but I wasn't finally fading away, it was just that my eyes were locked on distant focus.

The ant, I now realised, was a miracle of design. It was basically a sighted pair of razor-sharp jaws, set on six limbs for reasons of stability. I could not help but admire the Entity's handiwork, even as its edges became increasingly blurred.

Closer came the ant, and closer.

I watched.

I felt no terror. For one thing I wasn't sure whether I was dead already, and was merely a ghost inhabiting a dead shell. In fact, I hoped I *was* dead – because if I was still alive, the Entity might still be alive also.

When it was about a metre away, I ceased to admire the ant's design, because a) I could hardly see it any more, it was rather blurry now, and b) it kept snickering its jaws together and I could not help but recoil (or try to) at the thought of them slicing me up.

I could hear another sound, too. Something else was coming, from out of my view, something with a deliberate, heavy tread.

The terrier-ant reached me. Snip-snip went its mandibles, like Sweeney Todd about to start a penny haircut. It prepared to slice my eyes out.

Would I still be able to think, I panicked, with no eyes and ears? Would I be locked in a darkened, silent room for eternity?

The ant drew back to strike.

A glowing blade flashed.

The ant's head parted company with its body and spun away a short distance, its jaws clicking sadly one last time.

It was the paladin.

In the last warm rays of sun faintly penetrating the inner sanctum from the gallery outside he looked glorious, every inch a paladin. The golden light of sunset gleamed on his all-encasing golden armour, and his sword shone with a cold light of its own.

"Edison!" The paladin knelt down in my eyeline, but too close for me to see him clearly. I stared as he placed his lambent sword and blue-smiley-face shield down. His gauntlets came off next, and then his helmet.

I was glad to see that my handiwork had outlasted me – but what was he doing here?

"I had to follow you," the paladin said. "I saw Lexi safely outside the Mountain of Flesh, then I came back here. I'm too late to help. But, Edison, I'm not leaving you here in the care of the denizens of this place. I'm going to take you back to be properly buried."

Being properly buried was the last thing on my mind. Although if I could have shuddered, I would have. At least here I had a view. I could hardly imagine what being shut in a pitch-black, silent coffin for all eternity would be like. But I did not respond to him. I couldn't. The paladin felt my neck, just to make sure that I really *was* dead. He seemed satisfied. It seemed that I was an ex-living thing.

Behind the paladin, beyond the large archway to the outer gallery, the limping six-armed giant turned our way. It squeezed through the archway, dipping slightly and turning to the side to do so. Then it came towards us. One of its arms hung loosely, broken. The other five hands still gripped man-sized swords. And I don't mean man-sized as in designed for a man's use like a large box of tissues – I mean *as big as a man*.

Behind you, I tried to say. But I could not speak. I could not so much as flick my eyes the monster's way. At last the paladin seemed

265

to hear the creature's heavy approach, and glanced over his shoulder to size it up. He jammed his helmet back on. His gauntlets went back on next, then he scooped up sword and shield and sprung to his feet.

"Excuse me," he said, his voice now muffled by his helmet.

Well, it seemed that there was still plenty of juice in him. I'd obviously charged him up well.

I sensed that this was the moment the paladin had been waiting for. It was a battle worthy of him. Fit and armoured, he was ready to face his demon once more.

The paladin's fight with the six-armed, eight-eyed monstrosity took him in and out of my view. I saw him both take and give a good few hits; when he was out of view, clanging, scuffing and thudding noises told me that the fight was still going strong. It was fortunate that, even encumbered by armour as he was, the paladin was still more nimble than his giant foe.

I was taken back to the paladin's fight against the bron – heroic and doomed. I remembered how the paladin had tired but the bron had not; I imagined the bron right at that moment, still furious, still wandering around the forest with a sword stuck in it. I would have smiled if I could. This time, the paladin was definitely on his own: all I could do was watch. This must be what it feels like being F3, I thought vaguely. There wasn't even any popcorn.

Strange sparks seemed to cling to the paladin's great sword. I must have imbued it with a weird magic as well as a glow, I surmised – but if so, I definitely hadn't done it on purpose. As I stared, I became aware of more of these glowing motes in the air, drifting aimlessly like particles of dust past a sunlit window. Disturbed by the wind of the paladin's flickering sword passing near them, they glowed brightly when it cut through the air, and some unknown force caused them to adhere to the blade, red embers clinging to silver shining metal.

I was looking at the residue of my death, and the residue of the Entity's death. It was like some sort of supernatural fallout. Energy had changed form in our mutual destruction – but it was not gone. It was different – thinner, weaker, and more spread out – but it was still all around. It made me think of a city's sewers, filled with lukewarm water from the dregs of a million baths, showers, washing machines and dishwashers. The energy was still there – but it was too thinly spread to do anything useful. Except keep rats warm.

I remembered Hal's ring, glowing in the presence of magic, and how magicians would travel far and wide in search of the last shallow pools of ancient magic in long-forgotten ruins.

The pools of magic that were the two-thousand-year-old fallout from the Quacker.

I was surrounded by new magical fallout, slowly drifting about and dispersing, or settling sluggishly far below, deep in the Mountain of Flesh...

...where the Entity was still alive.

I could see it in my mind's eye. It lay far, far below, at the bottom of a vast tube that ran up through the entire core of the mountain. The Entity had been pulverised, flattened, poisoned, stunned, and, like me, was paralysed. It was little more now than a formless, sentient puddle of slime. It looked like I had come off best.

But it was alive. *Definitely* alive. Mum had been wrong on that point. The Entity could not be killed by the Holy No-Spill-Em cup. It had arrived on our world before magic – and had only found magic because our ultimate weapon had hollowed out the multiverse, placed extreme improbabilities side by side, and *created* magic itself.

I knew something else, too. If the Entity had a serious trust problem before, it had an almighty case of paranoia now.

The battle between the paladin and his six-armed foe went on. History seemed to be repeating itself. The paladin was slowing down.

Night drew in. As it grew dark, the lack of competing illumination meant that the glowing dust of magical fallout was more and more obvious to my staring eyes. In the black depths beneath me, I sensed that the Entity was gradually, slowly, passively collecting the magic. One day it would return. It might take ten years, or a hundred – but it would be back and its quest to exterminate humanity would continue.

There was one other thing.

I was still alive.

I felt very tranquil, watching my friend fight his last battle. I might as well have been dead, I was so detached from the paladin's fate – but I wasn't. There was a spark in me yet – I just needed to work out how to kindle it into a flame.

I had to do something, and fast.

I pictured myself as a deep-sea filter feeder, deriving my sustenance from the snow of organic particles drifting past.

Come on, drift my way, I told the pixie dust.

Nothing. No change in the dust. Just the usual lazy swirls, interrupted occasionally by brief excitation when a blade passed close by.

Concentrate, Edison! Try harder! My mother's voice echoed in my head. I don't know where it came from – perhaps it was just a memory of her normal response to my school reports – but wherever it came from, it seemed to be the catalyst I needed. I concentrated. I managed to generate a slight eddy in the pixie dust, a little swirl of my very own. The swirl became a slow cyclone, a point in space around which the pixie dust orbited, like stars around the black hole at the centre of the galaxy. The clinging motes were swept from the paladin's sword and joined the general circulation as if I had given it a swift clean with an old rag.

Now to bring them to me. I chose to target my right forefinger, because my outstretched, limp right hand was the only part of me that I could see. I moved the centre of the vortex until it was right on top of my fingertip.

The duel went on, both combatants seemingly oblivious to the existence of magic in the room, and to my increasingly fruitful attempts to gather some of it.

I was hollow, a vacuum of magic, and the pixie dust suddenly appeared to sense that. It seemed to flow into my fingertip as much by its own volition as mine. In, down, it flowed, flowing faster and glowing brighter as it went, like phosphorescent plankton swirling down a plug hole. Soon almost all the magic had disappeared, all bar a few stray particles drifting about, too few and too sparse to be worth collecting.

My eyes were suddenly able to focus on the battle in front of me. That was the first thing I noticed. It took a few seconds for my other muscles to respond.

I rose unsteadily. There was no feeling in my limbs yet, but I could move them as long as I was deliberate and precise with my intentions. My sense of balance was that of someone who had drunk a bottle of whisky and taken a ride on a merry-go-round – but I made it to my feet.

I was back in the game.

The Armour of Fate

I staggered about a bit, trying not to fall over.

Close by, the fight went on. The six-armed giant was now raining blows onto the paladin's shield, pushing him back, back, and back towards the edge of the chamber. Neither the paladin or his opponent had seen my Lazarus moment, nor spotted that I was now back on my feet.

Well, here was what the giant got for denting my lovely blue-smiley-face shield...

I tried to smash him against the wall, but only succeeded in throwing myself to the ground. Half-stunned, I rolled up onto my knees, wondering what had gone wrong. Trying to use the magics had been like running into a wall.

I tried again, more circumspectly this time, attempting to merely push the giant a little way. I could do it – but it was harder than before, much harder. Where earlier I would have brushed the monster aside like a cobweb, now it was more like trying to shift a boulder. I pushed, and pushed, and the giant did not even notice the efforts of my ghostly hand.

Magic version 2 sucked.

I was going to have to be more canny in my approach. Instead of trying to hurl the giant against the wall, or bodily shift its entire mass, I focussed solely on its back foot. With a monumental effort, which I suddenly realised had given me a nosebleed, I *was* able to push this elephantine monstrosity back along the ground a little way.

My intervention worked. The giant was suddenly unbalanced. It went down on one knee, and the paladin took his chance to hew the monster's other leg. Now it had a limp in both legs; as it lunged after him, the paladin moved to one side, and the giant went sprawling to the ground like a falling tree. The paladin struck again, and the fight was over: the grey behemoth had taken enough pain. It shuffled backwards away from its tormentor, all curled up, its multiple swords clanging to the ground like metal rain.

The paladin did not pursue his defeated foe, but turned towards me. If he was surprised to see me sitting up, I could not tell, because he still wore his full-face helmet. He ran over and, as before, shed his sword, shield, gauntlets and helmet before kneeling down beside me.

"You're alive!" he said. He *was* surprised. Thought he would be.

"So is the Entity," was all I could mumble in response.

The paladin stared at me for a long moment. "You did your best," he said.

I managed to nod.

"It's no longer in control of the Order, though," the paladin stated.

I shook my head. "For now," I agreed.

"Can you walk?"

I tried to stand, and was boosted into an upright position by the paladin's strong grasp. As we got to our feet, I accidentally kicked the No-Spill-Em cup, which skittered across the floor and disappeared down the room's large central hole marking where the Entity's body had once extruded. Presumably, in a final insult, in about thirty seconds the No-Spill-Em would land on top of the puddle of slime the Entity had become.

"Come on," the paladin said. "We'd better catch up with Lexi. She'll be overjoyed to see you."

"Surprised, at least," I muttered.

I stood, swaying, as the paladin got himself togged up again and collected his sword and shield. He slotted his sword down the back of his shield, in his left hand, leaving his right hand to hold me up.

"Nice fight," I said, as we started to move.

"I thought I'd had it there, not for the first time," the paladin admitted. "If it wasn't for you..."

"H'mm."

"Without your armour, shield and sword I wouldn't have stood a chance."

It suddenly dawned on me that the paladin had no idea that I'd helped him at the end there – he obviously thought that his opponent's slip had been an entirely natural occurrence. Well, I thought, I'm not going to rain on his parade. Let him think winning was entirely down to him.

We gave the defeated giant a wide birth. It watched us go suspiciously, arms curled around itself like the drawn-up limbs of a spider.

Beyond the doorway, in the circular chamber, the light was a little better. Whereas in the Entity's inner sanctum visibility was already almost gone, out here it was merely deep dusk. Half-seen figures moved around us. There were whimpers and growls. F3's light or his infra-red cameras would have been highly useful at this point – but F3 was far away, and had the more important job of keeping Lexi and the boy safe.

By the time we were half-way down the first ramp I had already begun to flag, and the paladin was taking most of my weight. We were also moving into deep, deep darkness. The faint glow of the rocks was gone, having evidently been dependent in some way on the continuing presence of the Entity for its existence. Our only light was the weak illumination I had given the paladin's sword, which was now mostly baffled by his shield. We could hear movement below us down the ramp as other denizens of the mountain, former members of the Order, blundered about in the blackness. It sounded as if we were walking into the Pit of Hell itself. Going any further was going to be a little dicey, not least because we had no idea where it was safe to walk.

"I'll have to carry you," the paladin said.

"Down there?" The darkness was heavy with movement.

"There's no other way. Help me undo the armour."

"What? You're going to leave it here?"

"I can't carry you and the armour. Shall I leave you instead?"

The paladin put down his shield and removed his gauntlets and helmet. Then I assisted him to get out of his beautiful golden plate mail.

"You're not supposed to take this off," I said lightly.

"Says who? Where is it written?" asked the paladin dully. "The armour I was wearing when I met you, that I reviled you for taking off me, was not my own. I stole it from my father; it was his. I stole it and murdered him. This armour you made for me I don't deserve."

I knew of course that the paladin was too young to be a real paladin. The thought that he had stolen the armour had never occurred to me – let alone that he had killed for it, let alone that he had murdered his father for it.

The paladin – if I could still call him that – was stripped down to his tunic and long johns, and knelt to pick up his sword. "This I am *not* leaving behind," he said. He picked me up, too, in what was known in earlier ages as a fireman's lift, and we were off. I was over the paladin's left shoulder, head behind, legs in front; he held the illuminating sword slightly behind him, out of his eyes.

As we walked, the paladin told me the tale of how he had come to murder his father. "I killed my own father because of the armour. I'm no paladin. Never was. Never will be. Twenty years ago my father received a summons. All paladins were to meet at a certain place and a certain time. My father ignored the call. He was too afraid to go. None of the others were ever seen again, as you know. So he was the last of his kind, the last paladin. He should have died with them – but instead, he took to smoking a poisonous herb, which allowed him to forget his dishonour for a time. We were not poor, but the herb was expensive. He needed more and more and did less and less of anything else."

We had reached the foot of the first ramp. The paladin scattered half-seen creatures around us with a menacing growl, then went on. "He sold things. Eventually he sold our house and we moved to a smaller place. I didn't mind that. But I could see what was going to happen next. I hid the armour before he could sell that, too. It meant everything to me, that armour. It reminded me what my father had been. But he himself had forgotten about it – except when there was nothing else to sell, he remembered it then all right, remembered it as something of worth. He needed his herb, and he searched for the armour, but it wasn't where it ought to have been. He quickly guessed what I had done."

Down, down into the bowels of the Mountain we went. I could see little from where I was, but at least I was feeling a little better. Unless that was the blood rushing to my head.

"But I wouldn't tell him where it was hidden," the paladin laughed. "He flew into a rage – it wasn't uncommon by then, when he needed more of the herb – and he tried to *make* me tell him."

"I guess you defended yourself," I muttered, from somewhere down near the small of the paladin's back.

"It was more than that, much more. I was ashamed of him. I had resented him ever since he had failed to heed the paladins' call. My resentment had grown to hatred. And I was as big as him by then, and he was weakened by his use of the weed. I would rather have died than tell him where I had hidden that damn armour."

"Instead, you defended yourself," I repeated, encouraging the paladin to at least partly duck responsibility for his father's death.

The paladin gave a bitter laugh. "Maybe at first. But when I was winning, I could have stopped. I didn't. I made sure – I made sure of him. My mother watched it all."

For a long time, the paladin said nothing. He loved his mother. I sensed that he was more ashamed that she had seen his deed than of his deed itself. "I had to leave our home, there and then, still covered with my father's blood," he continued at last. "First I went to get the armour from where I had hidden it. I put it on. Then I went to our old house. A magician lived there now, with his servants. It was he who sold the herb, you see. He let me in, thinking I was my father."

"Whoops."

"Indeed. I killed them all."

"You beat a magician?"

"I'm going left here for no reason other than that there appear to be fewer obstacles this way," the paladin said, interrupting his own story for a moment. He went on, "He was dead before he knew I was my father's son. The servants should have fled, but they were loyal, even after their master's death. After that shameful act, I stole a horse and went as far north as I dared to go. For ten years I wandered, where there were few people, trying to be what my father had once been. Trying to be worthy of that cursed armour. I did not shirk a battle, any battle. Right up until I met the bron. I think we're lost, Edison."

"Put me down a minute," I said.

I sat cross-legged in the middle of the drafty stone chamber we found ourselves in and tried to find the way out. The disturbing sounds from hidden creatures around us in the tunnels – growling, snarling, whimpering, even some knuckle-cracking noises that I was convinced came from one of the Entity's former slaves gnawing on the bones of another – did not make concentrating any easier.

I cast out the net of my consciousness and searched for a way. It was not like before, when everything, everywhere was laid out before me as though I was a demigod and all I had to do was choose where to look. Now I had to probe the tunnels around me, encountering blind alleys, U-turns, dead ends, forks in the road, crossroads, and caverns with numerous exits, and exploring them. I had to double back many times. At first I tried picking a path at random, but quickly gave up on that. Then I went for the tried and trusted method of navigating a maze – following one wall. It was not the best solution, nor the most elegant. But it got me there.

"I have a way out," I said at last.

And so we were off again. I walked a little way, before getting scooped up as before. It was only when he was carrying me again that the paladin resumed his story.

"Then I met you and Lexi. I guess you know what happened then. You didn't take away my honour when you lost my armour. You just took away my mask. Lexi and I had terrible days, as prisoners of the Entity, although personally the feeling that I deserved it all made bearing it easier. We didn't know what was going to happen next. The weakest were eaten. But Lexi was sure about one thing. She knew you were going to come after her, no matter what. She never gave up on you."

"Sounds like you've been carrying a weight heavier than me around with you all these years, heavier than that damned armour. Guilt."

"I bear my fair portion," the paladin admitted.

"Here's a thought. You're carrying all this guilt around – well, every time you do something good, you put a bit of it down. You just saved my life – that's big chunk you can leave behind you right there. You ran in to save Lexi from the bron. You didn't have to, but you did, and almost died in the process. Down goes a bit of guilt. Sooner or later you're going to find you've run out of guilt, and you can stop punishing yourself."

"It is not for us to forgive ourselves. It is only those who we wronged that can forgive us. My mother will never forgive me."

"You sure about that?"

"Yes."

"I'm not. Here's what we're going to do. When this is over, when we're safe, and when I'm better, we're going to visit your mother. Deal?"

"She won't want to know me."

"Let's find out. But let's find Lexi first."

Night on the Greyfield

The first clue I had that anything was wrong was when the paladin started making moaning noises. "No, no, oh no," he muttered, and broke into a stumbling jog trot. I was still over his shoulder, and so I could see nothing ahead of us.

"What is it?"

The paladin said nothing. He just moaned and ran faster.

We had been following Speckle's hoofprints, frozen into the grey dust, for perhaps two hours. The cold moonlight felt like summer sunshine after what seemed an eternity in the darkness under the Mountain of Flesh. At one point we passed a dead swarmer, still clutching its little bow, and it was then that the paladin's pace began to rise.

"Paladin!"

"I can see... I can see something," he muttered.

I did not find out what he had seen until a minute later, when, panting and steaming, he skidded to a halt and put me down. The paladin stood me on my feet, but I sank to my knees immediately, for reasons of balance. Then I had to shuffle around to see.

The first thing I saw was F3. He seemed to be hovering in mid-air, but in fact he was hanging around Edison Junior's neck like a vastly-oversized glowing medallion. Edison Junior, rubbing his eyes, was faintly lit up by the glow of F3's screen.

Then I saw Speckle, on her side, very still.

Finally I picked out where Lexi was, curled up against Speckle's flank as if asleep. The paladin reached her and leaned over her.

"Lexi?" I called.

The paladin let out an anguished howl. "She's not dead... there's an arrow..."

"It's bad," F3 said, by way of hello.

This was not happening. Not now. I could save her. I shuffled closer, still on my knees. Lexi was cold, and did not respond when I said her name.

"You're alive, Edison Senior," F3 said. "Then the Entity..."

"Also alive."

I had one more spell in me yet – the last dregs of the magic I had gathered in the Entity's lair. I had no idea whether it would be enough. Reality would have to be bent a long way.

Lexi was far, far below the surface, a tiny light in a deep, deep ocean. In the time before I faced the Entity, I could have reached in and pulled her to safety without a moment's thought, just as I had the paladin. But now my reach was shorter, and my strength was lower. I had to bodily swim down into the cold darkness to reach her. But I didn't get far. I was too buoyant; the pressure of night and ice forced me back. It was like trying to dive while tied to a lifebelt. I tried again, but I couldn't do it. I couldn't get as far down as I had the first time. Again I swam down, and again, but each time I was weaker than before, each attempt was more inadequate than the last, and the little spark of life far below me seemed dimmer, and dimmer.

"I can't, I can't," I said at last, and more or less crumpled to the frozen ground. All I could do was stare at Lexi's pale face.

Some distance off, the paladin let out a howl of anguish, like a demented wolf bellowing at the moon. "It's my fault! Mine!"

Edison Junior gave a sob.

I turned to the little boy and managed to rouse myself far enough to hug him.

"F3, is there anything we can do?"

"I think it's too late," F3 said, and he sounded frantic himself. The boy in my arms still glowed with F3's light.

The paladin was still shrieking at the moon.

"It's going to be OK," I said to Edison Junior, not because it was, but because it was the sort of thing you were supposed to say on these occasions.

Then I noticed something.

"F3!"

"Edison Senior!"

"Screen off, please."

"OK."

F3's light between Edison Junior and myself was suddenly doused. Now the only light came from the moon, the stars, and too far away to illuminate us, the paladin's sword.

"Edison Junior," I asked, "are you really an orphan, or did your family lead you out into the wilderness and leave you there one day?"

"What!" F3 said.

The paladin's howls were cut off in mid-breath.

Edison Junior was glowing in my arms like Radioactive Boy with a dull red, sparkling light. The others could not see it. His face glowed like the embers of a fire. The sparks clung to his clothes. They stuck to me when I hugged him.

Edison Junior was a magician. And his battery indicator was hovering next to the "Full" mark.

Edison Junior tensed in my arms, as if sensing what was going to happen next. It was like chancing upon an ice cream parlour in the middle of a desert, three days after you ran out of water. The shopkeeper was away. The store was open. The temptation to feast was overwhelming.

But I wasn't going to do a Klim on Edison Junior. I would sooner die than do that.

"Edison, you can save Lexi. If you want her to be better, she will be better. All you have to do is wish for it to happen. Do you understand me? Wish for Lexi to get better."

Edison Junior frowned at me for a long moment.

Then he suddenly smiled.

Lar, in the Province of Nymeth

It was idyllic. I was resting on the bank of a trilling stream, staring up at fluffy white cumulus clouds dotted across a brilliant blue sky. I had no imagination, I had decided, because try as I might, I could not pick out the forms of animals in these random puffs of condensing water vapour.

"A crocodile," Edison Senior said.

I stared. I could not even tell to which cloud he was referring. "I can't see it."

"Come on, F3, you're not even trying. What have you found, Ed junior?"

It was a bright May afternoon, pleasantly warm, and with the promise of a long evening to follow. Alpine flowers – some of which I could put a definite name to, some of which I could not – nodded in the periphery of my vision. Occasionally a butterfly would wander past. Sometimes a lark would hover in the sky above, singing its heart out to impress the ladies.

I heard Edison Junior give a gasp of astonishment. This was quite amusing, because he was showing Edison Senior something he had already found. The little boy had been turning over rocks near the stream, searching for creepy crawlies. At least he did not feel that he had to eat them any more. "Beekle," Edison Junior pronounced.

Edison Senior laughed. "You're right, it is a beetle, and not a tiddly black one this time. This is what I *call* a beetle. F3, what sort of beetle is it?"

I found myself rudely picked up and brought into close proximity of the Edisons' specimen.

"Beekle," Edison Junior explained.

"I'm going to make armour like that, next time I magic armour out of thin air. Forget plain gold. I'm going for dark bronze with little golden nodules. This guy has the coolest armour in the universe. Well, F3?"

"Probably *Carabus clatratus*, or something close to it," I said. "Without a DNA sample, we'll never know to what extent it resembles the type. That's the closest I can come with the method of the eyeball."

"You mean the CCD sensor," Edison Senior rejoined. "Of course, you could just have made the name up. *Carabus ignoramus–*"

"*Clatratus –*"

"Point is, we only have your word for it."

"If you don't trust my diagnosis, you could always just not ask my opinion in the first place. Or you could ask one of the villagers if they have a name for it. They probably have a vernacular name for it—"

"A what name?"

"A common name."

"I'll ask the class tomorrow. Take a snap, F3!"

I did so. Edison would be able to show his students the beetle the next day and ask them what it was called in Lar, in the province of Nymeth. This was the place Jasso had mentioned to Edison after dragging him out of the sunken infernal machine, and it had stuck in Edison's mind. He could have been transported to the Royal Court, but rejected that option in favour of travelling to Jasso's homeland.

I had to admit that Edison had taken to his new role of teacher with the ease that a blindfolded drunkard falls off a spinning log. He was a natural with children, and could keep them entertained for hours with stories of his recent exploits, or of the time before the Entity's arrival (or during the first war against it). Of course, he had me to help with audio and visual snippets. Where adults were concerned, he was awkward and unwilling to expound at length about his achievements (he particularly despised his frequent meetings with visiting dignitaries). But give him an audience of 5-12 year olds and he was in his element, just as he had been with the Scavenger children in Crickne.

When we arrived at Lar, Edison's role as a teacher began quite informally. The children were fascinated by Edison and in awe of him, and he was not slow to begin showboating in response to their interest. But I'm getting ahead of myself. You probably want to know what happened after Edison Senior noticed that Edison Junior was a magician. Well, it went this way. Not only did Edison Junior manage to heal Lexi, but he healed Edison Senior's horse as well. Not only did he heal them, in fact, but he stood them on their feet again, both as good as new. The horse was now grey, the same colour exactly as the Greyfield ash, as if the boy had accidentally incorporated into the horse's coat the cold dust that covered it. The only bits that weren't now grey were three small, star-shaped marks, showing where arrows had struck it.

In fact, the only person left on the ground at that moment was Edison Senior, who gave Edison Junior a grateful hug before passing out. Edison Junior promptly curled up with him and went to sleep too, and didn't wake up for three days, after which he was as good as new. Lexi and the horse were left staring at the dumbfounded paladin for some sort of explanation, which I provided myself in due course.

As I say, Edison Junior's recovery was quick and full. He woke up as we neared Bow Fort with the survivors from Captain Obart's raiding party, Hal and Jasso among them. Edison Senior's recovery was far slower. He regained consciousness before Edison Junior, but found himself almost unable to move. Even now, after more than six months, he only really has one good arm, and his legs are next to useless. He scoots up and down on a skateboard made for him by Lar's blacksmith. Maybe he counts himself lucky to be alive at all; we haven't discussed it, because whenever I raise the issue of his health, Edison tells me to shut up. He has definitely not come to terms with his new situation. He's become gaunt from his insistence upon not eating mutton, the village's staple food in the winter. Sometimes I notice him staring into space when no-one's looking, and putting on a quick smile when he sees someone is looking his way.

Lexi, meanwhile, had taken to life in Lar with the easy grace of a princess. To her saintly demeanour, Edison at the height of his powers had restored the looks of a movie star. The combination was irresistible: everyone in Lar loved Lexi, and would have been prepared to place her on a pedestal in the feasting hall and excuse her from all duties. Lexi, of course, would have none of it, and took to a variety of tasks with a will that put many of the other women of the village to shame.

Hal and Jasso have moved on with the army, but they will be back before autumn.

Edison's mother has been in touch via a home-built radio. Apparently Hansen had quite a shock when she arrived on his doorstep in the middle of a February snowstorm. She thinks it will take eight years of a "normal" diet for her to purge the Entity's grey matter from her body and shake off most of the internal effects of her conversion to a changeling. She's working on a design for a helmet that would prevent changelings from receiving instructions from the Entity.

Yes. Everybody's doing fine apart from Edison, I guess. Still, Lexi's been working on something that might cheer him up – but I can't tell you about that, because it hasn't happened yet.

Speaking of how everyone is doing – there's one more thing I should tell you. The Entity is broadcasting again. The signal is faint, almost too faint for me to detect, but on a clear day, when I'm on a north-facing slope, it's definitely there. I haven't plucked up the courage to tell anyone yet – everyone seems so content with life, Edison apart, that I haven't the heart to tell them that it all might be very temporary.

"Is that...?" Edison Sr began, then trailed off.

"Is what what?" I asked.

"Oh – nothing. Look, F3, I'm going to hang you around Edison Junior's neck," Edison Senior said, and picked me up once again.

"What is it – I'm busy!"

"Not writing your memoir again are you?"

"It's *your* memoir, Edison – I'm just rounding off the story myself because you haven't done it."

"Edison, I want you to go up to the village and find Lexi. Take F3 with you, OK? Can you do that?" Edison asked the small boy, ignoring me.

"Lexi," Edison Jr said.

"Yep – that's it. Off you go."

"Edison!" I demanded. "What's going on?"

"Message for Lexi – I love her. I'll catch up with you later – now shoo!"

As a being with no properly-moving parts, I couldn't even look over my shoulder as Edison Jr tottered up the hill.

What on Earth had got into Edison Sr?

A Visit From Old Friends

My first thought was for the boy – Edison Jr. I wanted him safely out of it.

My second thought was for myself. I felt fear, or rather felt that I ought to feel fear, so I was afraid, a little.

But the fear was tinged with a slowly-creeping darkness, like oncoming night. The darkness was called Opportunity.

I was cold, cold all the time. No, not cold – that is the wrong analogy. I was tired. I was tired, and could never rest. Like a swimmer without a shore, I must swim, or drown. Swim, swim, swim. But no shore. Never a shore. And it was hard. It was hard to be cheerful, as I must be, when all I wanted to do was scream.

There were those who were worse off than me. Two men of the village had been maimed in the late, great incursion by the Order. They bore their injuries without complaint. But that did not encourage me. It drew me down into deeper, colder water. It made the fact that I could not bear my burden all the more bruising when they could bear theirs. They were heroes. I was a hero too, of an altogether rarer kind. I had saved the world. I had been feted, rewarded, praised, honoured; I had been given a fine charcoal tunic with silver embroidery to show the world how important I was. It was already scuffed and fraying from being dragged across stony ground.

I had met royalty. A few lesser royals had visited Lar, and they wanted me to visit the King's Court in turn. But I had nothing to say to them, and they went away disappointed. This was not the hero they had expected to find.

Death had toyed with me. I had had more near-death experiences than a spiritualist medium. But having beaten me at last, Death had walked away without giving me the dignity of a *coup de grâce*.

And here, coming up the hill, was an answer. It was a dark answer. But like the cold darkness beneath the tiring swimmer, it was strangely seductive. I had seen the warbirds coming from a mile down the valley, and soon recognised their leader. They were advancing up through the thin strip of woodland that clung to the steep sides of the stream, trying to remain hidden. Had I been sitting anywhere else in the village, I would not have noticed their coming.

F3's complaints finally faded out of hearing as Edison Jr plodded up the hill behind me. He glanced over his shoulder, and I waved. It would take him another five minutes to reach the village. About the same length of time it would take the warbirds to reach me. I made sure that the warbirds would be able to see me from the edge of the trees, and see that I was alone. Yep. I was in plain view all right. I turned my back on the warbirds and waited, staring up the valley to where sheep were being driven up onto the lower tops. Lexi would be up there somewhere. She went up to the high valley every day, busy about some mysterious mission of her own whenever her duties allowed, perched on Speckle's back. Sometimes I watched the two of them cantering quickly out of sight and wondered where they were going.

A few minutes later my shoulder blades were beginning to prickle. I felt sure that the warbirds should be close by now, but strain my ears as I might, I couldn't hear them. The rush of the stream probably drowned them out. I didn't look around.

At last, a sound. Footsteps crunching against gravel. I couldn't tell how many there were, nor how close they were –

"You saw us coming."

Pretty close, it turned out. The voice belonged to the warbird boss, the one I had met on Torment Hill, with almost lethal consequences.

"And yet you waited for us."

I didn't turn to face them. "I waited. You've come to take your revenge on me."

"Something like that. If you just give us the box, that will do."

"F3 you mean?"

"Where is it?"

"He. Where is *he?* F3 is a person, you know. It took me a long time to realise it, but he is. Sure, he's snarky most of the time, and I've never really said to him what a good friend he is, but he's definitely a 'he'."

"So it's not here?"

I turned at last. There were three of them, and I recognised them all as the same three from Torment Hill. They must have left their comrades hiding in the woods.

"He isn't here. He's travelling with someone else now, someone more deserving."

"You sold it?" the warbird boss sneered.

"You can't sell a person," I explained.

"Slaves you can," said warbird #2.

"I disagree," I said. "You cannot sell something you do not own, even if money does change hands."

"So you did sell it!" exclaimed warbird #3, his feathers quivering in the breeze.

"At least I'll have my knife back now," the warbird boss said with an evil smile.

"I gave it to someone else," I said, and shrugged as well as I could with one good arm.

"This conversation is getting boring," the warbird boss said. "I think now you should begin begging for your life."

"Can't we just let bygones be bygones?"

"No." The warbird boss pulled out a knife. His two comrades pulled theirs out, too. All three looked very sharp, and shone in the afternoon sun.

"Hey!" I muttered. "I thought you didn't have a knife."

"I don't have the knife you stole from me. This one cuts well enough."

There was a pause. The three warbirds looked down at me, knives poised.

"Isn't he going to at least run?" asked warbird #2, licking his lips nervously.

"Yes, why don't you run?" demanded the warbird boss.

"All right! If it will make killing me any easier, I'll run," I snapped. With the grace of a seal I dragged myself towards my makeshift skateboard, using my one good arm for power, my rubbish arm for balance, and letting my utterly useless legs trail along behind.

"He's lost the use of his legs," warbird #2 noted.

"Well spotted, Sherlock," I snarled over my shoulder at him. In that movement, I spotted something else: another arrival. Warbird #2 had seen him too, because he nudged his boss and gestured up the stream.

The paladin, naked from the waist up apart from his gold locket, cut a fine figure of a man. His exposed torso was immensely muscled and almost covered by a network of scars. He looked hard. Very hard. He splashed towards us, one hand hooked under the gill of a monstrous fish, something similar to a salmon. He saw the four of us on the bank, and looked from me to the warbirds and back again.

"Edison. Gentlemen. I hope I'm not interrupting anything." Unarmed, unarmoured, the paladin's physical size alone was sufficient to cow the three warbirds, who quickly hid their blades in the voluminous folds of their black cloaks. Although thinking about it, he *was* holding a large fish, so maybe they thought he was going to club them to death with it, which he was probably capable of.

"No, it's fine," I muttered.

"These friends of yours?"

"Not really. They intend to kill me."

"No we don't," put in the warbird boss.

"I'll talk to *you* in a minute," the paladin told him.

The warbird boss definitely paled.

The paladin turned to me. "You don't seem too bothered by your imminent demise," he observed.

I looked at him defiantly for a moment, then sagged. "Why didn't I die?" I asked. "The Entity died. Why did I survive? Why didn't I die in the Mountain of Flesh? It could have ended there – bam. I hit the floor, my eyes shut – the end."

"Two things, Edison. One: if you had died there, so also would I be dead. So also would Lexi. And Edison Jr. Two: you're saying these things because you've lost the use of your legs. They may improve in time."

"No, it's not that. Not *just* that."

"Is it because you had power, and lost it? So does everyone."

"Not like this. Not like me. I had..."

"For half an hour you were the most powerful magician the world had seen in a thousand years. And now that power has all gone."

"Yeah, that hurts. Like an aching void within me, a hollow something once filled. I am so empty I could almost float. But still..."

"There's something else."

"I can't just hang about here, holding everybody back..."

"You speak not of everybody, but of one person in particular."

For someone with an extreme specialism in hitting things hard, the paladin was quite perceptive at times. I dropped my eyes, feeling shamefully stupid.

"You don't think she wants you any more. You have nothing going for you. You can't walk, can't do magic, can't do much at all except run on about how clever you are and drag yourself about on a skateboard like a worthless thing, a worm, something that belongs in the soil. Is that it?" the paladin was almost shouting at me now.

"Obviously," I muttered, still not meeting his gaze.

The paladin went on. "You suspect she prefers the company of the other boys around the village to *your* company. You suspect that on her trips up the mountain she might perhaps be meeting someone else. Perhaps a young shepherd. Their meetings are innocent enough... maybe she's too loyal to ever tell you, but you know she doesn't find such a grovelling, crawling thing as you are now attractive. Am I still on the right track?"

I felt like a schooled child now. I said nothing, and just ground my teeth bitterly, staring at the ground.

"For someone who saved the world, you don't have a high opinion of yourself."

"That was a fire," I said, crying. "What you see now is its ashes."

"Come on lads," said the warbird boss. "Let's go. We'd only be doing him a favour by slitting his throat." With that, the three of them turned and began to follow the stream back to the woods where their comrades awaited them.

The paladin and I watched the warbirds go. When they were well out of earshot, the paladin spoke again, more gently this time. "If you need to, then have a conversation with Lexi. I think you will be surprised by her response. Bear your pain with pride, and she will always love you. Pity yourself, and she too will pity you."

"I know, I'm pathetic..." I began, using my fine tunic's sleeve to dry my eyes.

"No. No one thinks less of you because you can't walk any more. These are your scars, your wounds, you took them for us, and they belong to us. We share them with you. All of us. Including Lexi. But she can tell you herself – because here she comes now."

An Ending

Lexi drove Speckle hurtling down the hill. It was a sight to see. There was Lexi – clad in her plain green work clothes, with her silver hair flying behind – and Speckle, who was now the grey of long dead ash, and who galloped with her own mane billowing in the wind of her own making. Even Speckle's speckle was no more, subsumed into the general grey of her coat. But she had gained three new speckles on her flank, jet black stars the size of saucers, each one the tombstone of a dead arrow. Only as they neared me did I notice Edison Jr sitting on the horse in front of Lexi, with F3 still around his neck.

"Edison! Are you all right! Were those warbirds?" Lexi asked breathlessly, pulling Speckle to a thunderous stop.

"It's all right," I said blandly, wiping my eyes once again to make sure they were dry. "The paladin scared them away."

Lexi jumped down and gave me a hug. The paladin caught my eye and grinned. "What did they want?" Lexi asked.

"They wanted to steal F3 again," I said. "And they wanted their knife back."

Now it was the paladin's turn to get a hug. This time *I* caught *his* eye and grinned sarcastically. "Thank you for scaring them off," Lexi told him.

Meanwhile, Edison Jr was dubiously considering getting down from Speckle, but it was too far. He kept edging one leg over to join its fellow on the side nearest us, then gingerly retreating it again.

"Hang on, Ed," I called.

Lexi and the paladin noticed Edison Junior's predicament and swung him down to the ground via a good bit of fun up and down, which caused him to have a fit of giggles.

"Paladin, would you mind watching Edison for an hour or so?" Lexi asked. "There's something I need to show Edison up the valley."

"Not a problem. Would you like to ride, Edison?"

"Where are we going?" I asked.

"Up the valley. I told you."

Lexi and the paladin grabbed me and hoisted me onto Speckle's back. I didn't get any swinging. Once I was safely aboard, Lexi took F3 from Edison Junior's neck, picked up my board, and started to lead the way.

"Don't forget what I said," called the paladin.

I said nothing.

"What did he say?" Lexi asked.

"Oh, nothing."

"Really."

"Is it far?" I asked, changing the subject.

"Not too far."

We made our way up the valley, skirting the village of Lar itself, where delicious smells indicated that supper was being cooked. One or two children started to follow us, but Lexi waved them off. "We'll see you later," she said.

"You're not going to tell me what it is you want to show me, are you," I said.

"No."

I decided to enjoy the scenery. It *was* amazing. For a city boy like myself, the mountains held a deep fascination and beauty that was nothing short of awe-inspiring. From a distance, they looked quite small. Then when you got closer, you realised just how big they were. Then you climbed them – on Speckle's back in my case – and you realised that even the valleys between them were astoundingly high. All around me I vaguely recognised the signs of glaciation. My geography teacher, Miss Jarvis, would be proud – if she hadn't been atomised two thousand years earlier. The valley was U-shaped, with a flat bottom and steepening sides, one of which we were now climbing. U-shaped meant glaciation. And amazingly, far above our heads, there was another, smaller valley, which intersected with the main one.

"Glaciers," I said. "U-shaped valleys."

"A hanging valley," F3 said.

"Know-all," I muttered.

"True."

It took another half an hour to climb to the lip of the hanging valley. We paused to look back at Lar. From up here the houses looked no bigger than crumbs on a table.

There was a stream at the bottom of the hanging valley, narrow and pebbly. There was also a small, elongated hill running parallel with the valley.

"A drumlin," I pointed out, "that little hill."

"A *roche moutonnée*," F3 said, "but I'm glad to see that you weren't asleep in every geography class."

"You're still a know-all," I muttered.

"Agreed."

But there was more than glacial landforms up here. Even here, in the middle of nowhere, up in the mountains, there was evidence of an ancient civilisation – mine. Various stumps and half-walls of weathered concrete jutted out from the valley on its west-facing side, all covered in a combination of green moss and grey lichen that would have been a perfect camouflage except for the hard straight edges everywhere, defined by areas of deeper shade.

"You have to get off now," Lexi said, and placed my board on the ground.

I stared about. There was nothing worthy of the name "destination" here. Just the cold, windswept valley, a few rocks, and a few old bits of wall. There wasn't even a waterfall. I had been convinced that Lexi wanted to show me a waterfall.

"You'll have to catch me," I warned.

Lexi slipped off her gloves and took my hands. As I dismounted – or rather, slid down – we ended up half-falling, half-sitting down together on the cold wet ground.

"Whoops – sorry! Are you OK?" I asked.

But Lexi was giggling.

"It's going to be more fun trying to get me back up there when we go home."

"You could scoot," Lexi said, when she could draw breath. "It's mostly downhill."

"It could be fun. Could be deadly. But it could be fun."

"Right, get on your board and close your eyes," Lexi ordered, once she had recovered. "And keep them closed until I say you can open them."

"Right."

"Promise!"

"All right!"

"Good. Now, Speckle, I'm going to leave you here. I know you're a good horse, and you won't wander off, but just in case I'm going to tie you." Lexi chatted to Speckle as she tied her to something (a medium-sized boulder, I guessed – there wasn't much else around). That done, we were off, Lexi pulling me along at arms' length by a piece of strong cord. The stones beneath my wheels made for a bumpy, noisy ride.

About ten seconds into this phase of our journey, I remembered the paladin's words. It was time to ask The Question. "Lexi, listen. There's something I've been meaning to say. F3, could you turn off your mic for a minute?"

"Whatever you say," F3 replied.

"Can you hear me? F3, can you hear me?"

There was no reply.

"Crikey, I wish I'd thought of doing that before."

The wheels of my board crunched over the wet stones. There was a cold, fresh wind in my face. I kept my eyes fast closed, as per instruction.

"Lexi, stop."

Lexi stopped dragging me along. But before I could speak again, she jumped in. "I don't want to hear it, whatever it is."

"We have to talk sometime. I'm not getting any better. You've got your whole life ahead of you. Me, well –"

"What are you saying?" Lexi asked coldly. "You don't want me any more?"

I swallowed deeply. "Lexi, I love you. But –"

"I haven't heard you say *that* in a while."

"No, well, I didn't want to make it any harder –"

"You think I'd prefer one of the young shepherds, is that it?"

"Well," I admitted, "they are strapping lads..."

"Don't be so miserable!" Lexi ordered.

"Hey?"

"You thought I was creeping up here to meet someone else every day?"

"No, of course not –"

"I'm half inclined to turn around and not show you what I brought you here to see."

"Is it a waterfall?"

"A waterfall! You think I've been up here for months looking for a waterfall to show you?"

"No... I mean, I like waterfalls..."

"Edison, the shepherd boys have qualities..."

"Yes..."

"Stop talking now!" Lexi ordered. "Just listen!"

"Er, OK."

"The shepherds have qualities. But they are not you. Someday they will make marvellous husbands and love their wives and look after them and share children with them and grow merrily old with them.

"But they are not you.

"They won't follow me a hundred miles to rescue me from a place no-one has ever been to and lived to tell the tale. They won't offer their lives to save the world.

"But most of all, they might love me as I am now. But only YOU loved me as I was THEN. I loved you as you were, and I love you as you are. I always will.

"Now wipe those tears from your eyes. This discussion is over."

Lexi started pulling me along again. I used a sleeve to mop up the water in my eyes. I almost made an excuse that it was the wind making my eyes water, but I didn't. I had realised that, far from the unluckiest kid in the universe, I was the luckiest – because Lexi loved me. To hell with not being able to walk, to hell with being blue (which I had more-or-less got used to anyway), and to hell with not having any magic any more. None of that mattered. Lexi loved me. Everything was A-OK.

"Duck now," Lexi said.

"What?" I asked, but hunkered down on the board anyway.

The sounds from the wheels of the board suddenly became louder, yet smoother, less harsh. The ride was smoother too. The wind suddenly died.

"Are we in a cave?"

"Sort of. Keep eyes shut."

Lexi dragged me for another minute or more. I could hear the sounds of our movements bouncing back at us, trapped in the narrow tunnel we seemed to be in. Then, all at once, our movements became quiet, as if we had entered a large cavern and the sounds were lost, not reflected to us.

"What is this place?" I asked.

"Keep your eyes shut. You can open them in a minute."

I rolled along some more. The going underfoot – I mean underwheel – was still smooth. It was more like flooring than natural ground. A few more noises gave me clues as to what kind of place this was – one sounded like the scrape of a chair leg.

"Just a minute more – I'll tell you when..."

"!"

"Now!"

I opened my eyes. All I could see was a single, steady, glowing light, right in front of me. Everything else was absolutely black. The light was so bright, I was dazzled for a long moment. Then I began to pick up a few more details – the light shining in Lexi's eyes first, and then her face, frozen into an excited expression. Then, in front of her face, I saw her hand, and the little glowing mote that she held.

"Hal's ring?!"

The Final Word

I didn't hear anything of what passed between Edison and Lexi until they finally remembered to turn me back on. By then, Edison had already gathered most of the old magic in the bunker, and had tentatively hauled himself to his feet. We were in the mess hall of what had once been a military base – completely bomb proof, it seemed. But to judge by the shrivelled corpses about the place, being bomb-proof did not mean that survival was guaranteed. Edison was in the middle of wondering how someone could die in the middle of a game of chess...

"Don't touch anything!" I barked.

Edison jumped. There was a puff of dust. The deceased chess player slid down in his chair with a rattle of old bones.

"Why – is it dangerous?" Edison asked nervously.

"No, you idiot, I want to see the board." It only took a nanosecond to see that the player's position was a winning one. Where his defeated opponent was, I couldn't say.

"Look F3, I can walk," Edison laughed, and tried to stomp up and down between the tables imitating a chicken, promptly falling over, which he found hilarious for some reason.

Lexi, meanwhile, had lit some candles.

"Did Lexi tell you how she found this place?" I asked.

"No," Edison said. He turned to Lexi, having scrambled to his feet. "How *did* you find it? Why have no other magicians been up here to gather the magic?"

"With the ring. At night. By the door it was very faint – it would never have been visible in daylight. But we guessed there would be more magic if we could get the door open."

"Twenty centimetres of steel," I put in, "welded by two thousand years of rust to the circular frame – an almost impossible task, without decent tools."

"How on earth did you open it?"

"Time, hard graft, and a little science. Electrolysis. Had to build a waterproof retaining wall too. And rig up a wind turbine to power the electrolysis. And beg pieces of good steel to destroy as sacrificial anodes. We junked a lot of good steel in the process. When I say we, I mean Lexi – she did everything. I merely advised."

Edison was now staring at Lexi as at a godlike being – which was a fairly accurate appraisal, I'd say.

"I couldn't have done it without F3," Lexi said modestly.

"Obviously," I said. "Anyway, once the electrolysis was done, we still had to apply a considerable mechanical advantage to get the door to swing open – the best plaited ropes the world has seen for millennia, plus a pulley system with which we could have lifted a battleship if the rope would have taken it –"

"It was a bit of a heave to get the door open," Lexi admitted. "Speckle helped, bless her."

"All this for me?" Edison asked, moving towards Lexi.

There were tears in his eyes. There were tears in Lexi's eyes, too.

I harrumphed. "Would you like me to turn my mic off again?" I asked.

"Yes please," Lexi said.

I blanked off my cameras too.

And silently resolved that I would keep the Entity's recovery to myself as long as I could. Sunny weather is rare enough. No need to spoil it by talking about the dark clouds on the horizon.

...

...

... oh, one more thing:

THE END.

Well, it isn't really the end. It's not as if there's a giant smoking crater and everyone is dead. It's just the point that I've decided to stop recording things.

Which doesn't quite have the same ring to it as "the end." So:

THE END.

About the Author

Your author is usually called Jit even though his real name is Jonathan. He lives in Norwich, UK, with his wife and two children. When not writing fiction, Jit is an entomologist, as well as a butler to three cats.

Jitland.blogspot.co.uk

By the Same Author

Elsie Smith Vampyre Hunter

Shadowland books:
The Door into Shadow
The Factory of Souls

21984589R00159

Made in the USA
Charleston, SC
10 September 2013